NASHVILLE NIGHTS 2

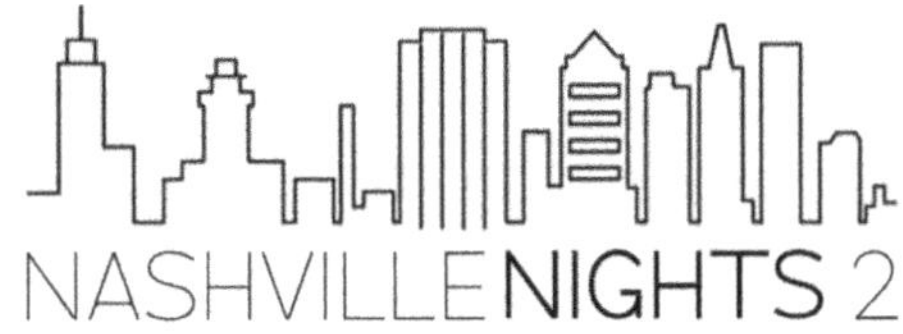

Waiting for Healing

SARAH PIRTLE

*To the ones who have spent their whole life healing others,
when all they want is to be healed.
This one's for you.*

Content Warning

Please note, this book contains sensitive subject matter.
My hope is that I have handled all subjects delicately and respectfully,
in the process of bringing our characters their happily ever after.
Please visit www.authorsarahpirtle.com for a full list of trigger
warnings.

Playlist

listen on spotify

Flirt – NEFFEX
Slow Dance – AJ Mitchell
Let Me Down Slowly – Alec Benjamin
Beyond (ft. Luke Combs) – Leon Bridges
Big Plans – Why Don't We
Love You Better – John De Sohn & Rasmus Hagan
The High – Bryce Savage
One Man Band – Old Dominion
Beautiful Crazy – Luke Combs
Take Me To Church – Tommy Vext
Weeping Willow – Warren Zeiders
Nervous – John Legend
Wrapped Around Your Finger – Post Malone
Fallin Up – SoMo
Baby I Am – Dalton Dover
Paper Rings – Taylor Swift

Chapter 1

It never fails that Nashville General Hospital is always busiest during the holidays, which is seriously depressing. Not only are we dealing with regular patients coming in sick, but the number of wrecks happening due to people trying to drive on slick streets is astronomical.

When you add all of the homeless folks coming in to seek warmth and shelter, this place is packed from Thanksgiving until New Years. My heart aches for every single one of them and my only hope is that I can help every person that comes under my care. Though I know a lot of times it's out of my control and there's simply no help to be given.

When I need a mental decompression I'll sometimes sneak away to the Labor & Delivery wing. Seeing the new babies getting strolled to their recovery rooms with their moms gives me a sense of hope that not everything happening in this hospital is always so tragic.

The last patient I admitted was an elderly woman who was diagnosed with dementia, so shortly after I left her I went for a visit to the babies. Those diagnoses always hit me so hard. Thinking about there coming a time you will forget those you love the most, it's heartbreaking. I've just returned to my station after my attempt at a serotonin boost, trying to keep my mind off of my patient's diagnosis. I grab my phone to check in with the girls before sitting down to finish charting, with the end of my shift near.

ME

Shane, you're making the margs tonight right?

SHANE

Taylor, name one time in the last year and a half I have come to girls' night and not made margaritas.

LEAH

I have the food, be there soon. We wanted the large cheese dip right?

LAUREN

If Shane isn't making the drinks and the queso isn't in a container as big as my head then I'm not coming.

RUBY

Yeah, this guac is looking a little ick so that queso is carrying the meal at this point.

ME

Perfect! See everyone in half an hour.

The group text is always mass chaos and I wouldn't change it for anything. It's the perfect written representation of how insane we actually are when we're all together. Tonight is our annual Christmas Eve eve girls' night and I have been looking forward to it all day. Since last year's attempt to go out dancing was such a fiasco, we decided to stick to what we know and do dinner with our favorite Christmas movie—*The Grinch.*

I am about to finish charting and ditch this hellhole when I start to feel the presence of someone behind me.

"You know you'd probably get that done a lot faster if you weren't so distracted," Zander teases as my phone continues to buzz while the girls text back and forth about which pajamas they're wearing tonight.

"Lurking isn't a good look on you Zander." I raise a brow at him as I lock my phone before turning back to my chart. When he leans against the desk I am working at, standing close enough for me to notice the subtle shake to his leg, I look up to find him a little more nervous than usual.

"Everything okay?" I spin in my chair to face him. Concerned by the way he looks like he might hurl at any moment.

"Uh, yeah." He clears his throat, standing up straighter now.

"Okay then." I furrow my brow turning back to my chart. Before my pen can make contact with the paper he is spinning my chair to face him.

"No, actually," he says, correcting himself from before.

"What's up, Zander? You're freaking me out a little," I ask, trying to get to the bottom of whatever has him acting a little unhinged tonight.

"Speaking of distractions, there's something I have been wanting to ask you for a while now," he starts, making me a little more nervous, "I know you've told me before that you like to focus on work and that's why we should keep things… *casual.*" He lowers his voice and glances around for eavesdroppers. "But I would really like to take you out on a date. A proper one. I feel like maybe there could be something *more* to us. What do you say?" he asks, his brown eyes reflecting the same nerves with a hint of pleading. Almost like he's… *scared?* Is he really that worried I'll say no? It's kind of endearing in a way, but also a little comical causing me to snicker at the thought.

Zander and I have had a no strings attached relationship going on for a while now, and though he isn't exactly rocking my world, he's easy on the eyes and gets the job done much better than my little purple friend.

It's not a harsh statement when you both take the situation for what it is – just sex.

I was sure to make it *very* clear that all I was looking for was a casual hookup when we made this agreement. I haven't had many *serious* relationships in my life since I've always focused more on school and work than anything else. Casual dating is where I have always felt most comfortable because there's an easy out waiting for me whenever I need it.

What's crazy is, lately, I have been wondering if maybe I'm ready to take the next step into adulthood and actually try to *date*. Like, really date, seeing as how I haven't since high school. Could he sense that or something? Because his timing is eerie.

"Wow, okay. Not what I was expecting at all," I tell him honestly, staring blankly past him. My mind tries to run through all the pros and cons of saying yes to this, something I tend to do a lot when I get asked out, which is probably why I prefer to stay single. I will over-think something to death and then end up saying no. Which is exactly why this time I skip overthinking and say, "Yes."

The look of surprise and relief that washes over him is adorable.

"Really? Okay. So are you free tonight?" he asks on a heavy exhale, running a hand through his dirty blonde hair.

"Um, no. Not only did Mrs. Winthrop pee on me earlier tonight making me desperate for a shower, or two. But that distraction you mentioned earlier is actually waiting for me," I say with an apologetic grin. Then it hits me. "Shit, what time is it?"

"It's 6:15," he says, showing me his watch.

"Shit, shit, shit. I have to go." I stand to gather my things franti-cally before turning around to see him smiling at me.

"So you really will go out with me?" he asks again.

"Yes. I really will go out with you. Your timing could use work since I'll be decking the halls and shit for the next few days. Should I just text you and let you know when I'm free?" I ask hesitantly. "I'm not sure how this is supposed to work now," I say, waving a finger between the two of us.

"Um, yeah. That works for me. Have a great night Taylor." He dips his chin and glances back up at me before I wave and rush out the door. When I get in my car my mind immediately goes to the one place I'd tried to keep it from going when Zander first asked me out.

All the freaking *what ifs*.

What if it's horrible?

What if he's completely different outside of work? And sex.

What if I'm completely different outside of work and sex?

What if I scare him off?

Because it wouldn't be the first time that happened.

When I grab my phone to start my playlist I see the messages from our group chat and decide to check it before heading home. Ignoring all the pajama and slipper talk I respond instead to the collective *where are you* text.

ME

Sorry I was getting asked out on a date.

LEAH

What's new? You're hot and unattached but like, how long does it take to say fuck off??

ME

Well, it takes longer to say yes I guess.

SHANE

GET OUT!

LEAH

YOU'RE LYING.

LAUREN

BACK. THE FUCK. UP.

RUBY

GET YOUR ASS HOME.

ME

I knew that would get them. My friends know I prefer to stick to casual dating – mostly they're aware of the breakup that pushed me to embrace my new way of life and ended my desire to date. So the fact that I've agreed to go on one, officially, for the first time in 10 years probably has them losing their damn minds. I toss my phone in the cup holder and start my car before making a swift trip home.

When I was looking to buy a house I made sure it was one close enough to work so I didn't have to worry about rush-hour every week. Plus it works out well when I'm on call and am needed in the ER as fast as humanly possible. I purchased a cute little cornflower blue house that's about 10 minutes away from the hospital and I absolutely love it. When I pull into my driveway I barely make it through the door before I am bombarded with questions.

Who asked you out?

You actually said YES?

Was it a dare?

"First of all, I got peed on tonight so I suggest you all take a couple of steps back until I have changed," I say, making all four of them back up with disgusted looks on their faces.

"Second of all, Zander asked me out. Yes, I said yes. And no, it wasn't a *dare*. Do people even still do that?" I ask, kicking my shoes off and placing them in the basket I keep at the door.

"Okay, well forgive us for our state of shock over this information.

It's just so unlike you," Lauren says, cocking her head to the side as if she's choosing her words carefully.

"I know… I – actually, can I shower before we dive into this? I think I need to be sitting down for it, and I refuse to do anything else while in these scrubs."

"Of course. I'll have your marg waiting for you when you get out," Shane offers, blowing me a kiss before heading off to the kitchen.

"You're a doll," I shout as I run back to my bathroom to strip out of my scrubs as quickly as possible. I toss them into the hamper and turn the water to its hottest temperature before stepping in.

I think I zone out for my entire shower because by the time I am stepping out, smelling like fresh peaches, I don't remember shaving or putting my hair mask on, but both things have been done. Shrugging I wrap a towel around my body and one around my hair before digging through my closet for my Christmas pajamas.

"We set them on your bed for you," Leah says, appearing in the doorway startling me a bit.

"You guys literally think of everything." I wink at her on my way past.

"So you really said yes? This is big Tay." She crosses her arms with an excited grin, her tone sweet and supportive in true Leah fashion. She was there right alongside Shane and Lauren when I got my heart broken and swore I would never date again. It wasn't just a childish proclamation either. At that moment I meant every word. I knew that I couldn't handle putting myself through that again. They know just as well as I do that this is a decision I'm not taking lightly.

"Do you think I made the right decision though?" I lean on the doorway, picking at the chipped polish on my nails.

"I wish I knew babe. You're the only one who knows for sure if this is something you want to do. Something you're ready to try again. What does your gut say?" Leah asks, plopping down on my bed. I let out a heavy sigh before joining her.

"I guess it's saying– this is a pretty safe bet. I mean I work with Zander so I know him pretty well, I think. Plus we've already slept together so there won't be any surprises there. I feel like we know each other well enough that it won't end *disastrously* ya know?" I process out loud.

"Is that what you're wanting? Something safe?" Her question is valid. I've always been the risk taker and limit pusher. The one always ready to try new things no matter how crazy they sound. But the one thing I won't play fast and loose with is my heart. I protect it like the Declaration of Independence. So as long as Nick Cage isn't after it, I think things will be okay.

"Honestly, I don't know what I want. But safe feels good… at least for now."

"Can you get your fine ass dressed? We're starving over here," Ruby says, appearing in the doorway in her Rudolph onesie pajamas. "Shane's stomach has been growling for about five minutes straight and I'm about to start shoveling food in her mouth myself just to make it stop."

"Okay okay, I'm coming. I swear." I laugh, knowing damn well how serious it is when we start hearing Shane's stomach growl. Ruby disappears to the living room again as Leah stands up to follow behind her.

"Hey, Le," I call after her.

"Yeah?" Her long auburn locks swish as she turns to face me again.

"Thanks. For checking on me. For listening to me process everything. You're a great friend." I smile in appreciation at her.

"That's what best friends are for, Tay. Now get dressed so I can squeeze you!"

When we're all bundled up on the couch with our food from my favorite local Mexican restaurant, Casa Taco, and Shane's famous margaritas, Lauren mutes the TV before starting the questioning about Zander.

"Okay, spill woman. We've heard little to nothing about this guy the whole time you've been hooking up and now you're dating him? We need details."

"Yeah, I would be lying if I said I wasn't curious about him myself. I mean, we've never even met this guy," Shane joins in, before scooping another chip into her mouth.

"I don't know. There's not much to tell right now." They all look at me in disapproval, clearly not liking my answer. A silent plea for me to divulge more information fills their stares.

"Okay, fine!" I dust the salt from my hands as I begin to think. "Well for starters, he's cute. Definitely the best-looking of all the guys I work with and he's so chill. He has that subtle confidence that makes him appealing to me. So when he mentioned wanting to hook up at a work party a year ago, I was open to the idea. Then once turned into twice so I told him where I stood with relationships, and he was cool with it just being a no strings attached relationship. It works for us." I shrug before grabbing my drink from its Chattahoochies coaster on my coffee table.

"Until now?" Lauren asks.

"I mean, it's not like it *stopped* working, he just said he thinks we could be more and asked if we could give it a shot," I explain further.

"So he's cute huh? What's he look like?" Shane asks, wagging her brows at me, making me laugh.

"He's a little bit taller than me, maybe like five-foot-nine? He has dirty blonde hair and brown eyes. He's fit too. Like you can tell he makes it to the gym. Plus he's not too bad in bed," I say, making the room erupt in laughter.

"You know, it's not often that you already know you're gonna have good sex with someone *before* the first date." Lauren winks in approval.

"Which is gonna be *when* exactly?" Shane asks, conjuring an expectant look from every face in the room.

"I have no idea. Despite his good looks, his timing kind of sucks. He only asked me out on the *busiest* freaking week of the year." I roll my eyes before settling back into the couch.

"Well… it's still exciting. If you're happy, then we're happy." Ruby raises her glass before bringing it to her lips.

Happy– there's a word I never thought I would associate with dating again. I guess only time will tell if it's an accurate prediction or not.

Chapter 2

Tucker

"THAT'S A LOVELY CHOICE." The gray haired woman behind the ring counter smiles, as Max looks at yet another engagement ring. He grunts at her without ever looking up. His gaze fixated on the giant ass square-shaped ring in his hand. I'm no jewelry connoisseur but I already know that ring is not what he's looking for. I start walking around the jewelry store, glancing through all of the brightly lit cases. Suddenly something catches my eye, making me huff out a laugh when I spot it.

"Max." I wave him over, breaking his focus from the five rings the woman has lined up in front of him – that all look exactly the fucking same. When he looks my way I nod to the case I'm stopped in front of. It's a small standalone case that's been placed by itself in the corner of the store.

"You can put these back," he says flatly, offering a fake smile to the woman behind the counter. "I'd be better off trying to make a ring my damn self," he mutters on the way over. "What's up, Tuck?" he asks when he reaches me.

"Look." I cut my eyes to the case, not specifying which ring caught my eye because I'm certain he'll spot it himself. By the pleased look that washes over his face, I'd say he has.

There's a ring front and center that is more than likely everything he didn't even know he was looking for. The center stone is sapphire blue, shaped a little bit like a raindrop, or maybe even a pear, with smaller diamonds surrounding it. A few of the bigger raindrop-shaped diamonds are set at the top, bottom, and sides while smaller round diamonds fill in the space between. Making it look an awful lot like the sun.

"That's it," he says with a small smile.

"No shit it is." I look up and see the woman still placing the other rings back in their case and wave her over.

"Excuse me, madam, I believe he's found one." I give her my most charming smile, making a rose color creep over her frail, wrinkled cheeks.

"Flirting with the jeweler, Tucker, really?" Max accuses.

"What? She looked scared after dealing with your grumpy ass. I felt the need to smooth any feathers you might have ruffled." I lower my voice as Glenda makes her way to the case. "You're welcome," I add. He huffs and rolls his eyes at me before turning his attention to sweet old Glenda. He slaps on his best, non-forced smile and points to the ring.

"I'll take that one. *Please.*" He quirks his brow at me as if to say *see, I can be polite.* The most sarcastic-looking smile spreads across my face and I give him a thumbs-up before my phone starts to ring. I look down to see Taylor's name flashing across my phone.

"Hello?" I answer, walking out of the jewelry store as if she'd be able to see or hear where I am. I'm the only one who knows Max's plan to pop the question to Shane at Christmas and I will *not* be the one to let it slip.

"Where are you? It's loud as hell," she nags instantly.

"Buying your Christmas gift actually," I tease, making her gasp in excitement.

"Reallyy?" she drags out.

"Sure, but I can't seem to find the coal factory anywhere. Would you settle for charcoal? I could hit up The Home Depot and call it a day." I try to contain my laughter.

"Asshole." I can almost hear her eyes rolling through the phone. "I was calling to see if you're helping set up tomorrow night while Shane and Max finish at the bar?"

"Yeah, I am going to be over there cooking the turkey so I can help with whatever," I answer as my gaze falls on a display in a shoe store window.

"So don't eat the turkey, got it," she notes to herself. I just laugh and shake my head. There's never a conversation between the two of us that isn't seeing who can aggravate the other more. I kind of love it. She's witty as hell and the conversations are never boring. "The girls and I are gonna roll in a little early to help prepare the rest of the food and bring gifts in."

"By *prepare the rest of the food*, do you mean transfer it from the take out containers and put them in pretty bowls while taking credit for the mashed potatoes you *didn't* make?" I tease, knowing damn well I've seen the pots and pans in her house that still have the plastic wrap on them.

"First of all, Lauren and Ruby are excellent cooks. Second of all, I did not ask for your negativity. See you tomorrow." I smirk at her defensive comeback.

"Yup. See ya." I hang up the phone and walk into the store to make my final Christmas gift purchase.

Hopefully.

I wasn't lying when I said I was shopping for her. I have gotten everyone else's gift except Taylor's because I have absolutely no clue what to get her. But I may be in luck because the shoes she hasn't shut up about needing for work are right in front of my face.

The last time she was talking about these damn shoes– that in her words *feel like you're walking on clouds*– they were apparently sold out everywhere.

"Hi, is there anything I can help you with?" the Foot Locker employee asks from right beside me. When she got there is a mystery to me.

"Yeah, actually. Do you have any more of these around here?" I ask, pointing at the display I've stopped in front of.

"Unfortunately we don't, that's our last pair," she says with a frown.

"Well, can I buy these then?" I pick up the shoes to check the size. *Size 7.*

Here's to hoping. She's pretty tiny though so maybe they'll fit. Hell, I don't know how women's feet work. She could be two sizes up or down and I wouldn't have a damn clue.

"Of course!" She exclaims, reaching for the pair of white Cloud-foam shoes with a leopard print band around the bottom. Maybe Taylor wasn't exaggerating about the *walking on clouds* feeling of these shoes. It *is* in the name after all.

"I'll take them." She's either going to look at me with her *disappointed Taylor face* or she's going to be ecstatic that I actually found them. It's a 50/50 shot and I'm tapped out with shopping. It's the shoes or a gift card to Amazon. Maybe I'll grab both just to be safe.

I shake my head as we make our way to the counter so I can check out and get the hell out of here.

"That'll be $126.84," the cashier says, beaming up at me from behind the register. She better fucking live in these shoes.

"Fuck an Amazon gift card," I mutter under my breath after hearing the total.

"I'm sorry?" The sweet little cashier asks with a puzzled look on her face. I swipe my card and listen for it to weep or curse at me for how much I just spent on some damn sneakers.

"Nothing, thank you. Merry Christmas." I smile at her and grab the bag while still receiving the same confused look from before. Tucking my wallet into my back pocket I make my way out into the bustling mall to look for Max.

"There you are, where the hell did you go?" Max asks, angrily walking up beside me.

"Had one last gift to buy. Why do you look grumpier than usual?" I ask, noting his tone and body language.

"Well, in case you forgot, I brought you along because I'm not exactly a people person. But when you dipped out *Glenda* had me on the hook to buy a matching necklace and bracelet set," Max scolds, making me laugh.

"Is it really so hard to just say, *no thanks, this is all I need?*"

"I may or may not have faked an emergency phone call before asking her to wrap up just the ring because I had to go," he admits sheepishly.

"OH. My. God. You're pathetic. You should really see someone about that," I mock.

"Can we get the hell out of here now?" he asks, glancing back over towards the jewelry store. He ducks his head pulling his cap further down his head, probably making sure Glenda doesn't see him just chilling out here while whatever fake emergency he came up with unfolds.

"You read my mind." We start off toward the entrance on the west wing where the truck is parked before I stop him with the back of my hand.

"Wait. What emergency, excuse me, *fake* emergency, did you tell poor sweet Glenda you had?" His jaw tightens and his nostrils flare at my question.

"I told her my girlfriend was in labor," he bites out.

"And you just stood out there looking for me after that?" I bark out a laugh.

"I will leave your ass here if you don't start moving." He turns to keep walking toward the door.

"Well yeah man, you have to get to the hospital. Big day happening for you. You're gonna be a papa." I rush up next to him shaking his shoulders.

"He's gonna be a papa!" I announce to a couple walking in the doors as we're walking out. They nod and congratulate him, making his face turn so red I am actually waiting for smoke to come out of his ears, making it impossible for me to contain my laughter.

"I hate you." Max shakes his head as a small grin creeps onto his face.

"Yeah, yeah. Sure you do." When we make it back to the truck I toss the shoe box in the back and Max pulls out the ring he bought for Shane to look at it. His smile is much more prominent now that we're out of the mall.

"I'm really happy for you man." He takes a deep breath and looks over at me.

"She hasn't said yes yet, Tuck," he says, snapping the ring box shut.

"And is there any part of you that thinks she *won't* say yes?"

"No, I guess not. It's just still hard to believe sometimes that she's mine. I've never felt like I couldn't live another day without someone before her. But now the only thing I see in my future is Shane."

"Wow…" I say exasperated, looking at him in amused disappointment, "I won't say that didn't hurt." Max throws a half-drunk Gatorade at me as his phone begins to ring. As always he answers it on speaker so he can drive while it's mounted to the dash.

"Hello?" he answers as we make our way through the bumper-to-bumper traffic in the mall parking lot.

"Hi, I'm gonna be crazy for a minute, but I am *bothered,* okay?" Shane's voice fills the truck.

"You're always crazy. How can we help?" I shout from the passenger seat causing Max to shake his head in disapproval.

"Shove it, Tucker. I'm in a crisis," Shane fires back.

"What's the matter, Sunshine?" Max asks. I sit back and let them have their conversation in peace.

"The extra pillowcases I bought for our room are like two shades lighter than the green on the sheets we already have. And since I didn't buy a full set now we're either going to have two different colors on the bed at a time or I have to try and match them perfectly to another set since you've had them since the dawn of time apparently and there's no tag to know where to buy more. Also, the curtain rod in the living room isn't centered and I can't stop looking at it."

Damn, she is a little crazy.

"Is anything else out of order?" Max asks calmly.

"Not that I have noticed. But I'm really struggling to get this curtain rod situation out of my head." That pulls a silent laugh from Max, bringing a smile to my own face.

"Alright. Just return the pillowcases and buy a new full set. That way when one's in the wash we just use the new ones and they'll all match. And as far as the *curtain rod situation…*" he mocks her playfully.

"Don't tease. You're just not looking at it or you'd be stressed too." Shane pouts through her laugh.

"As far as the curtain rod goes, I'll be home after I drop Tucker off and I'll get it straight. Sound good?"

"Thanks for dealing with my crazy so well," she says, releasing a long breath.

"You know I love your crazy ass. I'll see you in a bit." He shakes his head in laughter.

"I love you too."

"I love you guys too. Yup, I'm *still* here. Though that conversation did make me want to tuck and roll out onto the highway," I insert myself back into their conversation.

"Don't be bitter, Tucker." Shane laughs and Max rolls his eyes at me before they say bye and hang up the phone.

Watching Max with Shane is like watching an alternate version of my best friend living his life. Not only does she bring so much joy into his life, but he brings calmness to her chaos too and it's weirdly fucking beautiful. When we get to my house I get out, grabbing the shoes I bought Taylor before leaning back down to look at Max through the window.

"She's gonna say yes," I assure him with a smile.

"Thanks, Tuck. See you tomorrow." I nod and back away from his old Chevy as he pulls off down the road.

Shit. I have nothing to wrap these damn shoes with.

Chapter 3

Taylor

It's finally time to open presents and this *is* hands down my favorite part about Christmas. Not the getting so much as the *giving*, because I love being able to spoil all of my favorite people around the holidays.

We're all completely stuffed and gathered in the living room while little Hendrix, also known as Ruby's pride and joy, is snuggled up with Riley on the sofa, barely keeping his eyes open. I remember when Max tried telling Shane that Riley wasn't fond of new people, but she is hands down the sweetest dog I've ever met.

This really has become some sort of family dynamic friend group and it makes me feel so fortunate any time we're all together.

We all go around the room opening gifts one at a time and I can't stop smiling while seeing everyone so happy. I got Leah a self-care kit complete with stationary– because for teachers that shit is like crack– facial scrubs, hair masks, and some comfy socks. Lauren got the newest Dime beauty collection she's been raving about. For Shane, I couldn't choose between a gorgeous matching blue workout set or the new paint brushes she's had in her cart for over a month, so I just got her both, and Ruby got an at-home gel manicure set with all her favorite color polishes. Like I said, I love spoiling them. The guys all got custom pens with funny/ borderline inappropriate sayings on them, which Tank of all people was super stoked about.

"Hell yeah, I'm using this pen for every damn thing." He laughed, holding up the pen that said *fuck around and find out.* Hendrix got a remote control monster truck because it's *literally* all he talks about.

"Your turn Tay!" Lauren shouts as she puts her gifts into the biggest gift bag she can find. I do a little shoulder shuffle as I start to grab gifts from my pile. I'm blown away by how much my friends spoil me. I also got some self-care items, the phone case I have been wanting, a *Schitts Creek* coffee mug, and some new black silk pajamas. Max got me a stethoscope charm for my keychain, which is actually the cutest thing ever. Even though his unnecessary explanation *"Because you know, you're a nurse and shit"* made me want to die of laughter.

"Okay, last one," I sing-song, glaring over at Tucker. My last gift is from him and judging by the size of the box that is wrapped in *newspaper*, I have no idea what it could be. When I open it my eyes go wide and for the first time in… ever probably– I have no words.

"Show us what you got!" Shane yells from the couch.

"Um…" is all I can get out before turning the box around to show everyone the shoes I have been wanting for months.

"*Damnnnn.* Okay Tucker, coming for Taylor's title of best gift giver I see." Lauren glances between us but I pay her no mind.

"How… where did you find these?" I ask, finally able to form a coherent sentence. He crosses his foot over his knee as he sinks back into the couch.

"Lucky stop in front of a Foot Locker window." He grins before taking a sip of his whiskey. "Hope you like them, they were the last pair in the store."

"How did you know what size to get?" Glancing down I notice he's picked my exact size, though I've never mentioned my shoe size around him. I glance around at the girls to see if any of them look guilty of helping him, but they all look just as shocked as I am.

"Also luck. Like I said, it was the last pair they had so I took a chance hoping they'd work." He shrugs like it's nothing, but he has no idea how much this actually means to me. I have been wearing the same shoes to work every day since I got out of college. They're completely falling apart; with rent, all my other bills, and just not wanting to spend the money on myself, I have suffered through the pain of being on my feet for 12 hours at a time in shoes that have long lost their soles.

"This is amazing, Tucker. I can't believe you actually remembered that I wanted these. Thank you." I smile at him as everyone else's attention moves around the room. He nods in return but I see the look of satisfaction on his face when he realizes how much I love his gift. Which makes me feel like an asshole for only getting him some pens that say *I stole this motherfucker* and *That idea is garbage*. My focus is broken when Max comes back into the room with another gift box. Sitting down in the chair by the couch, he hands the box to Shane and we all look their way.

"For meeee?" she asks playfully as she settles onto the edge of the couch. "My very own leather jacket." She smiles over at Max, but when she lifts it from the box, everyone in the room gasps.

"Oh my god, have you never seen a leather jacket before?" she asks, looking around the room like we're crazy.

"Turn it around, bitch!" I all but scream at her. Because the back of the jacket has me on the verge of tears. When she does, Max drops to his knee and pulls out a ring box. When she drops the jacket that has *Mrs. Mullins* stitched on its back down in her lap, the sweetest proposal I've ever seen unfolds before me. And just like that, my best friend is a fianceé.

"Alright, get a room," Tucker yells from the same couch they're seated on. I roll my eyes at his facade of annoyance because I know I just saw that man grinning ear to ear during that sweet ass proposal.

"Merry Christmas everyone, now get the fuck out. I'm taking my fianceé to bed."

"And on that note, we're out." I clap my hands together before rushing to gather my things. I'm happy for my bestie but I don't need to stick around for the fireworks. Everyone hoots and hollers and says bye as they disappear down the hallway. We all decide to try and clean up as best as we can before hauling ass out of here.

As I am gathering all of my bags I hear my phone ding from my back pocket.

ZANDER

Merry Christmas. I can't wait for our first date, whenever that may be. 😉

ME

Merry Christmas. Is it still okay that I text you when I'm available?

ZANDER

Of course. No rush. Just letting you know I'm excited.

I smile at his last message. *He's excited.* Maybe I don't have as much to worry about as I thought.

"Damn girl, you need a pack mule for all this shit." Tucker's voice vibrates from right above me. I slide my phone back into my pocket before tossing my hair over my shoulder dramatically.

"I can't help that I'm well loved." I smile up at him but when I look into his eyes there's something there that usually isn't. A new intensity replacing his normal lighthearted charm.

"That you are, Darlin'." The sexiness and suggestive tone of his voice feel like a weighted blanket being draped over me. His forest green eyes never waver from my own, and I can't help but wonder what's going through his head. And maybe mine too. Because for the second time tonight, Tucker Landry has me rendered speechless. His very direct comment brings my attention back to our surroundings. I look around the living room for watchful eyes or listening ears, but everyone is going about gathering their own things.

"I am still seeing someone, Mr. Landry..." I tell him in a half-hearted playful tone. Not only have I been seeing the same person since he asked for my number a year ago, I just agreed to actually start dating this guy. Or at least try to. I'd thought about Tucker in that capacity more than once over the past year, I'll admit. But it all comes down to the fact that I wouldn't want to make things awkward in our friend group if it didn't work out. I just told Leah that safe felt right for now, and starting something with Tucker would be the farthest thing from safe. And now, our best friends are getting married. If things blew up between us it could ruin everything.

Zander is a safe choice. Tucker would be too... complicated.

He offers me his hand to help me back on my feet. I take it willingly, trying to keep my mind from wandering any farther than it already has. My stomach does a somersault at the feeling of his warm hand in mine. He pulls me up, swiftly bringing his lips close to my ear.

"Maybe you are, but if you spent one night with me, you'd never remember his name." He gives me a wink before walking out the door, packing my gifts in my car for me before he and Tank hop into his Bronco to head home.

Make that three times rendered speechless.

I drive the whole way home with no music playing, something I usually never do, replaying the events of the night with Tucker.

First, he buys me the shoes I've been dying to get for work, basically saving my feet from further abuse. Then he says he could make me forget about any other man after one night with him. Sure I could have rolled my eyes and told him that'll happen in his dreams, but it's hard to ignore the way his statement made me...feel things. Is there a possibility that the whole conversation could be chalked up to how much he drank tonight? Because that would make this a lot simpler and I could just move on to my date with Zander, whenever that happens, without another thought about this.

SHANE

We're having a NYE wedding.

LAUREN

Please say you mean next year.

LEAH

Damn, that proposal sex must have been ⭐

ME

Do not tell me you're making me plan a wedding in 6 days. Tell me you still love me.

RUBY

She definitely means in 6 days. I have some Xanax if you need one.

SHANE

Yayyyy so we're all on board then.

ME

Of course we are. Congrats bestie!

LAUREN

Dress shopping TOMORROW.

LEAH

Mimosas first.

RUBY

I'll see if Hen can hang with someone but I'm down.

SHANE

My besties are the BEST. 🐨 🤍

It only took us *two weeks* to plan Lauren's *birthday* party. Not even her 30th at that. And this is a whole-ass wedding. For a couple that deserves the wedding of the decade. And I have six days to plan it.

Deep breaths Taylor.

My phone dings again as I am taking cleansing breaths still seated in the driver's seat of my car. I look down to see another message from Zander.

ZANDER

Okay, I know you'd get back to me when you were free. But do you have plans for NYE yet?

ME

Actually, I do.

ME

Want to be my date to a wedding that night?

I immediately start to panic after sending my invitation.

It's too short notice.

He probably already has plans and was going to invite me to go too.

Is a wedding too formal for a first date?

Right as I am about to retract my invitation his message comes through.

ZANDER

I'd be happy to. 😊 What time should I pick you up?

ME

Well, we're planning it this week so let me get back to you on that.

ZANDER

Sounds good. Goodnight Taylor, Merry Christmas again.

ME

Goodnight. Merry Christmas.

I take a deep breath in, relieved that I'll be able to spend this week helping my best friend plan the wedding of her dreams. Not to mention Zander and I officially have a first date in motion and I can put any thoughts I may have of Tucker to rest. I bring all my gifts inside and drop them by my bed, too tired to put anything away tonight. But when my shoe box falls off the top of the pile, spilling the gorgeous new shoes from within, I can't help but jump up and slide them on my feet.

"Oh. My. God," I say aloud to myself. These shoes are a *dream*. I actually want to sleep in them. This is by far the best gift I've ever received. When did Tucker start paying such close attention to the things I talk about? For a reason other than to poke fun or see who can outwit the other. So much for putting any thoughts of Tucker to rest. Especially since the only thing I see when I close my eyes for the night, are his forest green ones staring back at me.

Fuck my life.

Chapter 4

Taylor

SOMETIMES I REALLY HATE THE incompetent idiots I work with at this hospital. It's almost not worth being the best at my job when literally every single task gets handed over to me because of it. I am on my last 12-hour shift of the week and am beyond ready to leave this place and get my best friend hitched. Planning the world's most spontaneous wedding and working three 12-hour shifts this week is about to kill me. The only reason I haven't hidden in a storage closet to cry is because this is the first time in forever my feet aren't screaming for relief. Trying not to think of the person behind that relief has not been an easy task.

We are all going to Topgolf tonight to hang out as a group before the *real* bachelor/bachelorette parties begin. Max in all his love-drunk grumpiness didn't even want to have parties but I'd insisted. My bestie is only getting married once, so she deserves to have one last hoorah. As her maid of honor and best friend, I am making sure that happens.

Tucker being Max's best man is no surprise, and neither is the fact that he was also trying with every ounce of his might to get Max to do something for a bachelor party as well. *"It's not like I'm going to hire a stripper. I want to actually live to see the wedding, plus your brooding would kill that buzz anyways. But we're doing* something." Tucker had argued. Max grumbled at the idea but finally agreed to do something as long as he and Shane got to be together for most of it. Freaking lovesick teddy bear.

I am finishing up my shift now before heading home to shower and change. I'm *hoping* to meet everyone on time for drinks. If only Lillith knew how to chart properly, I would have been out of here 20 minutes ago. I'm not really sure how she ever graduated nursing school.

"Okay, after you finish that you should be good to go." I make no effort to hide what a hurry I am in to leave.

"You're the best, thanks Taylor." She smiles over at me so appreciatively, it almost makes me feel bad for mentally being a bitch to her. *Almost.*

"It's no problem, if you need any more help after that Zander is around," I offer as my parting advice. Just as I turn to leave, I'm met by said nurse.

"Slow down there, gorgeous. Might cause a wreck." Zander grabs me by the shoulders to keep our bodies from colliding, sliding his fingers down the back of my biceps before looking around and taking a few steps back.

"Well if I was able to leave when I was supposed to, I might not be in such a damn hurry." I glance toward Lillith out of the corner of my eyes. When I bring my attention back over to him he's absentmindedly flipping through his chart.

"Sounds like maybe you could use something to help you relax. Unwind a little bit," he offers, lifting a brow as he looks up from his chart, bringing his eyes only briefly to mine.

"I might take you up on that, on any other day, but I'm actually late for my best friend's bachelorette party," I remind him, looking down at my watch and seeing just how late I'm going to be.

"Right, I forgot about that," he says nodding his head, remembering the event I have talked about non-stop all week. "What time am I picking you up tomorrow?" He finally tucks his chart underneath his arm.

When Zander asked me out a week ago I was still full of all the reservations that usually have me terrified at the thought of dating. But I wanted to step out of my comfort zone and give it a shot. I figured my best friend's wedding would be the perfect place to test the waters. Because if it went poorly then I would have literally a crowd of people I could choose from to hide away with.

Hide. Wow, it's *definitely* time for me to try dating again.

"I'll actually be at the venue all day setting up, so is it okay if I just meet up with you there?" I ask as he begins backing away.

"Sure. Maybe we can dip out a little early too." He winks at me before turning to walk down the hall. Dip out of my best friend's wedding early? Unlikely. But I don't have time to explain that to him.

"Maybe." I smile at him before rushing out the doors to head home. I grab my phone from my scrub pocket to update the girls on my whereabouts as I rush across the parking lot.

ME

No one hate me if I'm late. I work with imbeciles and I just left. 😔

SHANE

No worries babe. The party doesn't start til you're there. 😊

LAUREN

I feel your pain, no judgment here.

RUBY

I feel it's safest I don't comment on this one. 👀

LEAH

I literally had to explain how an instruction sheet works for the third time today. I gave instructions for instructions.

ME

You're a teacher & they're only 5.

LEAH

It was another teacher... 😬

ME

You win. See you guys soon!

I throw my 4Runner into drive, trying to see if I can beat my record for quickest trip home. My now empty home. It's been feeling a little lonely now that Shane's officially moved out and is getting *married*. That's still so wild to me. She's gonna be a whole-ass wife. My favorite song ends as I am pulling into my driveway which feels like it's setting the tone just right for the rest of my night.

Rushing to beat the clock I all but stumble through the front door and run straight to my bathroom, tossing my scrubs in the hamper and pulling my hair back into a bun. Seeing as I don't exactly want to show up with sopping wet curls, my hair wash day will just have to wait until tomorrow.

Dry shampoo for the win.

Once I'm done taking the fastest shower ever recorded, I do my everyday makeup of foundation, mascara, and blush, which I have dwindled down to a ten-minute routine, throw on the outfit I picked out with Shane via FaceTime last night, and I'm out the door.

When I pull into the Topgolf parking lot about 20 minutes later it's 7:45. We were supposed to meet at 7:30. I despise being late for things, which is ironic since I find myself late to pretty much every-thing. I walk in and see our group hanging out at the bar, all laughing and carrying on like we always do. I take a deep breath and walk over, trying to relax and get out of rush mode, which feels like my default setting here lately.

"There she is!" Tucker's deep and playful voice fills the room as he announces my arrival.

"The party has arrived," I announce dramatically before leaning in to hug Shane. "Sorry I'm so late," I whisper.

"Don't worry about it. We are in no rush." She flashes her bright, reassuring smile.

"You are, however, going to need to catch up." Tucker's voice catches my attention again, but this time he's much closer. When I turn around noting how our shoulders are almost touching he hands me a key lime martini, my favorite, and winks at me.

A rush of heat creeps over my cheeks, something that never happens when Zander, or any other man for that matter, winks at me. Suddenly his statement from Christmas is playing at full volume in my mind.

"If you spent one night with me, you'd never remember his name."

My stomach flutters all over again as I recount the night. I look around nervously as if people could actually hear the sentence from within my mind. He hasn't brought it up again since that night and has been perfectly normal around me during all the wedding planning. So I assumed my original thought– to blame it on the whiskey– had been correct.

I shake my head trying to remove the memory disrupting my focus. Tonight is not the night to dissect that thought to death. Tonight is about my bestie. No matter how much my heart is racing right now from the simple thought of Tucker.

"Thanks." Taking the drink from his hands I try to keep my poker face firmly in place. The last thing I need is for all of my tipsy friends to notice me acting weird around Tucker all of a sudden. Because they would have absolutely no chill about it.

"You got it, Darlin'." He tips his beer in my direction before taking a swig.

"Okay, are we ready to go up?" Leah chimes as she slides her now empty margarita glass back on the bar.

"Ready when you guys are." Max drapes his arm over Shane's shoulder, pulling her in closer to his side and planting a kiss on her temple. Making me equal parts jealous and extremely happy for my best friend.

It's no surprise that Tucker and Max tie for first. Their egotistical need to win was quite the entertainment for the rest of the group who was basically just there to get drunk and try to make *any* kind of contact with the ball. As we are all walking out, Leah takes the opportunity to completely roast my ass regarding my golf game.

"Taylor, you probably would have been better off picking up the ball and throwing it," she barely gets out through her laughter.

"You do realize I know more than one medical way to make a death look accidental, right?" I playfully glare at her as we walk out the front doors.

"Don't be a sore loser Darlin', I can teach you how to golf." Tucker smirks at me as we make our way to the exit. I try to act annoyed by the death glare I give him, but my body is so not on the same page. I keep trying to tell myself that his smile, the leather jacket, and the ripped jeans aren't the cause of my broken focus tonight, but they definitely are.

"Calm down there Tucker, you did *tie* for first. I'd rather have Max teach me." I lift my brow at him.

"Mmm. Pass," Max mumbles, drawing a laugh from Tucker, making my jaw drop open.

"Rude." I cut my eyes to Max who is snickering at his own comment.

"Maybe *Zander* could teach you how. Does he golf?" Leah chimes from behind me. For some god-forsaken reason, my eyes dart to Tucker as he holds the door open for us to exit. He cocks his head to the side, his eyes narrowing on mine. As if he's looking for an explanation for her comment. I look away as I make my way through the doors, linking my arm with Leah's when we're out in the cool night air.

"Great idea Le, I'll have to ask him." I try to ignore the way I can feel Tucker's eyes still on me. But it has blood rushing to my cheeks.

"I can't wait to meet him tomorrow," she adds, making the heat on my cheeks burn even deeper. Oh my gosh, she's cut off for the night. Tipsy Leah is a little too chatty tonight.

My eyes cut back to Tucker for a moment and that's all it takes to see the disapproval on his face. On his whole body, actually. He's standing tall with his arms folded over his chest and his eyes boring into me as I turn back to face Shane and Max.

"Okay, mister and soon-to-be missus, say your goodbyes, we've got some dancing to do!" I clap my hands together as I take a step closer to Shane. She and Max say goodbye and we make our way over to the Uber we called. I steal one more look at Tucker, unable to deny the temptation I have to try and figure out what he's thinking. His whole demeanor changed at the mention of Zander. The guy that he *apparently* wants to make me forget. He gives me a smile that doesn't quite reach his eyes before grabbing his helmet to get on his motorcycle. Maybe it wasn't the whiskey talking that night.

Chapter 5

Taylor

Girls night is in full swing and I am making sure we do it right. We decided to come dancing at the same club we came to for the black hearts event on Valentine's Day before we head home for skin care, movies, and more food than we can probably eat. I am so grateful to have a best friend who isn't obsessing over a diet before her wedding because the meal I came up with wouldn't be the same without dick-shaped pasta for the chicken alfredo.

We finish another round of shots at our table as Ruby looks over at Shane, who is grinning so big at her phone it's impossible to miss.

"I tell you what, that man has become a total simp for you." Ruby is the newest part of our crew and since Max agreed to close the bar for the weekend she's able to join us for the bachelorette party, thank God. Since more than half of the staff was going to be attending the bachelor/bachelorette parties and the wedding, it just made sense to close for the whole weekend. Shane smiles even bigger now, tucking her phone away.

"But it's only you. He still grumps at everyone else." Ruby laughs.

"Is it bad that I kind of love that?" Shane scrunches her nose.

"Hell no," I chime in eagerly. "We love a man who's only got eyes for you." I wink at her.

"And *believe me,* he only has eyes for you," Lauren's tone is a knowing one, which has us all turning to her a little confused.

"What do you mean?" Shane raises a brow, the universal sign for *elaborate.*

"Well," Lauren starts as she finishes off her spicy margarita. "When I got back in town from visiting you in San Francisco, I went to the bar to return his dog tags, as you'd asked. When I did, he got into it with some random guy who was talking very disturbingly, albeit accurately, about your ass. Then some girl at the other end of the bar not so subtly offered to help him *calm down,* sliding him her phone number on a napkin. He shut her down and threw the napkin in the garbage. Right in front of her face." She finishes and we all start laughing. Shane's face is a deep red and her mouth is hanging open.

"Oh, my god. And you're just telling me this now?" She yells, playfully shoving Lauren. "I had honestly forgotten about it until Ruby said what she did. That poor girl." Lauren shakes her head.

"Don't feel too bad for her, the alternative was her sleeping with my fiance; or at least something of the sort." Shane tosses back playfully. "I'm sure she's fine."

"Yeah, she probably used the same tactic at another bar down the street and ended up just fine. It's not her fault she hit on the one emotionally unavailable bartender in town." Leah's eyes widen as she takes a sip of her drink, making us all laugh.

"He's not emotionally unavailable. He was just emotionally invested in someone else," Shane argues, tipping her chin up confidently with a smirk on her lips.

"Okay, who's ready to go stuff our faces and rejuvenate our pores?" I close my eyes taking in a dramatic cleansing breath. When I peek my eyes open, the whole table nods in agreement so we close out our tab and pile into the Uber.

When we get back to my house, we all migrate to the master bedroom and bathroom to get our sweats on and wash our faces. I know a lot of bridal parties do the cutesy matching pajamas before a wedding, but not us. Leah, Lauren and I are all wearing our college sweats. Shane is wearing her usual Chattahoochies sweatshirt, and Ruby is sporting a Bad Bunnies hoodie from a strip club in Vegas. It has a cartoon rabbit in stilettos leaning against a pole, and I have serious questions about it. But that will have to wait.

Once we're all cozied up on the couch we turn on, what's surprisingly a group favorite, 'How To Lose A Guy In 10 Days' and let our face masks tighten our t-zones. I walk over to the kitchen to get the alfredo bake out of the oven, and I can barely contain my excitement for Shane to see it.

"I made your favorite, Chicken Alfredo – but with a bit of a twist." I try to wag my eyebrows at her, but my stiffening forehead is making that movement difficult so I just have crazy murderer eyes instead.

"*You* made it? Oh, I am beyond scared to know what the twist is." Shane laughs, "But I'm also starving so gimme," She holds her hands out with a grabbing motion as I pass her a bowl. She forks some of the pasta from the bowl and inspects it before she busts out laughing. "Oh my god, Taylor. Only you!" When the other girls look into their bowls there's a mix of amusement and shock, but if Shane thinks it's funny, then I've accomplished my goal.

"Are we really eating this?" Leah asks, with an unamused look on her face.

"You should, it's freaking bomb." Ruby says with her mouth already full of alfredo.

"If you're hungry you are, it's the only pasta I bought," I reply, shoving a bite of alfredo covered pasta dicks in my mouth. Lauren shrugs her shoulders and takes a bite before reaching for a piece of garlic bread.

"It's so… girthy." Leah says, staring at a piece before finally biting it off the fork. We all fall into a fit of laughter at her comment. I finally catch my breath and turn to my best friend.

"So, Shaney. How are you feeling about tomorrow? Are you nervous at all?" I ask, taking a sip of my water. No one likes a hungover Maid of Honor, so I went ahead and made the switch to good ole H2O.

"Honestly? No, not at all. I am so excited I feel like I could throw up, but I'm not nervous or getting cold feet at all." She smiles, sinking deeper into her fleece blanket. "Everything with Max just feels right, ya know?" She asks, looking around.

There's a unified response of "No," from the rest of us before she continues.

"It's just… I don't know. It's hard to describe. You guys remember what I was going through when I first came back. I had sworn off all men, but the very same day couldn't take my eyes off of Max. Every time I was with him he was gaining my trust. The way he showed up anytime I needed him, whether he knew I did or not is just… he's everything I didn't know I needed to be happy again. I still can't believe I get to marry him." She smiles, as she takes another bite of her wildly inappropriate but damn good pasta. I've never seen my best friend happier and I'm honored to be able to witness it firsthand.

When we finish our pasta, we rinse off the face masks and snuggle into each corner of the couch to continue watching our movie before calling it a night. Tomorrow my best friend is getting married to the man who completely changed her life. And I have a shit list a mile long to help make it happen.

Chapter 6

Tucker

It probably would have been easier to get a class of rookie SEALs through their first combat mission than it was to get Max to agree to a bachelor party and seem happy about it. Happy is a stretch, the simple fact that he isn't grumbling or trying to leave is as close to *happy* as we're gonna get. After leaving Topgolf with the girls we came straight to the cigar lounge. Max isn't big on smoking, but I know he enjoys a decent cigar every once in a while. And it's been a damn while.

I'm sitting in the chair across from him, noting the peace that's been presenting itself more and more in his life this past year. He's been my best friend since middle school, and I know every ounce of shit he's been through. I never thought I'd see the day the man was actually happy. Truly, completely happy. But Shane brought that into his life. She *is* that in his life. I'm just glad the fucker stopped being so ignorant of the fact and was able to see it for himself. It was painful to watch there for a while.

"Big day tomorrow man, how are you feeling?" Tank asks from beside him.

"Man, I'm counting down the minutes," Max answers, puffing his cigar. "She's it for me, you know? Has been since the first day I met her," he adds, smiling with his cigar gripped in his hand.

"You big softy." I pick at him, taking a sip of my whiskey.

"Oh shut up, Tucker. We can't all be players like you." He picks right back, making Tank snicker. I roll my eyes at the two of them as I sit back taking a puff from my cigar.

I'm not sure my best friend even knows I haven't been with anyone in almost two years. After the one semi-serious relationship I had ended, I would date casually here and there, but it just got to be so– unfulfilling. I never had anything in common with the women I met, and sex just got to be some routine thing. Which is the last thing it should be. I no longer have the desire to go out and try to meet someone. So I just focus on my work and hang out with the guys. Well, I should say the *group*. Ever since Max met Shane it hasn't been just the guys. She came with her own tribe of friends who we've accepted as our own now.

"Alright, what's next?" Max asks, picking up his whiskey glass, and raising a brow at me.

"What do you mean what's next?" I question, glancing over accusingly at Tank. But he just shrugs, warding off any potential blame.

"I know you've got something else planned, Tuck. So let's get on with it." Max exhales as he puts his cigar out. I grin at Max and clap my hands together.

"Well if you insist, let's go."

When we get to the next location Max looks at me with his regular, unimpressed stare.

"You understand we are way too old to be doing this right? What if we trample some nine-year-olds?" He holds his arm out toward the indoor paintball arena.

"Well, lucky for us, there won't be any nine-year-olds in there, I rented the place out tonight. Also, it's like 11 PM. I don't think nine-year-olds are allowed to be out this late. Are they?" I question looking between Max and Tank.

"Fuck if I know. Do I look like I spend my time hanging out with nine-year-olds?' Tank asks brashly. I open my mouth to rip on him about that statement but I'm cut off before I get the chance.

"Tucker," Max says, bringing my attention back to him, "why did you rent out an entire paintball arena for the three of us? That's kind of... weird. Plus we won't have even teams. What, is it every man for himself? Also, why the fuck do you have a duffle bag?" He fires off his questions while holding his arms out to his sides. Right then Max's arms get pulled behind his back in restraint. The look of anger on his face is quickly wiped when he hears one of the guys behind him shout –

"Every man for himself? You taught us better than that boss," Rip's raspy voice has Max's face lighting up. He turns around seeing Rip, Ram, and Johnny standing there smiling at him. "*'Work as a team or the team won't work'* wasn't drilled into our brains for as long as it was to go every man for himself this soon after getting out."

"Son of a bitch, what the hell are you guys doing here?" Max looks at me and then back at them, bringing them each in for a hug.

"What, you thought you were just gonna get married and us *not* be here?" Ram crosses his arms staring back at Max. He looks back at me and I shrug.

"Look, it's a miracle you even got Shane to marry you. We all know this is only happening once, they needed to be here," I tease, nodding to the group of guys from our old SEAL team.

"This means a lot, brother." Max nods appreciatively at me. "So, let's get in there then."

"Not so fast," I interject as they all move to go inside, "if we're doing late-night paintball. Then, fellas, we're doing it fuckin SEAL style." I drop the duffle bag, carefully, and pull out night vision goggles. Max grins and looks at Tank, then at Rip, Ram, and Johnny who all brought theirs with them too.

"Oh hell yeah." Max laughs as he grabs his NODs from my hand. We go in and play three rounds of 3 v. 3 – Me, Max, and Rip against Tank, Ram, and Johnny, and we smoked them all three times.

"Well, I call bullshit, you have the two of you, who have known each other long enough you probably share a brain or some shit, and one of the SEAL's best Goddamn snipers on one team, what do you expect to happen?" Tank whines. "No offense guys." He looks at Ram and Johnny half-ass apologetically.

"Shit that was a good time," Ram yells, brushing the sweat from his forehead into his dirty blonde hair.

"It really was, Tuck. Thanks again, man," Max says as he downs a bottle of water. Just then my phone goes off with a text alert. Who the fuck is texting me at 1 AM when everyone I talk to is standing in this parking lot with me?

TAYLOR

> Please don't let the groom be hungover tomorrow.
> I'm ensuring the bride is radiant and refreshed, you'd better do the same with the groom.

Well, I guess not *everyone* I talk to.

ME

> Hmm... you should have said something sooner Darlin', he's fucking hammered playing lawn darts in his underwear.

TAYLOR

> A visual I did NOT need & for the love of God, say that you're kidding.

. . .

I send a photo of me and Max to make sure she doesn't stroke out on me. He's perfectly sober, grinning ear to ear, with his water bottle conveniently visible for her sanity.

ME

What would you recommend? The seaweed scrub or a mud bath? Not sure he'll go for either but for you, I'll try.

TAYLOR

😶

ME

Come on, give me a little credit here. He's fine.

TAYLOR

I hate you.

ME

You ever gonna let me change your mind about that?

TAYLOR

Goodnight Tucker.

ME

Night Darlin'.

I smirk as I slip my phone back into my pocket just as a water bottle is chucked at my head. I look up to see Rip staring at me expectantly.

"What the fuck Rip?" I rub the top of my head as the guys all laugh.

"I thought Max here was the only one smitten and settling down." He raises an accusing brow at me. "What's got you smiling like an idiot at your phone over there Tuck?"

"That would be none of your Goddamn business." I throw the water bottle back at him. "She claims she hates me anyways, but I plan to change her mind," I tease, giving just enough information for Max to pick up on who I was talking to.

"Please do not fuck my future wife's best friend," Max says firmly. "Because God knows I will never hear the end of it when you do something to piss Taylor off. You redheads are insufferable." Max throws his empty water bottle at me.

"Because you're such a walk in the park. And my hair is barely red so you'll have to find a different reason to find me unbearable," I say, tossing the water bottle into the driver-side window of my Bronco. We ditched the bikes before coming here so we could all ride together. Not to mention I had the duffle bag hidden in the back so Max wouldn't be suspicious.

I never really thought about the effect being with Taylor, in any capacity, may have on the other people in our lives. Maybe that's selfish of me, but it's just the facts. No one else I've ever been with has had any kind of connection to my friends or family. So it never crossed my mind with her.

After learning she was seeing someone when I first asked for her number, I backed off. Though I'm starting to grow impatient waiting for this unbearably long-lasting *fling* to pass. Not to mention I was less than thrilled to learn he would be accompanying her to the wedding tomorrow. I'm not sure why this guy is showing up and meeting her friends all of a sudden. Not that it changes my intentions in the slightest. I'll be polite to *Zander* and keep playing the role of just her friend if I must, but my interest in her hasn't changed and seems to be growing more every time I am in her presence.

"Alright, we better get going, Taylor will have us by the balls if we look too tired tomorrow," I direct, doing my best to quiet the thoughts running through my mind.

"You'd like that wouldn't you *lover boy*," Johnny says, making kissing noises at me.

"Johnny, you're 45 years old. Grow the hell up." I shake my head as

I clap him on the shoulder. "See you boys at the ceremony tomorrow. Be safe getting back to the hotel." We say our goodbyes, toss our shit in the back and grab a couple of bottled waters from the cooler I keep in the back before hopping in the truck.

"Seriously Tucker. This was the most fun I've had in a while. You're a good friend putting this all together," Max says, shaking his head with an appreciative grin on his face.

"That's what brothers are for man. Now let's go get you married, huh?" I elbow him from the driver's seat before Tank gets in, slamming the door behind himself.

"Seriously though, how was it fair to stick me on a team with Ram and *Johnny*?" Tank starts bitching again. Max and I share a look, grabbing our waters from the cup holders before opening them and soaking Tank in the backseat.

"Hey Tank, stop being a little bitch and just shoot better," I joke as I toss the now empty water bottle at him.

"Maybe some of those nine-year-olds could teach you a thing or two." Max joins in making fun of Tank like the second big brother he has become to him over the years.

"I hear Hendrix isn't busy after pre-school, maybe ask him?" He barely gets out through his laughter.

"Assholes." Tank shakes his head, trying to hide his smile as he throws a water bottle back at us.

Max and I can barely contain our laughter as Tank continues on with his whining while we drive back to his house. We skip the pillow fights and giddy laughter seeing as we're grown-ass men and all. So when Max and Tank are back home, I haul ass back to mine.

Despite my body telling me to lay the fuck down immediately, I take the shower I so desperately need before calling it a night. God only knows the shit list Taylor will have for me tomorrow before the ceremony. As I close my eyes, letting the water wash over me, my mind floods with thoughts of Taylor. It seems like she's the thing on my mind the most lately.

The way she tosses her wild red curls when she gets worked up about something, her smile that shines so brightly when she's around her friends, and the look of defiance she gets when we're in our battle of wits. My mind begins to wander into new territory when I picture her perfect full lips.

I'm enthralled by the thought of what it would be like to take them with mine, or how it would feel to have my arms wrapped around her tight little body. What it might be like to have my hands gripping tight in her hair or around her full breasts. With that thought my eyes shoot open, and I wipe the water from them trying to reel myself back into reality. I have to get my shit together. Because no matter how much I want her to be, she isn't mine. Not yet at least.

When I finally make it out of the shower *relieved* of my wandering thoughts it's well past 2 AM. Thank God this wedding is happening at night, because I won't be worth shit in the morning. Just as my body hits the mattress, I hear my phone begin to go off so many times I think it's glitching.

TAYLOR

Do you have your checklist for tomorrow?

TAYLOR

I know I gave you one, but did you lose it?

TAYLOR

I'm gonna resend it.

TAYLOR

1) Steam Tux

TAYLOR

2) Make sure rings are hidden from Hendrix until it's time to walk down the aisle.

TAYLOR

3) Don't forget Riley's flower pup bandana

Max must really love Shane to let Riley wear a damn flower-covered bandana for her.

TAYLOR

4) don't forget your speech.

TAYLOR

DO. NOT. FORGET. YOUR SPEECH TUCKER!!!!

ME

Honestly Darlin', do you even need me for this conversation?

TAYLOR

This is serious. This is all important stuff. Everything has to be perfect.

ME

Look I'm not gonna forget. Some hellbent redhead has drilled my responsibilities for the day into my head. I still have my list, though I probably have it memorized now, and I have kind of a big day tomorrow. So I'm gonna go to bed now. Probably turn my phone off, but you two have fun.

TAYLOR

Two?

ME

You and whoever you're having this conversation with.

Go to sleep.

TAYLOR

I hate you.

ME

You'll change your mind one day.

The text bubbles come back for a moment before disappearing completely. I smirk and toss my phone to the side feeling a sense of pride in myself. I have never known Taylor to not have the last word. Just as I am dozing off I hear my phone ding once more. Unable to fight the urge to see if it was her, I pick it up. Peeking at the screen through one eye I can't help but smile.

TAYLOR

Unlikely.

There she is.

Chapter 7

Taylor

The day has gone about as smoothly as one could hope for a wedding planned in one week. Tucker and I grabbed coffee at Bruman's this morning and went over everything that needed to be done before it was time for Shane to walk down the aisle. I gotta say, I'm pretty damn proud of us for pulling this off.

"You are the most beautiful bride I've ever seen." Tears are welling in my eyes as I look at my best friend, minutes away from walking down the aisle. Her long blonde waves are pulled back halfway with a braid that has baby's breath woven into it perfectly. Lauren seriously missed her calling in the beauty industry. The wedding dress Shane chose is what bridal dreams are made of.

The bodice of the dress is a lace-covered corset with a sweetheart neckline, snatching her waist right above her hips. The skirt is full lace with a gorgeous whimsical flow to it with a thigh-high seam exposing her left leg. The peasant-style lace sleeves are the cherry on top. Everything about this dress screams *Shane*. I am convinced it was designed specifically for her. An artist that looks like a true work of art.

"Do not make me cry, Lauren will beat both of our asses if I mess up my makeup." Shane laughs, trying to fan away her tears.

"She's not wrong." Lauren glares playfully at us from her spot in front of the vanity. "But Taylor is right too, you're absolutely breath-taking babe!"

"I can't believe you're getting married, Shane!" Leah joins in. Now all of our makeup is threatening to be washed away by tears.

"You and Max make a beautiful couple. I am so glad you walked into the bar that day. No one else would have been able to remove the stick from his ass. At least not without surgery." Ruby takes Shane's hands as she makes her endearing comment. Our momentary threat of emotional takeover is now replaced by laughter.

"You guys are ones to talk, my besties look stunning." Shane admires us as we all strike poses in our silk gowns.

She chose the style of dress, letting us all pick our own colors. So while we all wear the same floor length, fitted spaghetti strap dress, I opted for *cerulean*, basically the most gorgeous shade of blue I've ever seen. Leah chose olive green, Lauren wears burgundy and Ruby is in plum.

"I am beyond grateful for each one of you ladies and the joy you bring to my life. I am honored to have all of you standing up there with me today." Shane pulls us in for the world's most gentle group hug, so as to not mess up hair, makeup, or dresses.

"It's time," the wedding coordinator says as she peeks her head in the bridal suite. She works in wedding planning at the hotel, and though we did all the planning ourselves, she's basically here to tell us when to walk and when to cut the cake. Deep breaths are taken all around as we line up to walk down the aisle.

"Come on Riles," Shane calls as Riley hops down wearing her floral bandana, as she is the official flower pup.

Attention whore. I swear she's my spirit animal.

We were able to book an absolutely gorgeous hotel that hosts weddings in downtown Nashville. It accommodated the last-minute timing and miraculously had rooms available for out-of-town guests and the wedding party for tonight after the reception. The banquet hall is set up beautifully with staggered candles in glass vases lining the aisle, white flower petals scattered down the runner, and white icicle lights strung all around the room.

White roses were Shane's flower of choice and they cover every inch of the room. The arch at the end of the aisle is full of roses and beautiful faux greenery. There are large, arched windows lining the back wall that make the room absolutely glow from the sun setting in the distance outside. The woodgrain seating she chose is a perfect contrast to all of the white that fills the room. Every seat is filled with family and friends, old and new, waiting to see the couple promise each other forever. When we finally get lined up, *"NeverStop (wedding version)" by Safetysuit* begins playing as our cue to walk.

I make my way down the aisle first, glancing around at all of the smiling faces, and seeing my brothers and parents in the crowd. Little Hendrix is standing up front with Max, Tucker, and Tank, looking so happy to be included. Even while pulling out a massive wedgie. *Cool move Hen.* When my gaze reaches Tucker my heart skips a beat. His green eyes are focused solely on me. So much so it feels like his gaze is burning my skin. The sexiest, most debonair smile comes across his face causing me to almost trip on my own feet. I quickly look away, trying to focus on *not* ruining my best friend's wedding by face-planting in the middle of the aisle. I watch as Leah, Lauren, Ruby, and Riley make their way down the aisle after me. But my favorite part comes when the doors have been closed as the song builds in anticipation of Shane's entrance.

When the doors open, I take a moment to appreciate my gorgeous best friend. I quickly turn my gaze to Max, who looks like it's taking everything in him to keep his feet planted. The emotion on his face, as he looks at his gorgeous bride, has a lump forming in my throat. The way he gazes at Shane through his tears is the way every girl dreams about being looked at. Anyone with eyes can see how in love he is with her. His actions speak even louder than his expressions when it comes to her too, and those speak pretty damn loud. When she finally reaches the front of the room, joining hands with Max, I hear him whisper not so quietly.

"You're a fucking vision, Sunshine. I'm the luckiest man in the world." Okay Max, a little louder and we'll *all* be crying. I wipe away my tears before grabbing her bouquet and smiling back at her as she beams brighter than ever, before exchanging vows with her soon-to-be husband. Seeing her at the beginning of her happily ever after–even with all the shit she's been through in life–makes me hopeful that it's in the cards for me one day too.

THE *Vows*

Max,

When I first met you a little over a year ago, I had just
moved back home. Broken and in need of a fresh start, I was
determined to swear off love for good and had made up my mind that
I would never trust my heart with another man ever again.
Within the first week of knowing you, you proved to me that I was
wrong in so many ways. You saved my life that week in more ways
than one, and I will never forget the impact that had on me.
You were there so many times when I was at my most vulnerable and
never made me feel anything but safe, loved, and heard.
You held me when my own anxiety threatened to take over me.
You stood with me as I opened an old wound and really faced
its reality for the first time. You let me in when it was hard for
you to do and encouraged me to chase my dreams no matter the cost.
Even though I'm still a little mad at you for that.
You told me once that you'd never let me go again, and that you
would fight for us no matter what. Today I vow to fight alongside you
against any battle we may face. I vow to be here, even when you may
not want me to be, and to fight for both of us when you feel
like you can't. I vow to love you in every way I know how and
to never let a day pass where I don't tell you how much
you mean to me. I vow to love you, honor you, and respect you
even when I'm mad at you. You told me once
I was your sunshine after a storm, well to me, you're the waves
in the sand. You're my fresh start, my new beginning,
and my love everlasting. I know life won't always be easy,
but I promise to help make it beautiful.

I love you forever. Pinky swear.

Shane,

Dammit, woman, you should have let me go first.
How am I supposed to stumble through these vows after that?
You're right, as always. You're the sunshine I needed when my life felt
like the most torrential storm with no end. The very moment I met you
I knew you were special, and when you walked away that day
I immediately needed more. I'm one lucky bastard that you walked
into my bar later that day. Every moment I spend around you
makes me a better man. You shine light and positivity in everything
that you do and everywhere that you go.
For someone with a stone-cold heart, well, that's life-changing.
I'm not sure I ever thanked you for pulling me from the brink
of darkness, but I promise to spend the rest of our lives showing
you how grateful I am for your love — the thing that saved me
from myself. You were there when I experienced my darkest day,
and you helped me come out on the other side. Loving you, and being
loved by you is undoubtedly the greatest thing that has ever
happened to me. Today I vow to always let you into every part
of my life, the good, the bad and the terrible, and never make you
wonder where you stand. I vow to give you every beautiful
memory you can imagine and experience all of life's greatest
adventures with you. I vow to keep our home stocked with
toaster strudel and iced coffee and to never let you give
up on your dreams. I vow to give you steadfast love and to be
there for you before you even have to call.
You're everything to me, Shane Mullins.
You always have been, and forever will be.

I love you forever. Pinky swear.

Chapter 8

Taylor

As the bride and groom are swaying to the song for their first dance, not a single person in the room can seem to tear their eyes from them. I've never seen my best friend happier than she is right now, and I'd bet the farm that this is the first time a smile this big has ever appeared on Max's face. Who would have thought when she came to live with me a year ago we would have ended up here? I'm jarred from my thoughts as someone snatches me up by my waist.

"Tater Tot!" His burly voice calls out as I am being spun around like a child. When my feet hit the ground I spin around to see the bright white grin spread across my brother's face.

"Sawyer, I swear to God if you ruin their first dance I'll kick your ass." I cross my arms over my chest, giving him an evil smile. He pulls me into him, squeezing me in his bear-like grip.

"Oh come on. I wouldn't do that to Shane, you know that." He pulls back glancing over my shoulder at the dance floor. "Plus, her husband would probably try to kick my ass if I did and I would hate to embarrass him on his wedding day." I snicker at the thought as he grins playfully at me. Sawyer could definitely hold his own in a fight. The man is six-foot-two, built like a house, and trains six days a week.

His long brown hair and clean-shaven face are no mask for the muscles and intimidating tattoos he hides beneath his hockey jersey. Max would still kick his ass if he ruined this for Shane though, of that I am sure.

"Yeah yeah. I'm glad you made it, where are JJ and Blaire? And Mom and Dad?" I ask, looking around the room for the rest of my crazy family.

Both of my older brothers, Sawyer and JJ, moved away for college and never really looked back. Sawyer got a hockey scholarship in Minnesota and now plays pro hockey for the Minnesota Bears and JJ went for nursing and is now a travel nurse along with his wife Blaire. I stayed local because Nashville will always be my home and it made me ill to think about living anywhere else. It really killed me when my parents decided to up and move to Colorado when I graduated from college. They always told us to chase our dreams so who was I to stop them from chasing theirs? Even though I'm not sure what dreams there are to chase in freaking Colorado, but whatever.

"I'm not sure. I came in with them but they disappeared. Who's your friend?" Sawyer nods behind me.

"Huh?" I ask, turning to see Zander closing the distance between us with a single rose in his hand. He looks handsome tonight. His sandy-colored hair is wavy and gelled back, and he's wearing a light blue button-down shirt, khaki pants with loafers and an apologetic smile. I probably would have chosen a different shoe with the outfit and I think Lauren's soul would actually leave her body if she saw them, but to each their own.

None of this excuses the fact that the reception is half an hour in, he just got here and I have not received one single text giving me a reason or heads up for his late arrival. I was beginning to think I was getting stood up.

"Sorry I'm late," he says, handing me the rose and kissing me on the cheek taking me by surprise. I find myself scanning the room for a certain pair of green eyes before turning my attention back to Zander.

"Um, it's fine. Sawyer, this is Zander. Zander, this is my older brother, Sawyer," I say, formally introducing them.

"Nice to meet you man," Zander says first.

"Yeah, you too." Sawyer takes his hand, narrowing his gaze as he assesses the situation. "Better treat Tot here right," he says, tightening his grip on Zander's hand while giving him his best *intimidating older brother* stare.

"Oh my god, Saw, it's not even like that. Calm down." I roll my eyes offering an apologetic smile to Zander to try and ease some of the awkward tension my brother dearest just created. Zander furrows his brow at me briefly before turning his attention back to Sawyer with a halfhearted laugh.

"If you'll excuse me, I think I am going to see what they have at the bar," he says, dismissing himself from the conversation. I feel a twinge of guilt as he walks away, but I'm not sure what for. He's the one that's hours late and already leaving me to go to the bar.

"Ah, there they are," Sawyer announces. I pull my gaze from Zander standing at the bar to look toward the entry to the reception hall. Heading our direction are JJ and Blaire.

I'm not sure how I got stuck with the petite gene in our family, because both of my brothers stand over six-foot tall and I am chilling at a whopping five-foot-three. I swear I must be adopted. If I didn't look exactly like my mother and JJ, I would be running tests.

"There's our favorite little spitfire," JJ calls out, sweeping me up in a hug much like Sawyer did just moments ago.

"Yes, I know, I'm crazy and small. Can we please keep my feet on the ground for the remainder of the evening?" I tease, shifting in my dress. JJ squeezes me before stepping back in line with Blaire.

"What's the matter, Tot? Not happy to see your older brothers?" Sawyer juts out his lip in a pout, leaning on JJ. I roll my eyes at the nickname.

"Sawyer, can you please call me anything else? *Anything* else," I plead. My brothers give each other a devious look that makes me immediately regret my choice of wording, as it gives them way too much freedom to come up with something much worse.

"Okay, you know what. I'm ignoring you now and I need a drink." I hold my hand up and turn to face my sister-in-law before heading over to the bar. "Blaire, so great to see you, as always." I lean in to hug her on my way past. "I still have no idea how you do this, but my praises to you." I raise my brows and cut my eyes toward JJ who gives me a shove, sending me even closer to the bar.

They all share a small laugh before I am too far out of earshot to hear where the conversation goes next. Hopefully it's not to think of a nickname *worse* than the one they've called me since I was a child. I'm a mere four feet from the bar, with my head still facing the direction of my perfectly dysfunctional family, when I bump into someone. I gasp, turning my head to see who it was just as two warm hands grab onto my arms to keep me from stumbling further.

"Careful there Darlin'." Tucker's voice sends butterflies to my stomach immediately. I smile as I take him in, relieved I didn't run into a stranger instead. His rugged and charming grin lights up his face immediately. Tucker is even taller than JJ and Sawyer, probably six-foot-five, and is built like what Shane once referred to as a Viking God. She wasn't wrong either. His muscles fill out every inch of his tux in a way that has every female's attention on him tonight. Though his attention is on...*me.*

"Sorry about that, I uh... Well, I just wasn't paying attention." I laugh, nervously brushing a loose strand of red curls out of my face.

"No worries." He picks a martini glass up off the bar table we're standing next to, "I was actually about to come over and bring you this." He hands me the most perfect-looking key lime martini and my eyes dart from the glass back up to his.

"Really? Why?" I ask in surprise, making his face twist in confusion.

"Just thought you might like a drink. You've been running around here without stopping all night, I thought it might help you to slow down," he answers, bringing his drink up to his lips.

"Right, well. Thank you." I shake my head, turning to face the crowd of people.

"Correct me if I'm wrong, but did someone call you Tater Tot?" Tucker looks at me from the corner of his eye, lifting a brow in question.

"*How* did you possibly hear that?" My eyes go wide as I turn to face a smirking Tucker. He shrugs without answering. Holding my stare as he continues to drink his beer. I sigh before looking over at my brothers, who are now engaged in conversation with Leah and Lauren. "Yes, unfortunately, you did." My eyes roll with the admission.

"Are you really going to make me ask?" Tucker laughs, leaning his elbow on the tabletop as all of his attention focuses on me, bringing a slight blush to my cheeks. I mirror his movement, facing him fully now.

"My older brothers, Sawyer and JJ over there, have called me Tater Tot for as long as I can remember. As you can *clearly* see, I am the runt of the Clark litter and therefore, a tot in their adolescent minds." I turn my head to face them again, as they all make their way onto the dance floor. "They always got a kick out of torturing me when we were younger, but I never gave them the satisfaction. I just acted like it didn't bother me." When I turn to look back at Tucker, he is staring down at me, his forest green eyes unwavering from my own. The look in them makes my heart begin to beat a little faster as the silence forms an unfamiliar tension between the two of us.

He opens his mouth to say something but another voice from behind me catches my attention before he can. This time my stomach drops for a different reason.

Zander. *Shit, I forgot about him.*

"Am I interrupting something?" Zander asks, in a more arrogant tone than I am used to. I quickly turn to face him, plastering a smile on my face that I *know* looks unnatural.

"No, not at all," I assure him before looking back at Tucker. His jaw is set and he looks more bothered than I've ever seen him. "Uh,

Zander this is Tucker, Tucker this is Zander." The two of them face off for a moment before Zander nods but neither of them speaks.

What the hell is happening right now?

"Well, this is for you." Zander clears his throat before smiling at me, handing me a glass of white wine.

"Oh, thank you." I accept the drink, trying my best to sound grateful, when in reality white wine and I do *not* get along. The migraines I get after drinking white wine are about as appealing as the cabbage patch my father is busting out on the dance floor right now. I feel the need for an aspirin just thinking about drinking this, but I'm not about to tell him that.

Especially in front of Tucker.

As I take the glass from him I hear a huff from beside me.

"Geez man, are you *trying* to kill her?" Tucker mumbles, under his breath, though I'm sure Zander still heard it.

Tucker is well aware of my battle with white wine after my overindulgence in it one night after Topgolf and the whole next day all I did was complain about how bad my head hurts when I drink it. He made sure to let me know how dumb I was and I made him promise he wouldn't let me drink it anymore if he could prevent it. Now I'm scared he'll actually follow through and embarrass my date in the process. I throw a threatening glare Tucker's way but he seems unfazed by it.

"Something funny?" Zander asks Tucker with a bite to his tone.

"Actually–" Tucker starts, with a smug look on his face. But before he can get the rest of his impending insult out, another familiar voice joins the mix.

"Pardon my interruption," Tank says, with a deep swagger to his voice. "Taylor, could I have this dance?" He smiles at me, offering his hand. I glance between Tucker and Zander who both look equally confused, then down at the drink in my hand.

I take this as a perfect out so that I don't have to bear witness to whatever was about to unfold here.

"I would love to. Do you mind?" I ask Zander as I give Tucker my wine glass and reach for Tank's hand. Zander looks pissed as Tank and I stride onto the dance floor. He spins me around, making me laugh before pulling me in closer, placing his hand respectfully on my waist.

"You have no idea how impeccable your timing is," I say, offering him a grateful smile.

"Oh, but I do. Believe me, I know when my brother is getting territorial. Someone needed to break his focus before things got out of hand." He raises a brow as he leads us effortlessly around the dance floor.

"Territorial? No, he was just giving Zander a hard time about the drink he ordered me," I correct. His timing may be impeccable but his assessment is way off.

"Whatever you say then." He smirks, before his eyes drift across the room. I glance over at where Tucker and Zander stand and notice the way Tucker seems more tense than before. His jaw is set, showing the sharp edges even from his side profile. I'm relieved when I see Max approach them and Zander finally turns his attention to him instead of Tucker. When I turn back to Tank, feeling rude for zoning out for so long, I notice I'm not the only one who's been distracted. I follow his gaze to where Ruby and Hendrix are dancing together. I see a little glimmer of joy in Tank's eye as he watches them, waiting a beat before I clear my throat.

"See something you like, Tank?" I playfully accuse. He turns back to me, no haste in his movements.

"I have no idea what you're talking about." He pulls away from me, spinning me once more before we continue our dance. "I was just looking at the little monster who apparently wore the wrong size underwear today. Dude had like five wedgies throughout the whole ceremony." That draws a laugh from deep within my stomach.

"Oh my God, I know. Poor kid. He probably put them on backwards again." The song ends and Tank brings my hand to his lips, planting a gentle kiss to my knuckles.

"Thank you for the dance." He winks at me, mirroring the same charm his brother seems to wield.

"Thank *you*." I smile at him as the rest of the bridesmaids rush our way.

"Hiii, we have a bridal emergency and we need you," Lauren says, taking me by the hand.

"Stat," Ruby urges. I hear Tank laugh and look over to see him giving Ruby a very flirtatious glance, but she seems oblivious to it.

"Okay, let's go," I agree as we all make our way out of the reception hall to the bridal suite.

Chapter 9

Tucker

"I'm uh, guessing you were going to harp on me for the drink choice then?" Zander clears his throat, starting our conversation back but I can't take my eyes off of my *brother* now dancing with Taylor.

I shrug as I place the wine glass on the table. "Eh, she just gets really shitty migraines if she drinks white wine. She wouldn't *actually* die." I turn to face the dance floor again before adding, "Though she may make everyone around her wish *they* were dead from listening to her complain the whole next day. Can't go wrong with a martini though." We stand in a somewhat awkward silence for a moment, before a laugh I can't contain escapes from my throat, remembering how she acted the last time she drank too much wine.

"You guys better never let me drink that shit again. I'm serious. I think my head is gonna fall off onto the floor."

A grin creeps over my face when I picture her wearing the ice pack eye mask thing that she *swore* would get rid of her headache faster.

"So, what? Are you fucking her too then?" Zander scoffs. The heat that immediately washes over my whole body could set this room on fire.

"Excuse me?" I ask through gritted teeth. This asshole better have a seriously good reason for the words that just left his mouth.

"I mean, you know her drink preference. The way you look at her. Hell, the way she acted when I interrupted your conversation a minute ago. *Something* must be going on," he accuses. I don't know who this jackass thinks he is, but I'm about to help him find his fucking place.

No one talks about my friends like that, *especially* not Taylor. Not to me. I turn to fully face him, closing what little distance is between us until we're almost toe to toe.

"Listen to me closely, *Zander*. Not only is Taylor way out of your fucking league, and way too sweet– albeit wild at times– to be with a condescending asshole like you. But she is also a *very* good friend of mine. And *no one* will disrespect *my* friends without serious repercussions." His brows draw in and nostrils flare at my words.

Oh, now he's pissed.

Good.

"Now, I suggest you find somewhere else to stand, before you get knocked on your ass," I finish just as Max approaches us from his place on the dance floor.

"Everything okay here, gentlemen?" I keep my stare locked on Zander until he finally breaks eye contact to respond to Max.

"Everything's fine. I was just about to go look for my date." He smirks, reminding me that she's here with him and not me. The one and *only* thing he'll be able to use to get under my skin. Because man, does it ever. When he finally leaves the room, my shoulders release tension I hadn't realized built up during our conversation. I turn to face Max as he pins me with a familiar look.

"Who the hell was that?" he asks as we approach the bar.

"*That* was Taylor's date. Great guy," I say sarcastically.

"Ah." He nods in realization. "And would the girl he's here with happen to be the reason it looked as though you were seconds away from rearranging some of his organs?"

"Maybe. Maybe it was the disrespectful way he spoke about her to me. Regardless, some rearranging would do him some good." I hold up two fingers to the bartender before plopping down on a barstool. Max takes the stool beside me, studying me as I stare blankly ahead.

"Something on your mind, Maxwell?" I ask with unamused charm.

"You like her." It's not a question and I don't quite know what to make of that. My facade drops instantly. My jaw is tight to keep me from saying…well, anything. I turn to watch as people cha cha slide on the dance floor, trying my best to ignore the way Max is staring at me, waiting for confirmation. Maybe if I don't answer he'll move on and leave it alone.

"Alright. You can ignore me, that's fine. Just do me a favor, and be sure if you are into her," he says, grabbing his beer as he lifts from his place seated next to me. Alright, I'll budge.

"What are you getting at?" He lets out a deep sigh, sitting back down beside me.

"From what I hear she hasn't had the best past with dating. She's all but protested against the idea up until now. So if you're into her, just be sure. Don't want anyone getting hurt at the end of it all. That means you too, man." He claps me on the shoulder like some old wise guy.

"Did something happen?" I ask, unable to stop the words before they leave my lips.

"I don't know the details. All I know is she got hurt, and she shut down." He lets out a *hmph*. "Pretty relatable huh?" He smirks at me, and I smile back. Though my heart isn't in it, because all I can think about is finding who hurt her. He smiles brighter as Shane and the bridesmaids come walking back through the doors to the reception hall.

"Excuse me, I have to go steal my bride," he says as he strides across the room. He pulls Shane onto the dance floor as the music slows down, the two of them smiling as they sway back and forth. I laugh at the sight of my best friend, the guy always known as *the grumpy one*, looking like a love-sick puppy with his new wife. From the corner of my eye, I notice gorgeous red curls and a perfect body wrapped in blue silk being escorted onto the dance floor as well.

When he pulls her body into his, I'm hit with an overwhelming sense of dread and annoyance.

When Leah and Lauren approach the bar, I tear my gaze from the dance floor giving them a nod as I turn to face my beer. Minding my own business has never been an issue, but tonight I can't ignore the conversation they have as they wait.

"I still can't believe she decided to start dating again," Lauren says quietly, her tone an endearing one.

"I know. This is big. Does she seem happy with him to you?" Leah asks, sounding a little more reserved.

"Yeah. I mean it's still new, but why wouldn't she be?" Lauren turns to face her, sounding as curious as I am at the question.

"I don't know. She just said he felt like the *safe* choice. But that just doesn't seem like Taylor does it? I mean if she's happy, then that's all that matters. I don't know. I just don't want her to get hurt again. Not after she finally put herself out there after all this time. You know?"

"I'll kick his ass if he does anything to hurt her," Lauren agrees as she grabs her drink from the bartender. I am on the edge of my seat, wanting to jump in and ask questions.

Who the fuck hurt her?

"Yeah, especially if it's anything like last time. He'll have taken his last breath if he's anything like *that* asshole." Leah grabs her margarita and they clink their glasses in agreement. I go from the edge of my seat to completely out of it; no holding back now.

"Do either of you lovely ladies know where I can find this asshole so *I* can kick his ass?" I smile at them humorlessly. They give each other *oh shit* glances, clearly not realizing that two seats away from where they were having this very private conversation, was still close enough for me to hear every word.

"Who are you talking about?" Leah asks, feigning ignorance.

"Whoever the guy is that I keep hearing about that hurt Taylor so badly she won't date. At least not until now, apparently." I shoot a displeased look over my shoulder where I see Zander and Taylor in deep conversation on the other side of the room.

"It's really not our place to say. Taylor doesn't talk about it and would kill us if she knew we were." Lauren glances at Leah, both of them now wearing a look of guilt.

"Please don't say anything to her. It would only open old wounds and end up hurting her," Lauren pleads with me. My jaw tightens and every fiber of my being wants to keep digging for information. But, like Max said, the last thing I want to do is end up hurting Taylor.

"Sure. I won't mention it to her," I agree. Relief washes over them as they make their way across the room. I, on the other hand, am quite unsettled by what I've heard tonight.

I grab my drink and head to my seat at the bridal party table when I see Zander's hands slide down Taylor's body, pulling her closer to him. My blood begins to heat at the sight of his hands mere inches above her perfect ass.

I hate the sight of it, and the way it reminds me they've actually slept together before. That thought alone has my feet moving before I even know where they're taking me. I place my drink on the table closest to me, and seconds after weaving through the crowded dance floor I'm standing directly behind Taylor.

"Mind if I cut in?" Taylor's head spins around, her grayish-blue eyes landing on mine. The blue in them is much more prominent tonight. Likely being pulled from the color of her dress. They're more rain and less rain-cloud tonight. "As best man and maid of honor, I feel it's only right for us to share at least *one* dance." I smirk as Taylor turns back to Zander. Just as I start to think she might be ignoring me, I find relief when I hear her ask,

"Do you mind?" Her tone is as sweet as honey, and completely wasted on him. He hesitates for a moment before nodding in agreement.

"Thanks, pal." I spin Taylor around to face me as we fall in step with the music seamlessly.

"What are you doing?" she hisses, trying to watch where her *date* wanders off to, but I move swiftly to block her view.

"Well, I'm not sure what the official name of this particular dance is, but I'm glad it's a slow one." I wink at her and she rolls her eyes dramatically.

"Don't play dumb, Tucker. I mean why are you interrupting my date?" She pins me with her curious stare. *Because I don't want you on it* is what I want to say. But in the spirit of not unpacking that statement in the middle of the dance floor, I decide against it.

"Just wanted a dance, Darlin'. I can leave if you want, just say the word," I offer. Hoping like hell she doesn't tell me to go. I'm not so sure I would keep my word if she did.

"No, it's fine." She takes in a deep breath, sounding as though she's relieving mounds of stress through her exhale.

"You know, if you ever get sick of being a nurse, you'd make a kick-ass wedding planner," I tell her as I look around the room. I may have given her shit about staying on me with the details, but she clearly knew what she was doing. The wedding she pulled off in a week's time is absolutely mind-blowing.

"Yeah right. I could have done so much more if I'd had the time." She looks around the room, but my eyes are glued to her. Noting the way her curls are falling out of the claw clip holding half of her hair up. The way the freckles on her face still peek through the makeup so pristinely painted on her cheeks. As though whoever applied it knew not to cover up their beauty. Most of all, I note the smile on her face as she admires the couple she pulled all of this off for.

"I think if you asked them, they'd say it was perfect." I nod toward Max and Shane who are clinging to each other on the other side of the dance floor.

"Well, I can't take all the credit. I didn't do it alone." She smiles, glancing over at the other bridesmaids all laughing at the bar.

"True. I did a pretty badass job too." The laugh that falls from her lips makes the smile on my face broadened. "I mean, look at this tux. Not a damn wrinkle in sight. Plus, my speech? Come on. That one old lady could barely catch her breath. I was making her laugh so hard," I add, making her laugh even harder now.

The way her body leans into mine as she laughs has me tightening my grip to keep her there. She looks up at me as she catches her breath, her arms draping over my shoulders now as we sway to the song filling the room. I hate that she's been hurt by love. That she was jaded for so long after. Most of all I hate that the person she's giving a chance to now is that pretentious asshole. But I know I'll change her mind. Maybe not yet. Maybe not *here*. But I will.

"So how long are you going to pretend to be interested in the guy you're here with tonight?" The boldness of my words sends shock across her face.

"What the hell is that supposed to mean?" she asks in a hushed demand.

"It means I want to know how long I'm going to have to wait for you to see that you should be with *me*." My lips brush her ear before I spin her body away from mine. I pull her back in, bringing her body even closer to mine. Her breasts brush against my abdomen and I can feel her perky nipples through the silk dress.

"Forever, probably. Because that's never gonna happen," she says very matter of factly.

"You keep telling yourself that, while your body is telling me something very different." I run the back of my knuckle along her nipple to prove my point. Her body jolts slightly, though she never backs away. I'm close enough to her now that her scent is invading every sense I have. The song we're dancing to comes to an end as I see Zander making his way toward us again.

"You're worth the wait. Have a good night, Peach." I pull away slightly, but her hand remains in mine.

"Peach?" she asks, her face twisting in confusion. I lean back in slightly, lowering my voice to ensure only she can hear it.

"You have no business smelling as good as you do tonight. Do you have any idea how badly I want to sink my teeth into you to see if you taste as good as you smell? All while you're here with another man." I tsk, giving her a playful disapproving shake of my head. She gasps and I pull away just as Zander steps behind Taylor. Her eyes are wildly searching mine as he wraps his arm around her shoulder.

"I heard someone say it's time for sparklers. Is that something you should be in charge of?" he asks with a laugh. She shakes her head as if to clear her thoughts before looking around the room frantically.

"Um, yeah we're supposed to gather everyone outside. Are you ready?" She looks at me still in a state of shock and I nod. Holding my hand out I usher her in front of me.

"As ready as I was trained to be." I wink at her, making her breathe out a relaxed laugh. We sent the happy couple off with so many sparklers it looked daylight out, and almost as if it was planned, as soon as the sparklers burned out, fireworks started right above the building. Apparently, the hotel we booked for the wedding has a firework show on New Year's Eve.

Who knew?

When Max's truck is no longer in sight and our wedding duties are done we all pile back inside the reception hall. Small groups start loading onto the elevators to make their way up to the rooms we rented for the night. When I see Taylor and Zander stepping onto one, I can feel all the blood draining from my face. I've been playing it cool tonight– as much as I could at least– but I am absolutely not okay with this. Knowing what will happen when they go to that room, and I have no reasonable way to stop it.

Chapter 10

Taylor

Waiting for the elevator isn't so boring when Tank is drunkenly trying to convince us he can moonwalk – as he repeatedly fails to do so. We all laugh, unable to hold it in any longer as he trips over his feet for the fifth time in a row.

"Catch me when I'm sober and I'll show you *all* that I can do it." He swats the air leaning against the wall across from the elevator doors. Zander leans down to whisper in my ear.

"Strange bunch you've got here, Taylor." My face twists in disapproval at his remark. Suddenly I'm very relieved that he's standing behind me and unable to see my face. I had been excited at the thought of having a room reserved for after the wedding. Hotel sex? Definitely here for it. But for whatever reason that excitement has turned into dread.

I can't pinpoint what's caused the dread exactly, if it was how awkward I felt while introducing him to Sawyer earlier. Or if maybe it's the new, *very* intense, vibe happening with Tucker. He's all but melted my brain with the way he's acted and the things he's said tonight. Or I could just be exhausted from going nonstop between work and wedding planning for a week straight and be in desperate need of some sleep. I suddenly care less about hotel sex and more about snuggling up with a face mask and some crappy TV.

The ding from the elevator finally arriving has me pulling my attention back to what's going on around me. The rest of the bridesmaids and Tank all file into the elevator before Zander and I but when I glance around to hold the door for Tucker he isn't anywhere to be seen. I could have sworn he had been standing in the hall with us though. When the doors close we ride to the fifth floor in silence, the night likely catching up with all of us now. I'm pretty sure Tank fell asleep standing up in the short amount of time it took us to get here. He almost falls over when we reach our floor and the elevator comes to a halt.

That's one thing I'll give Tank Landry, the boy knows how to have a good time. I take a deep breath as I unlock the door to my room, hoping Zander is cool with watching a movie and going to sleep. Because I absolutely have no energy for shenanigans tonight. His phone starts ringing loudly before we even step foot inside.

"Shit! I gotta go. I'm on call tonight and they need me at the hospital," he says in frustration. "I would say I'll come back if I get the chance, but with it already being so late I'm sure you'll be asleep by then," he adds. I try to hide the little bit of excitement I'm feeling from knowing I get to have some alone time tonight.

"Bummer." I frown with a dramatic pouty lip. "But that's okay. We can try to hang again another time." I run a hand along his arm giving him a reassuring smile.

"Sure, another time." He nods in agreement and smiles, kissing my cheek before he leaves. I wait as he makes his way back to the elevators, waving bye once more before the doors close. Once they're sealed I run into my room letting out a small squeal of excitement.

I throw my heels into the corner where my bag lays and strip out of my silk bridesmaids gown. It's gorgeous I'll give Shane that, but I cannot wait to be in my pajamas. I take a quick shower, not needing to pamper too much since a wax was part of my wedding prep. Once my charcoal face mask is in place, and my new favorite black silk pajama set is on, I snuggle into bed to see what I can find on TV.

I'm not even 30 minutes into The Real Housewives when I start to hear an unavoidable noise on the other side of my wall. I heard my loud ass neighbor stumbling around the hall about 15 minutes ago when I was in the bathroom washing charcoal off my face, but it's only gotten louder since then. I try to give it time and tell myself to calm down, it *is* New Year's Eve after all. But once they start yelling so loud that the wall lamp shakes, I'm throwing my covers off and storming out the door.

I bang on the door repeatedly to get them to answer, positive they can't hear me out here over their own obnoxious commotion. I'm ready to verbally light into whoever opens this door, only my mouth snaps shut when I see who it is.

"Hey there Darlin', what a nice surprise," Tucker drawls with a smug look on his face. I had no idea he was the one I was sharing a wall with tonight. He looked good in his tux but *damn* is the look of him in only his slacks and dress shirt– that's now unbuttoned sinfully low– putting up a fight. His chest is covered in tattoos and hair that is proudly on display. His sleeves are rolled up too, showcasing the muscles that flex beneath his tattooed forearm. I don't realize the way I'm leering at his arms and hands until a low chuckle escapes his lips.

"Something I can do for you?" he asks in amusement.

Um, yeah I can think of about a million things, all of them way too inappropriate to want from you.

I shake my head, trying to blink away all the dirty thoughts I'm having about Tucker, because *what the fuck?*

"Yes, actually. Could you keep it the hell down in here?" I cross my arms over my chest placing my usual Taylor attitude back where it belongs. In charge.

"I didn't realize we were bothering you. I figured you'd be making your own noise over there." He starts off teasing, but his voice sounds more venomous at the end.

"If you'd like, I can turn The Real Housewives up and disrupt *your* evening. Then we'll be even," I fire back. He scoffs in amusement, leaning against the doorway now bringing our bodies even closer together. He scans my face and I am suddenly mortified at the fact that I marched over here with zit cream strategically placed all over my face.

"Poor guy," he mutters under his breath. The realization hits me like a damn truck then.

"You think Zander is in there? *That's* the noise you were concerned about?" I see his whole body shift in discomfort, his eyes cutting to the room behind him.

"No." *Liar.*

"Because I'd have a guy in my room when I look like *this.*" I point to my face, drawing attention to the thing I was embarrassed by just moments ago.

"I don't know. Don't much care either. Now, we'll keep it down so you can watch your shitty TV show and scare away the zits trying to set up camp on your face. Do you need anything else?" His tone is dismissive and his words take me by surprise.

"No, there isn't," I bark back.

"Then sleep tight Darlin'." He winks at me before closing the door and I storm off to my room hating the way I love when he winks at me. Only when I snatch at my door knob do I realize – I rushed out without my key.

Shit.

I would ask the other girls for help or see if I can sleep in one of their rooms but they're inconveniently a floor below me and I don't exactly feel like traipsing through the hotel in my silk shorts and zit cream-covered face. The option to ask Tucker, my only reasonable option at this moment, has me wanting to sleep on the floor right here in the hallway. Especially after that exchange.

We never have actual arguments or fights. They've always been sarcastic exchanges or some sort of crazy battle of wits. Never has there been real tension between us. But tonight, he seems bothered and the tension feels real. I suck in a humbling breath as I approach his door again. This time it's much quieter on the other side. I knock three times, my heart pounding faster each time my knuckle hits the wood. When Tucker opens it again, I'm equally embarrassed and relieved it's him that opens it.

"Forget something?" He smiles as he leans against the door.

He must stop. At the very least he could wear the hotel comforter as a robe because the reaction I keep having when I see him like this– cannot be happening.

"I left my key in my room." I roll my eyes admitting my defeat.

"Aaand what do you want me to do about that?" he questions.

"I don't know Tucker, help me? At least let me wash this shit off my face so I can go downstairs and get a new one," I plead. He looks me up and down, making me very aware of every part of my skin that is showing.

"Absolutely not. You're not walking down there like that alone," he states, shaking his head in disapproval.

"I'm a big girl Tucker, I can go by myself. It's not like I'm naked," I quip. The raise of his brow and hint of hunger in his eyes have me feeling instantly sobered.

"Get in here." He glances around the hallway as he sidesteps from the entry. My feet stay planted as I watch in horror behind him.

"Who the hell is in there?" I whisper.

"Just the guys. Rip, Ram, Johnny, and Tank."

"So I can't walk downstairs to get my room key looking like this, but I can just waltz in there with every guy you know?" I take a step in the door, my voice returning to its normal octave.

"Just go to the bathroom and wash your face, Peach." The nickname he coined for me earlier makes my heart flutter again. He's so hot and cold tonight and I simply don't know what to make of it. I finally do as he says, slipping into the bathroom before anyone notices my presence.

I shut the door and wash the cream off my face, drying it with a hand towel folded neatly on the rack above the toilet. I'm just about to open the door when it swings open from the other side. Instinctively I gasp, jumping back a bit as Tucker appears in the doorway.

"Jesus Tucker, you scared me. What are you doing in here?" I ask, clutching my chest.

"Put these on." He hands me a pair of gray jogger-style sweatpants and a NAVY T-shirt. I look at the clothes neatly folded in his hands then back up at his face.

"And why would I do that?" I question, drawing a sigh from his lips.

"Dammit woman, can you just do as you're told?" My jaw drops slightly at his request because absolutely not. But also, that was sexy as hell. I love a man in charge.

Or at least that's what I would love. Seeing as how I've never had that before.

My expression urges him to elaborate further.

"I am way too exhausted and slightly too drunk to have to lay out any one of those guys for looking at you a little too long. Now, will you put the damn pants on? Please."

Umm, call it a red flag but I would do anything this man asked me to do right now. Maybe because I too am exhausted and clearly not of sound mind. I nod before going to shut the door. Ushering him out while trying to hide the effect his words are having on me. Once I'm changed I place my silk pajamas on the counter and make my way out into Tucker's room. I'm relieved to see some of the other guys dressed more casually in jeans and T-shirts, Tucker being the only one still in any of his wedding attire. Those slacks must be hella comfortable for him to still be in them at almost two in the morning.

"Oh my God, for the last time. She was so *not* into you dude," Tank yells from his seat closest to the window.

"You don't know shit about dick, you were drunk half the night," another guy argues back. "Maybe you can chime in. The bridesmaid, purple hair, black dress." He stumbles to get his words out. I glance around confused, looking to someone, *anyone* for help.

"She has black hair and was wearing a purple dress, and if you even *try* to make a move on her I will drop you, you clown," Tank barks, kicking the guys chair.

Damn Tank.

"Ah, so you're talking about Ruby?" I tread carefully into the conversation, unsure of where exactly it's going.

"Ruby," drunk guy repeats in a daze. "You think she'd be into me?" he asks, looking at me pleadingly. My instincts tell me that's a hard no. But I am also pretty positive this guy isn't in the condition to hear that. Or even recall this conversation tomorrow. I cross my arms over my chest, taking a few steps closer to where they're all seated around the room.

"Well, first I think it might help to be able to decipher a girl's hair color from the color dress she's wearing," I start, making Tank snicker. "But also, I'm afraid unless your name is Hendrix–"

"I can change my name," he cuts me off.

"*Or* you're three, obsessed with monster trucks, and share her DNA. Probably gonna be a no," I continue. The empty look on his face tells me my statement more than likely went directly over his head.

"No Rip, she said no." Tucker claps his shoulder as he takes a seat on the bed. He nods me over so I take a seat on the bed next to him.

"Taylor, I'm sure you remember Rip, Ram, and Johnny. They were on Max and my SEAL team. They're like family. The distant kind you don't claim, but family nonetheless." He smirks at them, making me smile.

"Of course. Nice to see you guys again. Sorry for crashing your little after party, I uh… locked myself out of my room," I sheepishly admit.

"Oh don't worry about it, I'm just glad we didn't show up in the *exact* same outfit." Ram winks at me, as I notice he's wearing the same T-shirt Tucker gave me to wear. "You wear it better anyhow." I hold my arms out to my side as Tucker's shirt *swallows* me, and laugh.

"Alright, cool it, Ramone," Tucker bites from beside me. *Touch-y.*

"Yeah yeah, we gonna play or what?" Ram pulls a deck of cards off the table and begins shuffling.

"What are you playing?" I ask, peeking up over Tucker's shoulder.

"Poker. You know how to play?" Tucker asks, cutting his eyes to me.

"Not anymore. I used to know how a long time ago but I'm a little too rusty to be playing with a group," I admit.

"Well, you can watch for a bit and if it comes back to you and you wanna deal in then that's alright. Right, fellas?" Tucker encourages as he sifts through his hand. They collectively agree and I sit back watching them play round after round. I catch myself nodding off around 3 AM but when I go to tell Tucker I need to get back to my room, no words come out. One final blink and I'm down for the count.

Chapter 11

Tucker

PLAYING poker until sunup is not something I should be doing well into my thirties. Once the guys left I nodded off for a couple of hours in the chair, not wanting to wake Taylor by getting in the bed. No matter how tempted I was to do so. Footsteps in the hallway jolted me awake right at 9 AM. I was surprised to see Taylor sleeping through it. The sound was similar to elephants marching down the halls. I figure I'll take advantage of the time, and hop in the shower before she wakes up.

I like the look of her in my clothes, in my bed. She may sleep like a bear in hibernation, but she's quiet as a mouse. I forgot she was even behind me a few times last night. I take my time in the shower, letting the water do its best to wake me up. Though I'm more desperate for coffee with each passing minute. Once I step out, wrapping a towel around my waist I realize I gave her my only other shirt last night. When I open the door to the bathroom to grab my jeans, I am met with a sleepy-eyed Taylor. She jumps back startled when the door swings open.

"Oh, my god. You almost gave me a heart attack." Her eyes are sealed shut as she places her palm to her chest.

"Is that your professional diagnosis?" I tease.

"Yes. It is." She rubs her eyes trying to clear her vision. Once they open, she lets them slowly rake over my body until she meets my gaze.

"Like what you see, Darlin'?" My voice is deep, making her eyes go wide when she realizes she's been caught. Her phone dings in her hand as she opens her mouth to answer. She looks down to read whatever came through before locking the screen.

"I need to use the bathroom." She tilts her head to look up at me, completely ignoring my previous question.

"All yours," I answer, side stepping just enough that she has to squeeze past me. Her shoulder brushes my abdomen on her way past and when my feet are firmly placed on the carpeted floor she slams the door shut in my face.

I like seeing her bothered. Not in the way she's normally bothered by me. Bothered in a way that makes her nipples as hard for me as they were last night. I walk across the room grabbing my boxers and blue jeans from my bag, sliding them on and discarding my towel on the floor. Just as I am walking towards the bathroom to let her know I'll be needing my shirt back she rushes out of the bathroom and into the hallway with her phone to her ear. She's still wearing my shirt, but the sweatpants I let her borrow no longer cover her porcelain skin. I glance in the bathroom and see them on the floor and her black silk shorts missing. Well thank God she's got *something* on underneath the shirt she's wearing like a dress.

"Wait, you're where?" she asks, her voice sounding panicked as the door closes behind her. I don't think much of it until I realize we share a friend group, and my mind starts thinking the worst.

I grab my key off the dresser, sliding it into my front pocket before rushing out the door behind her. Hoping I catch her in the hallway so I'm not galavanting around shirtless. To my surprise she's standing right outside the door, holding her phone down to her side. I quickly realize all of our friends are fine. Taylor's head whips around to face me, her eyes going wide when she sees my shirtless body. She turns back to face Zander who looks pissed as hell right now. I can't help but smirk seeing the way he turns red after seeing me. I didn't forget what an asshole he was being last night and the way he talked about Taylor.

"I swear it's not what it looks like," she starts to explain.

"Really? I would love to hear what it is then." He frowns, crossing his arms over his chest expectantly.

"I just... Well last night...I..." she stutters her words. She turns back to me again, huffing when she does. "Do you need something, Tucker?" As if my presence in the hallway is the problem. I'm pretty sure they've got bigger issues than me, but sure.

"You're wearing my only other shirt." I glance at Zander and I think I see smoke emerge from his ears.

"Then can't you just wear your dress shirt or something?"

"I would much prefer to wear that one, Darlin'." Her whole face goes red at my comment. Zander scoffs, turning to make his way down the hall.

So long douchebag.

Much to my surprise though, Taylor runs after him.

"Zander, wait. Please let me explain what happened..." she calls out before they're out of earshot. I'm not sure why she's running after this guy. The way he's acting is insanely immature in my opinion. Though I know I'm not helping the situation much.

Do I care? No.

I don't want Taylor upset or trying to explain herself over a simple misunderstanding, but I also don't want her with him.

Selfish? Probably.

But the sooner this guy is out of the picture, the sooner I can paint her a better one.

I'm still reeling over the conversation I heard between Leah and Lauren during the reception last night. I want to know who hurt her. Why she would still be mending wounds from so long ago. It must have been pretty bad for it to still affect her. I want her to be happy and taken care of. But I'll be damned if it's anyone else but me doing it.

I tap my key on the handle, walking back into the room once it's unlocked. I guess I will be waiting out their argument–or whatever is happening out there– in here. I *could* put my dress shirt back on as Taylor suggested. But I will still need to get my shirt back from her and she'll need the other half of her black silk pajamas. God the way she looked in those silk shorts and button-up. There was no way I was letting the guys see her like that. I love them like family no doubt, but they have no business even trying to look at her the way I do. I'm almost done tidying the room when I hear a knock at the door. It's the most aggravated and slow three-pound knock I've ever heard.

I walk over and look through the peephole, double-checking that it's her. I plaster a smile on my face when I see that it is.

"Hey there Darlin', what a nice surprise," I repeat my opening statement from last night. "Wow, this kinda feels like déjà vu," I tease. She rolls her eyes before storming into the room, pushing her tiny little body past mine as she does.

"Ugh, Tucker what the hell was that?" she grumbles.

"Not an invitation to come in and yell at me." I close the door before turning to face her.

"Zander was already being weird about you and I talking last night. Now *this*. He thinks we're sleeping together or something," she yells as she gestures her arms between us.

"And that would be a bad thing, why?" I narrow my gaze at her, taking a few steps closer. She stands up straighter now, swallowing hard as her eyes slip briefly from my face to my exposed chest. When her eyes are locked firmly on mine again, she looks like she's ready for battle. Here we go. I love when Taylor's fired up.

"Really? Why would it be bad for you and I to sleep together? You mean *outside* of the fact that I don't sleep around with more than one person at a time? Or the fact that last night was *supposed* to be our first date and it went borderline disastrously, ending with him coming to take me to breakfast and thinking I slept with someone else. Someone that's *not* him. And what the hell was all that about calling me a peach? Do I seem peachy to you now, Tucker?" She raises her brows, awaiting my answer. It takes everything in me not to laugh at that last part.

"Well. When you put it that way, yeah it seems a little bad," I admit in a mocking tone. She grumbles at me, rolling her eyes.

"I mean, do you really not see it? How would you feel if you were dating someone or *trying* to date someone and the night after your first date she came out of another guy's hotel room? Wearing his clothes. Then that guy shows up half-naked behind her?" She waves a hand up and down my *half-naked* body.

Point made, and now I'm pissed. Not because I feel bad for putting a strain on the relationship at hand. I give zero fucks about Zander and his feelings and I don't care who knows it. But I'm imagining that happening to me with *her*. And I know for a fact I'd take out anyone I thought touched her when she was mine. I'm silent for a moment, letting my mind sift through the facts. One of them being—she *isn't* mine. At least not right now. If I really want her to be happy then I need to stop actively trying to ruin her efforts to do so. Even if I hate every minute she spends with someone else. I'll never stop looking for my chance. For my moment to show her that she should be mine.

"Are you short circuiting?" Taylor snaps her fingers in front of my face.

"No." I clear my throat. "All good." The frustrated look on her face is one I've never seen directed at me and I hate it. I hate being on the receiving end of her anger. But I'd rather fight with Taylor than laugh with anyone else. "I'm sorry if things got complicated because of me." I strain to get the words out. "Did you guys fix it, or whatever?" I ask, waving towards the door.

"Yeah. It's fine. We decided to have a first date re-do," she answers, looking down at her feet over her crossed arms. My jaw tightens hearing her words.

"Good. Then consider me officially out of the way." I force a smile before handing over her clothes. She reaches for them, but I tighten my grip. Her eyes dart to mine when I don't let them go.

"But I will never stop waiting for you." Before she can respond and tell me my efforts will be pointless, I nod to the bathroom door.

"If you'll hand me my shirt I'll go get you a new key so you can grab your things. Check-out is in an hour." She takes the clothes nodding in agreement, as she walks into the bathroom. She tosses my shirt at me, promptly slamming the door in my face. I throw it on before heading downstairs. I swear to God it's like the universe is laughing in my face because every time I inhale I'm overwhelmed by the scent of fresh peaches.

TANK

The guys wanna go to the range. You down?

ME

Sure, what time?

TANK

Ram said they're heading there now. Pick me up?

ME

On my way.

We pull up to the local shooting range and the guys are already getting things laid out. I can already hear Rip bitching through the rolled-down windows when we pull up.

"It ain't my place but it'll do."

When Rip got out of the Navy he had this dream to open up his own gun range. When he told us he was naming it RIP's - standing for

Rounding In Precision, we told him it should probably be *Rounding WITH Precision.* He wouldn't hear it though. I distinctly remember him saying *"Nahh, this is my place I can call it whatever the hell I want."* So he did just that. We love it out there though. It's another place just like Chattahoochies that feels like an extension of us. Like a home away from home. Here's to hoping he doesn't spend the whole day comparing this place to his. We hop out of the Bronco and make our way over to the guys.

"You guys aren't still drunk are you?" I ask, studying the way Rip seems a little distant.

"No, *Dad.* We're all sobered up," Ram jests as he loads up his mags. I raise a brow looking over at Rip.

"Mhm. Rip?"

"Yeah?" His head shoots up like he just came back to reality.

"What was the name of the girl you were trying to get with last night?" I ask.

"I was with a girl?" His eyes are wide with worry.

"Jesus Christ." I shake my head in amused disapproval.

"What about you, player? You're the one who had a girl sleeping in your room all night. Did she *just* sleep?" Johnny wags his brows, pairing it with boisterous laughter.

"Johnny, I swear to God I will lay your ass out right here in this dirt if you do not shut up," I warn. They collectively *ooohhh*, making me roll my eyes.

Everyone except Tank. He just looks at me with concern from the corner of his eye.

"Alright boys, let's lock and load," Rip announces as they all start making their way over to get on line.

"Yeah, be right there," Tank calls out, stopping me with the back of his hand. When everyone is out of sight he looks at me with his concerned baby brother face. Which has grown up way too fucking fast. "Everything alright with you man?" he asks, his face searching mine for truth.

"Yeah. Why wouldn't it be?" I'm telling a half-truth. Getting my conversation with Taylor out of my head has proven more difficult than I thought.

"Don't chew my ass out for saying it, alright? But you've been real defensive about a certain redhead here lately. Just wondering what's going on there," he presses.

"Not a damn thing," I bite back a little more harshly than intended. I sigh and face him again. "Just didn't get much sleep. Thanks for checking in bud." I bump him with my elbow before we head off to our lanes.

We spend the rest of the day clinking and shooting the shit. It was a nice distraction for a little while. After I drop Tank off and head towards home, *finally*, I get a call about a project my company is in the middle of working on. There was an issue with the plans we drew up and the way the plumbing would be run so we're having to make adjustments. When I started The Landry Architect Group, I really thought owning my own company was the way to go, but now I'm starting to feel worn down by everything this job takes out of me.

I grab the small notebook I keep in my truck to make a note to get the plans fixed this week and the only pen I can find is the one that says *that idea is garbage*. I laugh at the irony behind me just having that exact thought to Ben's first suggestion on how to fix the problem we're having. Her gift may have been a joke, but she still did a damn good job. As I hang up the phone, she floods my thoughts all over again. I still get a whiff of fresh peaches any time I shift in my seat. Even after spending all day at the range. I should smell like gunpowder, sweat, and dirt. But no, this woman and her insanely overpowering peach scented whatever it is, has a stronghold on my senses. And my shirt, apparently. What the hell is that about?

Chapter 12

Taylor

After two months of scheduling and rescheduling our re-do first date, it's finally happening. Between work, Sawyer's hockey games that he played in town, and everyday life, we have just been on opposite schedules until tonight. I had the day off work and have been getting pampered since I got up. I went and got my favorite coffee from Bruman's, got my nails done, got a wax, and have been cleaning my house to make sure everything is looking its best. After standing in my closet staring hopelessly for a good 15 minutes, I pick up my phone and FaceTime Shane and Ruby. They're the only two who will be available during work hours to help with my fashion crisis. Shane and Max got in last night from their extended honeymoon and if I'm not mistaken Ruby is off work today.

"Yess?" Shane sings as she props her phone on her tripod beside the canvas she's painting.

"Hendrix, please don't shove those in your nose. Auntie Taylor isn't at the hospital today to remove them…" she pauses for a minute staring over her phone. "Thank you, love you!" she yells before looking down at Shane and me. "What's up boo?"

"Thank God, I have no idea what to wear tonight. I need help," I whine propping my phone up on my dresser as I sift through the hanging clothes.

"Well, if you're looking to get laid, just wear that." Ruby laughs before sipping on her energy drink. I look down at the red lace bra and underwear set I am wearing.

"Very cute. Don't think I wouldn't if the date didn't involve a very nice restaurant." I raise a brow challenging her remark.

"You might get your appetizers free that way," Shane offers, making us all laugh.

"This is serious! Okay, so do I do the slinky top, ripped jeans, and booties orrr… the mini dress and thigh-high boots?" I hold up the top and dress to show them through the phone.

"Slinky top and jeans for sure," Shane answers.

"Yeah, make him work for it," Ruby chimes in. I shake my head in agreement. "The mini dress is a little *you've got it* and less *come and get it*. You wanna keep the message clear," she adds.

"Plus my boobs look great in this top, so it's still sexy." I grab my favorite ripped jeans and black booties from the closet before getting dressed.

"Damn girl, you look fine as hell," Ruby says when I show them the final look.

"Smoking. Zander is a lucky guy." Shane whistles.

"Okay, gotta finish the face before he gets here. Love you!" I walk over to the phone, blowing them kisses before hanging up.

"Love you," they yell back in unison. My favorite part was Hendrix hollering "I LOVE YOU TOO!" as he ran across the living room toward Ruby's phone. It hung up just as he collided with it making me spew out a laugh.

Zander pulls up just as I am finishing getting ready and sending a picture to the group chat so Leah and Lauren can give their approval. He said we were going somewhere *awesome,* so I can't wait to see where we end up.

"No, oh come on. This ref has his head up his ass so far I'm surprised he can blow a whistle," Zander yells before shoving another bunch of fries in his mouth. Benji's Sports Bar & Grill. The *amazing place* he brought me was a sports bar where TV's cover every wall including the one behind me that Zander's eyes have been glued to since we got here.

Actually, that's not true. He looks away every time his phone goes off. He'll respond, ask me how my food or drink is, wink at me, then his attention is back on the game.

"Everything okay over here?" The waiter comes over just as Zander finishes his second beer. I smile at him and nod. As Zander points to his empty glass.

"One more," he says, barely taking his eyes off the TV.

How freaking rude.

I smile at the waiter apologetically. I'm pretty sure I saw his eyes dart away from my boobs just as I turned to face him. Well, at least *someone* noticed them. He rushes away from the table and I grab my phone from my crossbody.

ME

My tits look amazing and are basically propped up on this tabletop but you'd think I was wearing a turtleneck.

ME

He hasn't looked away from the TV above me except to respond to texts.

ME

Maybe I'll just run off with the waiter since I'll apparently be taking his eyeballs with me.

ME

Cause they're glued to the girls.

SHANE

Yeah no we caught that part. What an asshole.

SHANE

Zander, not the waiter.

LAUREN

You look hot AF. Screw him

RUBY

▶▶▶

LEAH

Want me to come by and motorboat you & see if he looks up then?

ME

The waiter might actually jizz himself, but rain check.

LEAH

My girls always have my back. And apparently, my front where Leah is concerned. A smile creeps across my face as I think of how amazing my friends are. I glance back at Zander who is less than graceful with his burger, ketchup spilling out as he digs into it. I place my phone back into my bag before excusing myself from the table.

I slide out of the booth and head to the bathroom, to likely question my taste in men and who I chose to explore dating again with. As soon as I'm upright and turning around, the waiter with velcro eyes runs into me, spilling Zanders beer all over me. Gasps come from people all around the restaurant as I stand frozen in place.

Could this night get any worse?

I hear Zander say "Oh, shit" from behind me, making me roll my eyes at the remark.

"I am so *so* sorry," the waiter starts, "let me go grab you a towel or something." I close my eyes, fighting back the tears that are creeping up. I don't know if I want to cry from amusement or embarrassment but they're coming either way. I take a deep breath in to compose myself, the smell of beer is overwhelming as it seeps through my shirt. Just as my eyes open I look down to see a towel in front of me, only it's not the waiter holding it. There's a familiar, tattooed forearm reaching out in front of me. My heart begins to race as I look up and see Tucker.

"Are you okay?" he asks, his eyes locked on mine studying them for an answer. He must find it before I can speak because he's taking action before my mouth ever opens. "Come on, I have an extra shirt in my truck. I can give you a ride," he offers.

"I'm on a date," I offer quietly. Probably because I'm a little in shock and a little embarrassed by the person I'm on it with. He glances over my head at our booth, his jaw flexes before he looks back down at me.

"And do you want to stay on it?" he asks, taking me by surprise. The last time Tucker and I talked where Zander was concerned, he *did* say he would stay out of the way. But I guess I didn't think he meant it. I shake my head staring back up at him.

"Then let's go." He holds a hand out to usher me before him. As we turn to walk toward the door, Zander finally gets out of the booth, stopping right in front of us. Did it really take him this long to figure out what was happening?

"Hey, where are you going?" I look at him dumbfounded, as he takes in my beer-soaked clothes. "Let me pay and I can help you out of those when we get back to your house." He winks at me as if I should be excited by his offer. I'm not sure how a person can actually be so stupid, but he's managed to soar way off the charts in that area. I look at Tucker, trying to get a read on his expression but it's stoic tonight. There's no hint of him about to fly off the handle and tell this guy off. So I guess I will do it myself.

"So you noticed that I was covered in beer and didn't bother to stand up until I was leaving with someone else?" I'm bordering on hostile at this moment. He turns his head to see who may be listening, laughing off my question in embarrassment. But I'm not letting up now. "You haven't taken your eyes off that damn TV unless it was to answer your phone, all night. I'll bet you probably have no idea what I ordered or what the name of our waiter is either." He scoffs, crossing his arms over his chest defensively.

"Calm down, okay? I didn't realize you'd care about that stuff. But I still don't want you to leave with *him*," he bites out.

"First of all, you don't get to tell me to calm down. Second of all, Tucker is my *friend* Zander. At least he noticed when I was drenched in beer and offered to do something about it. *He* probably would have noticed how bomb my tits look in this shirt too because his face wouldn't have been glued to a screen all night."

"Whoa!" Tucker expresses his surprise. I'm pretty much the main event in Benji's right now but I don't really care.

"This has been the *worst* first date re-do. It's definitely worse than the first one. I *am* leaving with Tucker. I'd suggest you find a ride too. You shouldn't drive after drinking so damn much." I snatch my purse from the booth and march toward the door. Tucker rushes in front of me to open the door, doing the same with the door to his Bronco when we reach it outside. He walks around the back, ruffling through a bag before getting into the driver's seat.

"Here you go," he says, handing me a plain black T-shirt.

"Thanks," I say, grabbing it from him.

"You alright?" he asks, looking at me from his seat behind the wheel.

"I'm so mad about this night. I put so much effort into myself today. I was excited. I finally tried my hand at dating again and *this* is what happens? Has Zander always been such an asshole and I just never realized it?"

"I'm not so sure you'd want my answer to that," Tucker mumbles.

Before I can think better of it, I am pulling my blue, beer-soaked shirt over my head, with my tits on full display through my red lace bra. When my head is in the shirt but not through the hole yet my heart drops into my stomach. I cannot believe I just did that. In front of Tucker. Who claimed to want to *sink his teeth into me* one of the last times I saw him. When I'm finally clothed again I hesitantly sneak a look in his direction.

A little curious, a little mortified.

He's staring at me with an intense look in his eyes and I wish I could climb into his mind and read his thoughts right now. It's only quiet for a few moments after my rant, but it feels like an eternity. He finally breaks the silence.

"You're right. I did notice," he turns to start the engine before taking me home.

Chapter 13

Tucker

"What were you even doing at Benji's tonight?" Taylor asks from the passenger seat as I park in front of her house.

"I was having a business meeting with a colleague," I answer, leaning back in my seat. Her eyes are wide in disbelief.

"And you just left with me? Is someone still there waiting for you to come back? You should have stayed Tucker, I would have been fine on my own," she says, sounding a mix between panicked and embarrassed.

"It was very laid back. No need to overthink it." I would have left dinner with the mayor himself after seeing what happened with Taylor on that cluster fuck of a date tonight. I was shocked she even left with me at all, but I can't deny the relief that washed over me when she did and I knew she wouldn't be going home with that prick.

"The meeting part was over, we were just watching the game and catching up when I left. I told him I had something important to tend to. He understood." I admit, staring out the window. I can feel the gaze of her raincloud eyes burning into the side of my head. She's tempting every last bit of my self-control not to look over at her.

Afraid I'll find some sort of pity on her face over the fact that I left a business dinner to come to her aide.

"How much did you see?" She asks timidly. I steal a glance at her, seeing her pull at a loose string on the T-shirt she's wearing. It just about swallows her petite body, and I've never seen my shirt look so good.

"Enough." I fight the urge to tell her I barely took my eyes off of her. From the time I noticed her walk into the restaurant to the time I was handing her that towel, my attention was hers.

"That's vague." She laughs nervously. "Thank you though. For showing up. For noticing when I needed a friend, and not being embarrassed by me causing a scene. I know it was probably a little much." She bites the inside of her cheek like she's trying to keep from saying more.

"Well, I wasn't too keen on the idea of letting you stay in beer-soaked clothes while your *date* sat there cursing refs on a TV screen." Every word is laced with venom as I recount watching tonight's events. Her cheeks flush at my words when she realizes that I saw it all and she grows quiet. Things with Taylor used to be so easy. We were always joking around and there was always a flirty energy between us. But ever since she started dating Zander things are different. And I hate him for it.

"And for the record, your reaction wasn't *too much*. I would have liked to see more, actually. Maybe pour a pitcher of beer on *him* and see how he liked it." I make no effort to hide the annoyance in my voice. She snickers then leans back into the headrest.

"Tucker…" she sighs. She sounds exhausted when she says my name now. Her phone dings repeatedly in the seat next to her and instinctively I look down. I regret it immediately when I see Zander's messages coming through. The last one reads *"I could still come over and help you shower."*

Jesus. Is this guy serious?

Is *she* serious?

I let out a humorless laugh. "What a tool…"

"Tucker," she repeats, more shocked by my words now.

"Do you disagree?"

"I mean… I don't know. He's so different now from when we were just sleeping together. It's like our dating has made him a completely different person." I can see the pained expression on her face while she tries to pinpoint where things went wrong, or when he changed. The only part sticking with me from what she said was that they used to sleep together and suddenly I don't care too much for this conversation anymore.

"I really don't want to sit here listening to you talk about the asshole who has disrespected you more than once. He doesn't know what he's got with you, and doesn't deserve you in the slightest. If you want me to stay out of it, if you really want me to stay out of your way while you continue to try and make whatever this is work, then keep me out of it. I don't wanna hear it." The words are flying out of my mouth faster than I can stop them.

"I didn't ask you to walk over and help me tonight. I didn't ask you for a ride, or for your shirt. I didn't ask for anything from you. You just showed up.," she starts arguing back, "you know what, here –" She grabs the bottom of the shirt like she would if she were going to pull it back off over her head. My hand flies over to grab hers, stopping her in action.

"Taylor, I swear to God, if you take that shirt off in front of me again I will lose any self-control I have left. And I've barely been hanging onto it since you did it the first time." She stares at me with defiance burning in her eyes. For a moment things feel like they used to between us.

Playful, fun, *normal.*

Then she narrows her gaze and lifts her brow. "What if I want you to lose it?"

The way my dick hardens at her words lets me know I'm in it deep with this woman. My jaw flexes as I stare back at her. My hand falls from her grip on theT-shirt hem. I let my hand fall on her inner thigh, noting the way they clench slightly when I do.

"By all means then, take it off." She doesn't move a muscle as she stares into my eyes. Surely seeing every bit of desire burning behind them. I swear I can see her hand start to move, making my heart race, when her phone starts to ring loudly. She jumps in her seat, letting out a sigh when she sees it's the hospital calling.

"You've got to be fucking kidding me," I mumble under my breath.

"Hello?" she answers, her eyes bouncing around as she listens to whoever is on the other end of the line. "Ha, of course he is. Yeah I'll be about 20 minutes, is that soon enough? Okay. Bye." She hangs up the phone, shaking her head as a sinister laugh falls from her lips. "I have to go in to work. The on-call nurse is apparently too drunk to go in," she announces as she throws her phone into her bag.

"You upset by the interruption, Darlin'?" I smirk at her. Her cheeks grow red again as she twists her face in denial.

"No. I'm *annoyed* that the on-call nurse is such an asshole and can't stay sober when he has commitments to keep." She fusses with the door handle trying to escape my questioning. I clear my throat, bringing her attention to me as I hit the unlock button. She rolls her eyes, before snatching her wet shirt from the floorboard.

"Right, of course," I sarcastically agree, watching as she hops out of the truck.

"Now I have to speed shower the beer smell off of me before going in on a night I was supposed to have off." She tosses some of her red curls out of her eyes as she slams the door shut. "Will I see you at Chattahoochies this week?" she asks, looking through the now rolled-down passenger window. We all have drinks at Max's bar once a week to just catch up, though I won't be making it this week.

"Not this week. I'll see you guys at The Gallery for Shane's exhibit though."

"Oh…" She sounds confused, seeing as the event isn't for another week.

"You better hurry. You're down to 15 minutes," I tell her, making her check her watch.

"Shit. Well, thanks again for the ride. See you… later I guess," she says awkwardly. The way she seems nervous with me now is the cutest thing I've ever seen. When she's safely in the house I put the truck in drive and head home.

Chapter 14

Taylor

I HAVE KEPT myself busier than usual this week to avoid the current chaos that is my life. I've done my best to avoid Zander altogether since I left our last date with Tucker. And I haven't seen or heard from Tucker since that night either. While I haven't been worried about trying to avoid Tucker, I *have* been trying to wrap my head around the events that occurred in his truck before I got called into work.

We went from fighting to flirting within seconds and it was…. exciting. Though I am still trying to figure out if it was just the adrenaline from the night making me feel that way or if it's just *him*. He seemed to have clear intentions during Shane and Max's wedding, but after the fight in his hotel room he said he'd *back off and stay out of my way*, and until he showed up at the restaurant last week he'd done exactly that. I only saw him at our weekly hangouts at Chattahoochies but nothing outside of that until that night, and nothing since.

We're all getting ready to board our flights to San Francisco for Shane's military-inspired art exhibit. My best friend is freaking talented and I am so damn proud of her. Max shut down the bar and everyone but Leah is getting to attend. Since she's a school teacher and it's April she isn't able to come, and she is salty about it. But she said she'd be there in spirit and to take tons of photos. Well, everyone but Leah was *supposed* to be attending. As I look around, our group getting ready to board, I don't see Tucker anywhere. My heart sinks a little when I don't see him. I walk over to Tank who is standing closest to me. Surely his *brother* will know where he is.

"Hey, where's Tucker, he said he'd be here?" Tank adjusts his duffle bag over his shoulder.

"Ah, don't worry. He'll show." Is all he says, not bothering to look around for him.

"*Flight 429 to San Francisco, now boarding.*" Still no Tucker in sight. I will kick his ass if he misses this moment for Shane just because things got weird between us.

The Gallery is absolutely stunning tonight. Every detail compliments Shane's exhibit. She is absolutely beaming as people walk around admiring her paintings. Hugh makes his way to the center of The Gallery, Shane and Max not far behind him.

"If I could have everyone's attention for a moment, please. I know this is a little different than we normally do things around here, but the artist behind the pieces you see tonight is someone very dear to me. And I just wanted to take a moment to acknowledge the excellence and honor she put into this exhibit. Shane has informed me that she and her husband will donate all proceeds from tonight to the Hope For American Heroes Foundation." Applause erupts throughout the exhibit space. "From what I understand this was a passion project, and very close to Shane's heart, as she honored a fallen soldier who was a very good friend to her husband. So please, enjoy the evening as we remember the sacrifices made by the men and women depicted through this art." Hugh nods, as people sniffle and begin mingling once again.

My eyes are misty as I breathe out a calming breath. I make my way around the room, grabbing a glass of champagne from a tray before stopping in front of one of Shane's paintings. Tears are being shed and appreciation from Veterans and their families is being shown to Shane and Max at every turn. She did an outstanding job. I don't think I have ever been more proud of her. It makes me appreciate the friends we've made in Max, Tank and –

"She really is talented." *Tucker.* I turn to face him, my eyes drawing up to his forest green ones. They're locked on the painting we are standing in front of. It's the one where the soldiers are carrying a flag-covered casket. He swallows hard, his jaw ticking before he turns to me with a sad smile on his face. "You having a good time, Darlin'?"

I've never seen Tucker look so solemn before. I feel a pang of sadness in my chest for him, thinking what this exhibit may remind him of. Or where his mind might be while taking in these paintings.

I give myself a moment to take him in. He looks so damn good tonight. He's wearing a fitted blue dress shirt, oddly similar to the color of the dress I am wearing, paired with black slacks that hug his toned frame just right. His shirt sleeves are rolled up to his elbows displaying his tattoos that I've always been fascinated by, and the top two buttons on his shirt are open, showcasing just enough of his chest to be a tease. I turn back to the painting, quickly blink away my wandering thoughts. Oh, my god, what is happening to me? I've never looked at Tucker like that before. But I can't fight the urge, I have to let my eyes rake over him again. When I catch him looking over at me, I realize I've been silent far too long since he asked me a question. I clear my throat and turn my attention back to the painting.

"She really is, and yes, I am," I finally answer. "When did you get here? You weren't on our flight, did you catch a later one?" He takes a deep breath in, bringing his champagne glass to his lips.

"No, I don't fly much if I can help it. I got here early this morning," he says.

"Wait, you *drove* here?" My eyes widen slightly as I turn to face him. No wonder I didn't see or hear from him this week.

"It's not so bad. Gives me time to think." He smirks.

"Sure, but that seems like it would get awfully lonely. You can't have *that* many thoughts. It's like a four-day trip," I say before taking a sip of my champagne.

"I've had plenty to keep my mind busy lately." He glances down at me with a raised brow. Heat washes over my face at his comment. "But, if you're worried I'll get too lonely or think too hard, there's room for one more on the trip back." He winks at me before walking over to Max and Shane, bringing them both in for a hug. I scoff as he departs, stunned at his invitation. When he glances back over at me, I realize I am still staring right at him. Warmth seeps into my chest when he flashes me a smile showing off his gorgeous white teeth and the way one side of his smile reaches farther than the other. I turn away trying to play it cool. I can't even count the number of times Tucker has made me blush lately, but it's starting to stack up. I finish off my champagne just in time for a waiter to come and replace my empty glass with a full one as I make my way around the gallery.

By the end of the night, every single one of Shane's paintings had been purchased. I'm admiring the cards posted under each painting that read *SOLD* when tears fill my eyes knowing just how big of a difference they're setting out to make. A true power couple those two make. I glance around, wiping a tear from my cheek before heading to the bathroom to make sure I don't look a complete mess. The number of times I have welled up tonight is a new record for me. I'm not typically a crier but the detail and meaning behind each piece Shane created, along with stories from people tonight has me wishing I'd worn waterproof mascara.

I stop right outside the bathrooms when my phone starts buzzing from inside my clutch. When I take it out, I see Zander's name coming across my phone. A heavy sigh escapes me as I debate answering it or not. When I look up to see Tucker walking my way, I drop it back in my bag instantly. Not that I wanted to talk to him anyhow, but the tension that arises when both Zander and Tucker are involved is something I'd rather avoid tonight. Tucker closes the distance between us, stopping so close if it were anyone else it would be a total invasion of personal space. But we're friends so I don't mind it I guess. My breath hitches in surprise when his chest stops just inches from my face. I start to make a remark about him being so close I can smell his breath, but instead all I can think of is how fucking good he smells right now. The scent of musk, vanilla, and *apples?*

"Hi," he says, smirking down at me.

"Hi." I narrow my gaze at him.

"So, did you think any more about my offer?" My mind is TV static as I try to remember what he offered me. When I can't muster up a response he chuckles lightly. "To keep me company on the trip home."

"Oh, right." I shake my head, trying to clear the static and focus. "You were serious?"

"As a heart attack," he quips. "Can't have me thinking too hard now can we, Peach?" His tone is dripping with sex appeal and I feel my body come alive under his stare, which is slightly alarming to me.

There's no chance in hell that going on a road trip with Tucker is a good idea. We're always bickering or trying to outwit one another; we'd absolutely kill each other. Not to mention, I bought a round-trip ticket for this event, I didn't take enough time off of work for a road trip, and I only packed clothes for the event and the flight back home. Clearly, all signs point to *no.* So why do I say "Sure, that actually sounds fun" instead? Probably because the smirk that creeps across his face is worth every adjustment I'm going to have to make to ride with him. He must see the slight hesitation still in my eyes despite my answer.

"Don't worry Darlin', I'll make it worth your while." He runs his thumb across my bottom lip and winks at me again before backing away. My eyes are wide as saucers, my stomach doing somersaults as he disappears back into the gallery. He keeps doing insanely sexy things and giving me no time to respond to them. Objectively or otherwise. Which probably isn't such a bad thing since I seem to forget how to speak every time he does them. What the hell is wrong with me? I don't feel nervous or even appalled that he just had his finger on my lip either. I feel... *exhilarated*. Something I don't think I've ever felt around a man. Maybe this trip will be a good way for me to finally sort out all of the mixed feelings I've been having about Tucker lately. Because the way things have spiraled over the last couple of weeks has me desperate for clarity.

We've had this family dinner planned since we knew we'd be flying out to San Francisco for Shane's exhibit. Mario's is her favorite Italian restaurant on the west coast and we wouldn't dare deny her a celebratory dinner after the night she just had, because this is freaking *huge*. But the way I can't seem to escape Tucker's gaze has me stirring in my seat. I called to take off work for the rest of the week almost immediately after I finished talking to Tucker at the art gallery. The eagerness in which I did so is slightly concerning, but I'll deal with those feelings later. I hear Ruby whispering to Lauren about someone who seemed obsessed with her tonight, eager to get my mind off of the tension filling the air I decide to join their conversation.

"Who's obsessed with Lauren?" I ask, blinking the Tucker haze away.

"*No one.*" Lauren eyes Ruby accusingly and I lift a brow at her.

"Actually, Lu, everyone is obsessed with you. It would be better for everyone if you could just recognize it and own it," I tease as I sip my martini. The second the key lime taste hits my lips, my thoughts and eyes wander back to Tucker. He's caught up in conversation with Max and Tank, looking sinfully delicious as he grabs his beer from the table.

The bottle all but disappears in his large, tattooed hands when he grabs it. My mind flicks back to him running his thumb across my bottom lip. I find myself pulling my bottom lip in with my teeth, slightly missing the electricity it sent through me to have him so close.

"Um, bitch what *are* you staring at?" Lauren demands from beside me.

"Or *who* are you staring at?" Ruby adds presumptuously, her eyes following my previous line of sight. I feel my cheeks flush and a slight panic settles in my chest when I think she may catch who I was thinking about. I'm relieved to see our waiter refilling water glasses right beside Tucker, and she instantly thinks it was him who had my attention. *Whew*.

"Ohhh he's cute Tay," Lauren whisper-sings.

"Yeah, girl. Get served." Ruby shimmies her shoulders drawing a laugh from the both of us. When I look back to where the waiter was a moment ago, he's no longer there. Instead, I'm met with a disgruntled-looking Tucker. His jaw ticks before he turns to answer a question Max has asked him.

"What are we talking about?" Shane asks as she takes her seat next to me.

"Nothing," I answer quickly. Though I'm not sure why.

"Taylor's got eyes for the cute ass waiter," Ruby teases, sipping her margarita.

"Ohh is that so?" Shane asks, looking around the room for him.

"Oh my god you guys, no. And stop doing that." I pull on Shane's arm, urging her to stop being so damn obvious as her head swivels back and forth.

"How come? It's *clearly* not going to work out with Zander. You deserve to have some fun. You shouldn't stay upset over someone so... awful." She leans into me encouragingly.

"Right, cause I've never done *that* before," I scoff. Letting the tiniest part of my heart feel the depth of the brokenness it went through all those years ago. Shane gives me a sad smile and squeezes my hand. I shake my head and roll my eyes, shoving those feelings back down in the little box I keep them in.

I *would* normally flirt with the waiter even if it was just to see if he would leave his number on my bill at the end of the night. But tonight I'm not focused on the waiter. I haven't even thought about Zander or why he may have been calling me earlier for that matter.

I've been solely focused on the wave of butterflies in my stomach every time I lay eyes on Tucker, and how absolutely terrified that makes me. His forest green eyes were filled with desire when he approached me at the gallery tonight, removing all self-preservation I may have had with him. I agreed to road trip all the way back to Nashville with him, with absolutely no reason as to why.

I don't mind flying, I do it all the time. I love my job, so I'm not avoiding that. If anything I could say I'm avoiding being around Zander because things between us still haven't been fully put to rest. He's still under the impression I am cooling off from our disastrous second first date and that we'll be rescheduling it, *yet again*. Though I have no intention of that happening. I still haven't told my friends I won't be flying back with them tomorrow, for fear of having to explain why. Something *I* still don't fully understand. I'm saved from having to answer any further questions when Leah FaceTimes us.

"Aw man, bring me back some garlic bread," Leah says, immediately recognizing the atmosphere around us.

"Hey to you too, bitch." We laugh as she rolls her eyes, settling into the couch.

"I'm so sad I'm not there with you guys tonight. Shane, how did the exhibit go?" she asks. Shane's face lights up as she tells her about the night.

"Every single painting was purchased. We raised so much money, Le. I still can't believe it." She shakes her head in disbelief.

"We can!" she encourages through the screen. Lauren, Ruby and I all nod in agreement. "You're so incredibly talented, Shaney. I can't wait to see what you do next. But could the next event be like, I don't know. During the summer or a weekend or something?" she teases.

"I'll see what I can do." The conversation carries on a few more minutes before we hang up, all ordering one final drink for the night. I do my best to stay focused on my girls and the conversations happening between them. But my efforts are futile when all I can focus on is the burning gaze from the green eyes that haunt my every thought.

Chapter 15

Tucker

I NEVER THOUGHT Taylor would actually agree to ride back to Nashville with me all the way from California. On the trip here I only stopped to sleep, shower and eat. But I had plans to extend my trip back home, making more enjoyable, and adventurous stops along the way. I'm actually pretty glad to have the company. She wasn't wrong, despite having the radio, podcasts, and my own thoughts to keep me company, the trip does get a little lonely. Though I'm not sure she knows exactly what she's getting herself into or how I planned for this trip back home to go.

I'm standing at my Bronco, waiting for her to emerge from the hotel doors when I check my watch- 10:55 AM. Check out is at 11 AM, where the hell could she be? I see her walk out with a duffle and garment bag thrown over her shoulder. She wears her hair in wild curls, *my favorite*, cut-off jean shorts, and the sneakers I bought her for Christmas. She wears sunglasses over her raincloud eyes, making me wish I could see what color they present more of today. I smirk when I notice the shoes, but I feel something else entirely when I notice the shirt she's wearing– is mine. The very same one I gave her over a week ago that she almost took off for me, or so I think, before we were interrupted.

My dick jumps in excitement just thinking about it. I've had a hard on for her since I saw her in the blue velvet dress she wore last night. It was formed to her body as if someone custom-made it around every delicious curve. It doesn't matter what she's wearing or not wearing though, the woman is downright breathtaking. She storms up to the truck, shoving her bags into my chest.

"I know you noticed. I don't want to talk about it," she says, her usual fierce Taylor attitude is in full swing this morning. I draw my brows in confusion.

"Am I supposed to know what we're *not* talking about?" I ask. She huffs, sliding her sunglasses into her hair.

"It's like butter, Tucker." She pinches the fabric of her shirt, *my shirt*, right by her shoulder. "You gave me the softest shirt in the freaking world to replace a beer-soaked one. I packed it to sleep in and was gonna wear it on the plane ride home because I like to be comfortable when I fly. I'm probably gonna keep it forever. So you'll have to rip it off my body yourself if you want it back." She crosses her arms over her body, a look of finality on her face.

"Challenge accepted." I rake my eyes over her body before brushing past her to put her bags in the back.

I don't think I've ever seen a woman pack so light. Even for a one-night trip. I saw Ruby and Lauren's bags and they had wheels. When I make it back to Taylor's side of the truck, she's still standing frozen in her place. I open the door for her and she looks at me surprised. She doesn't move for a few seconds.

"You know, it'll be really hard to go home if you never get *in* the truck."

"I can open my own door, you know," she says, sliding into the passenger seat.

"I'm sure you can, Peach." I shut the door behind her. "But just let me." I see her cheeks pink a little as she pulls her seatbelt on. I hop in the driver's seat as she's pulling her sunglasses back in place over her eyes. When she reaches for the AUX cord my hand flies out to stop her.

"Whoa, what do you think you're doing?" I ask. She holds her phone and the cord together as if to explain.

"Passenger princesses get full music rights, everyone knows that." She continues to plug her phone in before I can object further. "Are we gonna get breakfast?" she asks while scrolling through her playlist.

"It's... it's 11 AM." I was up and done with breakfast by seven. Though I now understand why she strolled out five minutes before checkout.

"Okay... So can we get *brunch* then? I'm starving." She selects a song and turns the volume up.

"Sure." I shake my head in disapproval. This is going to be a long trip. She flashes a big ass smile at me, and I swear to God it's the cutest thing I've ever seen. We pull out of the parking lot as Taylor starts rapping every single word to "To Be Honest" by Young Dolph, leaving me absolutely speechless and making me realize there is so much I still don't know about this woman. And I want to know it all.

"Why are we stopping here?" Taylor asks as we pull into the Walmart parking lot. We've been on the road for hours, only stopping for gas and snacks. Her choices made me want to give her a salad and a bottle of water immediately. How someone looks as incredible as her while eating the amount of sugar she does, is mind-boggling. Though I would never dare to tell Taylor how she should or shouldn't eat. Instead I will continue to admire her tolerance for sweets while I have a carrot in her honor.

"Well, I assume you'll need more clothes than what you packed. Unless you're planning on wearing that T-shirt or your dress the whole trip." I pull into a parking spot and cut the engine.

"*Right.* Glad one of us was thinking about that." She unbuckles, hopping out of the truck and stretching her arms above her head.

We go in and grab a basket and she quickly begins to fill it. The jeans and shirts she chooses have me thoroughly aware that she has no idea what's in store during our trip back home. She tosses in a couple of short pajama sets that have me instantly excited to see her in them. My mind wanders back to the night she showed up at my hotel room in her silk pajamas that were very poor at hiding her perfect peaked nipples. When I push the basket over to the camping area she stops abruptly at the end of the aisle.

"What do we need over here?" She scrunches her face. I toss a sleeping bag, bug spray, water canteen, and a few other items into the basket before looking back at her with a smirk on my face. Her eyes widened with realization.

"We're *camping?*" She makes her way over to the basket.

"Did I not mention that?" I grin as she stares into the basket. "You might also want some different shoes to hike in." I glance down at the tennis shoes she's managed to keep pristinely white. She looks distraught over the thought of camping. I'm not sure if it's because it's with me, or just the concept in general. "Don't tell me you've never camped before," I inquire curiously.

"What? Of course I have. I'm a natural camper. A woodswoman of sorts." She plasters on a mask of confidence that I see right through. She walks over and begins grabbing things off the shelves, making me fight back laughter at her selections.

"And what, dear woodswoman, might we need a collapsible shovel or an ax for?" I draw my brows together, eager to hear her response.

"Duh, in case we have to dig for… or what if we need to chop…" She stops as the laughter falls from my lips. "What the hell, Tucker? I don't camp. I don't hike. Do I seem *outdoorsy* to you?" she whines. I continue laughing as I take the items from her, placing them back on the shelf fueling the fire behind her eyes. And I like it when Taylor is fired up.

"Guess now's a great time to learn." I start walking down the aisle but she stays unmoving. Right between the sleeping bags and lanterns stands a Taylor that would have smoke coming out of her ears if she were a cartoon. I let another small laugh escape my lips as I lean over the handle of the basket. "You getting some new hiking shoes or not?" She rolls her eyes, groaning as she finally starts walking in my direction.

"You're lucky I like shoes," she says through gritted teeth, brushing past me. She spends at least 30 minutes trying to decide which of the *two* pairs of women's hiking boots look the cutest. Only to decide they're both hideous, making me choose some while she isn't looking.

We head to the grocery department to grab food that we can make at the campsite, my eyes widening at her selections. I picked up a small crate of eggs, bacon, bread, and peanut butter and jelly. She picked up Rice Krispie Treats, chips, and chocolate. I toss a small pack of bottled water in the cart and we head to the checkout.

"I will be watching you drink no less than two of those bottles of water." She scrunches her face at me as she grabs a Red Bull from the refrigerator by the checkout.

"Some kind of new kink for you, Landry?" she quips, moving forward as the line moves.

"If you consider making sure you don't develop diabetes during this road trip a kink... then sure." She rolls her eyes as we begin placing our items on the conveyor belt.

Taylor cracks open the energy drink she bought as we head back to the truck.

"You're not going to sleep at all tonight if you drink that now." I shake my head as she sips the peach-flavored drink. Now she not only smells like peaches but knowing she would taste like them right now too has my mouth watering.

"Well, I probably won't sleep anyways. I'll be too worried about being eaten by a grizzly bear or something."

"There are no grizzly bears. You'll be fine." I laugh.

"You don't know that," she fires back, taking another sip from her drink. I unlock the back of the truck, opening the hatch as I look down at her.

"Actually, I do. We're in Nevada, there haven't been grizzly bears here since the 1930s." Her gaze narrows and she opens her mouth to speak but snaps it back shut when her eyes fall on the back of the Bronco. It's set up with a sleeping bag and pillow. Just enough room for one. She looks at it and then back at me.

"I don't seem to recall you purchasing a tent of any sort." She stares at me pointedly.

"Trust me Darlin', you're not gonna want to be in a tent." I place our grocery bags in the back as she stands there staring at me.

"I'm sorry, but you're literally on crack if you think I'm sleeping in the back of a truck with you." She tosses her bags in, grabs the box of Rice Krispie Treats, and walks to the passenger side door. I walk over with her, rushing to open her door before her.

"This is how I travel. I didn't know you'd be coming with me," I tell her honestly.

"You *invited* me to come with you," she argues, anger flashing behind her eyes.

"I didn't think you'd actually do it." I laugh. Her cheeks flush at my statement. Something similar to embarrassment creeps across her face.

"If you didn't want me to come, then you shouldn't have fucking asked, Tucker," she says and reaches for the door handle, barely getting the door open before I slam it shut again. Her head snaps in my direction and I grab her, spinning her until her back is against the door she just tried to escape me through. I tilt her chin to look back up at me, her eyes filled with hurt and annoyance.

"Let me be very clear." My voice is direct, free of any playfulness. "I didn't think you would come. But I *do* want you here, Peach. I definitely want you here." I run my thumb across her bottom lip, my eyes studying the natural pout they have. When my eyes meet hers again, the hurt and annoyance have disappeared. Desire quietly dancing behind them instead. I open her door, causing her to jump slightly at the sound.

"Thank you," she mutters, sliding over for me to shut the door behind her. I nod and close the door before putting our basket in the cart return. When I get back in the truck I notice a Rice Krispie Treat sitting in my cup holder. I smirk, looking over at her, but she just takes a bite out of her own snack doing her best to avert my glances. When I pull out of the lot and start down a back road she finally pipes up again.

"Where are we going anyways?" she asks, noting the lack of– anything around us.

"One of my favorite places to stay when I'm out this way." I glance over at her, unease settling on her face. "Don't worry, I think you'll like it." She sighs, sitting back in her seat as nerves start to seep into my chest. I didn't realize I would care so much whether or not Taylor would like this place. But it really is one of my favorite places and suddenly I'm hoping she'll appreciate it as much as I do.

Chapter 16

Taylor

SHANE

You guys okay? You haven't killed each other yet have you?

RUBY

I'm still thoroughly confused why you would go on a road trip with Tucker. If you're taking your chance to kill him, we're all much too far away to help with… things. 🪦

LEAH

Where are y'all staying? Your location looks sketchy as hell.

LAUREN

Don't forget to wash your face – traveling is poison for your pores. 💆

ME

We're fine. Everyone is still alive. You know you'd fly out if I called to help with the body. My location is sketch AF because we're in the fricken mountains. And unless you want me washing my face with bottled water or a stream I can hear running – chances are I'm screwing my pores over big time tonight.

RUBY

Damn. That was a lot. Hendrix is dino screaming though, so I gotta bounce. Good luck. Let me know if I am booking another flight. Love you bitches.

SHANE

Night Rubes. Tay. Please don't kill Tucker. I'm positive with your navigational skills we'd never see you again if you were responsible for getting yourself back home.

ME

First of all, rude. I'm basically Google Maps. Second of all. Love you bitches too.

ALL I CAN HEAR through the rolled-down window is a stream flowing. I hop out, walking around the front of Tucker's Bronco. There are no lights around, so whatever this campsite is doesn't value people's safety, that's for sure. I squint my eyes trying to make out anything. There is nothing but dirt in the distance. Except for a single car that drives down the road we must have pulled off of, but it's so far away that it looks like a firefly from here. Tucker comes around the front with me and leans on the hood of his truck.

"What do you think?" I can barely see him but I can almost *hear* the stupid grin on his face.

"Tucker. I am trying so hard not to sound all *first-world problemish* right now. But what the hell is this? We're sleeping in the back of your truck in a dirt field? I'm sorry but how is *this* your favorite place?" I hold my arm out in front of me, bringing his attention to the emptiness before us.

"You went the wrong way." He leans closer to me, making my breath hitch for a moment.

"What?" My breathlessness and confusion mix to form an unrecognizable tone. He nods behind us and grabs my hand, pulling me to the back of the Bronco. The spark I feel throughout my body at his hand enveloping mine isn't lost on me. I'm glad it's so dark because I can feel the heat spreading across my face.

"You walked the wrong way, Darlin'. *This* is what you were supposed to see." My eyes widen as I take in the view in front of me. The water I heard from the car is gently crashing up to shore from the brush of the night breeze. The moon is reflecting beautifully on the water, giving me a clearer view now of the mountains surrounding us. There's a few feet of dirt that looks so soft it might as well be sand between the back of Tucker's truck and the shoreline. My jaw drops slightly as I look up at Tucker. My heart skips a beat when I see him already smirking down at me.

"Better?" he asks, nodding toward the view.

"Much better." I look around, still barely able to see much else around us. Only focusing on what the moonlight above us illuminates. He lets go of my hand, making me miss the warmth from it immediately. I flex my fingers before wrapping my arms around myself, noting the cool air hitting me from standing so close to the water.

"I am going to grab some firewood." He takes a few steps back, his eyes still on me.

"Okay, see. *This* is when we would need the axe I picked up."

"Right. But we didn't need that one." He lifts a storage compartment in the floorboard of his truck that I had no idea existed. "Because I've already got one." He smirks at me, making me roll my eyes.

"Feel free to change while I'm gone if you want." He stops, looking over his shoulder at me. "Though I won't hold it against you if you wait until I get back." He winks at me, making me roll my eyes at him yet again. It's an involuntary action at this point.

"In your dreams, martini man," I scoff playfully.

"Every single one." He meets my wit with his own, the way he always does. Though the way he looks at me and the steady tone of his voice don't feel playful at all.

He disappears into the wooded area and I grab some of the new pajamas I bought. Though I'm beginning to wish I had picked some with pants. I hadn't counted on camping out in the cold Nevada air. It makes me a little mad at Tucker for not warning me about it when he saw what I was purchasing. Thank God for the sleeping bag I have at least. The camping inside the truck makes much more sense now.

I take a minute to study his truck. I never paid much attention until now. Even while we've been on the road all day I spent most of it sleeping and making sure he didn't steal the AUX cord from my phone. He has a vintage 90's model Bronco and it is *pristine*. The exterior is two-tone sage green and tan, with tires so big I have to basically jump into the truck. You can tell he's done work on the inside too. Though the radio still somehow looks vintage it has modern modifications– such as the AUX cord I've been hogging all day. It's immaculately clean, not a trace of dust or a stray air freshener in sight. The only accessory being his dog tags hanging from the rear view mirror. The back seats are leaning forward but not laying completely down for some reason and the very back still has an absurd amount of room. I grab my phone and walk back to the shoreline to take some photos of the view, my camera nowhere near doing it the justice it deserves. I jump at the sound of wood hitting the ground behind me, almost losing my phone in the process.

"What the hell, Tucker?" I gasp, clutching my phone to my chest.

"Jumpy little thing aren't you?" he mocks, as he begins stacking the firewood. I sit down on a conveniently placed log near where he's setting up.

"Well, you left me all alone out here to go be a damn lumber jack for forever, excuse me for being a little frightened when you come crashing back." I wrap my arms around my body trying to fight the cold that is embedding itself down to my very bones. "How do you walk so damn quietly?" He smirks at my question.

"Well, I spent a lot of years with my life depending on my ability to be stealthy. I guess old habits die hard."

"Okay fine. That makes sense." I bob my head in agreement.

"Here," Tucker says, walking to the back of his truck, rummaging through his duffle bag. He pulls a camouflage uniform jacket out of his bag, walking over to me, holding it in my direction.

"You're freezing, put this on."

"No, I'm fine," I say as my body betrays me, and a chill breaks out causing me to shiver.

"Will you stop being stubborn and just wear the damn jacket?" he demands. I groan in protest but take the jacket anyways. I can't deny the fact that I am getting cold. And if taking this jacket from him will help him get this fire going any faster, then I'll take it.

"Thank you." I smile tightly at him. He nods, pleased by my cooperation before heading back over to start the fire. It builds slowly, warming me to my core as it reaches me. I sigh in relief and my shoulders finally relax. He appears beside me, handing me one of the snacks I picked from the grocery store as he bites into a protein bar. He puts a six-pack of beer between us, offering me one before opening his own. We sit quietly for a few moments, watching the fire and listening to the quiet ripple of small waves.

"Hey, Tucker."

"Yes, Darlin'?"

"Why did you ask me to come with you?" I break the silence with my abrupt question, surprising even myself with its boldness. I am instantly worried to hear his response. He inhales deeply, looking over at me. The fire flickering in his forest green eyes reveals the ambers in them that I've never noticed before. I'm suddenly overtaken by nerves as he studies my face.

"Believe it or not Darlin', I do enjoy your company. You were right, it gets a little lonely after a while on the road alone." He turns back to face the fire, my curiosity piqued.

"Okay, but how come you don't fly?" I ask, taking a sip from my beer, still watching his face. But he doesn't meet my gaze.

He clears his throat. "Turbulence."

"Sure, cause that's not vague at all," I tease, but he doesn't elaborate further. We sit in a comfortable silence for a minute before he breaks it.

"You close with your family?" The question takes me by surprise because I've never really had to explain my family dynamic to anyone. All my closest friends grew up with me and just *know*.

"Uh, yeah I guess you could say that." His gaze narrows on me.

"You guys seemed to get along okay at the wedding. Is that a misperception?"

I narrow my gaze at him. "You weren't around us at the wedding."

"I pay attention to my surroundings." He shrugs.

"Tucker, I have literally lost count of how many doorframes you've run into in the time I've known you." I pester him.

"Okay, fair. I pay attention to the things that surround you." His words shock me silent. "Why are you avoiding my question?" He bumps my knee with his thigh and takes another sip of his beer. I follow suit before finally answering.

"Yeah, we're close. Always have been…"

"But–" he presses, picking up that there's more I'm not saying.

"But it's just hard trying to get past the feeling that I'm living in their shadows, ya know? Trying to keep up with the boys was always challenging and it got to be too much sometimes. *I* got to be too much."

"Isn't your oldest brother a nurse too? And the other plays hockey right? What shadow is there to live in? Did your parents want you to be a hockey star as well?" I snort at his response.

"Just their excellence in what they do, I guess. Sawyer plays pro hockey and JJ went into nursing because of the opportunity to travel. I envy him for that sometimes. I wish I was more adventurous that way.

But, I don't know. He has Blaire to travel with so they get to see the world *together*. I wouldn't want to do it alone. Being away from everyone I know and love for so long, would just be too lonely. That's why I just stay put. Though traveling is starting to make its appeal harder to resist. Especially after seeing this place." I wave my hand in the air, bringing attention to the moonlight and mountains in the distance. He chuckles, his deep voice rumbling when he looks over his shoulder at the view.

"You want a travel buddy, Darlin'? Just say the word and I'll take you anywhere you wanna go." The butterflies that swarm my stomach take me by surprise. I could easily see any one of my girlfriends offering the same thing. So why does Tucker offering feel so significant?

"You ready to go to bed?" he asks, grabbing water in his canteen from the lake to douse the fire.

"Uh, yeah sure," I answer. It's a damn lie though. After sleeping while we drove most of the day and the energy drink I had on the way here I could probably swim from one side of the lake to the other. When the fire is out I immediately miss its warmth.

"Ladies first," Tucker says, his deep voice sending a shiver of a different kind down my spine.

"You know, I can just sleep in the front..." Before I can finish my thought Tucker's hands wrap around my waist and hoist me up. "Tucker!" I squeal his name as my ass is planted on the back of the truck.

"You are not sleeping in the front of the truck. I saw how that went earlier and it made *my* neck hurt." He nods behind me, gesturing for me to lie down.

"Okay *Dad*," I mock, scooting back and sliding into my sleeping bag. When he grabs his duffle bag out of the back, my face twists in confusion. "Where are you going?" I ask.

"I'm not partial to sleeping in clothes I've been driving in all day. I was going to change if that's okay with you," he says, his attitude resembling the one I just gave him.

"Oh I see, so it's fine if I take *my* shirt off in front of *you*, but you don't dare change in front of me. That makes sense." My hand flies to my mouth, my eyes widening briefly in shock at the words that just left my mouth.

No more beer for Taylor on this trip.

My heart skips a beat when his duffle bag hits the ground, his eyes glimmering as he stares me down.

"You a little sour about that, Peach?" I scoff, unsure what to say because – yeah, maybe I am. Though I'll never admit that to Tucker. He twists his ball cap around to face forward, pulling his shirt over his head in one swift movement, his cap somehow unmoving. When his torso is stripped bare, his tattoos and abs on full display in front of me, he twists his cap backward again and I lose all control of my fine motor skills. His entire body is covered in tattoos and I think I just discovered a new turn-on. If I had a factory reset, now would be the time to use it. The smirk on his face has me completely weak. I swallow hard when he throws the shirt he just took off at me. I blink rapidly when it hits me in the face, and my senses finally start to come back.

"Go to bed, Darlin'." I throw his shirt to the side.

"You're an animal." I roll my eyes, trying to act as normal as possible in this situation. Though I'm beginning to question what normal is between us anymore. I lay down, doing my best to get comfortable. When I can't, I scroll my phone for a bit being a total fangirl on Shane's account now that she's gotten around to posting photos from the exhibit. Before I am done scrolling my phone alerts me that I have no reception, and everything stops working.

Lovely.

Once I realize how much time has passed and Tucker still isn't back, I begin to worry. I sit up in my sleeping bag, noticing I'm still wearing Tucker's jacket. It smells like him and even if I wasn't freezing I probably wouldn't take it off. When I hear a loud splash, I look out on the water just in time to see Tucker emerging in nothing but his boxers. If this trip was an elaborate plan to seduce me, then well done. It's fucking *working*.

He shakes his head before running up to shore to grab a towel. Where the hell did that come from? His duffle bag is in no way spacious. Did he purchase it from the same company as Mary Poppins? When I see his head turn in my direction I throw my body back into a lying down position, trying to disappear before he catches me leering at him. I stay unmoving in hopes I haven't been caught. I keep waiting for him to come and confront me about it, but he never does.

I lay here, looking out the back window of the truck, thinking about how intimate this all feels. Or *could* feel. The sky is so clear tonight, making all the stars shine brightly in the otherwise dark space. The moon is illuminating the mountains around us and reflecting on the lake in a way I could stare at it forever. All of this is in perfect view from our little back-of-the-Bronco campout. I lay back down, waiting anxiously for Tucker to come to bed.

God that sentence sounds weird.

When he never shows I close my eyes and let the sound of the water lull me to sleep.

Chapter 17

Tucker

"Don't leave me. Please. Come on. Stay with me!"

"Tucker!" I hear a voice as sweet as honey calling my name, "Tucker, wake up. Please." I feel cold hands on my chest jolting me awake. I blink a few times, taking in my surroundings and the concerned look on Taylor's face. Despite the cool breeze and the late-night plunge I took in the frigid lake, I am sweating when I wake from the dream that's haunted me for years.

"Thank God. Are you okay?" She still looks slightly panicked as she studies me.

"Yeah, I'm fine. Are you okay? Are you hurt?" I ask before catching a glimpse at where her gaze has fallen. My hand is gripping hers tightly to my chest. I let go, and she pauses a moment before retracting her hand. Warmth fills my chest at her hesitation.

"No. Why would I be hurt?" she asks cautiously. Still looking at me like I am made of glass. I had hoped I would have relief from the torment of my own mind while being here with Taylor. Though I should have known better. I'm not sure I'll ever be able to escape my brutal subconscious.

"I'm sorry if I woke you," I say, taking her face in my hands as I look her over. Confusion and a hint of fear settle on her beautiful, freckled face. "Are you sure you're not hurt?" She shakes her head, assuring me silently that she's remained unharmed. I wouldn't be able to live with myself had I hurt her all because of the things that haunt my past.

She rests her hand by mine, our bodies closer now than they had been when I climbed in the truck last night. The sun is rising now and the way the sunbeams shine on her untamed auburn curls has me utterly captivated. Completely forgetting what got us in this position, I brush a loose strand of hair back, and as I do her eyes fall shut briefly. When I run the back of my hand across her cheek they fly open again, her hand coming up to grip mine. Before she can say a word my eyes are wide at the realization of just how cold her hands are.

"Jesus Christ, Taylor. Your hands are freezing," I say, wrapping my much larger hands around both of hers. She laughs sleepily.

"That's nothing. You should feel my feet." I can tell she's trying to be playful but I am filled with rage as I realize she's freezing because of me. Because of my failure to better prepare her for what we were doing and where we would be staying. I'm used to the changing weather, and don't mind the cold so much. But I feel like a complete asshole for not thinking about her needing more desirable amenities.

"Come here," I say, trying to pull her to me. She stills when I try, giving me a hesitant look.

"Um, absolutely not." She shakes her head, sitting back on her knees.

"No funny business Darlin'. You're fucking freezing to death because of me. Please, let me help fix it. You may not be fond of the idea, but it's the only way I know how right now. But I promise we'll stay somewhere with a bed and heat tonight when we stop." She studies me skeptically for a moment before she gives in, sliding her tiny body into my sleeping bag with me. She's wearing a white pajama set with *shorts* and my uniform jacket. The thin sleeping bag I bought for her is likely doing nothing to keep her warm. I couldn't take my eyes off of her last night in that tiny pajama set, and my jacket that just about swallows her. But now I feel selfish, knowing I likely didn't speak up during our shopping trip in hopes of seeing her in the tiny little outfit. She hesitantly nestles into me before letting out a sleepy sigh. My heart squeezes in my chest at the way she seems so comfortable.

"I am so so sorry," I say, my jaw tightening as her ice-cold feet slide under my calves.

Holy shit, she wasn't lying.

"What for?" she asks, not moving her head from my chest. I know Taylor and her *fuck off* attitude wouldn't dare be this close to me, and definitely not in such a compromising position if she wasn't desperate for warmth.

"For this. For not having better prepared you to come with me. For not telling you your pajama choice was quite the opposite of what you would need." I huff out a sad laugh, but hers is genuine, easing a little bit of my guilt.

"Yeah, maybe next time you could mention I will need a heated blanket and socks instead of the barely there fabric pajamas. That'd be much appreciated," she teases. I smile, glad that she is still able to be herself with me. Glad she didn't freeze to death last night. And mostly glad she didn't ask more questions about the way we were woken up this morning.

I feel her body relax, and her hand drops, wrapping around my waist now. My dick hardens at the feeling of her touch. Fuck. I sure hope she's asleep otherwise this is going to make my statement about not trying any funny business with her fall flat. My eyes get heavy as our body heat brings comfort that I was lacking when trying to sleep last night. I try to fight off sleep, not wanting to fall back into the nightmare Taylor woke me from. Especially not with her this close to me now. But my efforts are futile. Before I know it I am back into a deep slumber. Only this time my dreams are filled with visions of Taylor.

Her hand slides from around my waist, into the sweatpants I'm wearing. She wraps her tiny hand around my dick, pumping up and down as she plants kisses all along my neck. "Fuck," I groan, loving the way her hand feels around my cock and her lips on my neck.

"I want you, Tucker," she whispers in my ear before climbing on top of my lap. Straddling me in those tiny little white sleep shorts. She slides my jacket off, showcasing her perky nipples through the sleep shirt she wears underneath. Shit, she's not wearing a bra. How did I not notice that last night? She takes her top off, giving me an unobstructed view of her perfect little body. Her tits are heavy with desire, looking like a place I would happily go to die.

"Dammit Darlin', you are too fucking beautiful." She bites her lip, her hair falling over her face when she looks down timidly. When her eyes meet mine again they're burning with the same lust and desire I feel. I sit up straight with her still on my lap, our lips so close that if either of us moved an inch I would finally get to taste her. To know if she tastes like peaches the way I always imagine she will. Her pouty lips are the perfect shade of pink and the subject of some of my wildest fantasies.

"Tucker." The way she whispers my name like a plea has my dick throbbing beneath her.

"Yes, Peach?" I ask everything in me wanting to know what she's about to ask of me.

SLAM.

My body flies forward, my heart beating erratically in my chest. I look to my side to see I am alone in the back of my truck.

It was just a dream.

I am equal parts relieved and devastated at the realization. Because damn that was good. But if I woke her up talking through the other dream I was having last night, there's no telling what I would have woken her up saying during *that one.*

"Where the hell did you put that towel? Do you have any more in that Marry Poppins duffle bag of yours?" Taylor whines from the front of the truck. I swallow hard, readjusting my rock-hard dick that is struggling to hide behind my gray sweatpants.

"In my what?" I ask in confusion.

"Oh come on, you pulled so much shit out of that bag last night. Don't act like you've never seen Marry Poppins." She rolls her eyes, holding her dripping wet hair up in her hands, shivering. "Tuckerrrr," she wines. *Fuck*. Why does everything she does make my dick even harder? Her eyes are pleading when I look over at her. I grab the towel from behind where I've been laying and hand it to her.

"Sorry, here you go." She takes it from me and begins scrunching it around her curls, doing her best to dry it. "Did you just wash your hair in the lake?" I question, just realizing why her hair would be wet.

"Well, *Tucker*. I am not sure if you've noticed or not but there are no showers here. I was desperate," she gets out through chattering teeth. I glance at what she's wearing, noticing that she's changed out of her pajamas and into a pair of leggings and... my T-shirt from yesterday. I'm going to end up with zero shirts at the end of this trip, and I couldn't be happier about it.

"Yeah, sorry about that. I'll make sure we have somewhere better to stay tonight. Did you ever get your feet warm?" I ask sliding my ball cap on before hopping out of the truck beside her. Her eyes fall to the bulge in my sweatpants I had briefly forgotten about. I smirk when a redness creeps across her cheeks before she averts her gaze to the mountains beyond the lake.

"Um, yeah. They're fine." Her body is betraying her words as I see the goosebumps covering her arms. I grab the same jacket I had given her last night from the back of the truck, putting it over her shoulders.

"Liar." I wink at her before grabbing the matching pants from my duffle bag to change into. Once I'm changed, I walk around the truck, grabbing everything I need to make the eggs and bacon from the cooler, along with my percolator and two mugs. I join her by the lake, starting the fire again to make our breakfast and coffee.

"So, if it's alright with you. I have something I want to show you before we head out today," I tell her, seeing the curiosity in her eyes.

"Sounds good. As long as I'm caffeinated first." Once the coffee is ready I take her mug over to her, stretching my back as we stand looking out over the lake.

"Oh my god, this is amazing," she says after taking a sip. Her eyes fall closed as she takes another. I smirk at her, before trying it too.

"Damn, that is good," I agree. She looks up at me, shaking her head and rolling her eyes at me all with a sweet smile on her face. My mind flashes back to the look in her eyes in my dream, so sexy and full of desire.

"I see why you love it out here. It's so peaceful. So breathtaking."

"Yeah, it is." She's looking out at the green grass and trees lining the lake at the base of the mountains.

But I'm looking at her.

In *my* T-shirt, *my* jacket. She looks like *mine* and it scares me how much I love that.

This is the most serene I have ever seen her look. I love Taylor fired up, don't get me wrong. But seeing a sense of calmness surrounding her is something special. I've always thought of Taylor as this untouchable, strong, confident woman. But after our conversation last night, I'm wondering if it's all a front she puts on to hide how she feels like she falls short. It's only been one night but I'm already thoroughly enjoying this trip with her.

When she agreed to come on this trip with me, it gave me a twinge of hope. To see if maybe there could be something between us with that Zander asshole out of the way, and our friends not hovering every second we're together. The way she's been acting is the same way she's always acted as my friend, but the ever-present blush on her cheeks is new. Though I still wonder if she'll ever see me as more than a friend. I'm not going to stop trying to change her mind. I have to be careful not to force anything that won't be reciprocated though. The last thing I want to do is lose her all because I want more than friendship and that's all she'll ever see with me.

Chapter 18

Taylor

I'm NOT sure what I was expecting when I agreed to come on this trip with Tucker, but it definitely wasn't him showing me one of the most beautiful places I've ever seen in my life. The hiking I'm not too fond of, but thankfully I started working out again recently, otherwise I would have told him to leave me to die about 20 minutes ago.

"How you holdin' up, Darlin'?" Tucker smiles back at me. His smile along with the way he calls me *Darlin'* has my heart skipping a beat.

"I thought you said you weren't bringing me out here to kill me. But I'm starting to think you were lying," I pant as we make it up the hill, "are we almost there?"

"We…are," he says as he helps me up one last step. I look up to see that we're standing at the base of the most magnificent waterfall I have ever seen. My eyes go wide as I take in how absolutely insane this place is. I look over at Tucker who is already staring back at me. Those forest green eyes always seem to find their way to mine.

"Tucker… this place is…" I can't even begin to come up with a way to describe it.

"Beautiful," he says. The way he's looking at me makes me question if he's really talking about the waterfall. I pull in a deep breath as the silent tension between us builds. He looks so gorgeous it's unreal. We're both sweating from the hike, but it's working in his favor. The way his reddish brown hair peeks through his backward ballcap, and his white T-shirt hugs his body makes me want to climb him like a jungle gym. He drops his backpack on the rocks right next to the water, breaking my focus.

"Let's go, Peach," he says as he begins unlacing his hiking boots.

"Go? Where? We *just* got here." I hold my hand out to the waterfall.

"We're going in." He smiles at me as he pulls his shirt over his head. "Unless you're scared," he teases.

"I'm not scared. Wildly unprepared, sure. *Someone* failed to inform me of all the things I would need during this impromptu camping trip. I don't have a swimsuit," I tell him, waving a hand down my body.

I am wearing a pair of denim shorts, the hiking boots he picked for me last night, and a band tee. He unzips his pants and drops them to the ground, standing in front of me in his boxer briefs and a ballcap. His massive dick not being the least bit shy behind the black fabric.

HOLY FU–

"Neither do I." He throws his pants to the side and raises a brow at me. The look on his face tells me he knows he's being a tease and I refuse to let him have that power over me. I lift a brow in return, dropping my bag next to his. I quickly unlace my boots, kicking them off and dropping my shorts before pulling my T-shirt over my head. The look on his face makes my decision *well* worth it because he looks like he can barely breathe. I'm suddenly very glad that I chose to wear my matching black sports bra and thong set today. I pull my hair out of the bun on top of my head and brush past Tucker.

"Ladies first, yeah?" I strut past him, completely unbothered by the fact that he has a perfect view of my almost bare ass. I jump in the water, letting the cold water embrace me before I reach the surface again. The way the sun is beating down is a perfect contrast to the cool water. Making it bearable to swim in without feeling like I'll freeze to death.

"Goddammit woman." Tucker shakes his head before jumping in after me. He comes out of the water right beside me, splashing water on me as he emerges. "Let's go." He starts swimming away from me.

"What? Where?" I ask as I swim a little further out, following his lead.

"To the waterfall," he calls back. I stop where I'm at, my toes barely touch the bottom to keep my head above water. Tucker notices and starts treading water. "You coming?" he calls.

"No. You go ahead, I'll stay here," I call out. He swims back over to me, standing up to expose the top of his chest.

"How come?" His face is sincere, as though he can sense it's more than me just not wanting to.

"I'm not a great swimmer and water makes me nervous." He smirks, making me feel embarrassed by the admission. "Not all of us are trained divers, okay? Just go without me, I'll hang out here." I push the water between us, sending a splash over his head. He grabs me around the wrist when I do, pulling me into him. He snakes his arm around my waist and brings our faces closer together than they've ever been before.

"Do you trust me?" he asks, his gaze falls to my lips before meeting my eyes again.

"Yes, I trust you." I nod as he turns around, placing me on his back.

"Good. Don't let go." He starts swimming with me wrapped around him until we are almost to the waterfall.

"I'm going under, are you ready?" he calls out as we approach the rushing water.

"Yes!" I hold my breath and close my eyes as he takes us both under the falls. My whole body squeezes him tighter before we emerge on the other side. He swims over to the ledge for us to sit, pulling me around to his front before hoisting me up like I weigh *nothing,* then pulling himself up to sit beside me. He takes his hat off, shaking his hair before placing it back on his head. I can see small red marks from where my fingers dug into his skin.

"Sorry if I held on too tight." I run my fingers along the mark on his skin. He chuckles and grabs my hand, looking deeply into my eyes.

"Oh, Darlin'. I'd let you do far worse to me." He winks and I'm rendered speechless. How does he do that? Say things that are so unbelievably sexy but make it sound like it's just another normal conversation between us. I'll catch myself wondering if he's really into me like that or if he's just being playful, flirty Tucker. Does he talk like this with other women? I mean, I've never heard him talk to any of our other friends this way, but they'd probably just shut him down, whereas I have always indulged in his little games.

"If you feel safe, that's all that matters."

We sit silently with our hands by our sides, his pinky brushes against mine and my eyes shoot up to see him already staring back at me.

"Tell me something, Peach." His deep voice makes me tingle all over.

"What do you want to know?" He sits there mulling over my question before answering.

"Why are you afraid of the water?" he asks cautiously, his pinky now rubbing mine in a soothing motion.

"I didn't say I was scared. I said it makes me nervous, there's a difference," I correct him. He nods his head up and down slowly as if he's trying to detect my lie. Before I know it he slides his body back into the water.

"What the hell, Tucker!" I yell as I try to avoid the splash from the water. But when I turn back, I don't see him. I keep waiting for him to resurface, but so much time has passed I'm sure he went back under the waterfall without me. Leaving me to own up to my lie. But I never see him emerge on the other side either.

"Tucker, this isn't funny!" I yell. Another minute passes and I am in full-blown panic mode when he finally comes back to the surface, taking a deep breath in when he does.

"You were saying?" he mocks as he lifts his body out of the water, sitting next to me once again.

"What the *hell* was that? Are you trying to give me a stroke?" I scold, swatting his arm with the back of my hand.

"Tell me why you're scared of the water," he presses, acting like nothing even happened. I roll my eyes, letting out a sigh before facing the waterfall as I answer.

"When I was eight, we took our annual family beach vacation. I always loved the beach. The way the ocean sounds, the sun beaming down on me while I would build sand castles, and playing in the waves with my brothers. This one year in particular I was determined I was old enough to not need my life jacket anymore. I felt like I had grown out of that stage, and it was embarrassing to see all the other girls my age in their cute bathing suits while I had this big life jacket on. I insisted on going without it. My parents didn't like the idea but I was persistent and swore I would stay close to the shore with JJ and Sawyer.

"We were playing on our boogie boards and I drifted a little farther out than I meant to. I turned around to try and paddle back, but I didn't see the massive wave coming up behind me. It wiped me out and I lost my board in the process. I couldn't touch the bottom and I wasn't the strongest swimmer so I panicked. It only took seconds for JJ to get to me and pull me up. But it was the most scared I had ever been in my life." I glance over at Tucker, and he's just watching me intently. No judgment or sense of mocking on his face at all. "Ever since then, I just don't go into water that I can't see the bottom of. Or where my feet can't reach with my head staying above water." I feel so vulnerable right now, though I don't know why. Tucker just picks the conversation up where I left off.

"I've always loved the water. Diving was one of my favorite parts of being a SEAL. The silence, the peace that being under the water brings. During training of course; during a mission, there's no peace to be found. I know plenty of people are afraid of the water and there's that sense of fear that surrounds it, but I don't know. I don't mind it." He shrugs.

"Well, at least you know where to go if you ever want to get away from me." I laugh, thinking of how I've driven Tucker crazy in times past. I wonder if I still do. Tucker wraps his arm around my waist, making me suck in a breath. I look up at him, my heart beating faster in my chest. "What are you doing?" I ask as he pulls me closer to him.

"Hold your breath." *Yeah, already doing that.* I nod and take a deep breath. He pulls us into the water again, and without instruction I wrap my body around him again as we dive under the waterfall. When he brings us to the surface, my legs are wrapped around his waist, my arms around his neck, and our noses are just inches from touching. "You still trust me, right?" he asks, as his hands hold my thighs tight against his abs. Adrenaline is coursing through my veins as I try to stay focused on anything other than how it feels to have his arms wrapped around me.

"Of course." Tucker has one of the most ruggedly handsome faces I think I have ever seen. His facial hair is more red than the thick locks hiding under his hat. When the sun hits just right the red highlights in his brown hair are unmistakable, but his dark red facial hair is always the same. Covering his strong jaw but not hiding its definition. The thick eyelashes, that would make any girl jealous, accentuate his forest green eyes that show a hint of amber when light reflects in them. I could stare at his face forever and never be bored by it.

"Squeeze my arm when you're ready to come up," he says before he takes us beneath the water again.

I hold my breath as I feel his feet touch the bottom of the river. My body tightens around him and his grip on me follows suit. His own way of reassuring me I'm safe with him. I try to clear my mind and find that same peace in the silence being underwater brings him. I can tell I won't be able to hold my breath much longer. When Tucker's hand slides up to my ass, I suddenly wish that weren't the case. I can't fight the way it feels so right to have his hands on my body. I squeeze his arm to let him know to resurface. When we reach the top I take in a deep breath as he brushes the wet hair from around my face.

"You okay?" he asks, letting the back of his hand graze my cheek, sending a shiver down my spine. I nod in reassurance. "See, you did great, Darlin'. Nothing to be afraid of." His gaze falls to my lips before he pulls my hands apart to loosen my grip around his neck. He turns his body to place me on his back, our bodies never losing contact when he does.

"Hold on tight." I do as he says as he starts to swim back toward our clothes. He grabs a towel from his backpack, handing it to me first before using it himself to dry off. Once I'm dressed again I grab my phone from my backpack and take a selfie in front of the waterfall to send to the girls. Before putting it back in my bag I look over my shoulder to see Tucker taking a drink of water from his canteen.

"Hey, come here," I call him over, "take a picture with me." I don't know why I feel so nervous to ask him to take a photo with me. We *are* friends after all. Even if the *things* I have been feeling for him lately are far from *things* I feel for any of my other friends. Tucker comes up behind me, towering over me as he always does. I hold my phone up trying my best to capture both us and the waterfall behind us. I snap a few in a row because, *options*, then slide my phone in my pocket. "Thanks." I smile at him, feeling the blush wash over my cheeks.

"Anytime." He winks at me before grabbing his backpack off the ground. "You gonna make it back down or will I have to carry you?" he teases.

"Don't make offers you can't uphold." I raise my brows as a warning. Walking down the mountain is far less straining than the walk up. Giving me enough stamina to hold a conversation and walk at the same time.

"Your turn. Tell me something." I watch as Tucker walks so confidently down the trail. There's no telling how many times he's walked this trail. I wonder who else he's come here with. Who else he's taken to that breathtaking waterfall? Wearing nothing but his boxers. A streak of jealousy rushes through me at the thought, though I have no business being jealous.

"What do you want to know?" He looks in my direction briefly as I think, *What is it I truly want to know about Tucker Landry? Everything.*

Chapter 19

Tucker

Seeing Taylor strip down and jump in the water was hands down the sexiest thing I have ever witnessed. When her perfect plump ass sauntered past me so confidently, I struggled to look anywhere else. I love the way her body felt wrapped around mine, and the look in her eyes when I asked her if she trusted me. There was no hint of reservation or doubt to be found.

Fuck, I'm so gone for this woman.

"What made you want to become a Navy SEAL?" I laugh as I remember how that career came to be.

"As I'm sure you know, Max and I have been friends since middle school. After we met we did pretty much everything together. We became like brothers in no time. We attended the same schools all throughout middle and high school. After we graduated he went to college, with absolutely *no* idea what he wanted to do. I, on the other hand– being the brilliant man that I am– went to school for architecture. On a dare." I look over at Taylor to assess her reaction. She's wide eyed and her jaw is hanging open.

"A *dare*? How scholarly of you." She lets out a little laugh as we keep moving.

"Yeah, well. It wasn't all that bad. I have always enjoyed my creative outlets. I would always be drawing plans for me and my friends during high school. We had a million-dollar idea every other week, and I was in charge of drawing up the plans. So when it came time for graduation and I was still undecided on what I wanted to do, as you can guess, someone dared me to go into architecture. So I did. After a couple of years, I was starting to get bored with it, so I decided to take a break. My plan was to have one year off and then finish my degree, but when Max told me he was enlisting, there was no way I was letting him go without me. It was one of the best decisions I ever made. It gave me a sense of purpose, you know? I made friends who were more like family through the Navy, and that's something I'll always be grateful for." I help Taylor over a fallen tree as we near our secluded campsite.

The way she squeezes my arms as I help her over reminds me of the way her body felt wrapped around mine while we were under the water. It took every bit of self-control I had not to kiss her then. I'm not sure I'll ever get another chance to, but dammit if I do, I'm taking it. Any moment of validation that she may want it too and this girl is mine.

"Yeah, I noticed how close you all seemed the night of Shane and Max's wedding. You definitely have friends for life there." She smiles at me before continuing, "That's really cool though, that you guys did that together. What branch did Tank serve in again?"

"Tank served in the Marine Corps. He was *not* happy when he had to leave." My heart sinks a little thinking about the day I got that call. I stop myself from divulging any further. I don't like speaking on other people's behalf. Even if that person is my little brother.

"I get that. It must have been hard. Feeling like he didn't have a choice. Feeling like his job wasn't done, but having to let it be."

"Yeah," I mutter, unable to come up with another response. Because I'm not sure I've ever thought about it that way. "If you're ready we can get everything loaded up and grab lunch before we hit the road. Maybe get a few hours under our belt before we stop again."

Taylor stops walking, making me come to a halt a few feet in front of her. I look around to see what caused her abrupt stop.

"Or we could try and drive through the night if you'd rather try and make better time," I offer, unsure what's going on in that pretty little mind of hers. She pulls at the hem of her shirt, looking around us before turning to face me again.

"Could we... could we stay here another night maybe?" she asks, shocking me. Her voice wavers a little as if she's nervous to ask. Though the look in her eyes is hopeful.

"You want to stay here again? After you almost froze to death last night?" I point to the truck trying to remind her that she was moments away from turning into an ice block by the way her feet felt this morning. She takes a few steps closer to me, invading the personal space that I've started to desire less and less when it comes to Taylor.

"Yeah, it's just so beautiful. I don't know, I just don't feel ready to go yet." Her voice is sincere and her raincloud eyes are locked on mine. "*But*, food does sound like a good idea. I'm starving." Me too. But not for something I can get at a drive-thru.

MAX

Just checking in. Everything ok brother?

ME

All good here man. Preciate it.

TANK

Hey Tuck, I really need to talk to you. Call me when you can.

ME

Will do little bro.

"Why do my marshmallows keep falling off, and yours stay perfectly in place on your stick thing?" Taylor groans. I slide my phone in my pocket and laugh as her third marshmallow hits the ashes from our little campfire.

"I'd say you're doing it wrong, but I'm not even sure *how* a person can roast a marshmallow the wrong way," I tease, as I slide my marshmallow off of my skewer and into the graham cracker and chocolate sandwich I have waiting.

I take a massive bite, showing off my master s'mores-making skills. Much to my surprise she leans in and takes a bite off the other end. My eyes go wide as an unhinged laugh falls from her lips, her marshmallow-covered lips. When she swallows her bite, my eyes fall to the small bit of sticky white sugar that has clung to her bottom lip. I swipe my tongue along my thumb and her eyes fall to my lips as well.

"You have some marshmallow right..." I wipe the marshmallow from her lip, "here." Her cheeks pink instantly when I lick the marshmallow off my finger. Her dainty fingers follow behind where I just wiped, pushing her pouty lips to the side. God, I bet she tastes delicious. She clears her throat, pulling my gaze away from her lips. She holds up a marshmallow and shoves it in my direction, silently demanding I make one for her.

"Umm, Tucker," she prompts, as I begin making another s'more.

"Yes, Darlin'?" I smile, as she scoots closer to me, no doubt to fight the breeze that just blew by, but her nearness feels good all the same.

"Why did you buy a tent today?" My body tenses at her question and I can feel her eyes on me. I keep staring ahead, putting more focus than is necessary on the marshmallow I am charring.

"I'm gonna sleep in it tonight. I just figured you'd prefer more space in the truck." She rears back a little, looking– if I'm not mistaken– hurt by my answer.

"Did I make you think I didn't have plenty of room?"

"No, I just–"

"Did I take up too much room for *you* to be comfortable?" The embarrassment in her tone makes me grimace.

"No," I assure her as I turn to face her.

"Then tell me why you really bought it, Tucker." Her pleading for my honesty has my jaw tightening. *Because in one of my dreams, I woke up afraid I had hurt you, and in the other I almost fucked you.*

"When I woke you this morning..." Her words have my heart racing. "You were saying some things... is that why you don't want to sleep in the same space as me?"

"What was I saying?" I had no idea I talked in my sleep.

"You said uh... *don't leave me.*" Her gaze narrows. "Is there someone else who should be on this trip with you?" She tries to hide the hint of disdain in her voice, but I still notice. I always notice when it's Taylor.

"No," I answer quickly, before letting out an exasperated sigh.

"Tucker, it's *me.* Okay? You can tell me anything," she assures me, placing her hand on my forearm. The intimate feel of her touch has me relaxing a little more now. I wrap my hand around hers, looking down into her beautiful eyes.

"Do you know what I did on our SEAL team? What my job was?"

"No, actually. What did you do?" Confusion flashes across her face.

"I was our team medic." Her expression twists as she works through her realization.

"Don't leave me," she whispers, likely recalling what she heard me saying in my sleep. "Oh, Tucker..."

Chapter 20

Taylor

"It was supposed to be a direct action mission. The last one before a few of us got out. We were clearing a compound, and the first four buildings were cleared easily. As we moved up to the fifth and last building, we started receiving heavy fire. Max had to subdue a civilian, but the rest of us moved in toward the open fire. Our buddy, Red, took point and was waiting for a second man to breach, but before anyone got there a grenade dropped from the roof. I got to him as fast as I could to render first aid, but he was… it was bad." I swallow past the lump forming in my throat, squeezing his hand reassuringly as he continues.

"We called for a medevac, and I kept working on him until it got there. I never stopped. Not for one second. We got to the helicopter and I was praying the whole time that he'd stay with us. But before the building that had just blown was even out of sight, he was gone. Just like that. His hand went limp in mine, but I couldn't let him go. I held onto him until they took him off the helicopter. I know I did everything I could. But knowing it wasn't enough still eats at me." He sniffles and my heart shatters.

"Max was point, basically the leader, on that mission up until that moment. He never has forgiven himself for not being the first one in. That's why he is the way he is. So fucked up by his past, and why he seems so jaded." I wrap my arms around his waist and he hugs me back tighter. There's never anything you can say in these situations to ease the pain. Not one he's felt for so long. Not when it haunts his dreams even still. So I just stay there, giving him any ounce of comfort I can manage through a hug. The thought of him buying a tent to suffer that nightmare alone, just to spare me the inconvenience, has me ready to throw it in the lake.

"Alright. Your turn." I look up at him confused.

"What?"

"I wanna know everything about you, Peach. Every little thing there is to learn." My heart skips a beat and we settle in for the night. He roasts marshmallows while I tell him all about my childhood.

I tell him about how I wanted to be a dancer when I was little and how when that dream died I thought I would be a vet because I loved animals so much. It wasn't until Sawyer told me I'd have to stick my hand in animal asses that I switched gears and decided my healing methods would be best elsewhere.

"Hense being an ER nurse. Where you have to deal with *human* asses," Tucker teased, almost falling off the log from his laughter. I told him about how Shane, Leah, Lauren, and I met– Shane and I knowing each other since birth because our moms were best friends, and then Leah and Lauren came into the picture when we were all put together for a group project in middle school. I even admitted the insane crush we all had on our history teacher, how we all fought over who would marry him, and how devastated we were when we found out he was already married.

He asked about past boyfriends and I told him about how I thought I had met my match in high school, only for that to end in heartbreak. I spared him the details, choosing only to tell him it was after that I decided not to date ever again. Which led to Zander being mentioned and Tucker was none too happy to hear his name.

We talked about my job and the stresses of being a nurse. Some of my favorite patients and some of the hardest losses I've faced. I told him how I've cried in the storage room on really hard days because everyone thinks I'm impenetrable when it comes to my emotions. Which couldn't be farther from the truth. But I carry myself in a professional way and people admire that so I take pride in it. After I'm spent and my throat hurts from talking, laughing, and bordering on crying. Tucker picks up the conversation. Never missing a beat.

He tells me about how he and Max became friends after Max was getting bullied and Tucker stepped in to help. It's hard for me to picture Max being bullied after only knowing him as someone who would punch a hole through concrete if necessary. He told me how he'd gone through a phase of trying *every* extracurricular activity he could in middle school to try and find something that stuck – but nothing did. I got to hear all about his dad who was Tucker's hero. He was a police officer Tucker's whole life and died in the line of duty. He tells me about how his mom fell apart after that and they basically lost her too. Seeing the pain on his face when he reminisced about how she used to be, made my heart ache.

"They had the kind of love that could survive a war, ya know? But when she lost him, I guess she lost her will to keep fighting. No matter how much Tank and I needed her to, she just– couldn't. So I started fighting for us on my own. I ensured Tank was taken care of. I never let him see how much I was hurting so that he would know that we could make it through the loss. I wanted him to know we didn't have to give up like our mom did. I made sure he did well in school and stayed out of trouble, as best I could at least." He laughs, but I can see it's to cover up the fact that he's crying.

"Max had become like a brother to us, and the three of us did everything together. My mom had turned into someone I didn't recognize so we hung out with Cecelia, Max's mom, every chance we got. She took care of us when our mom couldn't and I'll always be grateful for that. It broke my heart when she passed away. It felt like I lost a mom that day too. But again, I didn't let my hurt show. I knew Max would need someone to lean on and I'd be damned if I wasn't there for him. Not after the way he and his mom had been there for me all those years." The little bit of light still flickering from the fire shines on Tucker's face. He looks exhausted from recounting all of these painful memories tonight. He takes a deep breath as if a weight has physically been lifted from his shoulders.

"That's about it, Peach. That's all there is to me." He wraps his arm around my shoulder, pulling me into his body as he plants a kiss on the side of my hair. The gesture warms my heart and I wrap my hands around his middle.

"Tucker…" I say, finally lifting my head from his chest. His eyes are misty as he looks down at me.

"Yeah, Darlin'?" That damn nickname. I might die if he ever stops calling me that.

"Please don't sleep in that tent tonight. Just… stay with me." The smile he gives me eases the tension I had been holding in my shoulders over asking him that.

"If that's what you want." He nods. I smile at him and nod reassuringly.

"Stay right here," he says as he pushes to stand. He places another log in the fire causing the flames to dance back to life, then he walks to the front of the Bronco.

"Okay." I raise a brow at him, when he reappears with a guitar in his hands. "Seriously? What kind of magic storage space deal with the devil did you make?" He barks out a laugh.

"I have no idea what you're talking about." He brushes past me with a wink, sitting on the log we've accompanied the last two nights. "Playing guitar always helps me clear my head. My dad taught me how to play before he passed. It makes me feel connected to him, you know?"

He begins strumming and my mouth drops open a little. But I

could actually faint when he starts to sing. I mean I know he said he was in band and choir during his trial run of –everything– in middle school but *damn.*

The deep rasp to his voice makes every word to "Beyond" by Leon Bridges sound like a damn invitation to fall in love with him. I let him play a little more before I pull my phone out of my pocket and play the remainder of the song, boldly asking him to dance with me. He sets his guitar down and doesn't hesitate to take my hand in his. We slow dance by the fire, while the song quietly plays on my phone speaker.

I wake up a couple of hours after we finally turn in, to Tucker whimpering in his sleep. I was hopeful that after our talk tonight, his mind would be able to rest easy. I know from experience that sometimes just speaking things out loud is enough relief for our mind to let things go, even if just for a little while. Though that doesn't seem to be the case tonight.

"No. No. Don't go," he pleads in his sleep. Pure agony is written all over his face. The nightmare seems to be worse tonight. His body twitches and his brows are furrowed. I cup his face with my hands, running my thumbs along his cheekbones.

"Tucker. Tucker. Wake up. It's okay." I'm not sure how he'll respond when he wakes, so I do my best to keep my voice calm. He sucks in a deep breath and sits up quickly. I jump back a little to avoid our heads butting.

"Hey, hey. It's okay. It's just me." His eyes don't focus on me though, they're darting around in a panic. His breathing is heavier now than it was when he was sleeping. I suddenly have no idea what to do. I wrap my hands along his neckline letting my fingers run through his hair. "Tucker, it's okay. I'm here," I try reassuring him.

What he does next completely shocks me. He wraps one arm around my waist pulling me over so that I straddle his lap, as his free hand cups my face– and he kisses me.

Hard, fast, desperate.

Like I'm the only thing keeping him grounded. Meanwhile, I feel like my body is floating, watching us from above the truck. The pure electricity shooting through every nerve in my body has me completely entranced. My grip on his hair tightens as I pull him in closer. If he needs to be grounded then consider me an anchor.

When his tongue swipes against my lips, I gladly let him in. A pleased groan rumbles in his throat, in sync with the moan that falls from my lips. I can feel him harden beneath me and the ache that's building between my thighs is undeniable. His one hand is gripping my waist while his other holds its firm grip on my hair. I grind my hips to try and relieve some of the pressure, but I'm not granted that privilege. While the hand he had on my waist had begun to guide my movements in one second, he's pulling it away from me in the next.

"Shit, I'm so sorry Taylor," he apologizes. The way he uses my real name instead of one of the nicknames he's coined for me makes my heart sink a little. His breathing is still heavy, but the panic behind it has been replaced with desire. He drops his head, snatching his hands away from me. I feel redness wash over my face, slightly embarrassed by the urgency he seems to have to get away from me. When he meets my gaze again, there's a sense of guilt creeping over his features. Surely he knows I would have stopped him if I hadn't wanted that to happen. Right? His jaw twitches and he apologizes again.

"I don't know what got into me. I am so sorry." The conviction in his voice has me desperate to reassure him that I'm not mad about what happened. If anything I'm mad that it stopped.

"Don't you dare apologize." He looks at me as relief and confusion wash over him. I slip into his sleeping bag and lay my head on his chest, as his arms hesitantly wrap around me. I can hear the rapidness of his heartbeat begin to calm ever so slowly, until his body goes lax and he begins to snore. I softly giggle to myself and close my eyes–replaying the most incredible kiss I've ever had in my life. I may have started this trip confused about my feelings for Tucker, but after tonight they're becoming *much* clearer. Because all I can think about is having his lips on mine again.

Chapter 21

Taylor

WE HAVE BEEN on the road for hours, and Tucker has barely uttered a word to me. My phone lost reception after the first night we were there, so as we get further into civilization again, messages begin pouring in.

SHANE

> I'm hoping that no news is good news and everyone is still alive?

RUBY

> I thought we were always supposed to assume the worst? Have I been wrong about that?

LEAH

> Oh Rubes. You were running with the wrong crowd if you thought that.

LAUREN

> Plot twist: they're just fucking. 

SHANE

No chance.

RUBY

Oooohhh. Interesting.

LEAH

Taylor, care to share something with the class?

Good Lord. It's never a good idea to leave these four to their own imaginations. The absurd shit they come up with...

ME

You guys are clinically insane. I am admitting you all to a psych ward.

RUBY

She lives!!!

SHANE

Bout damn time bitch.

LAUREN

We need answers, ma'am.

ME

I had no service. We were camping.

LEAH

... oh they definitely fucked.

ME

CLINICAL. 😶

ME

We hiked up to this waterfall that was absolutely gorgeous.

LAUREN
Pics or it didn't happen.

I start scrolling through my phone to send them the selfie I took in front of it. When I see the ones I snapped with Tucker, my heart jumps a little in my chest. I glance over at him, but he's hyper-focused on the road. You'd think he was driving through a blizzard or something with how trained his focus is. But there's no blizzard, it's clear freaking skies for miles. He's just making himself seem very unapproachable. I roll my eyes and click on the picture to enlarge it.

He's holding up a shaka and his tongue is sticking out in the first one– very on-brand for Tucker. I swipe through the next few, checking for blurry ones to delete but my chest warms when I stop on the last one. I am smiling at the camera, looking surprisingly good to have just come out of a river, and Tucker is looking down at me with a sated smile on his face. I drop my phone in my lap, thinking back to last night. The way his hands wrapped around my hair so possessively. The way his mouth moved on mine so effortlessly. It felt like a turning point for us. So why the hell is he ignoring me today?

I quickly send the selfie of just me with the waterfall in the back to our group text and lock my phone. When I turn to face Tucker his posture is stiff and his eyes are still trained to the road behind his Ray-Ban sunglasses.

"Tucker."

"Yeah?" What? No *Yes, Darlin'*? Rude.

"Why are you being weird today?"

"Is my driving weird to you? Because I'm not doing much else."

"Okay, first of all. Having an attitude is *my* thing. Second of all, that's exactly my point. I have been playing all kinds of crap music. Nothing. I put my feet on the dash which you *hate*. Nothing. You've barely spared me a second glance. What's going on?" Still not a word.

This motherfu–

"You hungry?"

I narrow my gaze at him. "That's the only thing you have to say?"

"You seem hungry. I know this area. We can pull off here and eat." He veers off at the exit and I throw my hands up in defeat.

"Great," I answer. I feel him peeking over at me, but I'm not giving in now. We pull off on an exit that's got all of *one* gas station-restaurant combo, causing me to glare over at Tucker.

"I am not eating here."

"You having more first-world problems Darlin'?" I scoff as he swings his door open to step out. He makes his way around to my door, opening it for me as I stay firmly planted in my seat.

"This place looks like...like..."

"Like what, exactly?" He crosses his arms over his chest, my eyes landing on his muscular biceps that are all but ripping the sleeves of his T-shirt. Ugh.

"Like I need a tetanus shot just to be here."

"Are you not up to date on all your shots? Isn't that a little irresponsible for a nurse?" He smirks at me and I could literally choke him. What the hell is happening with him today?

"Come on. I eat here all the time and I'm just fine."

"Hardly," I mumble when I'm a few steps ahead of him.

"What's that?" He shuts my door behind me before meeting me step for step. When we walk in the... *establishment* it's actually not as bad as I'd imagined. Though I will *not* be giving Tucker that win. It's got a 70's diner vibe to it with black and white floor tiles, an old busted jukebox in the corner, and bright blue and white vinyl seating. It even has a counter with bar stools and a portrait of Elvis hanging right beside the menu on the wall.

"See, I told you it wasn't so bad." Tucker bumps my shoulder, making the small smile on my face fall. We slide into a booth and a waitress comes up to take our order.

What even is this place?

"Hey there. What can I get you started with?"

"Water please," Tucker tells her.

"I'll take a Diet Coke." I smile at the waitress, *Annie* according to her name tag.

"And a tetanus shot if you have them." Tucker smiles brightly at her.

"What's that?" she asks, a confused innocent look on her face. My eyes go wide as I kick Tucker's leg under the table, *hard.*

"Nothing, that'll be all Annie." He groans in pain. I smirk, a little proud of my ability to actually inflict pain on someone who's built like a grizzly bear. Once Annie has retreated behind the counter I lean over my folded arms on the table.

"What the hell is actually wrong with you?" I seethe, but he just laughs.

"Man, you should have seen your face." I roll my eyes and settle back into my seat. We order and to my surprise, the food isn't half bad. If I'm being completely honest it might be one of the best burgers I've ever tasted. Tucker pays the bill and fills up the Bronco while I'm in the restroom. I go to open my door but he stops me, holding my hiking boots out to me.

"Put these on." My face is unamused when I look up at him.

"Tucker, I just ate a whole cheeseburger. Do you really expect me to climb *anything* right now?" He shoves them into my hands regardless.

"We have to drive a little further. You'll be ready when we get there." He opens my door and before I can turn around to climb in, he lifts me by the waist and places me in my seat.

"I don't need your help." I protest.

He just keeps his smirk in place. "I know, but just let me."

Overlook Canyon Hiking Trail

I am so not in the mood to be hiking with him right now. He was weird in the truck for *hours*, but got all playful as soon as we got out at the gas station diner, and now he's dragging my ass on another hiking trail. I have my answer. He hates me. That's what it is. He turns me on, pushes me away then brings me to a hiking trail to die. It all makes sense now.

Tucker hikes effortlessly along the trail as I stagger behind him. He's wearing some dark green pants that accentuate his nice ass and muscular thighs, and a heather gray T-shirt that hugs him the way I wish I could. Or the way I would want to if I didn't hate him right now. His hair isn't hidden by a ballcap today. His copper brown locks reveal a heavy tint of red anytime the sun shines through the trees. The tattoos that wrap around both of his arms give me something to focus on as we make our way up the hill.

"You doing okay back there?" he calls from over his shoulder.

"Like you even care," I pant. He comes to a screeching halt but I march right past him.

"What is that supposed to mean?" I glance at his face before continuing forward, confusion and shock cover his features. I scoff at his play at ignorance. He finally starts walking after me again as I find a new rush of adrenaline to stay ahead of him.

"Please. You think I haven't noticed how fucking weird you've been acting since last night, Tucker? It's been *painfully* obvious." His footsteps come to a halt again and I turn my body to walk backward up the hill.

"Taylor, look…" he starts. Using my real name yet again. I can already tell I'm not going to like what he's got to say after that. It's the classic *about to get rejected* intro and I am not about to get rejected on the side of some mountain while I still have *days* on the road with him.

"I don't want to hear it, Tucker. Just–" As I turn to start hiking uphill again I trip over a big ass tree root that's unearthed. I hit the ground *hard,* landing on my knee and catching the rest of my weight on my shoulder. I let out a pained and frustrated groan.

"Shit, are you okay?" Tucker rushes over to me, sliding his backpack off his shoulders. I wipe the dirt from my knee and can see the blood starting to rush down my leg.

"I'm fine." I wince when I try to move the arm I landed on. Tucker unzips his backpack and grabs a small first aid kit out. I sit there stewing in my own anger and embarrassment as he wipes the gash clean and puts a bandage over it. I would like nothing more than to brush him off. To get up and storm right back down this mountain without him. But there's no way I am letting this get infected so I let him continue. Once I'm all bandaged up, Tucker thoroughly disinfects his hands. *Those freaking fantastic hands.* When I go to stand, Tucker offers to help.

"I got it." I wave him off.

"Will you stop being so stubborn and just let me help you?"

"I don't need your help, Tucker. I can do it on my own," I bite back.

"Dammit Taylor, you think I don't know that? Do you think I don't know that you would take care of every single one of your problems alone, along with everyone else's, and never bat an eye? Never once ask for help. You're the strongest, most independent woman I have ever met. And believe me, that's sexy as hell, but for once in your life will you just let someone take care of you? Let *me* take care of you?" I stare blankly at the man in front of me, demanding I let him take care of me. I scoff at him, folding my arms over my chest despite the pain I feel in my shoulder when I do.

"And what would that look like Tucker? Are you gonna kiss me again and then ignore me for the rest of the trip home? I'm sure you think kissing me was a mistake. Or maybe it was just a *heat of the moment, just woke up from a nightmare and wasn't thinking,* kind of thing. I know I'm a lot to handle, and you're probably trying to find a way to let me down gently. But why don't you grow a pair and talk to me about it instead of hyper-focusing on your driving and being an asshole by ignoring me when I ask you about it." The words feel like fire coming out of my mouth, but there's no taking them back now.

It feels good getting it off my chest, but I'm filled with anxiety that at any moment he'll confirm my accusations and tell me it was a mistake. I turn away from him just as he marches up to me. His movements are slow but sure as he comes to a stop towering over me.

His hands grip either side of my face as he takes my lips with his own. My hands wrap around his forearms to steady myself as I let myself give in to his touch. His tongue swipes out much like it did last night and I part my lips to deepen our kiss. His hands move from holding my face and just when I think he's going to pull away– he proves me wrong.

He grabs my legs, wrapping them around his waist as he presses me up against a tree. It's as if he's trying to put every single one of my doubts to rest without ever saying a word. His lips part from mine as he places kisses all along my jawline, nipping at my ear before he pulls away.

"If you think for one second I haven't wanted to kiss you again since the moment my lips left yours, that it didn't take every ounce of self-control I had to not take you right there in the back of my truck, you're wrong. It took *everything* in me to pull away from you last night. It wasn't because I didn't want you– because that is the furthest thing from true." He pulls my back off of the tree, sliding me down lower on his body until I'm seated directly on his hardening length.

"It was because I didn't want to cross a line you weren't ready to cross. Because you're too damn important to me to lose you over my own selfish desires." I swallow hard, seeing the way his green eyes burn with the same desire I know is in mine. "And whoever made you think you were too much to handle can go find less or go to hell. I don't have a preference because I'd gladly take it all. Every bit of yourself you'd be willing to give me and I'd still want more." I'm pretty sure I'm panting by this point. He runs the tip of his nose along the bridge of mine before kissing me once more. This time it's softer, a reassurance of the truth behind his words.

"Tucker..." I whisper, staring down at his lips.

"Yes, Darlin'?"

"I don't want to be friends anymore."

His jaw ticks as he studies my face. "Explain."

"Be selfish with me. Take what you want. Because I think… I want that too." With a growl escaping his chest, he kisses me again. Squeezing my thighs and pressing me into him harder. I moan as I feel how hard he is beneath me as he nips my bottom lip with his teeth.

"Get your ass to the truck. *Now*," he demands as he plants my feet back on the ground.

Chapter 22

Taylor

Tucker all but throws me onto the open tailgate of his Bronco when we make it back down to the base of the mountain. He slides my legs open to stand between them, as his hands tangle in my hair and his lips are back on mine. He kisses me like he needs this moment more than air, and I kiss him back the same. My arm wraps around his shoulders as I slide my body towards him. He lets his hands fall from my hair, gripping my thighs before he slides his fingers up to the hem of my black linen shorts. I let out a soft moan when he moves a hand into them and runs his fingers over the unmistakable wetness. He pulls his lips from mine, making me whimper at the loss.

"Already so wet for me," Tucker growls as he slides the thin fabric to the side. He runs a finger along my entrance, teasing my clit before pulling away.

"Why did you stop?" I pant, unable to hide the intense desire in my voice.

"I need you to tell me how badly you want this," he demands, as he kisses my neck, swiping a finger along my center once more. "Because I've been very patient. I've dreamed about the things I would do to you for far too long for you to change your mind." He nips at my neck, licking the pain away right after. "Tell me how much you want this, Peach. Do you want me to touch you? Do you want me to make you come with my name on those perfect, pouty lips of yours?" I can feel myself dripping with desire for this man. And all I want is for him to feel it too.

"Yes, Tucker. Please, please touch me." I grind my hips against his hand, trying to find relief that he's taunting me with. He finally slides one finger in, working me until I'm ready to take a second. My head falls back as a moan escapes my lips. He grabs me around the neck, pulling me back into him. His fingers curl inside me, swallowing each whimper that falls from my lips as he does. He moves his thumb to start circling my clit and my hips rotate with the movement of his hands.

"Oh, my god. Tucker." I can feel my orgasm building, but just as I'm reaching that high, he removes his hand. "*No,*" I whine. He pushes me on my back and rips my shorts and underwear off in a matter of seconds.

"Spread," he demands. I don't hesitate to do what he says. When my legs fall open he just stares, looking more primal than I've ever seen a man look with me.

"So fucking perfect." He slides his fingers back in effortlessly, and runs his tongue along my pussy. My hands find his hair and my eyes drift closed. His fingers curl hitting the spot that's bringing me closer to the edge, and his tongue works my clit like he's absolutely starved for me. I can feel his facial hair scratching against my lips and thighs which is turning me on even more. When I steal a glance down at him, his forest green eyes are already on mine. He winks at me with a sinful smirk on his face, his tongue never losing rhythm as he does.

"Oh God, Tucker, I'm gonna come," I say breathlessly.

"That's right baby. You keep my name on your lips while you come on my face." He kisses and sucks on my clit, making the pressure build even faster.

It doesn't take long until I am sent over the edge. Screaming his name just like he said I would. He doesn't stop until he knows I've ridden out every last second of pleasure— completely at his mercy. He stands up, licking every last drop of *me* from his fingers before grabbing my neck to pull me into him again.

"You taste sweeter than I could have ever imagined." He pulls me into another kiss with the evidence of my arousal still in his beard. Like I've staked my claim to him, and it feels so fucking good. That was easily the best orgasm I've ever had, and I am eager to return the favor.

He slides my shorts back over my legs, not bothering with my soaking wet underwear. He grabs my waist helping me to my feet as he pulls them into place over my ass.

"Your turn?" I ask, biting my lip as I run a hand over his rock hard, massive dick. I feel an ache between my legs just from touching him. Tucker Landry is going to be the ride of my fucking life. A low growl rumbles in his chest, but as he opens his mouth to respond– a family of hikers pulls up next to us. Like, literally right next to us in an empty ass parking lot.

Cock blockers.

Tucker glances over his shoulder at them then turns his gaze back to me. He slams the tailgate shut then takes me by the hand.

"Let's go, Darlin'." He pulls me to the passenger side, opening my door before tossing me in like always.

"Where are we going?"

"To get a room." He winks at me and shuts the door before darting around to his side.

When Tucker said we were getting a room, I fully believed we would be stopping a few miles up the road at the first place we could find.

Turns out, there have been zero places with vacancies that aren't campgrounds for *miles*. I'm starting to get offended by how much patience he seems to have, when I am shifting in my seat over how wet I am for him. I glance over at Tucker, noting the way his dick is still hard pressed against his pants. I never have been the type to shy away from what I want. So with a lick of my lips I do something bold. I slide over to the middle of the bucket seat, and run a hand along his length. He sucks in a deep breath and turns to face me briefly.

"What are you up to, Peach?" he asks in that deep, sexy voice.

"Nothing," I answer innocently, "just keep driving." I slide my hand up and undo his zipper. He shifts in his seat giving me easier access to free his dick without uttering a single word to me about it. I bite my lip and glance up at him after taking in his massive length. He smirks when he notices the way my eyes widen slightly at the sight.

I wrap my hand around him, pumping up and down a couple of times before I lower my lips to his head. The low *"FUCK"* he mutters when I run my tongue along his length is enough validation for me to keep going. I take him in my mouth in a painstakingly slow way, doing my best to tease him as I go. Once I begin bobbing my head up and down as my hand works at his base, I can feel his whole body shift. He presses himself into me, making me take him deeper down my throat. I follow his lead and take him as far as I can, swallowing when I can't take him any further.

"Get your ass in the air. Now!" he demands. I push to my knees and he slides his free hand in my shorts. Running a finger along my entrance.

"Does sucking my cock make you this wet Darlin'?" His voice is downright sinful. I nod my head with a muffled moan in response. "You're dripping for me baby." He slides two fingers in and I can't contain my moan. I continue bobbing my head up and down faster, with my tongue pressed flat to take all of him as deep as I can. He thrusts into me again and tears sting my eyes as I swallow him down– his fingers gripping me tighter when I do. I've never been a big fan of giving head before, but with Tucker I can't contain myself. I want to make him feel as good as he made me feel in that parking lot.

"Goddammit," he groans. I keep going, unrelenting as I hear the truck accelerate. "Don't you dare fucking stop." So I don't. Just as I can feel his body begin to tense like he may come at any second, he pulls me up stopping me.

"Hey," I pout. He gives me a warning look as he pulls me into him. He throws the truck in park and before I know it– he rips my linen shorts off. Completely torn down either side. My mouth drops open as he discards them to the backseat before grabbing my legs and straddling me on his lap.

"I'll buy you some new fucking shorts. I need to fuck you, right now." Heat washes over my face as he pulls me in for a kiss. "Arms up. I want to see those tits bouncing while you ride my cock." I lift my arms and he swipes the T-shirt I'm wearing over my head, quickly unclasping my bra before letting it fall into my lap. I'm on full display on Tucker's lap.

In his Bronco.

On the side of the road.

About to ride him.

Who even am I right now?

He reaches in his back pocket and pulls out his wallet. His head falling back in frustration when he looks inside.

"Shit. I don't have a condom." He tosses his wallet to the side as he runs a hand through his hair.

I quirk a brow at him. "You *don't?*"

He growls at me before gripping my ass so tight I'm sure it'll leave a mark. I bite my lip as I stare back at him.

"No, I don't. Believe it or not, I didn't actually think we'd get to this point."

"Well… lucky for us, I have an IUD and haven't been with anyone since I got tested last. So, technically we don't need one." He pulls me in hard, my soaking wet pussy sliding over his dick. I suck in a breath, the feeling sending an ache for him throughout my whole body.

"You got tested?" His tone borders anger and impatience.

"Yes, Tucker. It's a precaution. I'm never with anyone who doesn't wrap it up. But I'm a nurse, it would be dumb to have casual sex with someone without getting tested." I roll my eyes and his dick throbs against me. He wraps one hand around my neck and brings his lips to my ear, as his other hand fists his length teasing my entrance.

"I'm gonna make you pay for even thinking you should have been with anyone else but me." Before I can utter a word, he thrusts into me. A loud moan escapes my lips as I adjust to his full length. He grabs me by my ass, controlling our movements as I grip his shoulders. My nails dig into him as he pushes further into me. His hands run along my body caressing my waist before they reach my breasts. Their fullness completely fills his large, tattooed hands. He takes my left nipple into his mouth while he pinches and teases the right one with his fingers.

"Tucker!" I shout, unable to contain the ecstasy coursing through my body.

"Look at you, taking my cock like such a good girl."

"More," I whisper, looking deep into his eyes.

Passion.

Desire.

Need.

All the things burning in his gorgeous green eyes, are burning in mine too.

"Greedy greedy girl," he teases as he brings his thumb to my clit, firmly but gently rubbing circles while I continue to ride him. My tits bouncing just like he wanted. He pulls my neck to him, biting and kissing it until I feel myself on the brink of release. He grabs my hips, controlling our movements once again.

"Tell me, Darlin'. Has anyone else ever made you feel as good as I do when I'm inside you?" I'm nearing my breaking point when he demands my attention.

"N- No," I finally get out.

"That's right." He smirks. "And no one else ever will. Cause you're mine, Darlin'. I plan on ruining you for anyone else. Cause I'm already ruined for you." Just like that I'm pushed over the edge. The most intense orgasm I've ever had rips through my body. When I lean in to kiss Tucker– making my own silent promise that I'm his– he's sent right over the edge with me.

Chapter 23

Tucker

"Welcome to The Honeybee Motel. What can I do for you folks today?" the older woman behind the counter smiles at us as we step up to the counter.

"Hello, *Harriet*. We need a room, please." I smile at her, doing my best to stay focused on her and not on the fact that Taylor never put her bra on after our stop on the side of the road.

"Well, we just so happen to have one room available." She turns to grab our room key off of the wall behind her. "It's our Lover Bee suite, I hope that's alright. We just added a brand new tub and ceiling mirror last week." She looks at Taylor over the rim of her glasses and winks. Taylor turns red as a tomato when I glance over my shoulder, giving her a knowing look. Amazingly, the woman who was stripped down riding me on the side of the road in my truck not even an hour ago, blushes over a mirror on the ceiling.

"It's the end of this hallway here. Room number 13."

"That's perfect. Thank you." I take the key from her, grab our bags off the ground, and throw my arm around Taylor. "Let's go check out that mirror, Darlin'," I say just loud enough for Harriet to hear. Earning me an elbow in the ribs from Taylor.

"Oh my God, I'm going to strangle you," she says, looking behind her for a reaction.

I can't help but laugh as I press a kiss to the top of her head. When we reach the end of the hallway, I unlock the door and throw it open.

"After you." I motion for Taylor to walk in ahead of me, but she stops just inside the door.

"Oh. My. God." The mirror mounted above the bed is massive and in the shape of a beehive, and the tub mentioned is in the actual room. Not the bathroom.

"Oh hell yeah." I drop our bags in the corner and walk over to the bed, looking up at the mirror above it.

"Oh hell *no*," Taylor argues, "I am not sleeping here. What if that thing falls in the middle of the night? Death by mirror is not on my list of acceptable ways to go."

"I'm not even going to ask what *is* on the list because I find it a little disturbing that you have one. But you're definitely sleeping here." I walk over and pick her up by the thighs. She instantly wraps her hands around my neck with a hint of a smile on her lips.

"Oh, and how do you figure?" she asks, the tip of her nose brushing against mine. I throw her down on the bed and drop to my knees at the foot of it. I plant kisses all along her left leg, running my hand up the right one until I reach the hem of the T-shirt dress she put on to replace her ripped shorts. I slide it up her legs until I'm met with an unobstructed view of her pussy.

"Because you're not gonna want to miss a thing that's going to happen in this bed tonight." I swipe my tongue along her entrance and her head falls back with a moan. "You're going to experience every way I've dreamt of having you, and you're gonna watch yourself fall apart under my touch." I stand, leaning over her body as I bite and lick along her neck. "Over and over again." I nip at her ear. "Until you're screaming my name and begging for more." I grab her jaw, running my thumb along her bottom lip as her eyes are set ablaze from my words. "Any objections *now*?" I question with my lips brushing against hers.

She shakes her head, eyes landing on my lips before she meets my gaze again.

"Good girl." I smirk at her before taking her lips in mine. The way she whimpers as she tangles her fingers in my hair makes me want to rip this little dress off of her and never leave this room. But I have one more surprise for her that I've been dying to make happen. I pull away and she immediately has her pout in place.

God, this woman.

"Why did you stop?"

"I have another place I want to take you." I help her to her feet, letting her dress fall back over her thighs.

"Tucker, if you're taking me to climb another mountain I'll be honest– I'd much rather stay here and climb you." She wraps her arms around my waist and a deep growl sounds from my chest.

"Baby, I'll let you climb me all night long if that's what you want." I wrap my hands around her neck as I bring her lips to mine. Kissing her slowly and savoring every sweet moment. "But we gotta go before they close. Get dressed." I slap her ass and send her off to the bathroom to get ready. She glares back at me which just makes me laugh. "Don't worry Peach, I think you'll like our next stop."

I'm finding myself falling dangerously in love with this woman. I've told her all about my life– my dad who's always been my hero, even after he passed away. How my mom was completely disconnected after we lost him. All of that being *after* she heard everything I went through during my time as a SEAL. And she never made me feel pitied or gave me empty words to fill the silence.

There was never an awkward lull in conversation. She listened when I talked, and talked when I needed to be silent. She's one of very few people I've ever talked to about all the most important things in my life, and she has no idea how she's helping heal some of my old wounds, just by being here. By being *her*.

6 missed calls: **Tank.**

 Shit. I forgot to call him.

Tank has been acting weird ever since the exhibit in San Francisco. I'd be lying if I said I wasn't worried about him. But I also know he's just been pissed about not being able to find a job outside of the bar. Whatever is going on, I'm sure I'll get an ear full when I'm back home.

"Tucker, I'm starting to think you're not as in tune with the things I like as you think you are." Taylor stares out the window with an unimpressed look on her face.

"Maybe I'm just trying to help you experience more in life." I smirk at her as I hop out to open the door for her. She stays unmoving, cutting her gaze to me before turning her head to face me fully.

"Tucker, it is literally a *shack*. It looks like an outhouse that has a mother-in-law suite. I can assure you I don't need to experience whatever is living in there." She takes my hand and hops out of the truck, her actions defying her verbal protests. When she whips her head around my senses are overtaken by the smell of peaches. She's wearing cutoff denim shorts, another band tee, with her white sneakers and I'd be lying if I said my focus has been anywhere but on her legs today. Every time I look at them all I can think about is the way they feel when they're wrapped around me.

"Come on Darlin', quit your pouting. Joel is an old friend." I lean down, bringing my lips closer to her ear. "So be nice about his shack."

I pull open the door and the sign above that reads *Joel's Hat Shack* tilts a little further to the right. When we walk in, I watch closely as Taylor takes in her surroundings. Joel is one of the best custom cowboy hat makers on the west coast. I come back to visit him every time I'm out this way.

"Hey folks, how can I help you–" Joel starts before lifting his head to see me standing in front of him, "Well, son of a bitch. Is it that time already?" He smiles at me and I walk over to shake his hand.

"I suppose it is. How you doing Joel?" I smile as he wipes his forehead with his old ragged red bandana.

"Oh, well I'm hanging in there you know?" His eyes drift over to Taylor who is still turning around in circles taking in all the custom hats that line the walls. "I see you have a friend with you this time around?" he says in a knowing tone. Taylor's eyebrows draw in as her eyes meet mine. Full of questions, no doubt.

"I do. Joel, this is Taylor. Taylor, this is Joel. The best custom hat maker you'll ever meet." Joel makes a *pfft* noise as he extends his hand to Taylor.

"Nice to meet you, Darlin'." I see the way her eyes bounce to mine and the slightest scrunch of her nose. Almost as if she doesn't like hearing that nickname from someone other than me.

"It's nice to meet you, too. These hats are amazing," she compliments, waving her hand around the room.

"Much appreciated. Please tell me we're getting this fine young woman a hat made today." Joel turns his attention back to me now.

"Oh, no–" Taylor begins.

"Absolutely. That's why we're here." I wink at her and begin perusing for ideas.

"Tucker, no. You don't have to do this."

"I know. But if I'm being honest, I've been dying to see you in a cowboy hat again ever since you and your friends went to that wild west night or whatever the hell it was." I can see the wheels spinning behind those raincloud eyes of hers.

"That was like... six months ago," she voices her realization.

"I know. I told you, Peach, I've been very patient." I let my eyes drift over her body, remembering the way she looked in her bandana-style strapless top and bootcut jeans– that hugged her ass the way I'm dying to. Her mouth pops open like she's going to say something but I call for Joel before she can.

"What do we think of something like this?" There's a sand-colored cowboy hat that is the perfect size and shape for Taylor. He nods and gets to customizing it. She picks a thread detail for the top, a ribbon combination to go around the base, and some feathers for the side. He shows her options she can have burned into the bill– she picks one with mountains. I try not to read into it, but I can't help but smile at the familiarity of the mountain view she chose. Once he's finished she tries it on grinning ear to ear as she looks in the mirror. She turns to me and moves her head from side to side to give me a full view.

"What do you think?"

She looks fucking adorable.

"You look perfect." The redness that washes over her cheeks at my comment makes me want to see her blushing and bare, wearing nothing but that hat.

"Well, if you're all set then let me grab a box for you," Joel offers. Taylor takes the hat off and hands it to Joel, but before he places it in the box she stops him. She whispers something in his ear and he nods before taking the hat back over to the customizing table.

"Something wrong?" I nod to where Joel begins working on the hat again.

"No, just adding one little detail we forgot." Her smile is dripping with mischief but I don't press it any further. Joel finishes her last detail request, we pay for the hat and head out again. She grabs her phone from her pocket, wrapping her fingers around my arm before we make it to the truck.

"Picture first!" She shakes her phone but when I try to take it from her to take her photo in front of Joel's, she snatches it back to her chest. "What are you doing? Get in it with me." I walk behind her, wrapping my arms around her waist as she snaps away. I bury my face in the crook of her neck, kissing and biting as the most beautiful laugh falls from her lips.

"Tuckerrr." The sound of my name on her lips like that will never get old. I spin her around to face me, pulling her body flush with mine.

"Have I told you how fucking glad I am that you came on this trip with me?" I look down as the sun shines in her raincloud eyes, and her teeth pull her bottom lip in before she smiles.

"I'm really glad I came too." She stands on her toes, planting a slow, deep kiss to my lips. Like she has all the time in the world to just stand here and be mine. I can only hope whatever she's feeling for me lasts. That she won't wake up tomorrow and decide this was a mistake. Because being with Taylor then having to carry on without her, is something I'd never recover from.

Chapter 24

Taylor

After leaving Joel's I had a million questions about other insane places Tucker has visited while on his long ass lonely road trips. When he told me they had a Coyote Ugly type bar nearby I was dead set on going. We've been camping and secluded for two days, going to a bar with other people didn't sound so bad.

We stopped off at a little run-down shopping mall where I picked up an outfit for the occasion. I found the cutest black leather shorts, ankle-high cowboy boots, and a cropped T-shirt that hangs off of one shoulder. All coordinating with my new hat of course. I convinced Tucker to let me pick him an outfit too and to my surprise he put up very little of a fight. He looks fucking delicious in the light wash blue jeans, black T-shirt, and hat I picked for him to wear. After a few rounds of shots I am feeling the buzz spread through my body.

"I think this may be my new favorite place." I wag my index finger around in a circle as Tucker's gaze floats around the little run down bar. I'm confident it's the liquor talking because there's nothing special about this place.

"I'll be sure to let Max know you no longer like Chattahoochies." He smirks before picking up the beer he ordered.

"Don't you dare!" I say dramatically spinning back and forth on my barstool. With every turn to my left my knee bumps against Tucker's thigh. I don't realize I'm even doing it until he grips my stool on either side, bringing my attention to the hungry look in his eyes.

"I'm not sure if it's a nervous habit or an absentminded action, but with every bump of your knee I'm one second closer to pulling you off that stool and into my lap." He grabs my thighs, his grip firm right below the hemline of my leather shorts. I stare down at my lap and the way my thighs are completely covered by his tattoo covered hands. When my eyes snap up to his I involuntarily bite my lip.

"Don't be a tease, Darlin'." He tilts his head with a raised brow. I lean in closer, resting my arm on the bar top in front of him.

"What if I want to tease you though?" Shouts begin to erupt around the bar but it isn't until I hear the splash of water being poured into pitchers that my attention is dragged away from Tucker. I look around at all the drunken maniacs waving their fists in the air like they're favorite football team just won the super bowl as the bartenders make their way onto the bartop.

"No way. They actually do this here?" My eyes are wide with excitement as one of the girls leans down to ask me if I know the drill.

"They do what here?" Tucker asks, looking around the bar in confusion.

Before I can respond, the blonde on the bar is pulling me up with her. The infamous water dance. I watch as Tucker's eyes go from confused, to hungry, to downright feral. Seeing the effect I have on him is exhilarating. I wink at him and he gives me a *you're in trouble now* stare that has me ready to beg him to take me back to our motel. By the time the song ends I've danced myself to the other end of the bar, opposite of where Tucker and I had been seated. I am dripping wet and ready to hear what he has to say when a guy offers to help me down from the bar. Seeing as how I don't love the idea of busting my ass by trying to get down by myself I take him up on the offer.

"Those were some pretty amazing moves sweetheart," the guy says as soon as my feet hit the ground. When I look back up I see the perverted way his eyes rake over my body.

Barf.

"You here with anyone or can I buy you a drink?" he offers, running a hand along my arm. Before I can pull away or respond I hear a deep voice come from behind me.

"You can't buy her a drink, but you *can* take that hand off of her if you plan to keep it." I've never heard a threat to remove someone's hand sound so sexy.

"Look pal, I think the lady can speak for herself." He brushes Tucker's warning off, letting his gaze land on me again. Tucker snakes his arm around my waist, pulling me into him.

"Oh, I speak from experience when I tell you she can. But tonight I'm relieving her of the trouble. So why don't you take your drink offer to someone available and leave my girl to me." And now I'm wet for reasons entirely unrelated to the gallons of water that were just poured on me.

"Come find me when you get tired of this asshole barking orders for you sweetheart. I'll show you a good time." The guy reaches a hand out towards my face as if to brush it along my cheek, but never gets the chance. Tucker quickly moves his hand from around my waist, grabs the guy's arm and slams it into the bar top. The guy lets out a yell that luckily blends in with the rest of the noise from the bar.

"Oh my god, Tucker!" I exclaim. "You just broke his hand," I whisper-shout at him, looking around to see if anyone noticed what just happened.

"What the hell!" the guy yells as he clutches his broken hand to his chest.

"Have I not made it clear to you that I'm going to protect what's mine? And *you* are *mine*. He should have kept his hands to himself," he answers, before leaning in closer, grabbing the guy by the shirt. "You might want to get that looked at *pal*. Maybe get your hearing checked while you're at it because I said, don't. Touch. My. Girl." He shoves him back before throwing his arm around my shoulders.

"Let's get out of here Darlin'. Cause I can't wait any longer to see you in nothing but that hat." Tucker drops cash on the bar where we'd been sitting, then leads the way towards the exit.

Chapter 25

Tucker

"Oh, dear! What happened? You're soaking wet." Harriet adjusts her glasses from behind the counter, sounding like any concerned grandma would. Which is exactly what she reminds me of. A grandma who's every concern is your well being and whether or not you're fed. I would not be even the slightest bit surprised if she were to pull out a plate of freshly baked cookies from behind that desk.

"Don't you worry ma'am. I plan to get her out of these wet clothes as soon as possible." I wink at her and she and Taylor both turn an adorable shade of pink.

"Well, I'll send some extra towels down for you both. We'll just uh… leave them outside the door for you."

"You are too kind, Harriet," I thank her and grab Taylor by the hand before rushing us down the hallway to our room. I slam the door shut behind us before pinning Taylor against it. Her hat tips up slightly from hitting the door behind her, as I run the bridge of my nose along her jawline before resting my lips right by her ear.

"You looked so fucking good dancing on top of that bar tonight. But you're in some serious trouble for allowing anyone else to see how well you move this sweet little body of yours." My hands cup her face as my thumbs caress the apples of her cheeks. Her raincloud eyes are locked on me as she studies me carefully with every breath.

"Then allow me to apologize," she whispers. Her gaze falls to my lips– like a silent prayer for me to take them with my own. I smirk at her, bringing my lips close but not quite touching hers.

"That's my good girl." Then I give her what she wants. I claim her mouth with my own. My hands trail from her face down around her neck, tilting her head up as I kiss along her neck.

Biting her.

Marking her as mine.

She whimpers at the pain and moans at the pleasure that immediately follows when I lick the marks I'm making on her. I grab her legs, wrapping them around my middle as I press her harder against the door to our room. When I squeeze her ass hard enough to leave hand prints and bite at her already perky nipple– she begins grinding her hips against me. Shameless as she lets me know how much she wants this.

Knock. Knock. Knock.

"Housekeeping," someone calls from the other side of the door.

"Leave them on the floor," I call out as I slide the chain locked on the door. I carry her across the small space, planting her feet on the ground by the small chair in the corner. I remove her hat to discard the top that's been hanging haphazardly off of her shoulder all night and peel her leather shorts off, dropping them around her ankles. She kicks off her shoes, along with the shorts, and is left standing in the room in nothing but her blue lace lingerie– until I put her hat back on her.

"Fuck, you look beautiful." I kiss her again, this time swiping my tongue along her lips demanding she let me in. She does so instantly, letting me deepen our kiss. I squeeze her ass and a muffled moan sounds from her lips. When I pull away a pout instantly takes place on her face.

"On your knees, Darlin'." I wink at her and I see the excitement spark in her eye as she does what she's told. She looks up at me, with her hands placed delicately in her lap. Looking like a fucking vision. I run my thumb along her bottom lip, savoring every moment of this.

"I love how you look on your knees for me." I back up to the foot of the bed, not missing the confusion that flashes across her face.

I rip my shirt off over my head and unzip my pants before tossing them in the corner. I sit on the edge of the bed and begin stroking my length as I stare at the flawless woman in front of me.

"You said you would make it up to me?" She bites her lip and nods.

"Crawl to me, baby." She freezes in place.

"You're joking," she scoffs. My jaw tightens as my gaze narrows on her.

"You heard me Darlin'. I love seeing you on your knees for me. So you can either sit there and watch me fuck my hand, or you can bring that smart little mouth of yours over here and let me fuck your face." I see the way her legs tighten as she watches me stroking my cock.

"I'm not crawling on this floor." Her tone is unconvincing.

"Oh but I think you will. See, I think you've been waiting for a man who will take control. Someone to tell you what to do. Someone that will tell you exactly what he's going to do to you and actually follow through. You crawl over here, Darlin' and that's exactly what you're gonna get. That ride in the Bronco was nothing compared to what I have planned for you. Let me show you how good I can make you feel when *I'm* the one in control." Her chest rises and falls more quickly with every word that falls from my lips.

"Crawl to me." As if she can't contain her need any longer, she places her palms flat on the floor and crawls for me. When she makes it to the foot of the bed, she sits back on her knees– the image sending shock waves to my dick. I grip her face in my hand, tilting her head slightly so she looks only at me.

"That's my good girl." Her eyes move from my face to my cock that is standing at full attention. She starts to move her hand closer, hesitating momentarily.

"Take what you want baby." With that encouragement, she does as she's told. When her hands wrap around my length it throbs at her touch. She licks her lips before taking me down her throat. I toss her hat onto the bed, wrapping my hand around her red curls letting her take the lead as I watch her mouth work around me. She teases my head with her tongue then takes me as far as her throat will allow. The gagging noise she makes when she tries swallowing me down makes my head spin.

"Fuck, you know how to use that mouth baby." Her eyes raise to mine, completely filled with pride as she takes me down further. One hand pumps at my base as she takes me in her mouth eagerly. Her other hand gently grabs my balls and my jaw tightens at the sensation. When I feel myself getting close to coming all down her throat I pull myself from her lips and yank her up into my lap. She pants as she tries catching her breath.

"I wasn't done." She takes her index finger and wipes the wetness from around her mouth and I about come undone.

"I'm not ready to come yet, Darlin'. Not until I've tasted you again, and certainly not until I've railed you properly." I take her lips in mine as I spin her around laying her flat on the bed. Her red curls are fanned out around her as she looks up at me. I run a finger along the center of her lace underwear, feeling the pool of wetness between her legs.

"Look at my girl, already so wet and ready for me." She bites down on her fingernail and nods her head at me. I move the thin fabric to the side as I slide one finger into her. She moans as she lets her eyes fall closed, bringing her hands up to play with her breasts. I slide another finger in and watch as her lips part to suck in a breath. She's got my dick throbbing and I'm not even inside her yet. I curve my fingers to hit the spot that makes her squirm, getting a thrill from every noise she makes from my touch. I lean down to taste her as my fingers continue to thrust inside her. I kiss and lick her wetness as she grinds her hips in sync with my movements.

"Tucker, please," she whines.

"Oh, my girl has manners. Tell me what you need Darlin', and it's yours." I hook my fingers in her once more and she looks into my eyes, completely unhinged.

"I need you to fuck me, please." I slide my fingers out of her and lean in to kiss her.

"Oh I plan to. But first you're gonna ride me while you wear nothing but that hat." I pull her off the bed, standing toe to toe with her at the foot of it. I pull her lace underwear down and unhook her bra, letting her perfect tits fall free. I place her hat back on her head and sit back on the bed, as she crawls up to straddle me.

"Fuck, Darlin'," I mutter as my head teases her entrance.

"Is this what you wanted?" she asks in a sultry tone.

"You're all I've ever wanted," I answer honestly. "Now ride." I press my length into her, making her gasp as she begins rocking her hips. She rocks and rides, taking me fully with every thrust. Her tits are bouncing as her nails dig into my chest.

"Fuck, Tucker," she moans. There's no way I'll last with her riding like this and my name falling from her lips. I grip her ass as she bounces effortlessly on my dick. When I know I'm about to lose control, I stop her completely.

"Turn around Peach, ass in the air." She does as she's told, spreading her legs for me as I fist my length. I toss her hat to the side before leaning down over her. My chest flush with her back, as I bring my lips to her ear.

"I don't plan to be gentle with you. When I said I was ruining you for anyone else, I meant it. I've waited far too long to claim you as mine, and that's exactly what I plan to do. So if I do something you don't like, say water and I'll stop. Understand?"

"Why water?" I can hear the confusion in her voice, and I can't help but smirk.

"Because I know how much you hate the water." It's quiet for a moment, and I can see the apples of her cheeks fill out when she smiles. "Do you understand?" I repeat, needing confirmation.

"I understand," she whispers. Gasping when I tease her entrance.

I wrap a hand around her throat, tilting her head to look at me, my lips brushing over hers when I thrust into her completely. "Good girl." I take her lips in mine as I push into her.

Her hands grip the sheets, her head falling between her arms when I finally let go of her throat. I stand up as I pull all the way out and thrust back into her again. The echo from me slapping her ass and the *"Oh God"* that falls from her lips when I do only motivates me further. I grab ahold of her waist, moving her body with mine to reach even deeper. I wrap one hand around her hair, pulling her head back up off the bed as my other hand slaps the same ass cheek again.

"Tucker!" she shouts as the sound of my body slamming into hers fills the room.

"Look at you, baby. Taking my cock like such a good girl. Look up in that mirror." I tilt her head even further, noting the way she bites her lip as she takes in the view of me taking her from behind. "Tell me who this pussy belongs to, baby." She moans at my request but no words leave her lips.

I let go of her hair, placing my hand around her throat again, pulling her up to have her back flat against my chest. She moans again as my grip tightens and I pull out of her slick pussy, leaving just the tip in. Whimpering at the loss she tries guiding me back in. I hold her at the hips, stopping her from getting the relief she's chasing.

"Tell me and I'll let you come. I'll make you come so hard you'll forget anyone who's ever tried to make you feel this good before." I slide in a little further, and I feel her swallow against my grip.

"You," she whispers. I plunge into her fully, making her moan in satisfaction.

"Louder," I growl into her ear, "who's are you, Darlin'?" I begin to thrust even harder, letting one hand slide down her body to rub her clit.

"Yours, Tucker," she cries out, "only yours, I swear." Her words completely undo me.

All control I thought I had is now gone. Everything between us ignites.

Hard and fast.

Punishing and rewarding.

With my name on her lips– loud enough that not a single person in this motel is spared from its echoes– she comes for me, sending me right over the edge with her. I pull out and watch my come drip from her pussy with my handprint still bright on her ass, and she's never looked more like mine than she does right now. I run my hand gently across the mark and she rolls over to lay on her back exposing the red mark around her throat from my grip on it. I pull her to her feet, caressing her cheek with the back of my hand before running my thumb along my handprint around her throat.

"You didn't use your safe word," I whisper, searching for regret that may be hiding in her eyes. But I find none. She only bites her lip and grabs my wrist before leaning into my touch.

"That's because I didn't feel unsafe," she says simply. I bring her lips to mine, kissing her slow and gentle before wrapping her in my arms.

"Come on. Let me run you a bath." I nod to the tub on the other side of the room and she giggles in agreement. Once it's full of bubbles and bath salts, compliments of the motel, Taylor throws her hair into a clip on top of her head.

"Get in with me. You'll love it." I quirk a brow in disagreement.

"Darlin'. I am six foot five. I am not fitting in that tub." This draws an eye roll from her.

"Okay, first of all. I know you're a grizzly bear and all that, but this is the biggest tub I've ever seen. You'll fit. Get in," she argues. It's not until she juts that bottom lip out in a pout that I give in and get in the tub.

She sits between my legs and I pull her back flush against my chest as the bubbles begin to pop around us. She leans her head back on my chest and lets out the most satisfied and relaxed sigh. I wrap my arms around her, and kiss her neck, nipping at it just to hear her giggle. She turns to face me and lets her eyes roam over my torso. I reach my arms out to stroke hers, needing to touch her in any way possible. Her eyes then drift to my arms and hands before looking at me inquisitively.

"Tell me about your tattoos," she says, running her finger along the bone frog on my bicep.

"Which ones?"

"All of them."

I tell her about the bone frog and how it represents a fallen SEAL and the date tattooed on my hand in honor of the day Red died in my hands. Long live the brotherhood tattooed along the back of my forearm. The grim reaper medic sitting on a helicopter that I got when I returned home, my own twisted way of dealing with what had happened that day. The helm of awe viking tattoo on my hand. Max and I both got those shortly after joining the Navy. The diver wearing NODs that I have on my chest with water surrounding him– which she seemed to know the meaning behind after our trip to the waterfall. Then all the little tattoos I got just when I felt like it. Palm trees and the plumeria flowers I got just because I loved them. A guitar in honor of my dad since he's the one that taught me. And other tribal tattoos I got when I was younger because I thought they looked cool.

Once our water is free of bubbles and our fingers begin to resemble raisins, Taylor climbs up in my lap, straddling me as she wraps her arms around my neck.

"Tucker…" Her face turns pink as she runs a hand through my hair. "Thank you for asking me to come on this trip with you." She smiles sweetly, kissing me quickly before pulling away again.

"Taylor…" My use of her real name has her studying me carefully.

"Yeah?" She rears back slightly.

"I love you."

Chapter 26

Taylor

Oh my god.

I think I'm having a stroke.

My body is completely frozen as I let his words sink into the deepest parts of my brain. The parts that have been reminding me for so long that I'm too much to handle. That I'll only ever have casual dating relationships. The parts that tell me any love I would try to give someone would go unrequited or would only end in disappointment or heartbreak.

"Don't freak out on me, okay? I'm not trying to pressure you and I certainly don't want to scare you off. I just–" he sighs, running a hand through his copper brown locks, "it feels like I'm lying to you if I don't tell you how much you really mean to me."

Tucker loves me.

"Darlin'. Please say something." The stress in his voice and the worry in his face almost breaks my heart. He's interpreting my silence– my buffering– as rejection. Which is the last thing I want him feeling.

"I– I'.." Seriously Taylor. Words have never failed you before. Now is not the time.

"Shit." Tucker scrubs the scruff along his jawline, turning his face away from me.

"Tucker–" He turns to face me again.

"Is this really that big of a shock to you? Have you really not known how interested I've been in you over the last year?" He waits a beat for a response that fails to come. "I understood when you said you weren't interested in anything serious. I respected that. Then I sat back and watched you try to date the biggest asshole I've ever met, because I just wanted you to be happy." He sighs, looking me in the eyes. There's nowhere for me to run. No escape from the hold his stare has on me. "You have easily become one of my very best friends. Anytime I am around you, I don't have to pretend to be the fun guy who's always having a good time. It just comes naturally when you're there. The verbal sparring, the endless flirting, I loved you as a friend first, but I won't pretend like I don't love you as *so* much more now."

"Tucker–"

"I have imagined what it will feel like if we get back to Nashville and you forget all about the things that happened on this trip, and I fear that you'll want to go back to just being friends. But I am telling you right now Taylor, I can't do that. I won't."

"Tucker!–"

"Because I have fallen desperately in love with you. I love it when you're mad at me, and glare at me with those raincloud eyes. I love the fact that you have no filter around me. You say what you feel and you never apologize for it. I love that you've trusted me with stories of your past, even when they seemed to hurt you. I am helplessly in love with every single thing that makes you who you are." He runs his hands along my arms and I immediately sink into him.

"Tucker, are you done?" my voice breaks as tears fill my eyes. He nods hesitantly.

"Yeah, Peach. I'm done."

"Good, because I love you, too." His throat bobs and his jaw ticks as he swallows hard. Relief and disbelief washing over his face.

"Say that again." He cups my face in his hands, caressing my cheeks with his thumbs as if to see if I'm real.

"I love you, Tucker. I'll never forget how much I've fallen for you on this trip." He pulls me into him, kissing me with a passion I've only ever felt with *him*. His tongue swipes across my lips and I part them without hesitation. We stay like that a while before he pulls away, pressing his forehead to mine.

"Swear to me. Swear you won't change your mind."

"I swear." I take his face in mine, kissing along his cheek and down to his neck. This time when he takes us to the bed, he makes love to me in a way that I'll never forget. It's not rushed like we may miss our moment, or rough but in all the best ways. He takes his time with me–every kiss, every touch like a promise that he won't let me go. That he'll never tire of me, and that alone means more than he'll ever know. When I finally fall asleep, wrapped up in my tattoo covered safe haven, it's the happiest I have ever been.

45 New Messages.

Shit, I'm in trouble.

Scrolling through what feels like the never ending group chat messages I finally come across the one that's going to save my ass.

RUBY

Honestly, the only thing that's going to save your ass at this point is if you had earth shattering sex and haven't been able to walk to your phone.

ME

Well, thank god that's the case. So I'm forgiven?

SHANE

Shut the fuck up.

LAUREN

No you didn't!

LEAH

God, FINALLY!

RUBY

This is about to be the best girls night ever.

SHANE

When do you guys get home????

ME

Still a few days. We haven't been driving as much as we have been exploring.

LEAH

Exploring each other. 😏

LAUREN

When did you stop being the mother of the group Le?

LEAH

I'm in my cool mom era.

ME

LMFAO. Thanks mom.

"Alright Peach, you ready to hit the road?" Tucker calls as he emerges from the bathroom. He's wearing dark blue jeans, one of his Navy T-shirts and sneakers. Looking–and smelling– like a damn dream.

"Ready when you are." I smile at him, sliding my phone into the back pocket of my blue jeans.

"I got the bags, but I can't find the room key. Do you see it anywhere?" he asks, scanning the room.

"Yeah. I can return it to the front desk if you wanna take those to the truck," I offer.

"Sounds good. Let's go then." He nods toward the door and I follow him out. He slings one arm over my shoulder as we walk towards the front desk. He plants a kiss on my temple before heading to the truck.

"You take care of yourself Miss Harriet, you hear." Harriet smiles brightly at Tucker as she waves goodbye. Her cheeks turn a little rosy as he winks at her. That southern charm of his.

"Hi, just returning our room key. Sorry about the keychain. I guess it fell off? I couldn't find it anywhere," I explain as I hand the key to her with only a silver ring attached, trying to hide the smirk on my face. She gives me a warm smile and a nod as she takes it from my hand.

"No worries dear. We can replace that. I hope the two of you enjoyed your stay."

"We did, very much. Thank you." I wave goodbye and walk out to meet Tucker at the truck. It's no surprise that he's waiting at the passenger side door for me. When I make it over to him, he leans down to kiss me. Something that would have seemed unimaginable just a few days ago. But now, it just feels right in every single way.

"Where to next?" I ask, as he opens my door for me.

"What do you say we stop off in Colorado? It's about eight and a half hours out. I figure that'll be a good stopping point." I smile as an idea creeps into my mind.

"That sounds great, I may even know of a place for us to stay." He nods and closes my door, making his way around the truck. I pull out my phone as he pulls out of the parking lot, no doubt headed to get us breakfast as my stomach growls obnoxiously loud.

ME

Hey mom, you guys feel like having a couple of house guests tonight?

MOM

Of course! I didn't know you were coming to town.
Which one of the girls is with you?

ME

Um... Tucker.

MOM

Oh, my. She's new. 😉

MOM

What time will you be here?

ME

Around dinner time probably.

MOM

We'll set 2 more places at the table. I can't wait to
see you honey. And to meet this, Tucker. 😊

ME

Love you, Mom.

Chapter 27

Taylor

"Taylor. This looks like someone's house. Are you sure you put the address in right?"

"I'm sure."

"What, is it like an AirBnb?" He leans forward to look more closely at the house, as he puts the truck in park.

"Not exactly." I roll my lips together trying to hide my smile.

About the time he looks over with his eyes narrowed on mine, my mom comes walking out the front door to greet us.

"I am so glad you two made it okay!" Mom yells with her arms outstretched to me. I run into her embrace, breathing in her cherry blossom perfume, as Tucker follows closely behind.

I hated when my parents moved to Colorado. My mom has always been one of my best friends and not having her right down the road anymore is one of the hardest things I've ever had to endure.

"Hey Momma. Thank you for letting us stay here." I squeeze her tight before stepping back beside Tucker.

"Oh don't even mention it. You're welcome here anytime for as long as you need, you know that." She pulls back, resting her hands on my shoulders as she looks me over.

"You just get more beautiful every time I see you." Her soft smile reaches all the way to her eyes as she takes me in.

"Ah, so this is your parents house?" Tucker mumbles as I step back beside him. I can tell he's trying his best to only let me hear him, but Marilyn Clark has superhuman hearing.

"Taylor Paige, you didn't tell this boy where you were staying?" my mother scolds.

"I wanted it to be a surprise." I shrug innocently, earning me a disapproving look.

She looks at Tucker almost apologetically as he extends his hand to her.

"Mrs. Clark, Tucker Landry, it's a pleasure to meet you."

"Please, call me Marilyn. I recognize you from the wedding. You were the best man, right?" she asks with a smirk on her face.

"Yes ma'am. I'm sorry I must have missed you that night." He glances at me with a confused look.

"Oh, Tony and I didn't stay long. Us older folks can't quite keep up like we used to. But the pictures turned out beautifully." She gives me a knowing look, but I'm lost as to why.

"Well, let's not stand out here like perfect strangers, come in the house. Dinner is just about ready." She waves us in as Tucker bends to grab our bags from the driveway.

We walk up the sidewalk to the covered front porch–one of my favorite parts of the house– and mom leads us through the large wooden front door. I glance over at the oversized porch swing that my dad built for my mom last summer and smile. She mentioned wanting one *once* so she could sit on it and look out over the mountains, and dad made it happen.

"Tony, they're here!" Mom calls as we stop in the foyer.

The house they purchased out here isn't extravagant, but it isn't exactly modest either. It's a beautiful two story home that has Mom's style written all over it. The open floor plan and beige walls were no match for Marilyn Clark. She has a way of making any place feel like home. The foyer has a modern style chandelier with warm lighting, a bench with decorative throw pillows and the biggest photograph of a bull I've ever seen hanging above it.

Past the staircase is the open area that leads to the kitchen/living room area that's separated by a large island. The living room has brown leather chairs and an oversized, white, plush couch decorated with olive green, rust and blue accent pillows. The built-in book-shelves on either side of the floor to ceiling cobblestone veneer fire-place is filled with family photos, books, and succulents.

"Hey Tot, come here and give your old man a hug." I glance at Tucker who looks like he's holding in a laugh and roll my eyes. I walk up to my dad, letting the scent of old spice waft my senses as I wrap my arms around him.

"Hey Dad. Dinner smells great." I take in a big whiff of the steak that is sizzling on the stove.

The kitchen in my parents house is stunning. It makes my tiny little blue kitchen, that I love so much, look sad. The oversized kitchen island could fit a kindergarten class and still have some room to chop vegetables on the side. The sage green cabinets with dark wood countertops makes it so warm and inviting.

"Well when Mom told me you were coming I knew we had to have your favorite. It's not very often we get a visit from our favorite daughter." He winks at me and I roll my eyes.

"I'm your only daughter, Dad."

"Yeah, but have you seen Sawyer's hair lately? He may be coming for your title." He raises his brows, making me laugh. "And who's your friend?" Dad turns his gaze to Tucker, extending his hand to him.

"Tucker Landry, sir. Thank you for having me." Tucker smiles at him, but my dad just narrows his gaze at him.

"Yes, well. Can I get you something to drink?" Dad offers as he walks back to the kitchen. Tucker follows closely behind him, while mom and I hang back, leaning against the kitchen island.

"Water, please." Dad makes a *hmph* noise and Tucker clears his throat as if he's uncomfortable.

"Well, you already know what I want." I pipe up, trying to break any awkward tension as I slide onto a barstool and fold my arms on the countertop.

"Key lime martini," they say in unison.

My eyes quickly dart back and forth between them, waiting to see how this plays out. Dad glances at Tucker, but Tucker's gaze– accompanied by the half smirk I love so much– stays on me. Dad gives an approving nod before directing Tucker on where to find everything to mix my drink. Then we sit down and have the least awkward *first time meeting my parents* family style dinner. Dad tells him all about his years spent being a doctor, and asks Tucker about his time in the Navy. The conversation is flowing well until my dad asks him something I would never imagine he could consider appropriate.

So much for this not being awkward.

"Have you ever lost anyone in the field?" My stomach drops to my feet instantly at his question.

"Dad!" I warn under my breath. But good ole Tony doesn't see how this could be a sensitive topic.

"What?" he sounds generally confused by why that question may ruffle some feathers. Tucker grabs my hand, squeezing it in reassurance before he answers my dad.

"Unfortunately I have, sir. I've lost a few, actually. One of my closest friends was one of them and I still think about them daily." Everything about his outward appearance is calm and collected. Meanwhile I'm ready to yell at my own father for being so insensitive.

"I know the feeling. The losses never get easier."

"No, sir. They don't." He gives my dad a forced smile before taking a drink of his water.

I understand that Dad may just be trying to bond with him, and I give Tucker major credit for the way he handled that, but I need this conversation to end. Now.

"Mom, do you want help clearing the table?" I'm out of my chair before she can utter a response, but she follows my lead as we bring dinner to a swift end.

Dad pours both himself and Tucker a glass of whiskey as they walk outside to sit around the fire pit. I silently finish helping mom clean up the kitchen, then make my way to the front porch swing with some of the chocolate chip cookies she made. I'm still reeling over the last conversation at the dinner table when she walks out the front door to join me.

"This view never gets old, does it?" She sighs as she begins swinging us back and forth.

"No, it doesn't." I look out over the mountains, smiling as I think about how happy she must be here. All the mornings she probably spends sipping her coffee and watching the sunrise.

"You love him." Mom's voice is soft as she pulls my attention back to her. "I saw the way he looked at you and how you came to his defense in there. You were protecting him." She nudges my shoulder and winks at me.

I get butterflies in my stomach at the mere thought of Tucker, remembering the way he told me he loved me and wasn't shy about just how much.

"I do, Mom. I really love him." My voice wavers a bit, as tears form in my eyes.

"Oh, honey. Why does it seem like that scares you?" She wraps her arms around me, rubbing my arm in a comforting way.

Marilyn Clark, most in-tune mother a child has ever had.

"Because it *does*. He's so sure about me right now, but what happens if he changes his mind? What happens if one day he realizes I'm too crazy for him to handle? I haven't dated anyone since high school. I've been waiting–" I sniffle, trying to swallow past the lump in my throat as my mom swipes the tear that's running down my cheek. "I've spent all this time waiting for healing over a wound almost a decade old. But it was a deep one, you know? At the time I thought I'd never recover, but now... he makes me feel wanted and loved and...*whole* again, Mom. Like my heart is all healed now just for him. Ready to be placed in his hands, but I'm just so scared."

"Scared of what?" she asks the question like she already knows the answer.

"Scared that he'll break it. And I would never recover from getting my heart broken by Tucker. I've never loved anyone the way I love him." Admitting these feelings out loud has my heart about to beat out of my chest. The vulnerability of speaking the depths of my feelings for him, comes crashing down like a hurricane. Mom pats my leg and stands from her place on the porch swing.

"Stay right here," she says as she walks back into the house.

No, it's cool. I'll just sit here in a puddle of tears, shoving cookies in my mouth while you just…leave.

She comes back a few moments later with a photo book in her hand.

"Seriously Mom, I don't think now is the time to reminisce."

"Oh, will you hush? Look." I notice the photo book she is holding is from Shane's wedding. She must have sent this to my mom when she finally got her photos back from the photographer. I know how close they've always been, their bond grew even more after Shane lost her own mother years ago, so it's not unusual for her to include her like this. When I look at the picture she is pointing to, it's a group shot of the entire bridal party. Tucker's hand is around my waist and he's looking down at me with a familiar smile on his face. The same way he is looking at me in our picture by the waterfall.

"Something tells me that man in there won't be the one to hurt you. If I had to guess, he would probably take out anyone who dared to," she teases, as a memory resurfaces.

"Well, he did break someone's hand for touching me the other day." Her eyes go wide at my remark, making me laugh. "Don't worry, the guy deserved it." I wave a hand in front of myself dismissively. I can see she wants to ask questions, but she just shakes her head and continues.

"Taylor, the only way you're going to end up hurt, is if you don't let him love you the way you deserve to be loved. I know you are strong, fierce, and independent– I *did* raise you after all– but that doesn't mean you can't rely on someone else every now and then. So let him love you, and love him back. Channel the strong personality you wield so proudly, and love him fiercely." I lay my head on my moms shoulder, as we continue to swing.

"Thank you, Mom. I really needed this." She pats my hand and I can feel her cheek move as she smiles.

"Anytime, sweetheart. But Taylor…"

"Yeah Mom?"

"Please don't love him fiercely under this roof. Your father might have a stroke." I shoot up in my seat.

"Oh my god, Mom!" We both fall into a fit of laughter as Tucker comes walking out the front door. I wipe my face again, doing my best to hide the tear streaks on my face.

"Am I interrupting?" he asks cautiously, smiling as he takes us in.

"No! You're not," I answer quickly before my mom takes it upon herself to fill him in on her request. Tucker must hear the rasp in my voice and pick up on the fact that I've been crying, as he looks at me with concern.

"You ready for bed, Darlin'? We have a long trip ahead of us tomorrow." Those butterflies begin to flutter as I feel my mother's gaze on me. But I keep my eyes on him.

"Of course." I lean over and kiss my mom on the cheek. "Goodnight Mom. I love you. Thank you," I whisper as I stand back up, walking over to Tucker as he drapes his arm around my shoulder.

"Night, Marilyn. Thank you again for letting us stay here tonight."

"It's no problem at all." She smiles, picking up one of the cookies from the plate I left behind. As we walk up the stairs, Tucker plants a kiss to my forehead squeezing me closer to him as we go.

"Are you sure everything is okay?" When we reach the top of the stairs, I turn to face him. My chin tilted up to be able to look into his eyes.

"I'm sure. Hey, I'm really sorry about my dad earlier. I think he was trying to bond with you or something. I don't know, I just feel bad. That was so insensitive."

"It's okay. I've gotten used to the questions from people who don't always realize their impact. I appreciated him trying to get to know me better. I didn't mind answering."

He is absolutely perfect.

When he leans down to kiss me, I don't hold anything back. My fingers tangle in his hair as he bends down to lift me, wrapping my legs around his middle. He pulls away and looks at me curiously.

"I love you, Tucker." I run the tip of my nose along the bridge of his, and brush my lips gently across his again.

"I'm never going to tire of hearing you say that." He kisses me deeper, grabbing the nape of my neck as his fingers glide through my hair. He plants kisses along my jawline and down my neck until his lips brush against my ear.

"I love you, too, Darlin'. Even on the days you won't want me to. I will. I'll probably love you even harder then." He bites at my neck and I whimper, tightening my grip around him. When he takes me to bed, I do my best to follow Momma's rules. But I fail miserably. Maybe Tucker can punish me on her behalf later. We *do* still have a few days on the road. Never know what might happen.

Tucker.

Bzz. Bzzz. Bzz.
Who the hell is calling me this freaking late.
Incoming Call: Tank

. . .

"Tank, it's three o'clock in the morning," I whisper, my voice unrecognizable as I try not to wake up Taylor.

"And apparently that's the only time you answer your fucking phone anymore." Tank's words are slurred, bringing me out of my sleep a little more quickly.

"What's the matter? Are you okay?" I slip out of Taylor's bedroom and quietly make my way downstairs and out to the back patio.

"Oh, *now* you care? I have to be hammered and blow up your phone for you to pay attention? What am I some like, desperate sorority chick?" He snorts, laughing at his own joke.

"Where are you? And what the hell is going on? This isn't like you." I lean against the railing and run a hand through my hair. I hate that whatever is happening with him right now, is happening while I'm not there to fix it.

"I'm hanging with Lenny and the guys at their usual spot. They asked me to join the gang, wasn't that nice? Lenny is so nice." What the hell is happening right now? Tank has never been careless with alcohol, and never goes off with biker gangs he knows little to nothing about.

"Jesus. I'm calling Max to come pick you up. Just don't leave before he gets there."

"Don't bother. Lenny called him 10 minutes ago..." Tank goes quiet for a moment, but I can tell even through his drunken ramblings there's more he wants to say. Call it a brother's intuition. "I just really needed *you* man."

"Tank–"

"Max is here. Glad to know your phone still works though." He hangs up before I can utter a response. I immediately go to my texts, unable to shake the gut feeling I have that something is seriously wrong.

ME

What the hell is going on with him? Is he okay?

MAX

Man, I don't know. I've never seen him drunk like
this. I'll see what I can find out.

ME

Keep me posted. I'll be home in a few days.

MAX

You got it brother.

MAX

He rambled about being a bartender and doing more
with his life. Mentioned joining Drenger. Then passed
out snuggled up with a water bottle.

ME

Please tell me you told him not to join Lenny's biker
gang.

MAX

I'm not his mother.

ME

Otherwise he seemed okay though?

MAX

I mean, as good as a 32 year old can seem while that
drunk.

ME

Alright then. Thanks again.

MAX

Anytime.

Kansas
Missouri

Tennessee

Chapter 28

Tucker

WHEN WE PULL up to Chattahoochies, Taylor very *ungracefully* throws the truck into park.

"See! I told you I'd get the hang of it." She tosses her wild red curls over her shoulder while I hang on to the door handle for dear life.

"And I'm sure you will… One day. But I'm going to have to ask you to never shift gears like that again." She rolls her eyes as she hops out of the driver's seat. I make my way around the front, throwing an arm around her as we walk into the bar. Instantly I hear shrieks that could break glass as a blur of blonde and brown hair attacks my girl. I jump out of the way so I'm not caught in the crossfire of affection.

"Oh my god, you're alive!"

"Welcome home, bitch!"

The screams and excited greetings continue as I walk over to greet Max and Tank who are both standing behind the bar.

"You made it out alive. Congratulations." Max grabs three glasses from behind the counter and begins pouring us all a drink.

"I thought for sure she'd be bringing your head home in her purse," Tank snorts.

"Lovely to see you too, gentlemen." I pick up the white towel laying on the bar and throw it at them. Max sets a whiskey on the rocks in front of me, picking his own up with a nod. I wave Tank over and he takes a seat on the barstool beside me. When Max walks out of ear shot I turn to face my little brother completely, studying him closely.

"Hey, you alright? You really worried me the other night with that phone call then I didn't hear from you again. What was up?" He just laughs and shrugs.

"What, you've never had too much to drink before?" He looks straight ahead as he takes another sip of his whiskey.

"Tank, I'm serious. You can talk to me." I grab his shoulder, finally catching his attention.

"I'm fine big bro. Really." The vacant look on his face unsettles me. But one thing I know about Tank is, if he doesn't want to talk, he won't. No matter how hard I try. I'm just afraid I missed my chance to listen when I let those phone calls go unanswered.

Max walks back over, throwing the white towel over his shoulder as he leans against the counter on the back wall.

"So, how was the trip? Took you a little longer than normal to get back." His statement has Tank turning his attention back to me.

"Everything was good, actually. We stayed in Utah two nights instead of one, so it prolonged things a bit." I lean back spinning my glass on the bar top as the girls make their way over to us.

"And did I see you *driving* the Bronco?" Shane asks.

"You did. Tucker taught me how to drive a stick." Taylor beams from beside me.

"Oh, I'll bet he did," Ruby says, wagging her eyebrows in a not so subtle way. I can't hide from the looks Max and Tank are giving me from behind the bar.

"You let her drive your Bronco?" Max asks in disbelief.

"Wait, you two are together?" Tank looks between me and Taylor.

All the girls snicker as Taylor takes a seat in my lap. I wasn't sure how she would act once we got back home and around our friends. But I don't have to question it when she leans in and kisses me. Max smirks at me, giving me a nod of approval. I'm not sure why, but that gesture alone makes me able to relax a little better. I wrap my arm around Taylor's waist, my hand resting lazily on her thigh.

"That would be correct," I finally answer Tank's question.

He looks at Max a little frustrated. "Wait, *you* knew about this?"

"My wife is her best friend, of course I knew. I've hardly heard anything else this week." Max cuts his gaze to Shane who rolls her eyes at his comment. Tank looks perturbed but I can't quite figure out why. He sits back with his whiskey as we all continue to catch up about our trip.

I'm dead tired after being on the road eight plus hours every day to make it back home before Taylor and I had to get back to our jobs. But she insisted on coming straight here to see everyone and I'd never tell her no.

Max and I play a round of pool while the girls all talk and Tank sits at the other end of the bar looking through a shot glass like he's trying to appraise the bar top. The girls are looking at Taylor's phone and giggling every now and then and I can only imagine what unfiltered things Taylor is telling them. Right as our game ends, Taylor slides her petite frame under my arm.

"Can you take me home? I am desperate for a shower and to sleep in my own bed."

"Of course, Darlin'. Let's go." I kiss the top of her head and we say our goodbyes.

"Girls night, tomorrow?" Shane calls out as we're walking out the door.

"I'll order the food!" Taylor blows her friends kisses, looking so damn adorable when she does, and walks over to the passenger side of the truck.

"What's the matter, you don't want to drive again?" I mock as she leans against the truck with her eyes falling closed.

"Do you *want* me to drive?" She peeks one eye open at me as I lean in to open her door.

"Hop in, Darlin'."

"Mhm. That's what I thought. I can drive stick Tucker, you just gotta accept that I may not do it *exactly* how you do it," she says in a forced manly voice.

"Which is *exactly* what worries me, because the way I drive it is the *right* way." I wink at her and she rolls her eyes, then we head back to her house.

It's just occurring to me that this will be the first time in almost a week that I'll be spending the night without her. I'm not sure what it'll be like to wake up without those red curls tickling my nose, or her petite body wrapped around mine like a koala bear— with her frozen feet tucked into my calves for warmth. Most of all, I'm not sure how I'll like not having the smell of peaches overriding my senses. But I guess I'm gonna have to find out.

When we pull up to her little blue house, I park in the empty driveway and look over at Taylor as she sleepily sings along to the song she has playing. I haven't even attempted to plug my own phone up since the first day she got in the truck and told me the *passenger princess* rules. I knew the day she wrapped every word to a Young Dolph song that I'd never get bored around her, and so far I've been proven right.

I still can't believe things happened the way they did on the road trip home. How easy it was to talk to her and how effortlessly she seemed to open up to me, too. There's just one thing that's been heavy on my mind for the last few days and I just can't shake it.

"Hey Taylor?" She glares at me from the corner of her eye, as she hits pause on her phone screen. She turns to face me, and scrunches her nose.

"Uh oh, you used my government name. What's wrong?" she teases, but then her eyebrows draw in, showing her true concern when she takes in my expression.

"I wanted to ask you about something, but I don't want you getting mad about how I know to ask." Her gaze narrows again and she shifts in her seat uncomfortably.

"Okayyy," she drawls. My hands are literally sweating right now and I don't even know why I'm so nervous.

"When we were staying with your parents. I overheard you talking to your mom…" She crosses her arms defensively but remains silent. "I came inside after being out back with your dad and was looking for you. I remembered the way you had looked at the porch swing when we first arrived so I thought I would check there. When I cracked the door I could hear you crying and realized you were talking to your mom. I started to back away because I'm not one to eavesdrop and I didn't want to invade your privacy–"

"But…" she says in a dry tone.

"But the part of your conversation I heard, I just… I want to… I *need* to know what happened all those years ago that made you stop dating. What it was that hurt you so deeply, for so long. Under other circumstances, I wouldn't pry. I wouldn't even think to ask, but whatever it was, it has you scared to love me, and that doesn't sit right with me.

"I want you to know I would never do anything to hurt you, but I also need to know that you won't bail on me because you're trying to beat me to the punch. So, will you please tell me– what happened?" She's pulling at a thread on her T-shirt as I talk. Something I notice she does a lot when she's anxious or nervous.

I want to reach out and grab her hands in mine, but I'm still afraid she might be upset by my request. That she'll tell me I have no right to pry into her business and that I should have walked away that night when I heard voices on her parent's front porch.

But I'm hoping she won't. I'm hoping I can drive away from here tonight, understanding her a little better. That I can assure her I'm not going anywhere, and that I would never do anything to hurt her.

She lets out a heavy sigh and when her eyes meet mine, they're already filled with tears.

"When I was in high school, I had a huge crush on this guy, Michael. He was on the soccer team; he was smart and funny, he was the whole package to a sixteen year old me. I, of course, did what any sixteen year old girl would do; I talked about him constantly with my friends and we came up with this stupid plan to have him *accidentally* run into me in the hallway to see if anything would come of it. To *all* of our surprise, it actually worked. I backed up at the perfect time as he walked down the hallways, causing him to knock every book in my hands on the floor. Once he noticed me, I didn't spend much time off of his radar. We would flirt, and I would catch him staring at me during lunch or the few classes we had together. And one day, he *finally* asked me out." She lets out a sad laugh.

"Fast forward six months and it was my seventeenth birthday. He bought me a cheap little charm bracelet and it instantly became my most prized possession. I had thrown myself a little party while my parents were out of town for some conference for my dad's work. Sawyer was at a hockey camp and JJ had already moved out for college. A *little* party meaning, pretty much everyone in our class was there. When Michael showed up I was ecstatic, and since it was our six month anniversary *and* my birthday, what better time to finally sleep together right? So we did. I was sure I had met *the one*." She lets out a scoff, swiping a tear that's rolling down her cheek as I feel my face begin to heat.

"The next week, I uh– I got a butt dial from him after soccer practice. His voice was so close to the phone I didn't know it was a mistake until I heard what he was saying." Her tears start coming more rapidly now, and I make a mental note to hunt down *Michael* and rip his throat out for whatever he said that broke her heart so badly.

"He was *telling* people about our first time. *My* first time. He made fun of how I cried after and said I was *too much drama*. He told them he was going to break up with me, he just didn't know how to so soon after the fact. That he didn't want to seem like he'd just been using me but that there was no way he planned to stay with someone like me.

"I hung up the phone, ripped my bracelet off, and made sure I beat him to the punch. I put the bracelet, along with a note breaking up with him, in his locker the next day. He never found out why, and didn't try too hard to figure it out either. I refused to talk to him after that. I was so heartbroken, I swore I would never let myself go through that again. I gave my heart to him, I gave *everything* to him and he just– he just broke me." Her sobs overtake her and I can't take the sight of it, of her hurting. If I could go back and change things for her, I would do it in a heartbeat. I will also be knocking the fuck out of this guy if I ever get the chance. I pull her into my lap, hugging her tightly against my chest as she lets herself feel it all.

"I know it sounds so stupid, because we were just kids, but it was traumatizing for me. I just— I can't suffer another heartbreak, Tucker. Especially not from you. I would never get over you. You're the epic love I never thought I would have." She peeks up at me, her usual raincloud eyes now bloodshot from her tears.

"Baby, you listen to me. You told your mom you found healing from that wound by being with me, right?" I tuck strands of her fiery locks behind her ear as she nods. "You have no idea the wounds you've healed for me, too. I didn't know I could even love someone the way that I love you, Darlin'. Maybe I was waiting for healing too and didn't even know it. Not until you came along and patched me up. Every smart ass comeback, every eye roll, every flirty interaction. Every kiss, everytime I hear my name fall from your lips, you're mending my heart just to make it yours. And I want there to be *no* room for misinterpretation—it is. My heart is yours to do with as you please. And if you think yours is mended for me, as well, I promise you, I'll keep it safe. You're my epic love too, baby. I will do everything I can to protect that. To protect *you.*"

She draws in a deep breath, running her fingers through the mess of hair I haven't bothered brushing today, caressing my cheek before letting her hand fall.

"My heart is yours Tucker. To do with as you please." She smiles softly at me, exhaustion and relief washing over her. I wrap my fingers around her neck, my fingertips brushing the strands of hair along the nape of her neck, bringing her lips into mine. Tonight our kiss isn't rushed or passionately aggressive.

It's soft and slow.

Full of promise and trust.

Because I will never stop promising her that I love her more than anyone else I've ever met. Hoping along the way she trusts that, as I do my best to prove it to her everyday. Because with Taylor, I will give her nothing short of my everything. Complete and utter devotion to love her how she deserves to be loved. Fiercely.

Chapter 29

Taylor

No matter how tired I was from the long trip home and seeing our friends tonight, when Tucker got out to bring my things in the house for me, I didn't even want to protest. I could have easily grabbed my bag and the box my new hat is in and let him be on his way. I can only assume he's as tired as I am, if not more, from this trip, but if I'm being honest, I'm not sure I want to stay here alone after spending my nights with Tucker.

We step into the quiet house, and the familiar cupcake scent immediately makes me want to curl up on the couch and fall asleep while a movie plays in the background. That's always been my go-to when I need to decompress or let my body recharge after being over-worked. Only this time instead of turning my phone off and being left alone– I want to turn my phone off and drag Tucker to the couch with me. Maybe torture him with a rom-com until we fall asleep all tangled up under a massive knit blanket.

"You want something to drink?" I offer as I kick off my shoes and walk over to my fridge. "I would offer you something to eat, but unless you want to test the strength of your stomach against food that is now growing a new species, I think a drink will be the safest choice." I pull the refrigerator door open to see some bottled waters and canned margaritas shoved in the back as Tucker laughs.

"Yeah, I think I'm good." He sets my bag on the ground before placing my hat box on the small kitchen table. I am too busy rummaging for something to snack on to notice him approaching me. When I finally slam the last empty cabinet with a loud groan, I turn to see him holding my hat. Running his fingers over the burnt details.

"I love your new hat." He smiles, placing it on my head. "Every. Last. Detail." My cheeks heat immediately when I realize he's noticed what I had Joel burn in after Tucker thought it was finished.

"You don't think it's too much. Or a little... I don't know. *Girl obsessed.*" I make a stabbing motion with my hand, as he wraps his arms around my waist with a deep laugh.

"I think it's perfect. I consider myself lucky to have you so obsessed with me," he teases. I roll my eyes and swat at his arm, but I also feel a massive relief from his reaction to it. I wasn't sure when I would get around to showing him the guitar pick I had burned into the hat right by the mountain detail. But the night I heard him play for the first time was so special to me. I just felt like I needed some way to hold onto it.

"So, you liked the guitar?" He smirks.

"I liked the guy that was playing the guitar." I drag my teeth across my bottom lip as he tilts his head to the side. "And you kind of shocked the hell out of me with that voice of yours. Like, damn is there anything you *can't* do?" I laugh quietly but his expression is somber.

"I can't imagine having to go home and sleep in a bed that you aren't in." He cups my face with his hand as his thumb caresses the apple of my cheek. I lean into his touch letting my eyes flutter shut.

"I know. I feel the same way," I whisper.

"Then let me stay," he says, brushing the tips of our noses together.

"You can't, Tucker. You have to go home." He rears back, his eyebrows drawing together.

"Why? You have someone else on the way over?"

"That's literally not even funny." My face falls at his comment.

"Then tell me why I can't stay?" He pulls my body flush with his, no doubt an effort to make it harder for me to say no.

"Because I have worn *all* of your extra shirts and it's been a week since either of us has done laundry. You'd have nothing clean to wear." He pulls back, taking both of my hands in his.

"So, you don't own a washing machine?"

"Of course I do."

"What about a dryer? You have one of those?"

"Yes…" I smirk, seeing exactly where he's going with this.

"And surely your shower hasn't stopped working since you left."

"Unlikely."

"And who said either of us would need clothes tonight?" I swallow hard as my eyes are locked with his.

I've always been one who liked personal space. I enjoy being alone, watching trash TV, eating whatever I want and going to sleep whenever I feel like it– without worrying about what someone else thinks of my schedule– or lack thereof.

But Tucker doesn't disrupt my peace. He *is* my peace.

He backs me up to the counter before lifting me on top of it, running his hands along my thighs before gripping my waist. At this level we're almost eye to eye, though I still have to peek up a tiny bit to meet his gaze.

"If you want me to go, Darlin', say the word and I'm gone. I know you might want to do your own thing and be alone tonight. But–"

"No," I quickly cut him off, "I want you to stay."

"As you wish." His lips land on mine as he pulls me to the edge of the counter allowing my legs to wrap around his middle. My head falls back when he begins kissing my neck, and I moan when he licks from the base of my neck to my ear. Nipping at it when he stops.

"So, how about that shower?" he whispers in my ear. Chills run through my entire body and my eyes meet his as I nod my head in agreement. He plants a quick kiss to my lips then before I know it, he pulls me off the counter, and tosses me over his shoulder.

"Tucker, what are you doing?" I squeal. He slaps my ass as he walks through the door that leads to my bedroom.

"Looking for the bathroom. Where's the damn light-switch in here?" He runs his hand along the wall, trying to locate the switch.

"If you run me into something I swear to God–"

"Ah, there it is," he says in a delighted tone as he flicks the lights on. He tosses me onto my bed and I immediately remember how much I've missed it. The soft down comforter, the fluffy pillows that look like they came straight out of a Boll & Branch catalog. I prop myself up on my elbows to see Tucker pulling his shirt over his head.

Will this man ever stop being so delicious?

He nods to me as he begins unbuttoning his pants. "Your turn." I sit up completely now, pulling my shirt over my head slowly. When he sees the red lace bra underneath I hear a growl come from his chest. He takes a step toward me, but I stop him by putting my foot on his chest. I unclasp my bra, holding it in place as I let the straps fall down my shoulders. I can see his jaw tighten when I let the bra fall into my lap.

"You trying to tease me, woman?" he growls.

"Is it working?" I smirk up at him. He catches me off guard by gripping my ankle and pulling my foot off of his chest, no longer keeping him from getting to me.

He pulls me to the edge of the bed, one leg hanging off the side, the other propped up on his chest with my foot on his shoulder. He leans in, letting his erection settle between my legs. I bite my lip and bring my hands up to play with my tits, knowing just how to drive him crazy.

He rips my shorts off and drops to his knees, his scruffy face settling between my legs. He growls as he swipes his tongue along my wet center. He kisses and sucks my clit, tension building in my core with every swipe of his tongue.

The man doesn't just eat, he feasts.

He may be the only man I've ever been with who truly understands female pleasure. When his tongue begins to hit my clit repeatedly, I grind my hips in perfect rhythm with him.

"God, Tucker. Yes, yes, yes," I plead as my hands tangle in his hair. He continues his movement, an orgasm ripping through me as my back arches off of my bed. He stands up, dropping his boxers to the ground, passion burning bright in his forest green eyes.

"Turn around. Ass up, face down," he demands. I do as he asks and feel a firm slap to my right ass cheek before he slides the tip of his cock along my dripping wet entrance. My body jerks at the feeling, the sensitivity from a moment ago still lingering.

"Settle down, baby. You can take it." He swipes along my clit again and I do my best to stay still.

"Tucker, please," I whine, with my head turned to the side facing my headboard.

"God, I love it when you use your manners," he muses, as he slides the tip into me. A loud, aggravated groan escapes my lips when he does. "What's the matter, Darlin'? Are you getting impatient waiting for my cock?"

"Yes! Just fuck me already, Tucker. I'm begging you." He slides all the way into me, a relieved moan falling from my lips when he does. He grabs my jaw to guide me upward, my back arching as he brings his lips to my ear.

"You will *never* have to beg for me again. I'm yours for the taking. Though I *do* enjoy it when you say please." He nips at my ear before letting my head fall back to the bed, grabbing me by the hips as he thrusts into me.

"Dammit baby, your pussy was made for me." He grabs my ass so tight I'm sure he'll leave his handprint behind. He reaches around my front, grabbing me by the tits to pull me up. My back is flush with his chest as he continues to thrust. When he reaches around to rub my clit again my head falls back on his shoulder.

"Tucker, I can't," I say breathlessly.

"Yes you can, baby. One more. I want to feel you come all over my dick," he growls against my neck as he bites and licks all the way up to the spot right behind my ear that drives me crazy. "One more," he whispers just as I'm sent over the edge again. Screaming his name as I pulse around him. He grabs my hips, bending me forward as he finishes right along with me.

"Fuck, baby." He breathes out as he empties inside of me. My face is buried in my down comforter and my breathing is labored, my body unable to move from the pleasure taking its toll.

"Nightstand." I try to mumble with a mouth full of comforter.

"Say again Darlin'," Tucker says before trying to pull out. I turn my head, freeing my airway and back my ass up to him not letting him go yet.

"I said, nightstand." I nod, bringing his attention to the box of tissues sitting by my lamp. He chuckles and grabs them, raising an assuming brow my direction.

"I have allergies, I like sad movies, and I don't want to make a mess on this bed right now. I am too damn tired to change the bedding before we go to sleep tonight."

"You are insanely efficient and I fucking love you for it." He laughs.

When we got out of the shower we ordered food that wasn't trying to grow *new* food and ate in bed while watching Wedding Crashers.

"What was your first impression of me?" I ask, as I run my finger along the scar on Tucker's hand. I remember the night I stitched him up after he and Max stopped that attempted robbery at Chatta-hoochies. He was so funny that night, even with a huge gash in his hand. Leave it to Tucker to keep the mood light even when he's in pain.

"Love at first sight," he says simply. I shoot up in the bed and whip my head around to face him.

"What?" I all but shout, making him laugh.

"What, you're surprised?" He pulls me back down to rest my head on his chest. He sighs deeply as he runs his fingers through my hair. "At first, I thought *who the hell drinks key lime martinis anymore?*" I glare up at him.

"Tucker! Be serious. I want to know!" I slap his chest, making him laugh again.

"I thought you looked too beautiful to be real. Your wild red curls, your freckles, the raincloud color of your eyes. Then I heard you talking with your friends and noticed what a spit-fire you were and thought *I have to get to know her, because she might be the coolest chick I'll ever meet.*" I bite the inside of my cheek, trying to fight the smile and heat rushing to my face.

"You liar. You know *Ruby.* She's easily the coolest chick I've ever met. How many girls can rock a full sleeve of tattoos, be a badass bartender and also remain one of the most down to earth people you'll ever meet?" I'm deflecting his compliments because I'm not sure I know how to act having someone be so into *me,* crazy personality and all.

"Nah. Ruby scares me. Cause she's also got that mama bear *I'll cut your dick off* vibe." I snort unable to hide how accurate I find his statement.

"Fair enough."

"Alright. Your turn. What was your first impression of me?" A sinister grin creeps across my face as I remember the first night I met Tucker.

"Love at first sight," I tease. Tucker rears back to catch a glimpse of my face.

"Be real."

"Ask Shane. The moment you made me that key lime martini, I told her I was in love. But I was probably talking about the martini." I scrunch my nose at him and he narrows his gaze at me.

"Okay, your real answer now please." He tickles my side and I squeeze myself closer to him.

"The first time I met you I thought, *Super hot for a redhead. 10 points for the tattoos. Probably a playboy. Absolutely not going there,*" I admit. He stays unmoving so I reposition myself to look at him fully.

"And what do you think now?" he asks, his eyes searching mine.

"Still super hot. Even more obsessed with your tattoos now. I don't care who or how many girls came before me, I just want to be the only one with you now. Very glad I went there," I admit, trying to laugh as the vulnerability claws its way up my throat and my eyes become misty.

"There will never be anyone but you, Darlin'. I'll tell you until I'm blue in the face if I need to. My desires have all been for you ever since the day you walked into that bar. You may not think it was love at first sight. But whatever it was, you had my attention and you kept it. After a while, I knew friendship wouldn't be enough with you. I knew one day I would make you mine. And that's what you are, Peach. *Mine.*" He brushes my hair out of my face and his lips lock with mine.

The way a kiss with Tucker can feel like a promise for so much more, terrifies me.

I am helplessly in love with him, and I have no idea how not to fear him leaving me.

Chapter 30

Taylor

"So you're finally back I see." I jolt at the sound of Zander's voice, sending my phone flying across the desk.

"Shit, Zander. You scared me." I hold my hand over my chest as my heart races.

"You have a good vacation?" he asks nonchalantly, leaning against the desk.

"Umm. Yeah, I did." I hear my phone begin to buzz, and begin shuffling through papers to find it.

"I'm glad you're back, I missed you around here," he says, plastering on his flirty grin.

"Okay," I reply flatly, as I see Tucker's name lighting up my phone. "Excuse me." I walk around the desk and down the hall as I swipe my phone screen to answer.

"Hello?" A smile immediately creeps across my face when I hear his voice.

"Hello to you, Darlin'."

"What's up? Is everything okay?"

"It is unless you tell me I have to eat these sandwiches by myself," he says, and I can almost *hear* the smile on his face.

"What are you–" I start, turning around to see him walking up behind me. He wags his brows at me, holding a takeout bag from my favorite sub shop.

"Thought I'd see if you could join me for lunch. I hope I'm not imposing." He leans in and kisses me on the forehead, turning my cheeks rosy when he does. I can't hide the smile that takes over my face just from seeing him. He stands out in these stark white hallways with his dark jeans, olive green medic shirt, and combat boots on.

"Of course you're not imposing. I'd love to have lunch with you. Let me just tell the charge nurse I'm taking my break." I look to either side of me, seeing we're right by the courtyard. "Why don't you pick us a table and I'll be there in two seconds." I smile, pointing to the door that leads outside. He nods and winks at me before walking out.

The little courtyard is pretty much empty today so it's just the two of us out here with our sandwiches. I forgot how much I loved being out here. I started letting myself get so busy at work that I would just grab a protein bar or other snack foods I could eat on the go and never stop for a real break.

"So, how are the shoes? You really like them?" Tucker asks, nodding to the white and leopard print shoes he got me for Christmas.

"You have no idea how much these shoes have changed my life. I no longer want to rip my feet off when I get home at the end of a long shift." He laughs as he takes a big ass bite out of his sandwich. "I still soak them most nights because 12 hours of running non-stop isn't great on your feet, no matter how good the shoes are. But they've helped more than you know. Thank you again." Tucker just smiles and nods in response, as his phone starts ringing obnoxiously loud.

"Sorry Darlin'. It's work. Do you mind?" he asks as he pulls his phone out.

"Of course not. Take it." I wave dismissively as he answers the call. I take the opportunity to check my texts too.

SHANE

You're never allowed to be gone that long again. This girl's night can't happen fast enough.

RUBY

I'm not sure I'll make it. Hendrix's sitter canceled.

LAUREN

Booo. Betty needs to get it together.

SHANE

Max said he can hang with him and Tucker. They never do anything particularly exciting.

RUBY

I couldn't ask them to do that.

SHANE

You're not asking. He offered. I know, I was shocked too. But don't let the opportunity pass you by.

RUBY

Tell him thanks for me. I'll drop him off before heading to Taylors. Wanna ride together?

SHANE

Perfect!

ME

Is Leah even alive rn?

LEAH

It's field day. I'll be there. Lots of margs pls.

I laugh thinking about Leah being dragged around by 20 plus kids all day. I slide my phone back into my scrub pocket as Tucker pulls a tiny notepad from his back pocket.

"Yeah, I'm making a note to change it, I'll update everything when I get back to the office and have it sent over to you by the end of the day." My eyes are wide when I see him pull out a bright orange pen that says *That idea is garbage* on the side. "Thanks John. Bye."

"Sorry about that. How's your food?" he asks as he takes a sip of his drink.

"You actually use that pen?" I point a finger to the pen tucked snug behind his ear.

"Of course I do. Why wouldn't I?" he asks, drawing his brows together in confusion.

"Tucker, those were supposed to be like, a gag gift." I laugh.

"Well, it writes better than any other shitty pen I've ever used. The other one stays in my truck. They're my new favorites." He pops a chip into his mouth and smiles at me. Unable to find words, I shake my head and do the same.

"So, we've never really talked about it, but do you like your job?" I ask, just realizing how little Tucker talks about what he does.

"Eh... it's fine. Actually, I've been thinking–" Just as it seems like he's going to open up, I hear the air ambulance fly over us. I glance up instinctively, watching it hover before landing on the roof, and when I look back at Tucker he is as white as a ghost, his eyes are blank and he isn't moving. He looks like a perfect statue.

"Tucker."

Nothing.

"Tucker, are you okay?" I lean in closer to him, but he hasn't even blinked.

I place my hand on his thigh and squeeze gently. His gaze finally falls to where my hand is and he blinks a few times before his eyes land on mine. They're still the gorgeous forest green color I've come to obsess over, but there's no vibrancy behind them. They're... vacant.

"What?" he asks, his eyes beginning to bounce between mine.

"Are you okay?" I repeat.

"Yeah. Yeah." He shakes his head, smiling at me though it doesn't quite meet his eyes. He crumbles his trash and places it in the bag.

"I'm gonna head out. I need to get back to the office. I'll see you later though. Okay?" He leans in, kissing me on the forehead with his hand wrapped around the back of my head. I let my eyes fall closed at the feeling, then just as soon as it was there, it's gone.

"Hey, Tucker," I call out, before he disappears through the doors.

"Yeah Darlin'?"

"I love you."

"Love you too." He nods and walks away, leaving me with an ache in my chest that I can't shake the rest of the day.

The girls are all talking and laughing while they work around the kitchen getting the food set out. Shane's making her famous margaritas, Leah is telling us about the kid who got a crayon stuck up his nose last week, and Lauren is thumbing through nail polish colors to give manicures tonight. But I can't stop checking my phone, hoping Tucker responds to one of the several messages I've sent him since he left the courtyard today.

"Earth to Taylor." Leah waves her hands in my face.

"What?" I drop my phone on the counter and my head snaps up.

"Damn girl. Where is your head tonight?" she asks, bringing everyone else's attention to me too.

"Nowhere. Sorry, what were you saying?" I ask, tucking my phone away to try and refocus.

"I was *saying* that I've had three different kids try to give me reptiles or insects as gifts just this week. One of them going as far as to pull a lizard from his *pants*." She imitates the motion with a flicking method at the end.

"See. This is why I don't have kids." I point a finger in her direction, raising my brows as everyone laughs.

"That and the fact that you *just* started dating for the first time since high school," Lauren interjects. She quickly shoots me an apologetic look but I wave it off dismissively.

She shouldn't feel bad for her comment. A few weeks ago I would have swiftly changed the subject to avoid facing that topic of conversation at all costs. They all know how much I hate bringing up the past. But for some reason it doesn't hurt as much now.

I fully believe that reason has forest green eyes and calls me Darlin' in the most heart stopping way. So, instead of her comment feeling like a jab that reopens an old wound, it just sounds like a simple truth. And one thing you can always count on from Lauren, she speaks the truth.

"Umm yeah. Give us details woman, we're dying here!" Shane pins me with her stare as she puts the lid on the blender to start mixing the margaritas.

"Is this for real? You're not just having fun like you were with Zander?" I sigh, happily letting all the memories we made while on the road flood back to me.

"Not at *all* like things were with Zander. I fell in love with him. I fell *hard*." Nobody moves or blinks, or says anything. The only sound in the kitchen is the blender still running.

Then the screaming begins.

Everyone rushes around the bar, squeezing me into the middle of a group hug.

"This is the best news ever!" Shane exclaims.

"So, okay there's the freaking bomb drop. Now tell us *everything*," Leah says, tossing her long auburn hair behind her.

So I do.

I tell them about camping in his truck, the waterfall, the night we sat around the fire talking about anything and everything. How he played guitar and sang. The trip up the mountain, and what happened when we got back down. I told them about him breaking a guy's hand for trying to touch me and they all agreed on how hot they found that. I left out the part where I crawled on a motel floor for him, but pretty much everything else stayed. I told them about the talk I had with my mom and we all cried together. By the end of the night my feelings about Tucker were very clear–to everyone.

"Okay, well I'm a freaking faucet now. I'll be right back." We all laugh as I swipe tears from my eyes and run to the spare bathroom down the hall to grab some tissues. I blow my nose in the most unladylike way, and that's when I feel it.

Oh, shit.

I hurry to grab some toilet paper and drop my sweatpants.

"Hey! Can someone bring me a tampon? I don't have any in here," I shout. Ruby comes to the door and tosses me one and an extra pair of sweats with my comfy underwear.

"You freaking angel," I tell her as I begin changing. I walk back to the living room and plop down on the couch next to Shane, tossing my feet over Leah's legs. Lauren and Ruby sit on the floor as Lauren begins painting Ruby's nails.

"Thanks for the warning you brat." I glare at Shane as I check my phone for messages from Tucker.

0 unread messages. Boo.

I exit my messages and go to update my period tracker that I keep up with *religiously*.

"Okay, how are you blaming me for getting your period early?" Shane scoffs.

"Because it's not early and you've started a day before me every month since we were thirteen," I explain, turning my phone to show her the screen that reads '*0 days left until cycle.*' She blinks a few times as realization washes over her face.

Then the realization hits me too.

"Shane?" I say her name cautiously.

"But...I didn't start yesterday," she says quietly, but no one in the room misses it.

"Period math. Now," I demand. She shakes her head like she's one step ahead of me.

"Taylor..." She cuts her eyes to me. "I think I might be pregnant."

"Okay. Okay. How do we feel about this?" I try to keep my voice steady, but the adrenaline beginning to course through my veins has me ready to jump off the couch. Everyone in the room remains silent. When I see tears form in her eyes and a smile come across her face we all begin to scream.

"Oh my god!" Ruby and Lauren yell.

"You're pregnant!" Leah screams.

"We're having a baby?" I whisper in her ear as I squeeze her closer to me.

"Well, we don't know yet but unless I'm a month and a half late, I think so," Shane says, wiping tears that are falling down her face.

"Everyone up. Drugstore run. Now!" I demand.

Chapter 31

Taylor

"Well, there's no denying there's a bun in that cute little oven of yours," Ruby says gently poking Shane's stomach. We all stand around the bathroom studying the multiple tests we bought for Shane that all read positive within seconds of testing.

"Do you think Max will be mad that we knew first?" Lauren gasps from her place on the counter.

"Do you think he will be excited?" Leah asks curiously.

"I– I have no idea," Shane stutters, still clinging to the last test she took.

"Did you guys ever talk about having kids? When did this happen? *How* did this happen? Aren't you on birth control?" Leah continues with her questioning.

"Le, chill. Let her process," I stop her as I see the panic settle on Shane's face.

"I mean no, we never really talked about having any kids of our own. We both love Hendrix though. He's really the only kid we've ever been around. I'm guessing it happened sometime on our honeymoon? I would assume the food poisoning I got while we were gone made me throw up my birth control? Does that seem like something that could cause this?" Shane's eyes are wide as she looks at me for confirmation.

"Yeah, it's definitely a possibility," I confirm.

"I can't believe I'm pregnant. What should I do?" she asks as her breathing gets heavier. While I think she's talking to Ruby– the only other mother in the room– when I glance back at her, she's looking straight at me. And miraculously, I have an idea.

"Come with me." I pull her up from her place on the toilet, and lead her back to the couch. I grab my phone from the coffee table, heart sinking a little when I notice I still haven't heard from Tucker. Then I quickly shift my focus back to my best friend. I click the Face-Time icon next to *Mom* and it begins to ring.

"Hello?" my mom says, coming into view. Shane immediately begins crying when she sees my mom's face.

"Hey Momma Marilyn," she chokes out.

"Oh, honey. What's the matter?" she asks as she adjusts the reading glasses on her face. The comforting effect of my mother's voice will be something I try to accomplish for ages.

"I'm– I'm pregnant." Shane holds up the pregnancy test I hadn't realized she was still holding.

"Oh Shane, sweetie. That's wonderful news! You're going to make a great mother."

"I–I– I am?" Shane stutters and sniffles, wiping her nose on her sleeve.

"Of course you are. Are you kidding me? You're an artist. Kids love to make messes. It'll be a match made in heaven," she teases, making Shane laugh.

"Truly sweetheart– you'll be a great mother. Do you know how I know?" Shane shakes her head. "Because you're simply a wonderful person. You're kind, and loyal, you see the good in people, and you aren't scared to chase after your dreams. Those are all things you're going to teach that sweet little baby. I'm sure your husband agrees. He's going to have a thing or two to teach that little one as well. What does he think?" Shane looks down at her lap.

"I actually just found out. I have no idea what he'll think," she admits. The brave mask she's trying to wear slips momentarily showing the fear she's trying to hide.

"Well, don't wait too long to tell him. You two should process and *enjoy* this together. But don't underestimate your abilities just because you're scared. Every mother has that moment of fear. Realizing you'll be responsible for another human is rightfully terrifying. *But* having a child is such a blessing and such a beautiful experience. Let him experience it all with you. Okay?"

"Okay. I will." Shane nods her head again. Her default setting at this point I'm sure.

"And Shane…" Mom says, bringing Shane's attention back to the screen.

"Yes ma'am?"

"I love you, sweet girl. Your mom would be so proud and so excited for you."

Thanks Mom, now we're all crying.

"I love you too, Momma Marilyn. Thank you," Shane gets out through her sobs.

I see mom wipe her eyes from my place beside Shane, even though I'm not in frame for her to see me. The way my mom stepped in to be there for Shane when she lost her own mom was something I always admired and loved about my mom. She never let Shane feel like she was alone.

"And Taylor Clark, where are you?" her tone is more serious now.

"I'm right here Momma, thank you for–" I turn the phone to face me completely, leaving only me and Mom in frame. She cuts me off before I can finish thanking her for answering the phone and being there for Shane.

"Don't you think for one second I don't know what you did in this house. You are *not* quiet, young lady." The girl's cries immediately turn into laughter from hearing my moms words.

"I gotta go Mom. Love you, bye!"

"I am not done with you young la–"

Click.

"I don't know what she's talking about." I throw my phone across the couch as everyone laughs, still wiping their tears away. I pull Shane's body into mine and rub my hand along her arm. "You gonna be okay?" She rests her head on my shoulder and nods.

"Let's get you home little mama. Hmm?" I ask, making her smile.

"Can we just watch a movie or something first? I want to process this a little more before I tell Max."

"Of course we can. Just name the movie. And maybe give me your margarita and switch to water."

"Oh my god." She gasps. "Do you think the baby is okay?" She shoots up on the couch beside me with a worried look on her face and her hand on her stomach.

"Look at you, already acting like a mama bear. I think the baby will be just fine. Believe me, people have done way worse than drinking while pregnant and miraculously have healthy babies. Just don't have any more and make an appointment with your doctor soon," I assure her as she settles back into the couch.

When What To Expect When You're Expecting ends, I click the TV off and look over at Shane who's sound asleep on the couch.

"I don't even want to wake her, she looks so peaceful," I whisper to Ruby.

"I know the feeling. Hendrix has spent many nights on the couch to avoid me having to move him to his room." She laughs.

"How do you think he's doing with the guys?" I shoot her a knowing look and she shrugs.

"I have no idea, but I'm ready to go find out."

"I think I'll ride with you if that's okay. Tucker can just give me a ride back. He was coming over tonight anyways," I tell her before tuning to wake Shane.

"You little love birds," Ruby teases, making me roll my eyes.

"Shane, wake up. Let's go." Shane sits up on the couch looking around the room. Leah and Lauren are snuggled up under a blanket on the other end of the couch and Ruby is putting dishes away.

"Am I really pregnant?" Shane asks.

"Yeah babe, that one wasn't a dream. Are you ready to tell Max he's going to be a daddy?" A soft smile reaches Shane's lips.

"Yeah, I think I am."

I ride to Max and Shane's house with her and Ruby in hopes of catching Tucker and finding out why he's been MIA all day, but when we pull up and neither his Bronco or his bike are here I start getting a bad feeling about what happened when he left the hospital.

"I guess Tucker didn't make it tonight," Ruby says as we pull into the drive.

When we walk in the door Hendrix and Max are in cardboard battle armor, holding Nerf guns while Max squirts whipped cream directly into Hendrix's mouth. Both boys look our way when the door clicks shut and they freeze like they've been caught committing a crime.

"Mommy! Uncle Max is teaching me how to clear a room." Hendrix bounces excitedly over to his mom, while Ruby shoots Max her *disapproving mom look*.

"Gotta start em young." Max shrugs, propping his obscenely large Nerf gun on his shoulder. "Hey Sunshine, y'all have a good time?" He smiles at Shane and when I look her way she's already misty eyed.

"Yeah, we had a great time. I'll be right back." Shane rushes to the back towards their bedroom, leaving Max looking both confused and concerned. When Ruby takes Hendrix to get his pajamas on, I take the opportunity to ask Max about Tucker.

"Hey. I thought Tucker was supposed to be hanging out with you tonight?" I try to ask nonchalantly.

"Yeah, he called and said he wasn't going to make it," Max says as he takes off his cardboard attire.

"So you've talked to him recently?" I fail to hide the disappointment in my voice.

"Yeah. Why?" he asks, more concerned now.

"Oh, nothing. I just haven't heard from him since lunch. I'm sure he's just been busy." I force a smile, but Max only looks more concerned. Shane's footsteps grow closer as she makes her way back into the kitchen.

"What's going on?" she asks, slipping under Max's arm as he kisses the top of her head.

"Oh nothing. Just didn't know Tucker wasn't here. Sorry for tagging along."

"You didn't know he wasn't here?" Shane asks, concern settling on her face.

"No, he uh– I haven't heard from him much today."

"Well why didn't you say anything? I could have asked Max if he was here, or asked him to track him down for you," she offers.

"Yes, please involve me *more* in this weird foursome relationship we seem to have now," Max deadpans.

"Oh hush, you know you love us." Shane swats at his arm playfully.

"It was girls night, and we kind of had *other things* happening." I pull Shane's attention back to me, reminding her that she kind of has some big news to share. Her cheeks get rosy as Max looks between us suspiciously.

"Do I even want to know?" he asks hesitantly. Ruby and Hendrix come into the kitchen about that time and she takes it upon herself to answer him.

"Yes, believe me you do. We're out of here. Thanks again Max. I really appreciate it," Ruby says, carrying Hendrix in his dinosaur pajamas.

"Yeah, thanks Uncle Max!" Hendrix yells unnecessarily.

"No problem buddy. Any time." He smiles at Hendrix and I sneak Shane a knowing look.

He's totally ready to be a dad. And she gives me one back.

I know but shut up!

I smile at the fact that we can still have silent conversations with each other.

"Well, I'm gonna call an uber and get out of here so you two can enjoy your night." I give Shane a playful wink and her eyes go wide as she bites her lip in excitement.

"Don't call an uber, just take my jeep. I can get it from you tomorrow," she offers, tossing me her keys.

"Thanks Shane. I love you." I lean in and give her a kiss on the cheek before turning to face Max. "If you hear from him again will you tell him to call me, please?" I plead.

"You got it." Max nods. I smile and turn to walk out the door. I'm trying my best to stay focused on the fact that my best friend is about to tell her husband they're having a baby, and not on the fact that I have no idea where Tucker is, if he's okay, or why he hasn't tried to reach out to me today. I want to be there for him and remind him that he doesn't have to go through the hard things alone, but how am I supposed to be there for him, if I don't even know where he is?

Chapter 32

Tucker

I'm standing outside of Taylor's house, with my feet planted firmly on the welcome mat at her front door. I look down at my watch– **3:34 AM.**

Shit. I shouldn't be here. But there's nowhere else I want to go.

I run a hand through my hair before knocking on her door. My heart beats wildly in my chest as I wait. Hoping she opens the door, and praying she'll let me through it. I wait a beat before raising my fist to knock again, but just before my knuckles make contact with the wood, the door flies open.

"Tucker?" She stands in the doorway looking at me like she doesn't believe I'm really here. I rub the back of my neck, offering an apologetic smile.

"Hey, Darlin'. I'm sorry it's so late–" She flies across the threshold wrapping her arms around my neck, with her face nestled there. I wrap her tightly in an embrace; feeling her warmth and smelling her peach scent immediately calms my nerves. Just as I exhale from taking in a deep breath of *her* she pushes away from me abruptly.

"Where the hell have you been all day?" she yells, slapping at my arm making me bite back a smile. Leave it to Taylor to fight me as soon as she knows I'm okay enough for her to do so. "I have been texting you and calling you. You even text Max, but me? Nothing. Not even so much as a *go fuck yourself, Darlin' I'm fine.*" She crosses her arms over her chest, waiting impatiently for my explanation.

"Listen baby, I love it when you yell at me, but can I at least come in first? Don't want you waking the neighbors." She steps to the side, rolling her eyes as she motions for me to come in.

"I'm sorry I didn't call you," I begin my apology, but I don't get far before I see tears start to well in Taylor's eyes. "Baby, please don't cry." I reach out to try and comfort her, but she turns away from me before I can.

"I was so worried about you. You just took off right after that helicopter landed and–" She turns to face me again, tears falling down her rosy cheeks as she tries to choke back her sobs. "And I didn't know where you were, or if you were okay. I didn't want to blow up your phone or hunt you down because I know that's a lot. But I would do that for my friends and you were my friend before we got together. But now we're together and I don't know if it seems too crazy but I really wanted to–" I pull her into me and she lets her sobs break free.

"It's not a lot. It's exactly how any sane person would react in that situation. I'm so sorry I made you worry. That was the last thing I wanted to do." I stroke her red curls that are completely untamed, kissing the top of her head as she catches her breath. She pulls away, looking up at me with her watery gray eyes.

"No, I promise I'm not sane. If I were in that situation with any of my other friends I would have already had their location and sent out multiple search parties. I just didn't want to scare you off if you were just like... out with a colleague and didn't want to talk to me." She shrugs and stares down at her feet, while hugging her arms tightly around her own body.

"Look at me." I take her chin, tilting it up until her eyes meet mine. "I am so, so sorry I had you worried all day. Not only about where I was and if I was okay. But about who I may have been with or how I would react if you were to look for me." Her eyes dart away from mine briefly. "I thought it would be clear to you by now that nothing you could ever do will be *too much* for me. I will crave every text, every phone call, every search party you send, because that just shows me how much you care. And I will *never* ignore you over anyone else." I see her relax a little at my words.

"Then why *did* you ignore me today? I really needed to know if you were okay." Her voice cracks and my heart does the same. I hate that I had her so worried all day.

"If you're willing to hear me out, I really want to explain what happened and where I went after lunch." She nods her head and we head over to her couch.

"Okay, I'm listening." She tucks her feet beneath her, leaning her elbow on the back cushion, allowing herself to fully face me.

"I know you're aware of the story about how we lost Red, and that I was the one with him when he passed away on the medivac." She nods her head in confirmation. "But what I didn't tell you is how bad things were for me when I got back home. I was... fucked up. And it was *really* bad. The nightmare you saw me have while we were on the road, was about ten times better than how bad they were the first couple of years after I got back home. I would wake up at night having full blown panic attacks and sometimes it would take me so long to come back from them, I thought they might never end. I was heavily depressed and drinking all the time to try and numb the pain, unsure how else I could cope. I hid behind the fun guy facade for years, while no one knew how bad I was suffering. Then, one night, I had a panic attack so bad I passed out in the kitchen. I woke up with a severe concussion and had to go to the hospital, and that's where my recovery began. I started seeing a psychologist regularly, I joined a veterans support group in town, and I stopped drinking as much. The nightmares started happening less frequently, the panic attacks stopped, and I found people who could relate to my situation and my story." I sigh, leaning back onto the couch.

"It helped me to see that I wasn't suffering alone, and that I didn't have to suffer so severely. PTSD is a lifelong issue, and I know I'll never be rid of it completely. But the things that trigger me, trigger me hard. They can threaten to undo all the work I've put into getting my head right, and dare to drag me back to a dark place. And today was one of those days."

I don't realize how vigorously my knee is bouncing while I talk until Taylor drapes her leg over mine to help steady it. I smile at the gesture and look up at her.

She's just...*listening*.

Noticing the way I am anxious and calming it, having no idea this is exactly why I showed up on her doorstep tonight.

"Hearing that AirMed coming in so close to us today, took my mind right back to being on that medivac. It took me back to the entire mission, honestly. I just couldn't shake the images no matter how hard I tried. I knew if I was going to spiral, that I couldn't take you down with me. I felt like it would be best to take some time to be alone, and do what I thought would help. I went to a support group, went for a run and called my therapist– who is the one that suggested I try running to replace binge drinking. But at the end of the day, I still ended up with the same nightmare, and all I wanted– was to be with you." I run my hand along her bare leg, still draped comfortably over mine. "Because out of all of the things I did today to try and keep that nightmare at bay, none of it worked. But every night I've spent with you has been the most peaceful I've ever felt."

"How do you do that?" she asks, her gaze narrowed and searching.

"Do what?"

"Talk about everything you've been through, everything you felt today that tore you apart, as if you're...unbothered?" She treads carefully through her words, likely to make sure she doesn't upset me.

"Everyone deals with their shit differently, Darlin'. I had some time to process, and therapy has helped me find ways to cope without losing my damn mind. I'm not unbothered, I just refuse to let things I've worked so hard to heal from keep me captive in my destructive feelings." She swallows hard then shifts into a more playful tone, backtracking to an earlier part of our conversation.

"So! You've been using me like a nightmare catcher? I just keep the bad dreams away?" I let out a small laugh, but I won't be letting that joke slide. I refuse to allow her to think for one minute she's anything less than my everything.

"That's not funny. You should know by now you do more than keep the nightmares away." I lean over, grabbing her by the waist, pulling her to straddle my lap.

"You keep a smile on my face." I plant a chaste kiss on her lips. "You keep me on my damn toes." I kiss her again, squeezing her ass this time. When I pull away she bites her lip, making my cock jump in excitement. "You keep me hungry for you, and only you." I wrap my hand around her fiery curls, tilting her head back to kiss and lick her neck. "And you will *always* have me coming back for more," I whisper in her ear. Her nipples harden as goosebumps appear all down her arms.

"Because you, Darlin', are everything to me. I will never stop showing you just how much I want you. Every bit of you that you've been convinced for so long is *too much*, is exactly what I crave every single day. I'll never stop reminding you that you're perfect just the way you are."

"You make it so easy to love you, Tucker Landry," she says, running her fingers through my hair.

"Why don't you let me love you right back, *properly*?" I nip at her neck again, making her squeal.

"Can't, sorry," she says, pushing me back into the couch cushions.

"Can't? How come?" I frown.

"It's shark week." She shrugs.

"I'm pretty sure that's not until July." An unhinged laugh escapes her lips. "What are you laughing about?"

"*Shark week* is a euphemism for *I'm on my period*," she explains, making me feel like a complete idiot.

"Alright then. Making a mental note of *that*." I pick her up off my lap, placing her comfortably back on the couch.

"It's not contagious you know?" She lifts a brow as I stand from my place beside her.

"I know that. I'm getting snacks. Do you have Rice Krispie Treats here, or do I need to go searching for some?" I say, smirking at her. She bites on the inside of her cheek, trying to hide her smile.

"How do you know my comfort snack?" she asks, propping her chin on the back of her hands, watching as I pilfer through cabinets.

"Seriously? You mean *besides* the four boxes you went through while we were on the road?" I raise a brow at her and she scrunches her nose at me.

"Right…" she drawls. I finally find a box hidden behind a bag of Funyuns. I hold them in the air, shaking them back and forth. I grab a Dr. Pepper and a bottle of water from the fridge, giving her options. When I make it back over to the couch, she picks the Dr. Pepper.

I shake my head in disapproval. But she just grins from ear to ear.

"Please just drink some water today. Maybe let me witness it, for my own sanity." I sit down on the couch, handing her the box of snacks and her drink, as she nestles under my arm.

"Look at you, all worried about my health," she teases, taking a bite from the marshmallow treat.

"Severely." I cut my eyes at her as I grab one of the five knit blankets strewn about the couch and cover her legs. "So, tell me what I missed today." I begin rubbing her arm as she hums while thinking. Then she gasps, almost choking on her food.

"Oh, my god!" She sits straight up on the couch.

"What? What's wrong?" I ask, slightly panicked. She turns to face me, her eyes wild with excitement.

"Shane's pregnant," she says, wide eyed with her fingers covering her lips.

"Is this a sixth sense that just kicked in, orrr?" I ask, searching for further explanation.

"*Nooo.* We found out tonight. Can you believe that they're having a baby?" She squeals.

"Oh, my god. Wow. That's amazing. Are they excited? What did Max say?" I ask, hating that I missed all of this.

"Shane was excited after the initial shock, and I think she was planning on telling Max tonight. But I haven't heard anything so I don't know." She shrugs. "But don't say anything! You have to act surprised when they tell everyone," she demands. I smile and nod.

"I know nothing." I hold my hands up in surrender before I wink at her and she settles back under my arm. I grab the remote and flip through channels as we lay on her large sectional.

"Do you have to work today?" I ask, as Taylor turns her head to look at the clock on the wall that reads **4:30 AM.**

"Yeah, I have to be up in about an hour," she says through a yawn.

"Go to sleep baby, I'll be sure to wake you on time." She nods her head, nuzzling into me. "I'm so sorry I showed up so late and woke you." I kiss the top of her head glancing around to see her eyes already closed.

"You didn't wake me. I couldn't sleep without knowing whether or not you were okay," she whispers sleepily, wrapping her arms around my middle. I almost immediately feel her body fall limp, and just like that she's sound asleep in my arms. I hate knowing she lost sleep over me, but does it make me an asshole if I kind of love it, too?

I'm dangerously in love with her, and all I want is for her to fall that hard for me too.

Chapter 33

SHANE

It's someone's fucking BIRTHDAY WEEK! 🎉

RUBY

🎈 🎂 🦕 the last one is from Hendrix. He says it's a happy birthday dinosaur. I don't make the rules, I just follow them 🦖

LEAH

What do you wanna do to celebrate this year Tay?

LAUREN

Anything you want!

ME

You guys are the best friends a girl could wish for. I really want to go out. Go to a bar, listen to some music. Shane, is that okay? We can totally do something else if you're not up for it.

SHANE

Of course I'm up for it. I'm finally figuring out how to handle the nausea and it's usually gone after lunch anyways. Let's do it.

RUBY

Then it's a plan. Let me know what day and time you wanna go so I can see if Betty is available. 😊

LAUREN

Outfit shopping anyone? Theme Tay?

ME

Yes! Let's own the theme our city thrives on. Country.

LEAH

Yes!

RUBY

Yes!

SHANE

Like, is that even a question? None of my clothes fit. Which I feel like it's soon for that to happen and now I'm scared my baby is going to get its father's genes. 😂 😬

"WHAT ABOUT THESE? They're sooo cute and you have the little brown booties that will match." Lauren holds up a pair of dark wash bell bottom jeans that have a seam going all the way down the front of them.

"Ohhh. I love those, gimme." I grab them from her and she smiles from ear to ear. Lauren loves fashion the way kids love candy. And I've babysat Hendrix enough to know that love is a strong one.

"Does this make me look like a picnic table?" Shane comes out of the fitting room in the most adorable blue and white checkered baby-doll dress and white ankle cowboy boots. We all turn to face her as she does a sad little twirl.

"Oh my god, little mama. You look so fucking cute!" I fake cry, dropping my arms dramatically.

"Really? We like it?" She examines herself in the full length mirror again before looking at the others for confirmation. Lauren places a white cowboy hat on her head and smiles.

"Seriously, Shane. You're the cutest." She grins, making Shane's face light up too.

"What about you Tay, do you need a hat?" Lauren begins examining the ones on display around the little boutique we're at.

"No ma'am, I am wearing the one I got from Joel's." I smile, feeling the heat rise to my cheeks.

"*Oh yeahhh,*" she drags out. "I forgot about the custom hat Tucker the dreamboat bought you." I roll my eyes playfully and shake my head.

"What about you guys, are any of you bringing a date tonight?" I ask, glancing around at Leah, Lauren and Ruby.

"The only man in my life still wears Batman pajamas, and thinks goldfish are an acceptable meal. So that's a no for me," Ruby says, looking through the denim shorts on display.

"No for me too. No time to date with my schedule." Lauren shrugs.

"I *might* have someone I could ask, I just wasn't sure if it was a friend group only thing." Leah scrunches her nose.

"What! Say more," I press eagerly.

"I don't know. One of the guys I work with mentioned going out for drinks sometime and he's kinda cute. I don't know much else about him though, besides he's a teacher and doesn't give *'I'm gonna murder you in an alley'* vibes," she says, as if she's questioning whether it's a good idea or not.

"Well then invite him. That way you can try to get to know him but if it goes south or he *is* a total creep you have a literal army of people there to swoop in and save you," I encourage, seemingly putting her mind at ease.

"Yeah, you're right. Maybe I will." She gives a flirty look over her shoulder as she continues shopping.

"Okay, but I still need to find a top. I want something on theme, but still sexy," I say, thumbing through the rack of blouses. I finally stop when I see an aztec print bodysuit that will go perfectly with my hat and the jeans Lauren found for me.

"Oh, what about this?" I hold it up in the air and everyone nods in agreement.

With mine and Shane's outfits taken care of, we are able to help the rest of the girls shop. Leah finds flare jeans with rips in them, a white shirt that says *save a horse, ride a cowboy* and a black cowboy hat. Lauren and Ruby both go for the cutoff denim shorts; Lauren pairing hers with a bodysuit, a button up with cow print sleeves and black cowboy boots. Ruby chooses the knee high white boots with a Johnny Cash T-shirt and a white cowboy hat. It's been far too long since we all went out together and I can't wait to finally get dressed up for something again.

When I spot a shirt across the boutique that is all black with the same aztec print pocket as the bodysuit I'm holding, I immediately walk over and pick it up in Tucker's size. I don't care if he fights me on it, it's *my* birthday and I *will* fight him back on it. Plus he's gonna look sexy as hell in this.

"I am so glad Max got some more help at the bar so Ruby and Tank can come too!" I yell from my bathroom. I have music playing, applying my makeup, while Tucker puts on the shirt I bought for him.

"Yeah, me too. You deserve to have everyone you want there with you tonight," he says, as he makes his way into the bathroom with me. "This is the softest shirt I think I've ever worn. Which I *would* be excited about if I thought I would get to keep it longer than tonight." He raises a brow at me, making me pinch mine together in confusion.

"What do you mean? Are you going to return it?" I ask, as I swipe blush across my cheeks.

"Nooo, some little red headed shirt fairy keeps taking all my shirts. I think I am down to two in my own closet now." I laugh as he walks up behind me. "I'm serious, I had to order more," he continues, wrapping his arms around me in my plush bathrobe. He's not wrong though, more of his shirts are here than at his own house anymore.

"Did you bring your hat?" I ask, as I zip my makeup bag closed.

"Of course. Told Max and Tank they better not forget theirs either." He spins me around smiling down at me. "You look beautiful, Peach. Are you ready to get going?"

"Almost." He steps away so that I'm able to unsash my robe. I walk over to the closet door and hang it up, then turn around to get his reaction.

"Wait a second. Do we match?" His head rears back and his eyes narrow, his expression unreadable.

"We do. Just this once! I thought it would be so cute, and it's my birthday so you can't tell me no!" I begin my argument before he can even get a word out.

"First of all, your actual birthday isn't until Sunday. Second of all, I would never tell you no. Plus people will see us together and know who you belong to, that works for me." He pulls me into him, wrapping his hand around my neck as he kisses me.

I love how my body comes alive beneath his touch. He pulls his lips from mine, running his fingers gently along my jawline and pinching my chin with his thumb and index finger as he backs away. He grabs my hat from its stand on my counter and places it on my head.

"Damn baby, you look incredible." He grabs my hand, kissing the back of it before winking at me. "But I can't stop picturing what you look like in nothing but that hat." I bite my lip, anticipating what the rest of our night will look like.

"Let's go, Darlin'. I know you hate to be late." He winks at me again as he pulls me behind him out of the bathroom.

When we walk into the kitchen he picks his cowboy hat up off the counter and places it on his head. Suddenly I've forgotten any and all plans we made for the night. The sight of him in his new shirt–that is hugging his biceps in a way I go feral over– the fitted blue jeans and his square toed boots, has me wanting to just stay home and climb him like the gorgeous mountain that he is.

"Or we could just cancel. You know, just stay home. I would have just as much fun here," I bargain with him, but he just laughs and shakes his head. He walks back over to me, pulling me by my belt loops to bring my body flush against his.

"Oh absolutely not. Tonight is about celebrating you. And I'll be damned if I don't get to take my girl out looking this fine. Then, when we get home, I'll *celebrate* you all night long if that's what you wish. But your friends want to celebrate with you too, and I know you're looking forward to it. What do you say?" He moves his hands to my waist, twisting my hips back and forth in an effort to make me agree.

I roll my eyes and groan. "*Fine.* You win." I smile at him and he leans in to kiss me, causing me to hold my hat in place so it won't fall off my head.

"Any day that you're mine is a day that I'm winning, Peach." He kisses the tip of my nose sending butterflies swarming in my stomach. I don't know how I spent so long seeing Tucker as just a friend. I guess we found our groove as friends and that was enough for me. But I am so damn glad friendship wasn't enough for him, and that he didn't let my ignorance get in the way of his persistence. Because I wouldn't want to imagine having to live my whole life not knowing what it's like to be loved by Tucker. Because being with him is easily the happiest I've ever been.

Chapter 34

Tucker

Lyrical Blues Karaoke Bar is Taylor's choice of venue for her birthday outing. When she said she wanted to drink and hear some music this was not what I thought she meant, but here we are. The girls are all squished together as they try to take a selfie, not bothering to ask one of the three other people here with them to help.

"Would you like some help with that?" I ask, as Taylor reaches her arm out so far it looks like it could dislocate at any moment.

"You don't know our angles," she yells, looking at me over her phone.

"Darlin', I know for a fact you look good from every angle." I wink at her and her eyes go wide. They snap a few more photos until finally she gives up and hands me the phone.

"Ok, fine. Just make sure it looks good," she says, making her way back over to the girls. They all stand in front of the empty Karaoke stage–striking different poses, laughing, lifting their legs like flamingos.

Honestly, they look ridiculous.

But Taylor is having fun and that's all that matters.

"Okay, did you get it?" she asks, as she trots back over to me.

"I took about a hundred so I hope you can find one you like," I tease, handing her phone back to her. She narrows her gaze before spinning on her heels.

"Okay, one round of shots before we order our drinks!" Taylor claps, and Tank takes it upon himself to grab the waiter's attention.

"Eight shots of tequila." When the shots arrive at the table I notice how Shane looks over at Max and nods.

They haven't made the official baby announcement yet, and I'm wondering if this is going to be it. What other way would they explain Shane not taking a birthday shot with her best friend?

"We actually have some news." Max clears his throat. "Shane and I are having a baby." He pulls her in closer, but his eyes stay locked on mine while all of the girls begin to cheer.

"Holy shit, congratulations you two!" Tank exclaims, his eyes widening in shock. He gives Shane a hug and gives Max's shoulder a congratulatory shake. Max acknowledges him briefly, then he looks back over at me.

Taylor told me to act surprised– so I do.

"Are you kidding me, man? That's incredible. You're *actually* gonna be a Papa now!" I exclaim, holding a hand out toward him. He looks between Shane and Taylor, who are both very obviously rolling their lips to keep from laughing, then back at me.

"Wait, what do you mean *actually*?" Shane asks, clearly confused by my statement.

"Ah, don't worry about it." She gives me a playful *how dare you* look before quickly shifting her attention back to the girls.

"You already knew, didn't you?" he asks, sounding unimpressed.

"Yeah, I knew. But this is great news man, congratulations." I shrug as I walk around the table and give him a hug. We pat each other on the back a couple of times and when we pull away, he rubs his neck nervously.

"I wanted to tell you the night Shane told me, but then… I just wanted to make sure everything was okay with it first," Max says from beside me.

"Hey, no need to explain. I knew you'd tell me when you were ready." He smiles and nods, wrapping an arm around Shane's shoulder. "So, tell me. Are you excited?"

"More than I imagined I would be." He squeezes Shane's shoulder, bringing a smile to her lips as she looks up at him. The love that radiates between the two of them is something you only see in movies.

"Okay! The news is out, Max will do a shot for Shane," Taylor announces, passing the shot out and setting two glasses in front of Max.

"Don't tempt me with a good time," Max says playfully.

"Okay, we need to make a toast," Lauren says, bouncing back and forth on her feet. Taylor thinks for a minute, glancing over at me briefly.

"To the next year and new adventures." She smiles at me first, then winks at Shane who gets rosy cheeked as she places a hand on her stomach.

"Cheers!" *Hit. Clink. Hit. Drink.*

"Another round!" Tank yells. "We have a lot to celebrate tonight." Taylor and Shane both smile and squeeze him in a weird hug sandwich until the next round is brought out.

We all sit around the table talking and laughing as Max listens in horror as Ruby talks about colic, teething and diaper rashes.

Then he relaxes a little when she softens the blow with how good a newborn baby smells, what it feels like when you see them smile or hear them laugh for the first time. She also makes it a point to remind him about how well he handles Hendrix and reassures him that if he can handle a dinosaur obsessed, chicken nugget vacuum, that doesn't stop talking until his head hits the pillow, that he can handle anything.

"I am not drunk enough to listen to this," Tank mumbles from beside me, as a couple of drunk girls on stage scream sing the words to "Friends In Low Places" by Garth Brooks, to the point it is *almost* unrecognizable.

"I hear that." I laugh, ordering us both another beer. But before the waitress walks off he orders himself two more shots.

Unease creeps into my gut when I notice how much he's drunk already. I'm never one to judge when it comes to having a drink or two, but I know reckless when I see it. Mostly because I've been there myself, and I don't like the path I see him heading down. As bad as I want to drag him outside by his ear and knock some sense into him, it's not the time or the place. Which is confirmed when I see my girl heading my way.

"I know what I want for my birthday," a tipsy Taylor says, plopping down in my lap.

"You're ready to go already." I smirk, making the blush in her cheeks darken.

"*Nooo.*" She bobs her head, bringing her face just inches away from mine. "I want you to play. And sing, obviously," she sputters as she nods to the stage.

"I don't think so, Darlin'." I bring my beer bottle to my lips, taking a drink as Taylor rears back with a pouty frown on her face.

"Yeah, good luck with that one." Tank raises his brows, staring straight ahead as he finishes his beer.

"Please, Tucker." She doesn't demand or whine like she's entitled. She simply says please– which is my weak spot with Peach. All she has to do is ask, and I'd give her the goddamn world. I let out a deep exhale and set my beer on the table.

"Anything for you, Darlin'." I stand up, shocking even myself as I approach the stage. I ask the MC if I can use the guitar on stage, and he agrees. I strum the guitar a few times, getting it in tune before approaching the mic.

"Evening. I hope y'all don't mind. I'm gonna ditch the track and play something myself, at the request of my girl." People throughout the room cheer and a few claps sound off here and there. I look up and see Taylor smiling so bright it instantly lights up the dimly lit room.

"Happy Birthday, Darlin'. This one's for you."

TAYLOR

I didn't think it was possible to fall more in love with Tucker. But as he stands up on the karaoke stage, and begins to sing "One Man Band" by Old Dominion, I'm proven wrong. The twang in his deep, velvety voice that's present every time he calls me *Darlin'* is even stronger when he sings. I can't peel my eyes away from him. It's like he's been singing in front of people his whole life.

The otherwise noisy bar is completely quiet the whole time he plays. When he plays the last chord and sings the last note, the bar erupts in applause. I can't keep myself from running up to him when he walks off the stage. He instantly lifts me off the ground, wrapping his arms around my ass to pick me up. I lean in and kiss him, careful not to knock his hat off of his head.

"Best birthday gift ever."

"Anything for you, baby." He winks at me before placing my feet back on the ground.

"Hey! You made it," I hear Leah's sweet voice say, drawing my attention to a guy walking towards our table.

"Yeah, I'm sorry I'm late. Traffic was awful tonight," the guy says, leaning in to give her a gentle hug.

"Oh, no it's okay. Everybody, this is Jackson. Jackson, this is–well, everybody. There's Max, Shane, Taylor, Tucker, Tank, Ruby, and Lauren." We all say hello, and wave.

"Great to meet you all. Although I can guarantee I won't remember your names the first time, so you'll have to forgive me when I ask for them again." He laughs, and Leah smiles.

"So what are you drinking?" Leah asks as the two of them walk over to the bar together.

When we turn back around, all eyes are on Tucker. And none of the girls hide their shock from his performance.

"That was great, Tucker. I had no idea you could sing. *Or* play guitar," Shane says, giving me a little *he doesn't have to know we discussed it at great length,* eye roll and smirk.

"Yeah, that was badass. You should go on The Voice or something," Ruby says, sipping her rum and Coke.

"Yeah, Tucker. So you've just been walking around with all this hidden talent then?" Lauren says, making Tucker shake his head. I think I even notice a hint of embarrassment on his face in the form of a... *blush?* Before he can respond to any of them, someone grabs me by the waist, pulls me away from our table and spins me around in a circle.

"Hey, put me down, asshole!" I begin kicking my legs as I hear a deep laugh rumbling in the chest of the person holding me.

"What, you wanna fight me on your birthday, Tot?" I turn around to see Sawyer standing behind me. He sticks out his tongue, running a hand through his long brown hair.

"Oh my god, Saw. What are you doing here?" I squeal, wrapping my arms around him.

"No way I was missing my baby sis' birthday. You know that," Sawyer says, holding my shoulders as I step out of his hug.

One thing that we've done ever since we were kids, is show up for each other. Birthdays, graduations, big events– you name it we show up. On my sixth birthday I wanted to have a waterslide at my birthday party and invited every kid in my class. Shane got the chickenpox that weekend and couldn't make it– and no one else showed up. When Sawyer and JJ saw how sad I was they called all of their friends and *they* actually showed up. Some of them even brought presents. It was one of the best birthdays I ever had. Ever since then, we don't miss a single birthday if we can help it.

"Well come sit down, it's a tight squeeze but we can smush," I tell him, walking back over to the table.

"Hey Sawyer. I'm glad you could make it," Shane says from Max's lap.

"Of course you knew," I say, shaking my head at her. She shrugs her shoulders and lifts her water glass.

"I'm gonna grab you a drink Darlin', be right back." Tucker leans in and kisses me before walking over to the bar.

"I like this date much more than the last guy I saw you with," Sawyer says, nodding toward Tucker.

"First of all, don't make me discuss my mistakes on my birthday," I say, holding an index finger up in Sawyer's face.

"It's not your actual birthday, Tot," Sawyer laughs.

"People have to stop saying that to me tonight. It's close enough." I roll my eyes.

"Well, when I talked to Mom and Dad, they said he was something special. I'm just glad I'll get to see for myself now." Sawyer crosses his arms over his chest, giving his best *judgmental big brother* stare. He cracks, smirking at me from his towering height. I just laugh because that look never intimidated me, and it *sure* won't intimidate Tucker.

"Yeah…Tucker will be the one to make me forget about the rest," I say, admiring the man holding a key lime martini at the bar. When I turn back to face Sawyer his smile has faded, his features stone cold now. "Hey, everything okay?" I ask, grabbing Sawyer's arm. It's not often I see Sawyer looking this bothered, besides maybe when he's on the ice.

"Yeah. It's fine. I think I'm gonna grab a drink too." He looks down at me and forces a smile then heads over to the bar as Tucker makes his way back to the table. I shake my head, trying to shrug off the weird vibe coming from Sawyer.

"Is he okay?" Tucker asks with a concerned look on his face.

"I think so. You can never tell with Sawyer though." I shrug, carefully taking my drink from Tucker's hands. "You are my hero." I take a sip of my drink before scrunching up my nose.

"Is it not good?" Tucker asks.

"It's fine. They're never as good when you're not the one making them," I admit. Bringing a smile to his face.

He takes the glass out of my hand and sets it on the table. Then turns back pulling me into a kiss that most people would only have in private. His hands slide into the back pockets of my jeans, while mine wrap around his neck. His tongue swipes against my lips to deepen our kiss and I eagerly welcome it. About the time I'm thoroughly turned on I hear Leah's voice through the noise.

"Who's ready to go line dancing?" she calls out, pulling Jackson behind her. All the girls smile mischievously as the guys look between each other in confusion. A prominent *did you know about this* stare being passed between them.

"Hell yes!" Lauren, Ruby, Shane and I all call.

"Ah, fuck me," Max mumbles, causing Shane to whisper something in his ear. He nips at her neck, drawing the sweetest giggle from her.

They're the freaking cutest.

Chapter 35

Taylor

"So DO you have any idea what he's got planned tonight?" Shane asks from the pedicure chair beside me. I love that she owns her own business and was able to do girls day with me when everyone else has to work. It's been ages since she and I were able to hang out just the two of us.

"I have no idea. All I know is I have to be at his house at six. When I asked what to wear he said *anything you pick will be perfect Darlin',*" I say trying my hand at a Tucker impression. Shane and I both giggle when I fail miserably to execute it. "As if that's helpful information," I continue through my laughs. "Maybe I'll just show up in one of the fifteen T-shirts I have stolen from him since we left San Francisco."

"I don't see him complaining about that. However, if he was planning to take you out, you probably wouldn't make it out of the bedroom." Shane wags her eyebrows at me, while the perfect outfit appears in my mind. I am almost squirming in my seat with the eagerness to run home and try it on when Shane's phone begins to ring.

"Hello?" she answers in her inhumanly sweet voice.

"I guess strawberry is fine this time," she pouts. "Is that Tucker?" she asks, her brows drawing together as her head turns my direction. I match her confusion when I turn to face her.

"It does too matter," she yells into her phone before looking around the salon slightly embarrassed. "Tell him it's not the same and he's not the one with pregnancy cravings," she whispers into her phone making me and both nail techs laugh. "Love you too, bye."

"What the hell was that about?" I ask, laughing at the end of the conversation I *could* hear.

"Max and Tucker are apparently grocery shopping together. Max was telling me the store is out of apple toaster strudel and asked if strawberry was okay." We both scrunch our noses.

"Ugh. What's with the apple always being out of stock?" I ask.

"Right?" she exclaims. "Anyways, Tucker was just saying it didn't matter and that we could make them from *scratch.* Like who do I look like, Betty Crocker?" Shane quips. "Max maybe, but me? I could never."

"I love that he cooks. That's super hot." I rest my head back in my chair, closing my eyes as Maria massages my feet and legs.

"Wait a minute…" Shane thinks aloud, making me peek one eye open. "Do you think he's cooking for you tonight?" This has me sitting up a little straighter in my seat.

"Do you think?" I ask, as the wheels in my brain start turning. He did cook breakfast over a fire while we were camping. I've never asked and anytime we are together lately it's after work and we just end up ordering takeout.

"I mean, they're *grocery* shopping together. That doesn't exactly seem like a normal place for them to hangout. The gym, sure. Chatta-hoochies, always. But the grocery store?"

"Oh my god. He's cooking for me." I'm still not one hundred percent sure, but Shane has me all but convinced.

"We have got to learn to cook. I mean, our takeout ordering skills are impressive, but how amazing would it be to cook a bomb ass meal and be like *yeah, I did that*." I playfully point at the hypothetical meal in front of me.

"You're right," Shane says with sudden realization. "Let's sign up for a cooking class!" We immediately grab our phones, searching *cooking classes near me* and *beginner cooking classes in Nashville* until we find one. Lucky for us, it starts next week.

"How are we going to hide the fact that we're going to a cooking class once a week?" Shane asks.

"We'll just tell them we're doing hot yoga or something." I shrug as I inspect my sienna ombre nails.

"Oh, perfect!" she agrees, sitting back in her chair placing her hand on her stomach.

"Are you guys going to find out what you're having or are you going to wait?" I lean my head against the chair, admiring my glowing best friend.

"We both want to wait. Max says he really wants to be surprised and I agree. We're gonna love this baby no matter what and we can prepare without knowing."

"I think that is really cool. Aunt Tay loves you baby Shine. And you're gonna love me more than your other aunties I promise," I yell over to her stomach, not giving one single fuck about who thinks I am crazy in this nail salon.

"Baby Shine?" Shane laughs.

"Max calls you Sunshine, I had to come up with some kind of nickname so I'm not calling it *it* for the next seven and a half months. That's the best I've got. If I come up with something more suitable, I will amend it and let you know."

"It's weird, and cute, and perfect. Don't change a thing." Shane smiles as she reaches over squeezing my hand.

I look in the mirror at the outfit I put together for tonight completely satisfied. It turned out as cute as I had pictured and that almost never happens. I came straight home from lunch with Shane after getting our nails done to ensure I had the shirt I wanted to wear washed and ready. It's the same black shirt of Tucker's he gave me the night he rescued me at Benji's. Since he's a giant and I'm the size of a teacup chihuahua, I cinched the shirt at my waist with a simple belt, paired it with my black booties and I'm wearing my untamable curls in a claw clip. I check the clock on my nightstand– **5:45PM**– grab my purse from its usual place in the arm chair in the corner and head out the door.

Knock. Knock. Knock.

"Coming. I'm coming," I hear Tucker yell as he approaches the other side of the door.

"Already? I just got here." I smirk when the door swings open. He draws back slightly, his brows lifting towards his hairline.

"Wow. You look incredible." He lets his eyes rake over me and I let mine do the same. He is wearing a powder blue button up shirt with the sleeves rolled up, showcasing his tattooed, muscular forearms. The veins in them look like a roadmap straight to heaven. His shirt is unbuttoned at the top, giving me just a peek at his chest hair and tattoos. He has it untucked– stopping just at his waist– wearing black ripped jeans and combat boots. He's hands down the sexiest man I've ever seen in my life.

I see him toss the white dish towel over his shoulder, and I can't help but drag my teeth over my bottom lip. He takes a step forward, grabbing me by the wrist, pulling me into him. He leans down wrapping his arms around my waist and takes my lips in his. I can feel the T-shirt I am wearing as a dress raise a few inches when I wrap my arms around his neck.

"Happy Birthday Darlin'," he says, his lips brushing across mine with every word. He lifts me and spins around, bringing us both over the threshold, before shutting the door with his foot. Once inside, he quickly wraps my legs around his middle. His hands move to cup my ass, growling when he finds it bare.

"You're going to make me lose my fucking mind," he says, his mouth traveling down to bite along my neck. My eyes flutter closed and a moan escapes my lips when he licks from my collar bone all the way up my neck, stopping right at my cheek.

"Oh my god, something smells amazing." My eyes pop back open when the smell of fajitas overtakes my senses.

"Shit," Tucker says, gently but quickly placing my feet back on the ground.

He rushes to the kitchen as I trail in behind him. He begins moving food from the hibachi portion of his stove stop. Turning knobs off, and placing veggies, chicken, and steak in bowls on the counter. I look around and take in the full fiesta he has on the far side of his kitchen island.

I've always loved Tucker's house. It's modern but still cozy. The kitchen has black cabinets, stainless steel appliances and marble countertops. There is an original Shane masterpiece hanging over the dining table. It's a painting of the ocean– from surface level to the depths where you wouldn't be able to see your own hand in front of your face. It always made me feel queasy before, because the ocean has always scared me, but knowing Tucker better now and understanding his connection with the water, I can admire it through his eyes.

"You're a dangerous distraction, you know that?" He smirks, as he walks over to me.

"Hey, all I did was show up on time." I hold my hands up defensively.

"Your mere existence is enough to distract me from anything else requiring my attention," he says, walking over holding a perfectly frosty key lime martini. "I hope you're hungry." He smiles, a hint of nervousness flashing through his eyes.

"Tucker, this is amazing. Thank you." I smile at him as he takes me by my free hand.

"Don't thank me quite yet, you have to at least try the food first. You may be making me apologize later," he jokes as he leads me over to the dining table and pulls my chair out for me. He quickly brings the home made fajitas, queso, and tortilla chips over to the table.

"No one has ever cooked for me before. Besides my parents of course. This is the sweetest thing anyone has ever done for me. The food could taste like dirt and I would still thank you, simply because you made an effort to do something like this for me," I admit, as his forest green eyes ignite my heart, sending electricity throughout my body.

"Well then, you're welcome Darlin'. Let's hope the food is still good though." He winks at me and I melt in my seat.

"So, did you have a good time celebrating with Shane today?" he asks, wiping the corners of his mouth as he pushes his empty plate back on the table.

"We did. We're uh… going to start attending a hot yoga class once a week," I say, trying to get a read on him.

"That sounds… truly awful. But I hope you two enjoy it." His deep laugh rolls off his lips, simultaneously making me laugh and turning me on.

"I think it'll be great. We're looking forward to it." I sit back and adjust the top of my shirt as it starts to drape off of one shoulder. Tucker's gaze narrows and he leans across the table, sliding his pinky through a hole in the neck of the shirt.

"Is that one of my shirts?" he asks, examining it more closely now.

"It is. It's the one you let me borrow the night you took me home from Benji's."

"I think it's considered stolen at this point, not borrowed." He quirks a brow. I roll my eyes as he sits back in his chair, crossing his arms over his chest.

"You know, I thought I was going to lose my mind that night. When you ripped your shirt off, letting those perfect tits of yours tease me through that lace bra you wore," he recounts, as my cheeks begin to heat, "then I got so pissed when I realized you had worn it to impress someone that *wasn't* me." His jaw ticks, then a forced smirk comes across his face. Almost as if he's trying to rid the memory but his mind won't let him.

I stand from my seat at the table and walk around to his side. He pushes his chair back like he knows my next move before I ever make it. I straddle his lap, undo the belt that is keeping his shirt hugged tight to my waist and drop it on the floor. I reach down and lift the shirt over my head, much like I'd almost done that night before my phone interrupted the moment. I drop the shirt to the floor and Tucker sucks in a deep breath when he's met with the same lingerie I wore that night.

But tonight, I wore it for *him*.

I take his face in my hands and his eyes lock with mine.

"I am so glad I left with you that night. I hadn't stopped thinking about you since the night of Shane and Max's wedding. It scared me because you were so sure and so bold in how you felt about me. I was still processing what that meant. Unfortunately, I was trying to go about my dating life with someone else, when the whole time, it should have been you." He grabs me by the ass, and his jaw relaxes. He lets his eyes drift down my body before meeting my gaze again.

"You were worth the wait, Darlin'."

"I'm sorry I made you wait, Tucker." I lean in, running my hands through his wavy red hair. I kiss him gently first, then I begin grinding my hips against his growing erection. He squeezes my ass, pulling me harder against him. One hand wraps around the back of my neck as the other slowly guides my hips back and forth against him.

"Oh I know you'll make it up to me, baby," he says, taking my bottom lip in his teeth.

"On your knees, Darlin'."

Chapter 36

Tucker

I DON'T THINK there will ever be a sight I love more than Taylor's red curls splayed out across my pillows. The nights we spend together are always the nights I sleep the best. Our bodies intertwined, her peach scent lingering for days after she's gone, and the way the sun peeks through the window illuminating her freckles makes me wish we never had to leave this room.

"Stop staring at me, you're going to give me a complex," she grumbles with one eye barely open.

"Then stop being so damn intoxicating all the time." I lean over and kiss her forehead. "I realized that I never gave you your birthday gift since we got…*busy* after dinner." Her freckles are quickly accompanied by my favorite shade of pink.

"You got me a present?" She bites her lip eagerly as I pull her gift from my nightstand.

"Did you really think I wouldn't?" I frown, teasing her with the small wrapped package, pulling it back each time she tries to grab it.

"Of course not, I know you better than that. I just don't know how you'll top the dream shoes you got me for Christmas." She finally gets fed up with my teasing, jumping in my lap to reach her present.

She really *is* the most intoxicating thing I've ever seen. Her red curls are in perfect disarray around her bare face. She's wearing a white surf shop shirt–that she stole from my closet of course– and a blue cotton thong that gives me perfect access to squeeze her bare ass. If I could stop time and savor this moment forever, I would.

She looks triumphant as she rips the package open, while my hands stay busy kneading her bare skin. I have to keep busy somehow, otherwise the anxiety will win and I won't be able to stay still and take in her reaction. I was confident when I got her gift, but now I'm wondering if she'll even like it. If it will be enough.

The smile that lights up her whole face when she removes the tissue paper, has me instantly able to breathe easier.

"Tucker. When did you… Wait, *how* did you get this?" She looks up at me with a confused frown as she turns the frame around to show me the photo.

"I might have taken your phone and sent it to myself one night after you went to sleep. I hope you aren't mad." I admit.

"Of course I'm not mad. I love it." She smiles, running her dainty fingers along the frame.

It's the picture she took of us after we swam to the waterfall.

Well, I swam. She clung to me for dear life. Pressing her perfect body hard against mine.

In the photo her hair is soaking wet, there's not a trace of makeup on her face, and I'm looking at her the way I always do.

Completely and irrevocably in love with her. Even when she didn't know it, I was.

"I know it's not much, but–" Her index finger flies to my lips to silence me.

"Don't you dare. It's perfect. Thank you, Tucker." She smiles sweetly, running her fingers along my jaw as she leans in to kiss me.

I sit up straighter in the bed, taking the photo from her hands to set it to the side. Just as I slide her closer to me, deepening our kiss and ready to celebrate her all over again, she pulls away.

"What time is it?" she asks, looking over at the clock in a panic, "crap! I have to go." She scurries off the bed, eyes darting around the room for her clothes. "Shane and I have our first coo... uh, yoga class today and I will never hear the end of it if I'm late. And I still have to go home and change."

"Well, you have fun sweating your sweet little ass off. I'm actually running late to meet Max, too." She rolls her eyes as I make my way over to her side of the bed.

"I love you, Peach. I hope you had a great birthday." I run my fingers through the hair at the base of her neck and lean down and kiss her forehead. She stands on her tiptoes to kiss me, and runs her fingers through my hair.

"It was the best one yet."

MAX

Running a little late. Grabbing coffee. See you in 30.

ME

Looks like there's a theme today cause I'm running late too.

ME

Max and I are running late. Meet us there in 30 instead?

TANK

Actually, my ass already looks perfect today. Real firm. I think I'll sit this one out.

I walk into Hall's Gym and see Max talking to Jimmy at the counter. They seem deep in conversation so I don't bother walking over to say hello just yet. Instead I drop my stuff off at the treadmill, and start scrolling through my emails. The past few weeks at work have had me questioning why I've kept at this for so long. I used to enjoy the creative aspect and I was proud of myself for building this company from nothing. But this office project has me ready to throw in the towel.

Every day I am on back to back phone calls or answering a dozen emails about changes that need to be made before we can move forward. It just makes me wish I got to do something I really love. Like Max with the bar, Shane with her art, Leah teaching the sticky gremlins that she somehow adores, and Taylor getting to take care of people at the hospital. Only, I'm not even sure what it is that I love enough to pursue as a career.

"Hey, sorry about that. You ready?" Max says, walking up to the treadmill next to mine.

"No worries. Everything alright?" I ask, nodding to where he and Jimmy had been standing.

"Yeah, he was just telling me that Heidi hasn't been doing so well," he says in a hushed tone. Heidi Hall was diagnosed with stage four cervical cancer a month ago and was told she had one year left, give or take. It's maddening how the good ones get taken so soon. Heidi and Jimmy are both barely in their fifties, it's just not fair.

"Did he say if they need anything?" I ask, letting my gaze drift to Jimmy. He used to be so carefree, smiling and giving gym goers shit just for laughs. But, understandably, his light has dimmed severely over the last month. I just wish there was some way to help.

"Not really. He mentioned Heidi wanting to sell damn near everything they have to be able to travel more before... Before she can't anymore." Max's jaw ticks as he gets the words out. I know the topic of cancer is still hard for him, after losing his mom to it a little over 10 years ago. "But they would have to talk with her doctors about the possibility of that even happening," he continues, finally stepping up on the treadmill. He clears his throat, signaling a shift in conversation.

"So, I've been wanting to ask you something," he starts as we begin to jog.

"What's up?"

"How would you feel about being part owner of the bar?" Well, I definitely didn't expect *that*.

"Are you serious?" I rear my head back trying to get a read on him.

"Do I strike you as the joking type?" He gives me a smart ass grin.

"But why? Are your investments in any trouble?" He shakes his head.

"Nothing like that. You seem to like it there. You always get a kick out of bartending, you're *good at it*, and honestly man. Your job seems to be sucking the life out of you."

"Yeah, I'd prefer if Taylor was the only one doing that." I smirk.

"Jesus Christ, man." He closes his eyes, shaking his head at me.

"Is the burn out that obvious?"

"To me it is. Every time you take a phone call or check your emails I see the way it's getting to you. If I'm overstepping or misreading the situation then by all means–"

"No, you're definitely doing neither of those things," I cut him off, stopping my treadmill, as Max does the same.

"Just, think about it. If it's something you might be interested in then we can discuss details. I've been toying with the idea of possibly expanding, and it would be nice to not have to do it alone. I can't think of anyone better for the job."

"Let's discuss the details now," I say, curious as to how this might play out.

"Fair enough. What do you want to know?" Max agrees.

We spend the duration of our workout discussing what it would look like to be co-owners of Chattahoochies. He tells me where he wants to expand and who he would like to oversee that. We go over my buy in amount, position and pretty much anything else you could imagine. By the end of our workout, I have no doubt in my mind, this is something I'd want to do. I just have to figure out how to go about selling my company– while we're in the middle of a stalled project no less.

"Just keep me in the loop on what you're thinking. I would love to get things moving before the baby is born, but I don't want you to feel pressured. The offer doesn't have an expiration date. Like I said, I can't think of anyone else I'd wanna do this with," Max assures me as we walk out of the locker room.

"Thanks man, will do."

"You wanna grab lunch?" he asks, looking down at his watch.

"I actually have lunch plans today. Rain check."

"Sounds good." We bump fists then Max is out the door. I grab my phone from my bag, eager to talk to Taylor about my thoughts on a career change.

ME

Hey, what time is your hot yoga thing over?

TAYLOR

Well, we got the time mixed up. It starts at 11 not 10 so we should be done around 12 I think. Why, what's up?

ME

I just have something to talk to you about. Can we get together afterward?

TAYLOR

Of course. I'll call you after I'm home and showered.

ME

How about you tell me before you shower. I wouldn't wanna miss that.

TAYLOR

Yes sir.

ME

I love that my girl has manners.

Chapter 37

Taylor

"Welcome to your very first Beginners Baking class." The blonde at the front of the class wearing a white apron claps her hands together, with a grin on her face the size of Texas.

"I am Maggie, and I can't wait to help you get your foot in the door of the food world. Today we are starting with something simple that I think *everyone* will love– chocolate chip cookies."

"Hell yes. Do we get to eat what we make?" I lean over, whispering in Shane's ear.

"Are you confident that we're going to *want* to eat what we make today?" She scrunches her nose at me, making me think twice about my excitement.

"There are ingredients and the recipe we will be following at each of your counters. I will be using the same recipe up here and going over each step as we go, but if you have any questions please feel free to ask." Shane and I share an excited glance before putting our aprons on and grabbing the recipe.

> *Preheat oven to 350°*
> *Combine dry ingredients in a bowl; set aside.*
> *Combine butter, sugars, and vanilla in a large bowl; beat until*
>   *creamy.*
> *Beat in eggs.*
> *Add flour mixture; blend well.*
> *Stir in chocolate chips.*
> *Drop rounded spoonfuls onto a greased cookie sheet.*
> *Bake 8-10 minutes.*

Not on the recipe– *setting the kitchen on fire.* But did that stop Shane and I– the queens of natural disaster?

Absolutely not.

Five minutes later, class was dismissed.

"Does it not feel like some sort of freaky sign from the universe that maybe we *shouldn't* try cooking? Or baking? Honestly, I still don't fully understand the difference." I hold a hand out, while my other dips my fries in ranch before I devour them in one bite.

"Or maybe we should make sure we *don't* turn a stove on while reaching for the baking sheet, then proceed to leave a towel right next to it." Shane bobs her head as she takes a sip of her lemon water.

"Honestly, we need to just have your mom teach us how to cook. And bake. Her cookies are superior and *that way* we don't have to endure public humiliation."

"I'll say. Maybe I could have her do weekly FaceTime classes for us. I just don't understand–" my words stop, as does my heart, when I see Tucker sitting in a booth across the restaurant. With another woman.

"How someone can stop in the middle of a sentence, leaving you with a verbal cliffhanger?" Shane laughs.

"What?" I say, still not peeling my eyes from the two of them.

"Oh my god, Taylor. You look like you've seen a ghost. What's up?" she asks, turning around to find the answer for herself. "Do we know her?" she asks through her teeth, turning to face me again. The fierce mama bear mask I've worn for all of my friends while growing up has now landed on Shane's face.

"Nope. I've never seen her before." I continue watching as Tucker's gorgeous white smile lights up the room. The woman sitting across from him has shoulder length, straight brown hair. From what I can see she's dressed in business attire. White silk blouse, dark dress pants, and a pink statement heel you could see if you were blind. They don't seem particularly cozy, which does *nothing* to calm me down. They're sitting on opposite sides of the booth, no hands reaching across the table, no flirtatious smirks.

So help me God if I see him wink at her I will end up in jail for murder.

"I can see that something is about to unfold here. Though I'm not sure *what*, I just want you to know I fully support you," Shane says, nodding her head firmly as she approves of whatever action I am about to take.

I look around at the waitstaff and notice my all black attire matches theirs perfectly, and instantly know my next move. I grab a water pitcher from the small refill station behind our booth and make my way over to where they're seated. My heart is racing as I approach their table, unsure exactly what I want to say or even how I'm feeling besides *pissed the hell off*. But there's no turning back once I slam the pitcher down on their table. Drawing a gasp from the brunette sitting across from him.

"Anyone need a refill?" I ask, glaring down at Tucker. I'm watching his every move trying to pick up on any flash of guilt that may appear, but I get nothing. Just *pleasant surprise* written on his features.

"Hey Darlin', I thought you had hot yoga for another half hour or so," he says, glancing down at his watch.

"It ended early," I say, cutting my eyes to the woman sitting across from him who looks as though she's getting more uncomfortable by the minute.

"How was it?" he asks, shifting in his seat.

"We uh– we were burning it down," I say playfully, crossing my arms over my chest.

"Well I'll take that as a good thing." He smiles. Still failing to introduce me to the woman sitting across from him.

"Sure," I snap, turning my attention to *her*. "Hi, I'm Taylor. The girlfriend, the one who woke up in his bed this morning, and the one he was *very* eager to meet in the shower about 30 minutes from now. And believe me, he's not just interested in washing my hair. And *you are?*"

"Ah, so this is Taylor." She looks at Tucker who is smirking. He nods and she turns to face me again. "I'm Alice. It's a pleasure to meet you," she introduces herself as her face turns red.

"Mm, is it?" I sass, feeling my claws come out more with every passing second.

"Well, I actually have to get going. I'm glad you called Tucker, don't be a stranger." Alice points a finger at Tucker before turning back to me and winking.

Maybe Tucker isn't the only one who has to wink for me to feel homicidal.

Tucker nods and gives her an appreciative smile. I can feel my ears begin to heat as Alice slides out of the booth, gracefully making her way to the exit.

"Care to explain who the *hell* that was?" I seethe.

"*That* was Alice," Tucker says, standing from his seat. I roll my eyes, placing my hands on my hips.

"Yeah, I'm not stupid Tucker. Just ill informed. Alice is…" I wave my hand in the air impatiently.

"My therapist." His answer is so calm and collected. He doesn't even seem bothered by the fact that I…

"Oh. *oh shit.*" My hands fly up to my mouth as I spin to face the door that Alice has well passed by now. I glance over and see Shane, wide eyed and searching for answers.

"Yeah," he whispers.

"I basically just told your therapist we were going to have sex in the shower." My hands move from covering my mouth to covering my eyes. Wishing I could wipe the last few minutes from existence.

"Yes, you did. Wanna tell me what's got you all riled up today." I peek through my fingers to see Tucker smirking back at me. Amused by my unhinged actions as always.

"I don't know. I just... We were just over there having lunch and then I saw you over here with *her* and I... I just didn't like how it looked." Tucker glances behind me and my gaze follows to see Shane staring not so subtly at us. He salutes her with two fingers and she smiles awkwardly, before sinking back down into her seat.

"And how exactly did it look?" he asks, crossing his arms over his chest.

"It looked like you were with a woman that wasn't me, and I didn't know anything about it. Or anything about *her*." The vulnerability behind my words makes me feel like I'm standing naked in the middle of this restaurant.

"So you pretended to be a waitress because..." he trails off, letting me fill in the blanks.

"I thought I could catch you off guard and–" I stare down at my feet, unable to meet his gaze or finish my sentence.

"Catch me off guard and what? Catch me cheating on you?" He takes a step closer, gripping my chin to bring my gaze to his. "Do you really think I would do that to you? If you recall, I waited for a *year* just to have a chance with you, baby. Why would I throw away everything we have after that, huh?" Once again, Tucker is right. So sure about us. So sure nothing will go wrong. The thing that both terrifies and comforts me about him.

"Okay, I get it. I was acting crazy. You and your stupid, magic dick have made me crazier than ever. And I was pretty crazy *before* I ever rode you in your Bronco on the side of a highway." My mouth snaps shut as I realize we are still very much in a public place. Tucker laughs and places his hands on my arms, drawing my attention to his dreamy green eyes.

"And I fucking love every crazy thing you do. But one day you're gonna have to accept that and trust me, Darlin'. Because no matter how much I love watching you get all worked up and jealous, I'd much rather see you come to a point where you can completely trust me with that beautiful heart of yours." He leans in and kisses my forehead, making me feel relieved *and* like a total idiot for ever doubting him.

"Go enjoy your lunch with Shane. I'm gonna head out, but I'll see you later, alright?" I nod as he makes his way to the counter to pay. For the first time since Tucker and I got together, things feel off between us when he walks away.

That's the thing though, I *do* trust Tucker. I trust him more than I've ever trusted anyone. Which is why I went a little crazy when I saw him with another woman that I knew nothing about. I walk back over to Shane with my tail between my legs, and I can see that she's dying for information.

"Well you didn't scratch her eyes out, so that's a good sign. Who was that?" She picks up a french fry, popping in her mouth while she impatiently awaits my answer.

"Um, it was his therapist."

"Oh! So no sweat then. Whew," she says, relieved.

"Mmm. Maybe it *would have been* no sweat. If I hadn't acted like a dog marking its territory before I ever even knew her name." I bury my face in my hands, reliving the horrifying conversation all over again.

"You didn't." Shane freezes in her seat.

"Oh, but I did," I say, still not looking up.

"What did you say?" She pries my hands away from my face, forcing me to look at her.

"Nothing. Just that..." Shane's eyes are wide with anticipation. I roll mine when I finally admit. "That I was his girlfriend and I may have made it painfully clear that we would be having sex in the shower after their lunch date or whatever the hell this was."

"Oh my god, Taylor." Shane blinks like I just slapped her.

"*I know*," I grumble, dropping my head into my folded arms on the table. "What the hell is wrong with me? Why did I even go over there?" I mumble, unsure if Shane can even understand the words coming out of my mouth.

"Because you care, babe. The man you're in love with was sitting at a restaurant with another woman that you *don't* know. Any girl in your position would make the same assumption." Shane rubs my arm in a comforting motion. "Honestly, I probably would have poured the water *on* them. But maybe that's my hormones talking," she continues, making me laugh.

We finish our lunch while discussing how not to start any more kitchen fires, and how I probably should just see if my mom can teach us via FaceTime. Shane even pulled out her phone and schooled us both on the difference between cooking and baking.

Baking requires an oven. So simple.

All the while, I can't stop thinking about the massive apology I owe Tucker. His words from the night he showed up at my house after disappearing, start playing on a loop in my mind.

"I just refuse to let things I've worked so hard to heal from, keep me captive in my destructive feelings."

Because that's exactly what I'm doing. Letting things I claim I've healed from keep me captive in my destructive feelings. Which, unfortunately for me, means causing public scenes and discussing my sex life with a perfect stranger.

God I've got to get it together.

Chapter 38

Tucker

I'VE BEEN FIRMLY PLANTED at my kitchen counter since I got home from lunch, mulling over the details that will go into selling my company and becoming co-owner of the bar. I hated leaving things with Taylor the way we did, but my mind was elsewhere from the moment I left the gym. I knew I needed to see through the lunch I'd set up with Alice– talking through what happened at the hospital along with the thought of a major career change seemed like something that needed to be done. Though I never thought it would end up the way it did. I had told Alice all about Taylor, but had failed miserably at telling Taylor about Alice.

My eyes are going blurry from staring at my computer screen for hours on end, so when I hear a knock at the door, I welcome the interruption. I shuffle to the door in my black sweatpants, and turn my ball cap backwards to look through the peephole. When I see Taylor standing on the porch I don't bother looking for a shirt to put on. I open the door and her mouth immediately falls open as her eyes scan over my body.

"Umm, hi." She shakes her head, awkwardly raising a hand to wave at me.

"Hey there Darlin'. You alright?" I lean against the door and smirk at her. We've been together for weeks now and she still gets rosy in the face when she looks at me.

"I'll be great once you tell me you don't open the door for everyone looking like that." She waves a hand up and down my body, laughing nervously as she does.

"Nah, normally I don't get this dressed up. Most times I stick to just the ball cap. Seems to shorten the sales pitches." I wink at her and her face drops.

"Not funny." I step to the side, gesturing for her to come in. She steps in the door holding a Tupperware container in her hands.

"To what do I owe the pleasure of your unexpected visit?" I ask. She walks straight to the kitchen, taking in the computer and pile of paperwork on the island where I had been working. She sets the container on the counter, not bothering to ask about the mess, then she turns to me and lets out a deep breath.

"I owe you an apology."

"What for?" I lean against the counter, crossing my arms over my chest. I notice the way her gaze falls to my arms before she drags her eyes back up to mine.

"For acting the way I did at the restaurant today. You were right. I was worked up and I was jealous. Because as much as I wish this weren't the truth, I thought you were on a date with someone else. I know we've spent a *lot* of um… *quality time* together, but we haven't really been on a date yet. Like, out in public, just the two of us. So I got jealous thinking you were on one with someone else." She crosses her arms, staring down at her feet. Showing a vulnerability I know she hates.

"I do trust you though, Tucker. I think I trust you more than I've ever trusted anyone else. So when I was met with something that looked a lot like deceit, it hurt. It hurt a lot. But I admit, I could have handled it *much* better than the way I did. Like, just asking you about it instead of assuming." Her eyes are as gray as a storm cloud tonight, looking into mine with a raw truth I've never seen before.

"I am so sorry, Tucker. For making you think I didn't trust you. Will you forgive me?" I push from my place on the counter, walking over to take her in my arms.

"Of course I forgive you. Thank you for being honest about how you felt today. Just promise me that from now on, you'll talk to me before assuming the worst. Because I will *always* be honest with you. I'd rather die than do anything to hurt you. And before you say anything, I know that's a bold statement, but I need you to hear me when I say it. I will *never* purposefully do anything to hurt you. And if I ever do break your heart– God forbid–you have my permission to inflict one of those medical deaths you can make look like an accident." Taylor laughs, wiping away a tear that has rolled down her cheek.

"Deal." I lean down and kiss her, having missed the way her lips feel on mine. Even a few hours without Taylor is entirely too long. When I pull away from her the container she set on the counter catches my eye again.

"What do we have here?" I tap the box with my knuckle.

"Well, since we're on the topic of honesty..." I raise a brow at her awaiting further explanation. "Shane and I weren't at hot yoga today."

"Oh, no?"

"No. We, uh, were at a beginners baking class." She scrunches her nose at me.

"Is that so?"

"It is. Since you and Max can both cook, we started feeling rather inferior in that area. We thought we'd take cooking classes and surprise you both."

"You know there's a difference between baking and cooking, right?" I ask, genuinely curious.

"Yes, thanks to our best friend, Google, we figured that out." She rolls her eyes. More at herself than at me. "Anyways, we kind of set the classroom on fire. We thought it would be best for us *not* to return, and instead we recruited my mom to teach us a few things via

FaceTime. Today was our first class, and *those* are the product of our success." She beams, but my mind is still stuck on one small detail.

"You set the classroom on fire?" I repeat back to her.

"It was like a baby fire, it's fine." She waves a dismissive hand in front of her before reaching for the container. "So, do you want to try one or not?"

"Well, that depends. You still haven't told me what *that* is yet." She grins at me mischievously as she removes the lid.

"Marilyn's famous chocolate chip cookies." She bites her lip in excitement.

"Oh, I absolutely want one, are you kidding?" I remember how amazing her mom's cookies were when we were visiting them in Colorado. If Taylor and Shane's taste anything like that, these cookies won't last an hour here. She grabs one from the container and holds it up to my lips. I take the whole thing in my mouth, making her squeal when I nip at her finger.

"You animal!" She laughs. The cookie is still warm and is basically melting in my mouth. I wink at her as I swallow it down and her cheeks instantly blush.

"Baby, I'm not gonna lie to you. Those cookies–" I nod to the container, watching as nerves settle on her face. "Are even better than your moms." She throws her arms around me and squeals.

"Wait a second. You said you can't cook, but I thought you made something for Shane's bachelorette party? What was it, dick shaped pasta?" I pull her back by her hips, and she rolls her lips together to stifle a laugh.

"Yeahhh. That was the exception. It's Shane's favorite and it took *many* failed Pinterest recipes to finally get one to taste right," she groans.

"But you did it. I think you're more capable than you give yourself credit for. If you ever want to try a new recipe and Marilyn isn't available, you can always call me. I'd love to cook with you sometime." I kiss her forehead, bringing a soft smile to her lips.

"Now, I have something I need to ask you," I say, plastering a very serious look on my face.

"Okay…"

"Taylor, will you go on a date with me? A proper one." Her whole face lights up as she shakes her head eagerly.

"I would love that."

Taylor and I walk hand in hand down the sidewalk as the spring night's breeze blows her red curls away from her face. She looks fucking stunning as always, in her blue spaghetti strap dress and black platform heels, making it hard for me to look anywhere but at her.

"So what was all that paperwork on your counter the other day?" she asks, as her heels click against the concrete.

"Well, I was actually going to talk to you about that tonight." She turns her head to look up at me. "I think I'm selling The Landry Architect Group." She stops walking, keeping my hand firm in her grasp.

"What! Why?" She gapes at me, making me laugh.

"I'll explain more when we sit down. Do you have a preference of where we eat?" I ask, as we're stopped conveniently in front of a steakhouse.

"No preference, anything is fine with me." She smiles.

"Alright Darlin', right this way then." I open the door and place my hand on the small of her back to guide her in front of me.

"Wow, so you're going to sell your company and go into business with Max?" Taylor asks, taking a sip of her margarita. We're finally out on our first date, and we're discussing… work. We stopped in front of City Steakhouse, one of the nicer restaurants around town and they miraculously had a table for two available.

"I think so. I mean, I really want to." I sigh. "Max is right, I'm burnt out where I'm at now and I don't want to spend the rest of my life doing something I don't love. But I just don't know if I should. I'd be selling the company that *I* built, not to mention I'm in the middle of a contract that's going *nowhere* because the people keep wanting to make changes at every other corner."

"Well, if you find someone to buy the company, could they fulfill the contract? That way it's not technically broken, it just wouldn't be *you* finishing it."

"Maybe. I have a list of possible buyers that I could reach out to." I stop and watch as Taylor nods her head, listening intently and keeping up with the conversation that I'm sure isn't best suited for our first date.

"Then do it. Reach out. You're amazing at your job, and I know you worked hard to make it what it is. But Tucker, if you're not happy there anymore then don't let something as simple as pride hold you back from something better."

"You know, this is why I love you so damn much. I knew you were the person I needed to talk to about this." I bring her hand to my lips, planting a kiss on her fingers.

"Anytime." She smiles sweetly at me as the waiter approaches our table. I give her a wink before turning my attention to him.

"Good evening guys, I'm Michael and I'll be your waiter tonight. Have you had a chance to look over the menu yet?"

"No, sorry. We haven't." I look back at Taylor to ask if she needs a minute, but the state I find her in is alarming. She's frozen in place, all color has drained from her once rosy cheeks, and her eyes are locked on the waiter.

"You alright Darlin'?" I squeeze her hand and she turns her head woodenly to look at me.

"Excuse me." Is all she says before she exits the booth, headed straight for the restrooms. I want to take a moment to appreciate the way her knee length dress is hugging her in all the right places. But it's hard to focus on her body when I'm more worried about her state of panic.

"Taylor," I call after her as I stand to my feet. Whatever is wrong I'm not leaving her to deal with alone.

Or at least that's my plan until…

"I thought I recognized her," the waiter says in realization. "She hasn't changed a bit since high school." My jaw tightens with every word out of his mouth. I turn to face him and almost crack a molar when I read his name tag again.

Michael.

There's no fucking way. My intention to chase after Taylor gets put momentarily on old.

"You knew Taylor in high school?" I feign ignorance.

"Oh yeah. Well, I more than knew her, if you know what I mean. Careful with that one, she can be a little…*intense.*" The motherfucker nudges me with his shoulder like we're sharing some sort of inside joke. I take him by the arm, doing my best to stay composed.

The way I wish this dining room were a parking lot right now.

"Here's what I know about *that one.* She is undeniably the best thing that has ever happened to me. I waited *very* patiently just to have a chance with her. I know for a fact that I should rip your throat out right here and now for the things you've said about her. But I won't, simply because I can't love her properly from a jail cell. If you ever speak another ill word about her they'll be your last, I promise you that." I shove him back, dusting invisible lint from the shoulders of his white dress shirt.

"Jesus man, what is it you think I said about her?" He looks on in disbelief. Before I can tell him that he knows what the fuck he said, I'm saved the trouble.

"*She's too much, man. She's literally crazy. She even cried after. Who fucking does that? I've gotta break up with her, she's way too much drama. I just gotta play it right, can't have people thinking I just used her like that. I have a reputation to uphold.* Does any of *that* ring a bell?" Taylor's voice is stone cold and steady.

Michaels eyes go wide, all the color draining from his face with the realization. He turns around to face her, giving me a clearer view of her myself. Her arms are crossed over her chest, shoulders squared, chin lifted.

My girl is ready for battle.

"How did–" Michael starts.

"How did I know that? It's called a butt dial, Michael." Venom drips from every word.

I sit back watching her mend this old wound once and for all. She takes a few calculated steps toward him, stopping right at the edge of our table.

"Ugh. You were never worth my tears anyways. You know, the fact that you're still going around referring to women as *intense* just because we have feelings, tells me you never became man enough to handle one. Go to hell," she says, grabbing her water glass from the table and pouring it over his head. Gasps sound all around the restaurant but I just stand back smiling.

"Actually, I *do* have a preference." She smirks at me. "Can we go somewhere else? I'm not too fond of the waitstaff here," she requests, looking him up and down in disgust.

"I'll take you wherever you want to go, baby." I put some cash down on the table for our drinks, then drape my arm around Taylor's shoulder as we head towards the door. "I am so fucking proud of you. That was the sexiest thing I've ever seen." I lean down and take her lips captive in mine.

"Wait until you see what's under this dress," she teases, turning to face me as she walks backwards on the sidewalk.

Nothing she mouths.

Chapter 39

Taylor

Tucker rushes up to me, scooping me up in his arms as he dips into a dimly lit alleyway. We stop by the back door of the restaurant we were just at and he plants my feet back on the ground, pinning me against the brick wall.

"What are you doing?" I whisper, letting my eyes drift to his lips, that are a hair away from my nose. I can smell the whiskey on his breath and it turns me on thinking about how he'd taste like it if I leaned in an inch.

"I'm showing you just how fucking proud I am that you're mine," he growls, before sinking his teeth into my neck.

I whimper at the pain, but he eases it immediately like he always does. Licking and kissing along the spot he knows sends shivers down my spine. I arch my back, pressing my peaked nipples against his chest. He wraps one hand around my neck, taking my mouth captive with his own when my lips part at his touch. The warmth of his hand around my throat has wetness pooling between my bare thighs. As if he can sense it, he slides a hand up my dress, running his fingers along my slick entrance.

"You like having my hand around your throat, don't you baby?" he whispers against my lips. I keep my eyes locked with his as I shake my head. He smirks at me and my need for him feels more intense than ever before.

"That's my good girl." He slides a finger into my slick pussy, followed by a second moments later. He pumps and hooks them just right until I'm writhing beneath his touch. He teases my clit just barely with his thumb, making me weak in the knees.

"Tucker," I whine, needing the release he's teasing me with. He pulls his fingers away completely, picking me up and placing me on top of a wooden crate nearby.

"What are you doing?" I squeal, looking around frantically.

"We never made it to dinner, and I'm starving," he answers with desire burning in his gorgeous green eyes. He steps between my legs, tipping my chin so I can't look anywhere but at him.

"Mind if I feast on you, Darlin'?" He rubs the bridge of my nose with the tip of his, letting his hands glide up my thighs making my eyes flutter closed. My dress rises higher and higher on my legs until I can feel a slight breeze along the wetness he abandoned.

"I'd never let you starve." Tucker kisses me once before dropping to his knees.

He wraps his arms around my thighs, lifting me up to bring me to the edge of the crates where he needs me, and wastes no time making a meal out of me. The warmth of his tongue and the scruff from his beard work together to drive me wild. My head falls back as I savor every kiss along my clit, moaning when his tongue dives deep into me. My fingers tangle in his hair, as he slides two fingers back into me, kissing and sucking on my clit until I'm right on the edge of my orgasm.

"Oh my god, Tucker I'm gonna come." His fingers continue to hook inside me as his eyes find mine.

"That's right baby, let all of Nashville know who's good girl you are." His lips brush against my clit with every word, keeping the sensation there.

Right as his tongue goes back to work and I scream his name, the back door of the restaurant flies open. My eyes are sealed shut as I ride the waves of my orgasm, and Tucker doesn't let up until I'm completely satisfied. Zero fucks are given about who just came out of that door.

We're angled in a way that I'm not exposed to whomever it is, but when I finally open my eyes again Tucker is standing protectively between my legs. He pulls my dress back down to cover me better, and I look over to see Michael standing right outside the door. Wide eyed and holding a bag of trash.

"See, *real men* get on their knees for their women. Not bring them to theirs in tears." He holds a hand out for me to hop down from the crates. "Let's go Darlin'." I can feel the heat in my cheeks, though I'm not sure if it was from the insane orgasm or slight embarrassment that someone saw it.

Michael stays speechless as we make our way back down the alley, and onto the busy sidewalk. I glance up at Tucker, and see his face still glistening from my arousal.

"How's it feel, baby?" Tucker asks, draping his arm around my shoulder.

"What do you mean?"

"To have closure." He glances down at me, and I realize that he's right.

I stayed in a state of brokenness for so long over someone not worth a single second of my time. I was so young when Michael broke my heart, and instead of facing him about it, I ran away. Letting myself believe that the amount of hurt I endured at his hands was what awaited me in any future relationships. Now I have closure, *and* a man who isn't afraid to claim me proudly in the most delicious way.

"It feels pretty damn good." He plants a kiss on my temple.

"Okay, now *where* am I taking you to eat?" He squeezes me closer, giving me the same sense of security I always have when I'm with him.

"Honestly, I kind of just want to go home," I admit.

"Takeout it is. Let's go home, Peach." He smiles, as we approach his Bronco. He walks around to open my door, and I don't bother telling him I can do it myself. Because if there's one thing I've learned about Tucker– it's that he's well aware I can take care of myself and fight my own battles. He just loves me enough not to let me do it alone. He knows when to take control and when to let me lead. But no matter what he's always there. We ride back to my house with music playing quietly in the background as Tucker reenacts Michael's face when he looked at him from between my legs.

"You would have thought the man was looking straight at an alien," Tucker quips.

"Well, I'm sure understanding female pleasure *is* just as foreign to him." I glance out of the corner of my eye to see Tucker's mouth hanging open.

"Just when I thought you couldn't get any sexier you dish out a burn like that." He shakes his head as I double over in laughter. The good vibes stop when we pull into my driveway and I see someone lingering around my porch.

"Zander?" I say out loud, squinting to get a better look.

"This night has officially become the visitation for the ghost of boyfriends past." Tucker sighs as he puts the truck in park.

"They're not dead, Tucker." I roll my eyes as I unbuckle my seatbelt.

"Not yet, maybe," he mumbles under his breath as he hops out of the driver's seat. He comes around and opens my door, helping me out so I don't break my ankle in these heels. Before we can make it halfway up the sidewalk to the front door, Zander is stumbling on his feet and slurring his words.

"Oh, how chivalrous of you to open her door for her." It's no surprise that he's already being an asshole.

"What the hell are you doing here Zander?" I demand, crossing my arms over my chest and keeping a safe distance from his drunk ass.

"Well, *Taylor*. Funny you should ask. See, when you got back from your little vacation a while ago I tried talking to you at work. Maybe you'll remember, you got up in the middle of our conversation to answer your phone." He wags his finger between me and Tucker. "I was trying to tell you I'd been trying to contact you the whole week you were gone. I was trying to apologize for how horribly things went between us, but your phone went straight to voicemail. Every. Single. Time." He takes a step closer with each enunciated word.

Tucker takes a step slightly in front of me, but I just tip my chin up at him. Zander's eyes cut over to Tucker before landing on me again.

"Imagine my surprise when I went after you that day and saw you all cozied up with *him*," he snarls. "So what, you just ran off to start sleeping with him while you were still stringing me along?"

"Hey man, you're out of line," Tucker's deep voice booms from beside me. After the night we had, Zander has no idea what thin ice he's skating on right now.

"No, Zander. I didn't *string you along*. I'm not sure in what universe you'd think I was still interested after the way things ended on our last date. You let me get soaked in beer and didn't get out of the damn booth until someone else offered to help me. You grade A asshole." Zander rears back like I just slapped him, but from my peripheral I can see Tucker smirking.

"Whatever you say. I'll bet you left a date with me and fucked him in the parking lot, like the slut I'm sure you are." Without another word Tucker grabs Zander by the throat and backs him up until he reaches the support beam on my porch.

"I've heard more than enough slander towards my girl tonight to last me a lifetime. Apologize," Tucker snarls. His knuckles turn white as Zander's face keeps growing red.

"What," he struggles to get out.

"Did I fucking stutter? You will apologize for speaking down on her character just because she chose someone else over you. You pathetic piece of shit. Apologize. Now."

"I'm sorry." His voice is barely audible with Tucker's grip so tight around his throat.

"The reason she didn't answer your phone calls is because *I* blocked your number from her phone. I play dirty to get what I want, so you can talk shit about me all you want. But you keep *her* name out of your mouth if you wish to continue using it." Zander shakes his head but no words come out.

"Glad we understand each other. Have yourself a good night." And just like that, Zander's eyes flutter shut and Tucker lets go of his throat, letting him fall into my flower beds.

"Oh, my god!" I yell, as Zander's body hits the ground with a thud. "Did you actually kill him?" I ask, peeking over to see if he's still moving.

"You know, you don't sound as concerned as you do curious." Tucker raises a brow as he turns to face me again.

"Well… " I shrug.

"He's just passed out, unfortunately." He wraps me in his arms, kissing me as if there isn't a drunk ex-boyfriend passed out in the shrubs beside us.

"Takeout fajitas, right?" He smiles at me wagging his eyebrows

"Tucker!" I yell.

"What? No fajitas?" He frowns.

"There is a drunk person passed out in my flower beds. How do you plan to explain that to the fajita delivery guy?" I hold a hand out to Zander who finally shows proof of life with an involuntary groan.

"Fine. We'll call him an uber, *then* order you food."

"Thank you." We sit on the porch until the uber arrives for Zander. Tucker slaps him awake and shoves him into the car. The driver looks slightly panicked until I lean over his passenger window and turn on the charm.

"Thank you *so* much. I trust you'll get my friend here home safe? Poor thing can't handle his alcohol I guess." I smile and the guy nods, not taking his eyes off of my cleavage daring to spill out of my dress.

"Unless you're trying to get me into a *third* fight tonight, stand your ass up, now," Tucker growls from beside me. My spine straightens immediately and the car pulls away from the curb.

We go in the house and get changed into something more comfortable. Tucker and I officially have *the drawer* at each other's houses for nights just like tonight. When our food arrives we snuggle up on the couch and let Sons of Anarchy play while we eat. I absentmindedly keep watching the door, even though I know there are no other unhinged exes that could show up tonight. But I'm still rattled by what Zander did. Coming here that drunk, going off about something as wild as me being with Tucker. I don't even realize how zoned in on my own thoughts I am until Tucker's voice breaks me out of my daze.

"Move in with me."

"What?" I shake my head, thinking I may have misheard him.

"I want you to move in with me," he continues, rubbing my feet the way he has been since we finished our meal. His pace is steady, and his features are calm.

"If this is because of tonight, I can just get security cameras installed or something."

"It's not just about tonight, Darlin'. Though it *did* sell me on the fact even further," he says in a more serious tone. "We've spent more nights together than we have apart ever since we got back from San Francisco, and I don't know about you but I don't like the nights we spend apart. I'd rather wake up choking on a mouth full of your hair than wake up in an empty bed." He laughs, making me roll my eyes.

"Are you sure?" I bite my lip trying to contain my excitement.

"I've never been more sure of anything in my life. Move in with me baby." He pulls me over by my legs until they're laying on either side of his hips. His hands find my waist and his eyes dance with anticipation.

"Okay, yes!" I finally answer. Excitement fills his face as he brings me in for a kiss.

ME

Looking for a real estate agent. Anyone know of a good one?

LAUREN

Ha ha. Very funny. Are you selling your house?

ME

I will be.

RUBY

Mysterious.

ME

I'm moving in with Tucker.

LAUREN

Oh my god, that's amazing!

SHANE

Aww. I'm gonna miss that little house.

LEAH

Good job guys, you're making Shane cry.

ME

Everything makes Shane cry. It's called   baby
hormones

Chapter 40

Tucker

"Was a full brunch spread really necessary for us to pack up your house?" I tease Taylor as I look at the kitchen island covered in a variety of fruits, waffles, croissants, and breakfast meats. And let's not forget the mimosas she whipped up in a matter of seconds.

"Yes, it was necessary. All of our friends are coming to help us pack. The least we can do is offer to feed them," she insists, pouring herself a mimosa. "I mean, have you *seen* how much stuff is in just my closet alone?"

"Good point. Maybe we should get *more* food." I smirk, making her roll her eyes in the way I love. The way that tells me I'm pressing all the right buttons to get her worked up.

"So I guess maybe we should figure out what stuff I'm bringing, what can stay with the house, and what I need to get rid of. I mean, we won't need two couches, two beds, and two TV's," she rattles off, tapping a pen against the notebook in her hand.

"Well I vote we take your bed cause I like it better. We can keep whichever couch you prefer, or we can buy a new one together, and we can put one of the TV's in the spare room." I walk over wrapping my arms around her waist, brushing her hair to the side before planting kisses along her neck.

She has her hair down with her natural curls in perfect disarray, and the bandana she often wears like a headband tied around her wrist. She's wearing cutoff denim shorts with the black shirt I gave her tied in a knot at her waist–the same outfit she wore out of the hotel the first day of our road trip. I'll never stop being amazed at how she looks so incredibly beautiful no matter what she's wearing.

"How did I know you would be the one to make *moving,* of all things, something so simple and unproblematic?" she smiles, turning in my arms to wrap hers around my neck.

"Because I know you're already a little sad to be leaving this house and the memories you made here. I want to make everything else as enjoyable as I can," I tell her, kissing the tip of her nose. When she bites her lip I can't help but take them with my own, bringing my hand up to cup her face as I deepen our kiss. A loud cough and clearing of someone's throat tears us apart as we look up to see Shane and Max standing in the doorway.

"I will not be packing anything that you've had sex on top of," Max says, making Shane swat his arm. Riley whimpers before running over to the couch and making herself at home.

"Well then feel free to leave," I joke, making Taylor pinch the back of my arm. Max just grumbles at my witty response. "Don't be a prude, Maxwell." I smirk at him and he huffs, trying to hide a grin creeping across his face.

"Packing party is here!" Leah announces, walking in with bubble wrap and packing tape. Lauren comes in behind her holding disassembled brown boxes, followed by Ruby and Hendrix.

"*Roaaaaaar,*" Hendrix screeches when Ruby sets him down. He holds his arms in a T-Rex motion and stomps through the house, making all the girls giggle and scream in fake terror.

"We can put him on pillow duty or something," Ruby suggests, as she stands with both hands propped on her hips.

"Sounds like a plan. Right Hend-rex?" Taylor says, emphasizing the dinosaur nickname she gave him. He smiles and gives her a high five. "Alright, let's do this." Taylor takes a deep breath and all the girls go over and squeeze her in a group hug. I glance at Max and we share a knowing look. Two years ago he and I were going through the motions of life.

Work. Gym. Range. Repeat.

Then one night a group of girls helping their friend mourn the cluster fuck that was her life, came into Chattahoochies and changed our whole dynamic. The best friend I thought I'd never see genuinely smile again is now *married* and about to be a dad. I'm moving in with the girl of my dreams, and Ruby is thriving with her new group of friends instead of going it alone like she had for so long. We've built our own little dysfunctional family and I fucking love it. Though one dysfunctional piece is missing.

ME

Where you at brother? Thought you were joining the packing party.

TANK

I can't do it man. I'm sorry.

ME

Well, no worries. We'll probably catch up with you at the bar tonight then.

The three little dots pop up then disappear, and nothing else comes through. I get a weird feeling about the way he responded but before I can act on it, I hear glass shatter in the kitchen, derailing my train of thought.

"I'm sorry Aunt Taylor," Hendrix says quietly, as tears fill his little eyes.

"Oh don't you worry about it little man. I never liked that bowl anyways." She winks, bringing a sad smile to his face. He runs up to her, wrapping his arms around her waist.

"Okay, what do you say you help me pack up all my pillows and blankets into these boxes, while we let someone sweep up all this glass?" she asks him. He shakes his head in excitement and stomps off towards the spare bedroom.

"Tucker, you and Max are on heavy lifting, *obviously*. Ladies, do your thing." All the girls nod and playfully salute the woman in charge. *My* woman in charge.

After Hendrix completed his job of packing all non breakable items, he props up in the master bedroom with Max, Riley and I while we disassemble the bed.

"Feel like taking a trip to the mall between unloading? Maybe visit your old pal Glenda," I ask Max, as I drop screws into the bag Taylor labeled *bed frame*.

"Holy shit, man." Max looks at me, propping his arm up on his knee as he sits back on the floor. "You're all in aren't you?"

"I've never been anything less when it comes to Taylor, you know that." I continue working, trying not to make this moment seem as mushy as it probably is.

"Hell yeah man. Let's do it," Max agrees.

As our conversation ends we start hearing the girls' voices coming from the kitchen.

"I'm just gonna miss this house so much. It always smells like cupcakes when you walk in."

"This was where we finally got to be roomies when I moved back from California."

"Remember when we ate dick pasta here?"

· · ·

"Did someone just say dick pasta?" Max's head snaps up, making me snort.

"Yeah, don't ask."

"I have loved this house so much. All the girls nights, vent sessions, trash TV watched, sleepovers, and nights getting ready to go out that happened here will live in my heart forever. But this house isn't my home anymore, Tucker is. And I think I'm really ready to move onto the next chapter of my life. Something I truly never thought I would say."

I hear sniffles and sobs echoing through the hallway, making a lump form in my own throat.

"Alright. This one is ready to go. We got all the heavy stuff loaded right? The next trip is just boxes of clothes and shit?" Max asks. I clear my throat, trying to force the emotions out before I speak.

"Yeah. Which is probably a whole Uhaul's worth, with Taylor's wardrobe." I laugh. Max blows out a puff of air as he looks into the closet. We grab the bedframe and haul it out to the truck, just as we slide it into place, Max's phone starts to ring.

"Hello? He didn't? Alright. I'll see what's going on. Yeah, thanks. Bye." He hangs up the phone giving me a concerned look. "Tank didn't show up to open the bar. Have you heard from him today?" he asks as we walk back up to the house.

Suddenly the last couple of months start playing in my mind like a movie recap. And like pieces to a puzzle, every sign I failed to see has been right in front of my face the whole time. The heavy drinking, the playful facade, the drunk call while I was in Colorado. I feel like a fucking idiot for not seeing it for what it was sooner.

"I gotta go. Tell Taylor I'll be back." I grab the keys from my pocket and rush to my Bronco.

"Tucker." Max is right on my heels, his voice is laced with a knowing concern.

"How did I not fucking see it, man?" Panic shoots like lightning through my whole body when I see the look on his face.

"I'll tell her. Go. *Go!*" He nods me off urgently. I throw the Bronco in drive and hit 20 over the speed limit the whole way to Tank's apartment.

"*FUCK!*" I shout, punching the steering wheel.

Please don't let it be too late.

I don't bother knocking, or yelling for him to open the door. Because if he didn't answer, or yell at me to go away, I would crumble at his doorstep. I take the stairs two at a time when I get to his building, and when I push the door open–I hear it almost immediately.

Click.

I rush in, my ears ringing from the sheer panic I feel. My head is on a swivel as I look for him, and waves of anxiety and slight relief fight for control when I see him sitting on his couch. There's a void look in his eyes as he stares down at the side arm he's holding in his lap.

"Tank." I try to get his attention, though my feet are rooted so deeply to his floor I can't manage to walk over to him.

He doesn't move. He doesn't even blink.

"Tank!" I yell again, finally lifting my feet through the heaviness I feel in them. I walk over and take his firearm, setting it on the coffee table next to his dog tags and an envelope with my name on it. I feel bile trying to creep up my throat when the entirety of the situation hits me. I take his face in my hands as I look him over, ensuring there isn't a wound I have missed through my panic. The tiniest bit of life creeps back into his eyes as they make contact with my own.

"It didn't fire," he whispers. I feel bile in my throat and I can almost hear the sound of my heart shattering inside my chest.

"You–" I start, but I can't get the words to come out.

"It misfired." I see it happen. The dam of emotions breaks through the shock, and before I know it, he begins to fall apart. His eyes dart around the room and he pushes to his feet, making me stumble backwards as I stand with him. I quickly grab his gun from the table, putting the safety in place before holstering it in my waistband. He paces the room, running his hands through his hair.

"It didn't work. Why didn't it work? I can't do this. I can't fucking do this. Why the fuck can't I just be put out of my misery already?" he yells, as he pulls at his hair.

"Tank, look at me. *TANK!*" When his eyes meet mine, I can see him drowning. The plea for help that his voice kept silent is a deafening scream behind his darkened eyes. "Sit down, let me get you some water." I try to guide him to sit but he shoves me away and shakes his head.

"I don't want any fucking water. I don't want to sit down. I want *out!*" he yells.

"No you don't. You hear me? You're not leaving me like this, Tank. I won't let you." I grab him by the shoulders and shake him. "Look at me," I demand. "You are *not* giving up. You are a motherfucking Marine. You are *my* brother, and so help me, you will *not* leave this world without a fight. You're gonna fight, Tank, and if I have to fight for you until you're ready to do it yourself, then that's what I'll fucking do."

"Why bother? What's the point? I don't have a purpose here, not anymore," he chokes out.

"You think that just because you left the Marines you don't have a purpose? Try again. I left, Max left–" I begin trying to calm him down, but that only seems to make things escalate.

"Yeah, Tucker. You *chose* to leave. I wasn't given a fucking choice! One stupid fall and I was done. I *was* fighting my fight. I was making a difference over there, and just like that–it was taken away from me. I didn't get a fucking choice! *THIS* WAS MY FUCKING CHOICE!" He points to the spot I found him in. "And it was just taken away too."

"And I will be thankful every single *fucking* day that fate knew you weren't done here. Because you have so much to live for, brother. You just have to find something that you love, find a reason and fucking *live* for it. And you won't find it at the bottom of a bottle or a barrel."

His breaths are short and quick, his chest heaving as he struggles to get air into his lungs. His anger and adrenaline morph into severe panic.

"Tank!" Ruby calls as she runs through the door. I step aside as she rushes up to him.

"Ruby? What are you doing here?" I ask in confusion. She shoves her phone in my hands as she takes Tank's face in hers. I look down to see a text from Tank illuminated on the screen.

11:30AM
TANK

Thank you for being such a good friend. I think I'll miss you the most. I'm sorry I couldn't tell you in person.

He sent this five minutes before I walked in the door.

"Tank, look at me." Ruby's voice is steady as she looks up at him, still cradling his face in her hands. "Take a deep breath in through your nose." She rubs her thumbs along his jawline. Tank takes in a shaky breath. "Another one. Deeper." He draws in a deeper breath this time, steadier than the first.

"Good. Now, can you tell me what you smell?" she asks, encouraging Tank to take another breath in.

"You," he whispers. Ruby cuts her eyes to me briefly, then turns them back to Tank.

"More specifically."

"Cherries," he answers. I stand back and watch as Ruby brings Tank down from his panic attack.

"Now tell me what you can see."

Tank smirks now. "You."

Ruby lifts a brow in disapproval.

"Your brown eyes. Like melted chocolate and caramel."

"Good." She lets go of his face and Tank takes one final deep breath. "Don't you *ever* scare me like that again." The anger in her voice is accompanied by tears welling in her eyes.

"You're a lot of things, Tank Landry, but a quitter is not one of them. You better figure your shit out and realize that there are people who are counting on you being around."

"I will," he tells her, pulling her into an embrace, looking over at me with a reassuring nod. She swipes a fallen tear away angrily, her voice shifting into humored annoyance.

"I hate closing the bar with Marco, he still doesn't know how to make a gimlet and it's literally the easiest drink in the world to learn."

Not only did she calm him in a panic, but she's making him laugh too. I could be way off, but I think I'm staring at his reason. And she's a force to be reckoned with. We sit around the table silently, as we all process what just happened. When the silence is finally broken, Tank asks Ruby and I to keep this between the three of us, wanting to get his head right before dealing with anyone else knowing. We both agree before she rushes off to the coffee shop, then back to help the girls finish packing.

Chapter 41

WHEN I WALK OUT of my bedroom with my last box of shoes, all the girls are standing in front of the island in the kitchen.

"What's going on?" I ask, as they all smile back at me in a somewhat unnerving way. When they all scoot over I see a blender, five glasses and the ingredients for Shane's famous margaritas.

"We thought we could have one last margarita before we say goodbye to the house," Lauren says. Tears well in my eyes, as I drop my box of shoes on the floor shaking my head. Shane mixes the margaritas and we all sit on the living room floor, listening to our voices echo through the empty house.

"Okay okay. So Shane is married and having baby Shine, her destiny has been fulfilled. You're about to move in with Tucker, which I can only see getting better from here. What about you Leah? We haven't seen Jackson around since Taylor's birthday. What happened there?" Lauren asks, giving her a playful nudge.

"Nothing really. I mean he's still super nice, and he's cute or whatever but we literally had nothing to talk about outside of school. I am there all day, I don't want that to be the *only* thing we have to talk about when we leave," she explains, taking a sip of her drink.

"That's true. That would make for a very short relationship. What would you guys talk about all summer?" Ruby jokes.

"Well, what about you, miss thing? You have been spending an awful lot of time with Tank lately," Leah accuses. My eyes grow wide as I look in Ruby's direction, noting the pink hue to her cheeks as she promptly denies it.

"We're *friends*. And coworkers," she adds, as if that helps her case.

"Oh yeah, working on the *night shift*." Lauren rolls her body suggestively and we all burst out laughing. Ruby just shakes her head in response.

"Okay Lu, what about you? You expect us to believe you have had *zero* love interests in the last few *years*?" We all look at her expectantly as she brings her margarita glass to her lips.

"Yes, that's exactly what I expect you to believe," she says in her mysterious tone. Leave it to Lauren to always keep us guessing. My phone dings, reverberating through the living room and when I pick it up I notice two hours have passed since we sat down.

TUCKER

Did you change your mind about moving in?

Of course not, the girls just wanted to do one more margarita before we said goodbye. I'm leaving here in 5!

TUCKER

Take your time. I'll be here when you're ready.

"Time to go ladies." We clean up our mess, and walk out together. I hand my keys to Lauren after locking the door one last time and we say our goodbyes.

The trip to Tucker's house is quiet, as I let my memories fill my mind, as well as thoughts of what my future will look like now that I'm starting a new chapter. When I made the decision to start dating again a few months ago, I never imagined I would be where I am now. I thought the best case scenario was that I would be going out to dinner with the guy I was already sleeping with, and saying I had a plus one for events. It's almost comical now, seeing how things turned out.

When I pull up to the house, it's completely dark. Tucker's Bronco isn't in the driveway like it usually is, even though he said he would be here. When I open the door to walk in the house, I'm completely taken back by what I see.

There are candles and flower petals lining the floor from the front door all the way to the sliding doors that lead to the back yard. I toss my keys in the bowl that sits on the entryway table, and place my box of shoes on the floor beside it.

When I slide the doors open, I see Tucker standing by the small fire pit, waiting for me. He's still in the same clothes he wore earlier in the day. He has his olive green medic shirt on, one of my favorites that I've restrained from stealing because it looks so damn good on him, and his dark wash blue jeans with his lace up boots. He no longer wears the backward baseball cap, and his copper brown waves look perfectly messy.

The patio lights are turned on, accompanying the many battery operated candles lining the pathway to him. I close the distance between us, noticing the mini fajita bar and key lime martini ingredients set out on his outdoor dining table. His guitar is propped up on the swing right by the fire pit, and when I make it to him, he instantly pulls me into his embrace.

"Welcome home, Darlin'." Even his voice feels like home to me.

"Tucker, what is all of this?" I laugh, waving a hand around the yard. "How long have you been waiting for me?" I gasp, wondering just how long he's been out here.

"How many times do I have to tell you, you're worth the wait." He smiles. "I wanted your first night home to be special." He kisses the top of my head, and my eyes fall closed as I take a deep breath in. The smell of musk, vanilla and apples wafts around me. He pulls me back slightly, looking down at me with a serene yet serious look on face.

"Taylor…"

"Oh, serious," I tease.

"Something happened today, something that really opened my eyes and I realized I have never been happier than I am when I'm with you. For the duration of our friendship I savored every smart ass comment, every death glare you threw my way, and every time I knew I would see you I couldn't wait to get under your skin. The day you told me you didn't want to be friends anymore, was the best day of my life. Because I knew if you would just give me one chance, that I would do whatever it took to make you mine and that plan hasn't changed. I knew I was in love with you long before I told you, but I've only fallen deeper in love with you since then. When you told me you loved me and that your heart was healed just for me, I knew I would spend the rest of my life making sure it never broke. Not by me, not if I could help it." I'm crying so hard I can barely see the blurry outline of Tucker suddenly drop down on one knee.

"Darlin', I want to spend the rest of our lives traveling the world, taking you places you've never even dreamed of going. I want to play guitar and sing for you until you insist that I dance with you instead. I want to order takeout at 3 o'clock in the morning, and watch our favorite shows while you make fun of my favorite characters. I want to watch you learn to cook and yell at my therapist. I want to spend every single day loving you in a way that reminds you that you've always been it for me. Taylor Clark, will you make me the happiest man in the world, and be my wife?" When he opens the ring box I can't even see what's inside through the tears. But I don't need to. I would still marry Tucker if there was a paper ring inside the box.

"Yes, of course I will." I blink rapidly trying to clear my blurry vision. When the tears have fallen and I can finally see clearly, I find Tucker smiling up at me.

That gorgeous smile that keeps me falling for him every single day, and his forest green eyes glimmer from the tears that fill them. He slides the ring on my finger and when I finally get a look at it, the breath I am struggling to catch escapes me all over again. A peach sapphire is set on a rose gold band, lined with tiny diamonds all the way around. He stands up, picking me up by the waist as his lips come crashing down on mine.

"I love you baby. I promise I will never stop proving to you how much. Thank you for trusting me with your heart," Tucker says, as he presses his forehead to mine.

"I love you, Tucker. Thank you for making it so easy to trust you with it." I run my fingers through his wavy red hair, letting my eyes fall closed a moment before I lean back to look at him.

"So, what happened today?" I ask, unable to fight my curiosity. Clearly it was big if it made him want to *propose*. He lets out a deep sigh, as I see him contemplating his answer.

"Can you trust that I will tell you when the time is right? I made a promise to someone that I wouldn't speak about it, and it's a promise I need to keep." I can tell it bothers him to keep whatever it is from me, but I can respect his loyalty and the need he has to keep his word.

"Of course I trust you. But you already knew that." He smiles as he leads me over to the swing, picking up his guitar as we sit down in front of the fire.

"You want to pull a Max and Shane and get married next week?" he asks, catching a death glare from me as he does.

"You know how mentally unstable I was trying to plan that wedding in a week. No way in *hell* am I rushing through planning ours," I tell him.

"Well don't make me wait too long. You know how impatient I get when it comes to making you mine." He winks at me and I roll my eyes, involuntary blushing at his words. I push the swing with my tip toes as Tucker begins playing a Luke Combs song. Being here with Tucker, in *our* backyard, with his ring on my finger and our entire future in front of us, my heart feels whole.

Epilogue

"Tucker, I swear to God if we miss this I will postpone this wedding until Hendrix is in college," Taylor yells from the doorway as I hurry to get my shoes on.

"Damn Darlin', they just called two minutes ago, don't start threatening me already." I smirk at her as I slide my ball cap on.

"This is the birth of my first godchild, and I *will not* miss it," she says, tossing my truck keys at me. I smile when I see the keychain that my beautiful fiancée stole from the Honeybee Motel, attached to my key ring.

"Yes ma'am, let's get going then." I slap her ass as she scurries out to the truck. When I turn back around from locking the door, Taylor is already in the Bronco and buckled up. I smile and shake my head as I jog up to the driver's side door.

We arrive at the hospital first, even beating the woman in labor here. The rest of the crew files in shortly after, as we fill the waiting room. Taylor goes back with Max and Shane and the rest of us wait impatiently as Taylor sends text updates.

> TAYLOR
>
> She's doing great. She's at 7cm already and progressing quickly.
>
> TAYLOR
>
> 10cm. It's baby time.
>
> TAYLOR
>
> SHE'S HERE!

"IT'S A GIRL!" Leah, Lauren and Ruby scream. Tank and I startle at the noise just as Max comes into the waiting room.

"Congratulations, brother." I laugh, bringing Max in for a hug.

"Yeah, congratulations man. We're so happy for you," Tank adds, squeezing Max's shoulder. I can't help but smile when I see how far Tank has come these last six months. Having him here today, smiling and sharing in the joy of a new life, is a moment I don't dare take for granted.

"Alright. Who wants to go meet her?" The girls are rushing out the door before Max even finishes his sentence. When we walk into the room Taylor is propped up on the bed next to Shane, while they stare down at the baby swaddled in hospital blankets with a pink and blue bow hat on.

"Hey guys," Shane whispers, glancing up at everyone. "Come on in and meet the newest member of the crew." All the girls surround the bed, cooing at the baby and asking Shane how she is feeling.

"Oh I'm fine. Just a little tired. But I didn't want to wait to introduce her to everyone." Max and I walk over to the open spot by the bed, and he sits next to Shane as he tucks baby girl's blanket under her chin.

"You ready?" he asks, wrapping an arm around her shoulder. She shakes her head, looking down at their daughter.

"Everyone, we would like to introduce you to Cecelia "Cece" Paige Mullins." Shane says, looking up at Taylor.

Her goddaughter shares her middle name.

All the girls turn their attention to Taylor, as a small gasp escapes her lips.

"Are you serious?" Taylor asks on a sob. Shane shakes her head, fighting back tears of her own.

"Ah shit. We're going to spoil this girl rotten aren't we?" I say, running a hand through my hair. Taylor doesn't answer with words, she only shakes her head in agreement before wrapping her arms around her best friend.

"I love you so much. Thank you, I am so honored." Taylor sits back up and looks down at Cece. "I am going to love you so much. And I promise to pick you up from school when the girls are being mean or a stinky boy breaks your heart. And we will go get ice cream or our nails done as soon as I'm done kicking their ass," she proclaims as Cece holds onto Taylor's index finger.

"I would expect absolutely nothing less from you." Shane sniffles and laughs.

Max picks Cece up and brings her over to me, placing her in my arms. He adjusts my elbow and helps make sure I have her fully supported before he lets go. Taylor walks over resting her head on my bicep as she stares at her new goddaughter.

"You think you'll ever want any of these?" I whisper, glancing down to catch her reaction.

"I don't know. Maybe someday. I think I'd like to just be your wife for a while. Spend some time traveling and enjoy just being us. If that's okay with you," she says, looking up at me with those perfect raincloud eyes.

"Whatever you want, Darlin'. If you ever change your mind just say the word." I wink at her and she smiles, turning back to face Cece again. We each take a few minutes to hold her before leaving the new family of three to get some much needed rest. We walk out of the hospital hand in hand as Taylor gushes over how beautiful Cece is. She's not wrong, that's hands down the cutest baby I've ever seen. When we get to the truck I open Taylor's door, helping her in like I always do.

"There's somewhere I want to take you, if you're down for a little adventure?" I ask, bringing a curious grin to her lips.

"With you, always," she agrees.

My palms are sweating the whole drive here, and when we pull onto the gravel road Taylor frowns as she looks at her surroundings.

Trees. Lots and lots of trees.

She's on the edge of her seat until we make it to the clearing and her features soften. I put the truck in park and rush to open her door.

"What is this place?" she asks, looking over at me. I help her out of the truck as we walk around to the hood.

"This is… our new home." Her eyes grow wide as she looks back out into the clearing where the framework for our house sits. "Well, it *will* be. I've been working on it to surprise you. It's set to be done right before our wedding." Her hand comes up to cover her mouth, her raincloud eyes sparkling from the tears beginning to fill them. "Unless you actually postpone it until Hendrix graduates, then it'll be done well before that." She laughs as a tear falls down her cheek. I swipe it away with the pad of my thumb, tilting her chin to look up at me.

"Say something, Peach," I plead. Unable to take her silence.

"I don't know *what* to say, Tucker. This is… so incredible and thoughtful. You're building us a home?" she asks, like she still can't believe it.

"Home for me is anywhere you are Darlin', I just thought we should have a place that we build together, from the ground up. I want to decorate it and design it together. From the trim to the doorknobs I want this place to feel like *ours*. Not my house that you're just living in."

"I can't wait to build a new life here with you. I love it, Tucker. I love *you*."

"I love you, too, Darlin'. Since the first day we met."

The End.

Marilyn's Famous Chocolate Chip Cookies

Ingredients:

2 ¼ C unsifted all purpose flour
1 tsp. vanilla
1 tsp. Baking soda
2 eggs
1 tsp. Salt
1-12oz. Ghirardelli pack choc. chips
1 C butter, softened
¾ C sugar
¾ C brown sugar, firmly packed

1. Preheat oven to 375.
2. Combine flour, baking soda, and salt in a small bowl; set aside.
3. Combine butter, sugars, and vanilla in a large bowl; beat until creamy.
4. Beat in eggs. Gradually add flour mixture; blend well.
5. Stir in chocolate chips.
6. Drop rounded teaspoons of cookie dough onto a baking sheet.
7. Bake for 8-10 minutes.

Acknowledgments

First, I want to say a big ass thank you to you, my readers! When I released the first book in this series I never thought it would get the attention that it did. But the way Waiting for Healing has been on everyone's radar since I announced Taylor and Tucker were getting a story has blown me away. I am truly grateful for every single one of you, and can't wait to finish out this series for us.

To my husband, Pirtle (aka the real life book boyfriend) I truly could not do this without you. The encouragement and support you give me is what keeps me going when I want to give up, but more than that your involvement in my writing is something very special to me. From helping with music for each character's playlist, to the research for all things military and mental health, I couldn't ask for a better partner to do this with. I love you forever.

To Courtnee, without whom I wouldn't have a Taylor. I love you so much. Thank you for inspiring me to write and giving me the kind of friendship I hope everyone gets to experience in their lifetime.

To Kate, with Kate Decided to Design. I am so incredibly thankful for you, our friendship, and your creative mind. Thank you for giving me the perfect Taylor and Tucker proposal scene. This book wouldn't be what it is without you. You have absolutely gone above and beyond for me behind the scenes and I will never be able to thank you enough for the work you have put into this series right along side me.

To Erica, with Logophile Editing, my editor and friend. I am so so thankful that we connected when we did and that I now get the pleasure of working with you. I truly hope we will continue working together for a very long time!

To Taylor and Keri, my beta readers and hype girls. I can't even begin to describe how incredibly blessed I feel to have connected with you both through Waiting for Sunshine, and to have you both in my life and on my team now.

To my babies, for showing me just how strong I truly am. Being a stay at home mom, wife, and author is no small task. On the days I feel like I just can't do it anymore, your little hugs and "I love yous" remind me to slow down and take a deep breath. I am so blessed to be able to live out both dreams of being a mom and a writer, and I hope one day I can help you chase every one of your dreams as well. I love you one hundred.

Also by Sarah Pirtle

NASHVILLE NIGHTS SERIES

Waiting for Sunshine : Shane & Max's Story

Waiting for Healing : Taylor & Tucker's Story